4/10/21

BRENT LIBRARIES

Please return/renew this item
by the last date shown.
Books may also be renewed by
phone or online.
Tel: 0333 370 4700
On-line www.brent.gov.uk/libraryservice

ADDITIONAL PRAISE FOR *DETRANSITION, BABY*

'Writing with alarming insight, Torrey Peters captures the grandiose, heartfelt and sometimes mangled aspirations of queer and trans people facing an unprecedented array of personal choice. By showing how gender transition (like divorce, or any transformative life event) can be simultaneously destabilizing and liberating, Peters makes trans culture relatable to all. A voraciously knowing, compulsively readable novel'
CHRIS KRAUS, AUTHOR OF *I LOVE DICK*

'*Detransition, Baby* is a landmark piece of trans literature – brutally honest and yet incredibly sensitive about trans living, tremendously funny and sexy as hell'
JULIET JACQUES, AUTHOR OF *TRANS: A MEMOIR*

'Torrey Peters just took everything that couldn't be done and did it. Out of the vibrant particulars of trans experience, *Detransition, Baby* renews a fundamental novelistic ambition: to peel back the skin of social life and illuminate the captivating details of desire and family underneath. Plenty of books are good; this book is alive'
JORDY ROSENBERG, AUTHOR OF *CONFESSIONS OF THE FOX*

'I love *Detransition, Baby* for its wit, its irreverence. And I love it even more for its reverence – its reverence for the quest for womanhood, motherhood, self-hood. Torrey Peters evokes these characters with such fullness and compassion that they felt like dear friends to me. This is an important book, and I couldn't put it down'
HELEN PHILLIPS, AUTHOR OF *THE NEED*

'Smart, funny and big-hearted ... A wonderfully original exploration of desire and the evolving shape of family'
KIRKUS STARRED REVIEW

BY TORREY PETERS

Infect Your Friends and Loved Ones

The Masker

DETRANSITION,
BABY

DETRANSITION,
BABY

Torrey Peters

First published in Great Britain in 2021 by
Serpent's Tail,
an imprint of Profile Books Ltd
29 Cloth Fair
London
EC1A 7JQ
www.serpentstail.com

First published in the United States by One World,
an imprint of Random House, a division of
Penguin Random House.

Designed by Fritz Metsch

Detransition, Baby is a work of fiction. Names, characters, places, and incidents are
the products of the author's imagination or are used fictitiously. Any resemblance
to actual events, locales, or persons, living or dead, is entirely coincidental.

1 3 5 7 9 10 8 6 4 2

Printed and bound in Great Britain by
Clays Ltd, Elcograf S.p.A.

The moral right of the author has been asserted.

A CIP catalogue record for this book is available from the British Library.

ISBN 978 1 78816 720 8
eISBN 978 1 78283 812 8

To divorced cis women, who, like me,
had to face starting their life over without either
reinvesting in the illusions from the past,
or growing bitter about the future.

DETRANSITION,
BABY

CHAPTER ONE

One month after conception

THE QUESTION, FOR Reese: Were married men just desperately attractive to her? Or was the pool of men who were available to her as a trans woman only those who had already locked down a cis wife and could now "explore" with her? The easy answer, the one that all her girls advocated, was to call men dogs. But now, here's Reese—sneaking around with *another* handsome, charming, motherfucking cheater. Look at her, wearing a black lace dress and sitting in his parked Beamer, waiting while he goes into a Duane Reade to buy condoms. Then she's going to let him come over to her apartment, avoid the pointed glare of her roommate, Iris, and have him fuck her right on the trite floral bedspread that the *last* married dude bought her so that her room would seem a little more girly and naughty when he snuck away from his wife.

Reese had already diagnosed her own problem. She didn't know how to be alone. She fled from her own company, from her own solitude. Along with telling her how awful her cheating men were, her friends also told her that after two major breakups, she needed time to learn to be herself, by herself. But she couldn't be alone in any kind of moderate way. Give her a week to herself and she began to isolate, cultivating an ash pile of loneliness that built on itself exponentially, until she was daydreaming about selling everything and drifting away on a boat toward nowhere. To jolt herself back to life, she went on Grindr, or Tinder, or whatever—and administered ten thousand volts to the heart by chasing the most dramatic tachycardia of an affair she could find. Married men were the best for fleeing loneliness, because married men also didn't know how to be alone. Married men were experts at being together, at not letting go, no matter what, until death do us part. With the pretense of setting the boundaries of "just an affair," Reese would swan dive super deep, super hard. By telling herself it would just be a fling, she gave herself permission to fulfill every fetish the guy had ever dreamed of, to unearth his every secret hurt, to debase herself in the most lush, vicious, and unsustainable ways—then collapse into resentment, sadness, and spite that it had been just a fling, because hadn't she been brave enough and vulnerable enough to dive super deep, super hard?

She saw herself as attractive, round face and full figure, but she didn't pretend that she stopped traffic; nor did she frequently note people standing around to admire the harvests of her brain. But with the right kind of man, she bore a genius for drama. She could distill it and flame it like jet fuel when solitude chilled her bones.

Her man this time was similar to her others. A handsome, married alpha-type who put her on a leash in the bedroom. Only this one was better, because he was an HIV-positive cowboy-turned-lawyer. He had a thing for trans girls and had seroconverted while cheating on his wife with a trans woman, *and* the wife had stayed with him, *and* now he was at it again with Reese. *Wheeeee!*

"Did you bottom or something?" Reese had asked on their first date.

"Fuck no," he said. "My doctors said I had a one in ten thousand chance to contract it from getting head. You figure that at least ten thousand blow jobs are happening every minute, but that one in ten thousand was me. Also, she gave me a lot of blow jobs."

"Cool," said Reese, who knew that that explanation wasn't factual, but had only really agreed to make sure he wasn't going to try to bottom with her. Within the hour, she had him back in her room and confessing from whom he'd gotten HIV and where. Within two hours, Reese convinced him to talk about his wife's disappointment, how she was unwilling to let him fuck a child into her even though his HIV had declined to undetectable levels. He described how much his wife hated the IVF treatments, how their clinical nature reminded her over and over what he had done to put her on a cold doctor's table instead of in their warm marital bed.

"You're getting a lot more candor out of me than I'm used to," her cowboy said, sounding surprised at himself, even as he squeezed Reese's tits. "The power of pussy, I guess."

"You might get my pussy," she responded, enjoying herself and aping his cowboy drawl, "but a good woman'll flay your soul."

"Ain't that the truth," he drawled back. He lifted a big paw to the back of her neck and brought her face close to his. She sighed, went limp.

Her eyes glassily held his.

"Tell you what," he told her, "first I'm going to own your pussy . . ." He paused, and with his hand still on her neck, he slowly, firmly, pushed her face down into a pillow. "Then we'll see about my soul."

Now he slides back into the car, with a little brown bag full of lube and condoms, and a tickling of anticipation slides across Reese's stomach. "Do we really need these tonight?" he asks her, holding up the bag. "You know I'm gonna want to knock you up."

This was why she still put up with him: He got it. With him, she'd discovered sex that was really and truly dangerous. Cis women, she supposed, rubbed against a frisson of danger every time they had sex. The risk, the thrill, that they might get pregnant—a single fuck to fuck up (or bless?) their lives. For cis women, Reese imagined, sex was a game played at the precipice of a cliff. But until her cowboy, she hadn't ever had the pleasure of that particular danger. Only now, with his HIV, had she found an analogue to a cis woman's life changer. Her cowboy could fuck her and mark her forever. He could fuck her and end her. His cock could obliterate her.

His viral load was undetectable, he said, but she never asked to see any papers. That would kill the sweetness and danger of it. He liked to play close to the edge too, pushing to knock her up, to impregnate her with a viral seed. Make her the mommy, her body host to new life, part of her but not, just as mothers eternal.

"We agreed on condoms always. You said you didn't want it on your conscience," she said.

"Yeah, but that was before you started on your birth control."

She first called her PrEP "birth control" at a Chinese place in Sunset Park where he felt safe that none of his wife's friends would possibly run into him. It popped into her head as a joke, but he looked at her and said, "Fuck, I just got so hard." He signaled for the check, told her that she wouldn't get to see a movie that night, and drove her right home to put her facedown on her floral bedspread. In the morning, she sexted him one of the sexiest, but most ostensibly non-sexual, sexts of her life—a short video of her cramming a couple of her big blue Truvada pills into one of those distinctive pastel birth control day-of-the-month clamshell cases. From then on, her "birth control pills" were part of their sex life.

There was another reason, beyond the stigma, taboo, and eroticization, that their particular brand of bugchasing had bite for Reese: She really did want to be a mom. She wanted it worse than anything. She had spent her whole adulthood with the queers, ingesting their radical relationships and polyamory and gender roles, but somehow, she still never displaced from the pinnacle of womanhood those nice white Wisconsin moms who had populated her childhood. She never lost that secret fervor to grow up into one of them. In motherhood she could imagine herself apart from her loneliness and neediness, because as a mother, she believed, you were never truly alone. No matter that her own and her trans friends' actual experiences of unconditional parental love always turned out to be awfully conditional.

Perhaps equally important, as a mother, she saw herself finally granted the womanhood that she suspected the goddesses of her childhood took as their natural due. She'd set herself up for it, once. She'd been in a lesbian relationship with a trans woman named Amy—a woman with a good job in tech, and who became so suburban-presentable that when she spoke, you imagined her words in Martha Stewart's signature typeface. With Amy, Reese had gotten as close to domesticity as she figured possible for a trans girl—the trust and boredom and stability that now had the faded aspect of a dream recalled right after you wake. They even had an apartment by Prospect Park—the kind of bright, airy space that evinced enough good taste and stalwart respectability that the idea of showing adoption agencies where they lived had been one of the lesser obstacles to motherhood.

But now, three years later, as Reese's odometer clicked up into her midthirties, she began to think about what she called the *Sex and the City* Problem.

The *Sex and the City* Problem wasn't just Reese's problem, it was a problem for all women. But unlike millions of cis women before Reese, no generation of trans women had ever solved it. The problem could be described thusly: When a woman begins to notice herself aging, the prospect of making some meaning out of her life grows more and more urgent. A need to save herself, or be saved, as the joys of beauty and youth repeat themselves to lesser and lesser effect. But in finding meaning, Reese would argue—despite the changes wrought by feminism—women still found themselves with only four major options to save themselves, options represented by the story arcs of the four female characters of *Sex and the City*. Find a partner, and be a Charlotte. Have a career, and be a Samantha. Have a baby, and be a Miranda. Or finally, express oneself in art or writing, and be a Carrie. Every generation of women reinvented this formula over and over, Reese believed, blending it and twisting it, but never quite escaping it.

Yet, for every generation of trans women prior to Reese's, the *Sex and the City* Problem was an aspirational problem. Only the rarest, most stealth, most successful of trans women ever had the chance to even confront it. The rest were barred from all four options at the outset. No jobs, no lovers, no babies, and while a trans woman might have been a muse, no one wanted art in which she spoke for herself. And so, trans women defaulted into a kind of No Futurism, and while certain other queers might celebrate the irony, joy, and graves into which queers often rush, that rush into No Future looked a lot more glamorous when the beautiful corpse left behind was a wild and willful choice rather than a statistical probability.

When Reese lived with Amy, she aspired to the *Sex and the City* Problem herself. It felt radical for her, as a trans woman, to luxuriate in the contemplation of how bourgeois to become. It felt like a success not to have that choice made for her. Then Amy detransitioned and it all fell apart.

Now futurelessness had crept back into view. Now Reese made other women's prizes her own bliss, and made babies out of viruses.

"All right," she says, after they'd been driving for about ten minutes.

"All right, what?"

"All right. Let's see if you can get me pregnant."

"Really?"

"Yeah." Her cowboy starts to say something, but she cuts him off. "Only, if we're going to do this, you've got to start treating me better. You've got to treat me like the mother of your child."

He reaches over to pinch her side. "Mother of my child? C'mon. You don't want that. If I put a tadpole in the well, then you're gonna want to be the knocked-up sixteen-year-old from the bad side of town. You want everyone knowing it's 'cause you're an easy slut."

She squirms away from his pinch. "I'm serious. Treat me better."

He frowns, but keeps his eyes on the road. "Yeah. Okay. I will. Let's get some food," he says, braking at a red light.

"Really?" They were driving to her neighborhood, Greenpoint, and he often wouldn't eat with her in that area. He knew too many people who lived there. Once she forced him to go out to a vegan buffet by her house, and he barely made eye contact the whole time. His gaze instead jerked to the door whenever someone new came into the place. After that, she let him drive her south, or sometimes into Queens. Never Manhattan, never Williamsburg, where his wife made her social life.

But now, she says he can fuck her without a condom and all his rules go out the window. Reese has a moment of satisfaction. Her body is the ultimate trump card.

"Yeah," he says, "maybe you could run in somewhere and pick up some takeout."

Of course. Takeout. With him waiting in the car. She nods. "Sure, what would you like?"

In the Thai restaurant, she doesn't order anything for herself. He loves curries, spiced to a barely edible Scoville level. She does not. She'll make herself something at home after he leaves. She's scrolling through Instagram when her phone rings, and it's a number she doesn't recognize, some out-of-state area code. Her cowboy uses Google Voice so her texts don't show up on his iPad at home, which his wife sometimes borrows, and Google often routes the calls through weird numbers.

She hits the green Answer button and brings the phone to her ear. "I got you green curry with beef, five-star spiciness," she says by way of a greeting.

"Hey, that's nice of you, but if you remember, I was always such a wuss about spice." A man's voice. Warm and smooth, but none of her cowboy's drawl, which he somehow managed to keep, even through his years in New York.

She lowers the phone, checks the number. "Who is this?"

The man's tone changes, not quite apologetic, but inviting. "Reese. Hi. Sorry, it's Ames."

Out in the car she can see her cowboy, the glow of his own phone illuminating the glasses he only wore to read. She turns away, as if he might overhear her through the glass windows of his car, the plate glass of the restaurant, over the clang of the kitchen and the talk of the scattered customers.

"Why are you calling, Ames? I didn't think we were speaking anymore."

"I know."

She waits, holds her lips together. She can hear him breathing. She wants to make him talk first.

"I'm not calling to bother you," he presses on. "I was hoping for your help."

"My help? I didn't know I had anything left for you to take."

He pauses. "Take from you?" His bafflement sounds genuine. This was his whole problem. That he couldn't see what he had led her to lose. "Maybe I deserve that. But I promise I'm not calling for that. It's almost the opposite."

"I'm on a date. I've got some Thai food coming." She knows it's vindictive to say. But she can't help it. He's thrown her off, and she wants both to return the favor and to prove to him that her life has moved on.

"I can call at a different time?"

"No, you've got until my food gets here to explain yourself."

"Is there some guy watching us talk?"

"I'm getting takeout. He's waiting in the car." A thrum of satisfaction plays in Reese's chest. Clearly, however Ames had anticipated this conversation going, she has wrested it away from him.

"Okay," he says, "I'd hoped to explain this at length, but we'll do it your way. Remember how you always wanted us to have a baby together? That's what we had planned for?"

Something must be off with him that he'd call her about this. He wasn't the type to hurt people for fun, and he must know such a question, asked so directly, would hurt her. She feels stupid for having told him that she was on a date.

"Is that still something you'd want? A baby, I mean?" His question ends on an up note, as though he's slightly afraid of his audacity in having voiced it.

"Of course I still fucking want a baby," she snaps.

"That's so good to hear, Reese," he says. His tone is relieved.

She knows him so well, she can almost picture the way his body is relaxing. "Because something happened. Even after everything, you're the person I trust most to talk to me about it. For everything we had, please, please, can I see you? I badly need to talk to you."

"You'll have to tell me more than just this, Ames."

He exhales. "All right. I got a woman pregnant. I'm going to have a baby."

Reese can't believe it. She can't believe that Ames would call her to tell her that he had gotten the thing she so desperately wanted. She closes her eyes, counts to five.

The waitress behind the counter plops down a brown bag, and signals that it's her order. But Reese doesn't notice. Her cowboy, his five-star green curry, the birth control pill he'll feed her later— they're all lost to her. Somewhere, somehow, Amy did the impossible: She got herself a baby.

Katrina sits in the roller chair before Ames's desk. The moment has an air of uncommon inversion. Because she is his boss, Ames nearly always goes to her office and sits in front of her desk. Her office, corresponding to their relative places in the corporate hierarchy, is double the square footage of his, with two full windows looking out on two neighboring buildings, and between them, a sliver of East River view. By contrast, Ames's office has one window overlooking a small parking lot. Once, in the twilight, he saw a brown creature trotting spritely across the pavement—and has since maintained that it was an urban coyote. One takes one's excitements where one may.

Katrina rifles through a briefcase, pulls out a manila folder, and plops it on his desk. Her coming to his office makes him tense, like a teenager whose parents have entered his room.

"Well," she says. "It's real. This is happening." He reaches for the folder. He has good posture, and gives her an easy smile. The folder opens to reveal printouts from an online patient portal.

"My gyno," Katrina says, watching him closely. "She followed up with a blood test and a pelvic exam. She confirmed the home test results. Without an ultrasound, she can't say how far I am, so I had one scheduled for the Thursday after next. I mean, I know you maybe aren't sure yet how you feel about it, but maybe if you come, that'll help? If I'm more than four weeks into it, we'll be able to see the baby—or I guess, embryo?"

He is aware that she is scrutinizing him for a reaction. He had been unable to give one after the pregnancy test came back positive. He feels the same numbness that he felt then, only now, he can no longer delay by telling her that he wants to wait for official confirmation to get his emotions involved. "Amazing," he says, and tries out a smile that he fears might be coming off as a grimace. "I guess it's real! Especially since we have"—he searches briefly for a phrase, and then comes up with one—"an entire dossier of evidence."

Katrina shifts to cross her legs. She's wearing casual wedge heels. He always notices her clothing, half out of admiration, and half out of the habit of noting what's going on in the field of women's fashion. "Your reaction has been hard to read," she says carefully. "I don't know, I thought maybe if you saw it in black and white, I'd be able to gauge how you were actually feeling." She pauses and swallows. "But I still can't." He sees the effort it costs her to muster this level of assertion.

He stands up, walks around the desk, and half sits against it, just in front of her, so his leg is touching hers.

He rotates the printouts, there's a list of test results, but he can't make sense of them. His brain shorts out when he cross-references the data that they clearly show—he is a father-to-be—with the data he stores in his heart: He should not be a father.

Three years have passed since Ames stopped taking estrogen. He injected his last dose on Reese's thirty-second birthday. Reese, his ex, still lives in New York. They haven't spoken in two years, although he sent her a birthday card last year. He received no response. Throughout their relationship, she had always talked assuredly about how she'd have a kid by age thirty-five. As far as he knows, that hasn't happened.

It is only now, three years after their breakup, that Ames is able to talk about Reese casually, calling her "my ex" and moving the conversation along without dwelling. Because in truth, he still misses her in a way that talking about her, thinking about her, remains dangerous to indulge in—as an alcoholic can't think too much about how much she'd really like just one drink. When Ames thinks hard about Reese, he feels abandoned and grows angry, morose, and worst of all, ashamed. Because he has trouble explaining exactly what he still wants from her. For a while he thought it was romance, but his desire has lost any kind of sexual edge. Instead, he misses her in a familial way, in the way he missed and felt betrayed by his birth family when they cut off contact in the early years of his transition. His sense of abandonment plucked at a nerve deeper, more adolescent than that of jilted adult romantic love. Reese hadn't just been his lover, she'd been something like his mother. She had taught him to be a woman . . . or he'd learned to be a woman with her. She had found him in a plastic state of early development, a second puberty, and she'd molded him to her tastes. And now she was gone, but the imprint of her hands remained, so that he could never forget her.

He hadn't understood how little sense he made as a person without Reese until after she began to detach from him, until the lack of her became so painful that he started to once again want the armor of masculinity and, somewhat haphazardly, detransitioned to fully suit up in it.

So now, three years have passed living once again in a testosterone-dependent body. Yet even without the shots or pills, Ames had believed that he'd been on androgen-blockers long enough to have atrophied his testicles into permanent sterility. That's what he told Katrina when they hooked up the first time, the night of the agency's annual Easter Keg Hunt. He told her that he was sterile—not that he'd been a transsexual woman with atrophied balls.

Ames sifts through the papers in the manila folder Katrina has brought. Beneath the printouts from her doctor are more printouts, from what look like Reddit forums. "What are these?"

She drops her hand to her stomach. It's flat, no baby bump, but she's already holding herself like a pregnant woman. "Well, I know you said you were sterile now. I was looking it up, and vasectomies are like ninety-nine percent effective, but I found some message boards, from men who still got women pregnant—"

He raises a hand. "Wait a sec. I never said I had a vasectomy."

His office, like all the offices in this row, has only a glass wall to separate it from the hallway. He's at the end of the row, beside an alcove into which is tucked the copy machine, water cooler, coffee maker, and a little kitchenette stocked with—due to a recent human resources campaign—only healthy organic snacks. Coworker hallway traffic remains constant throughout the day. He would not consider his office to be an ideal location to come out as a former transsexual.

"No? But we haven't used condoms for months and this whole time I thought—what did you mean, then? Like low sperm count?"

"I had very low testosterone for a while." He works to keep his voice casual, to resist the urge to lower it nervously. "And during that time, my testicles atrophied, and my doctor told me that none of my sperm would ever again be viable."

When Ames first went in for an estrogen prescription, he saw a gentle, elderly endocrinologist, who had taken on trans patients not because of any special interest in gender, but because trans patients were, in his words, "so happy to come see me for treatment." The bulk of the doctor's other patients suffered from hormonal disorders that made them emotionally volatile. After this endo discovered trans gratitude, he filled his appointments with as many transsexuals as he could find.

Ames, who had no history with trans therapy, and none of the paperwork that the hormone gatekeepers tended to require, had spent weeks before the appointment fretting that the endo would declare him "not really trans" and deny him hormones. Upon hearing that the doctor appreciated appreciation, Ames therefore gushed with gratitude, and duly walked out with a prescription for injectable estrogen. At his next appointment, the endo confided, "Perhaps, last time, I prescribed somewhat hastily. I should have said more about sterility." He told Ames that permanent sterility would set in within the first six months of a hormone replacement therapy regimen, and he gave Ames a recommendation for a sperm bank.

The next day, Ames mustered great bravery and called the sperm bank. He did not want to think about fatherhood, that final plume in the cap of manhood, but he forced himself to call anyway. A receptionist on the other end of the line quoted annual prices for sperm storage akin to his cable subscription, which he supposed was a reasonable cost for preserving the viability of his future genetic line. The receptionist put him on hold to make an appointment and as Vivaldi played, Ames pondered whether he ought to cancel his subscription to HBO in order to afford this sperm bank. He couldn't fully comprehend the enormous weight of fatherhood and generational lineage, but he could easily comprehend how much he did not want to cancel HBO.

Without further consideration, he hung up. By the time his nipples began to ache that spring, he figured it was too late anyhow. The more his nipples hurt, the less he suffocated from the dread that came from thoughts of fatherhood. Now, with Katrina sitting in his office, for the first time in a long time, he had to think about the possibility of having sired a child. Shortly, very shortly, he was going to be called upon to make some decision, which would lead to other decisions, generations of decisions generated by this decision.

"Your testicles atrophied?" Katrina asks, baffled. "But they felt normal to me!"

"Yes," he agrees. "I mean, they're not huge or anything."

"No, not huge," Katrina affirms, and then adds encouragingly, "but fine!"

On the other side of his office's glass wall, Karen from the art department pauses in the hallway to unwrap a granola bar. Ames becomes suddenly aware that Katrina and he are casually discussing his balls in the middle of a workday.

Coworkers had shared the office gossip about Katrina almost immediately after Ames had joined the agency: bad divorce. She'd left her husband a few months before he'd interviewed. She cried in her office, the coworkers told him, then told her secretary not to put her husband's calls through. He had cheated on her, said one. No, no, she'd had a miscarriage. Incorrect, said another, they'd had money problems. The speculation took on a tone both lurid and compulsory—to have a boss is so commonplace that one rarely remarks on its strangeness, yet its structure compels a cult of personality around even the most quotidian of managers. As an underling, one needs to furnish an epistemology of how it came to pass that she has sway over one's precious autonomy. Basic comprehension of capitalism's arbitrary mechanics doesn't satisfy—the heart demands a human explanation. Or at least that's what Ames said to justify his initial crush.

Still, over that first year that Ames worked for Katrina, she kept her personal life just that. Instead of talking about her divorce, Ames intuited it. He noted the slight woundedness and exasperation that clung to her, the nearly teenage angst and willingness to test bad ideas that led to a certain oh-fuck-it-ness about her work and a straightforward honesty with her employees.

She developed a visceral suspicion of conventional narratives. The anodyne corporate clients who came to the agency occasionally saw one or two much darker and more experimental pitches for their online marketing campaigns slipped in among the conventional fare. Dadaism for the Clorox bleach campaign. Cyborgian despair for Anker batteries. A series of radio ads for Purina in which Jon Lovitz catered to nineties nostalgia by reprising his cult role as critic Jay Sherman in order to give negative reviews to various puppies. It made her good at her work. Ames interpreted her tendency to re-narrativize as divorce-induced.

Well into their romance, after they'd already slept together numerous times, she brought up the subject of her divorce. They were in his bed, on their sides, facing each other, he propped up on an elbow, she with her face resting on one of his forest-green pillowcases, her glossy brown hair stepping down from head to pillow to bed. The bedside light shining behind her illuminated the outer crescents of her face—he still instinctively noticed the curve of a brow.

"I know that people in the office probably told you about the miscarriage," she said. "I stupidly talked about it with a few people. Telling Abby anything is a mistake." He laughed, because, yeah, Abby was a gossip.

"When you get a divorce," she said after a moment, "everyone expects you to provide a story to justify it. Every woman I've ever met who has had a divorce has a story to explain herself. But in real life the story and actual reasons for the divorce diverge. In reality, everything is more ambivalent. My own reasons are closer to a tone than a series of causes and effects. But when I talk about it, I know people want a cause and effect, a clear *why*."

"All right," Ames said. "So what's the tone of your divorce?"

"I like to call it the Ennui of Heterosexuality."

"I see. Do you still suffer from the ennui of heterosexuality?" Ames asked, gesturing grandly at their postcoital bedroom tableau.

"I suffered from a miscarriage," she replied defiantly, puncturing his irony.

Ames quickly apologized.

Katrina shifted a pillow, and when she turned back to Ames, her face was . . . amused? "See, you proved my point. When I said 'ennui of heterosexuality,' you challenged me, but when I said 'miscarriage,' you immediately apologized. That's why the miscarriage is the official story of my divorce. No one ever challenges it. Miscarriages are private, and so my miscarriage is a clean get-out-free card. It makes for a divorce in which Danny was blameless—grief where you lose something you can't quite name. People assume that mourning drove a sad wedge between a couple—no one's fault. Everything is assumed. No one ever asks how I actually felt about the miscarriage."

"How did you feel about the miscarriage?" Ames asked.

"I felt relief."

"Relief?"

"Yes. I was relieved. Which made me feel like a psychopath. I read all these articles in women's magazines about miscarriages, and they all said that I would feel grief and guilt. They assured me that it wasn't my fault: that it wasn't because of that glass of wine I had once, or that Italian sub full of processed meat. But I never thought it was my fault. My own guilt came from not having guilt. After a while of feeling that way, I began to ask why. Why should I feel relieved? It caused me to look harder at my marriage. I was relieved because of something I didn't want to admit: I didn't want to be with Danny anymore and if we had a kid together I would have to be. Danny was a good boyfriend to have when I was younger, when we were in college. Like, in the same way that a Saint Bernard would be a good dog to have if you were lost in the mountains. A big amiable body that a girl could shelter behind. Danny was an idea I inherited, maybe from growing up in Vermont, of what a man was supposed to be. We looked good together; like, early on I knew any photo for our wedding announcement was going to look like it came from a magazine. So when he proposed, I accepted, even though we had been dating two years, and I don't think that sex ever lasted longer than fifteen minutes, including foreplay, and despite the fact that by the three-month point in our relationship, I had somehow already ended up doing his laundry.

"One time, I made this joke that my marriage was like a push-up bra: It looked pretty good underneath a shirt, but you know it's all just padding and by the end of the day you can't wait to take the damn thing off. My friends laughed, but I felt icy, because I realized I had inadvertently told the truth and it was awful."

Ames listened. She had once told him that she liked how he didn't seem to feel a need to speak or give advice when she was working through a thought out loud.

Katrina removed her earrings and set them on the nightstand. "Danny and I went to Dartmouth with this couple—Pete and Lia. When they moved to New York from Seattle, they did this thing where they invited other married couples over to watch *Cheers* and eat pie. The couples were the kind of people who liked rock climbing and called themselves foodies. Everyone but me was very, very white. Watching *Cheers* was part of their weird hipster irony. We all snorted at the eighties-era sexual politics like we were better than that, like we'd really come so far since then. Pussy-hound Sam Malone and shrill, wannabe-feminist-but-secretly-dick-crazed what's her name? Oh! I can't remember what her name was."

"Diane," said Ames.

"Yeah, Diane. I just remember this one night, after I lost the baby, all the men, once the show started, sort of unfurled themselves around their wives, and each wife settled into her respective husband's arms contentedly. These bonded animal pairs. And suddenly they all looked like apes grooming each other. I was revolted. And Danny, you could see that he was leaning back on the sectional, opening his long arms so that I would place myself in them like all the other good wives. But I wouldn't do it. I sat stiffly next to him on the couch with a foot of space between us. Our hosts put on *Cheers,* and we watched men and women say horrible things to each other and we laughed like that wasn't what we also did. Or do."

"Yeah," Ames said, nodding.

"All through it," Katrina went on, "Danny kept sneaking me this hurt expression. I'm sure he didn't know what was worse: what

I thought or what all our friends thought. But I didn't care. There was nothing that could ever have induced me to care about his hurt feelings just then. At that moment I blamed him for ruining me. For making me a psychopath. My thoughts were focused on him like I was psychically stabbing him with them. Over and over I thought the words, *If you didn't annoy me, I wouldn't be glad to have lost the baby.*

"I don't think it was fair or even logical, but I understood that I had felt that way for a long time. I had never even dared to think it in words. Just something about the smugness of that situation released it, of having to be his pet lap ape, while pretending we were evolved."

Katrina cut off her own story with a mirthless laugh. "Also, I think it was around then that I found his secret Asian porn collection."

"He had a secret Asian porn collection?"

"A bunch on his computer and some DVDs titled *Anal Asians* or something."

"I dunno," Ames said. "If I were an Asian woman, and my husband had a collection of Asian porn, maybe I'd be flattered. At least it means he's attracted to me."

"No," she said. "You don't get it. It means you begin to entertain creeping suspicions that after all you've been through together, years of learning to be adults together, the man who you married might only be with you because he fetishizes Asians—even though I have felt not quite Asian enough my whole life. He couldn't even fetishize me accurately."

"What's that kind of chaser called?" Ames asked.

"That kind of what?"

He pulled the covers around him, suddenly cold. He had the sense of having wandered out blindly in a winter storm to discover that he'd stumbled onto a thinly frozen lake. He had only ever encountered chasers in one context. "Like, uh, a tranny chaser. What's an Asian chaser called?"

She appraised him with a strange look. "A rice chaser," she said flatly. "In Vermont, growing up, the kids who saw my dad with my mom—their favorite way to bully me was by saying my dad had yellow fever."

Ames saw suddenly that she thought he was asking about himself. That she thought he wanted to know the slur for what having slept with her made him. He stifled an overwhelming urge to protest in horror. To tell her: *God, no, I would never think having sex with a certain person could mark me as something—I just really do get what it's like to be fetishized. I get what it's like to have someone think that his desire for me degrades or lowers him.*

But even at that moment, such an admission seemed too risky. What if coming out as a former transsexual meant never getting into bed with her again? What if it meant the end of their professional relationship? No, better to wait for the opportune moment.

Now and again, Ames scrutinized Katrina, and imagined what it would be like to tell her. How she would react. When he was alone, he told himself that maybe, maybe, she'd even be into it. That maybe the deepest reason for her divorce from Danny had been sexual. That while not exactly queer—she wasn't totally into the married straight life either.

For real, she was a freak in bed. Their sex was way wilder than he had imagined in his crush stage. Their first hookup had been drunken, and involved pretty typical hetero dynamics. Their second hookup—which occurred dead sober, midday a week later after she took a day to "work from home" and told him, as her employee, to do the same—had been decidedly bent.

In her kitchen, she had opened her fridge and leaned into it. The shape of her from behind, along with the thick sexual tension, sunk him to his knees and he half kissed, half nuzzled her jean-clad ass. She looked back from the fridge, with an expression of near concern, at the same time she reached behind her and grabbed a handful of his hair.

"Are you sure you're okay with this?" she asked. "If the genders were reversed, and some man had told his female employee to take a day off of work and come over I'd be appalled."

She had her fingers entwined in his hair even as she asked, so he couldn't pull back his head, and ended up responding to her ass, his mouth speaking an inch from her right ass cheek as if it were a microphone.

"Trust me, I love it," he told her ass. "I'm in heaven. I've always had a thing for bossy women. Getting with my actual boss is like secret-hotness level unlocked. You have consent or whatever, just please let me keep my face here."

"Should I be more of your boss about this, then?"

He looked up at her, unable to believe his luck. To find a toppy femme who was already literally in charge of him? Lotto odds. "Yes," he said. "Please."

"Fine." She laughed, and turned to face him, so that his nose was level with her crotch. "Make me a PowerPoint presentation about why I should let you stay down there with your face in my pussy." He closed his eyes, inhaled happily; a dawning awareness that this play turned her on as much as it did him chiseled loose a layer of the calcification that had begun to encrust his libido, and by extension, his heart, and by extension, his life.

The next day she sent him an email while they were both at the office. *Still waiting on that PowerPoint deck we discussed. When can I expect it to be delivered?*

He wasn't sure whether to respond openly. Here he was, with all his secret queer credentials, and this divorced straight woman had completely wrong-footed him. Which, of course, was so insanely hot that he briefly considered finding an out-of-the-way bathroom in which to jerk off. *LOL,* he responded weakly.

No, I'm serious. I'll expect you to present your slides to me by close of day Tuesday. If you're late, I'll make you present them in a conference room. Your choice.

．　．　．

This thing he had with Katrina—their power games, the thrill of sneaking around at the office and the explicitness of their flirting—it had all come together to make for really good sex. In his previous life, Ames had transitioned to live as a woman before he had ever had really good sex, and he wasn't sure that post-detransition, he'd ever have truly good sex again. Every other dalliance he'd attempted as a heterosexual man had disconnected his body and mind, fostering an inability to display real excitement or joy even as he performed all the necessary acts, until eventually, his partner took that disconnect as indifference and let go of him. When that happened he'd drift away without effort, like in shipwreck movies, that ubiquitous shot when the lover's body floats slowly down into the oceanic void. But not Katrina; for Katrina and her bossy games, he was fully here, electrified, daydreaming about it even when they were apart. Amazingly, his desire hadn't faded over the whole of the five months they had been together. If anything it had grown, gotten wild: lush unruly green life that overran the tidily landscaped paths and garden beds of proper behavior.

He suspected that, although Katrina was too proud to openly say so, they had been having a type of sex that she had long craved but never before known to ask for. That this was the first time in her life that she was experiencing the mind-scrambling effects of good sex—the kind of sex where you travel across the country for just a couple hours together, after which you talk about buying property, or moving in together, or just generally entwining lives in a way logistically unjustified by a short period of intimacy. In short, the sex that Katrina and he were having was in the category that meant that when a pregnancy test comes up positive—keeping the baby is very much an option.

Except for two caveats: First, she didn't know that he was once a transsexual, and second, after all his mental gymnastics, after all the lessons of transition and detransition, fatherhood remained the one affront to his gender that he still couldn't stomach without a creeping sense of horror. To become a father by his own body, as his father was to him, and his father before him, and on and on, would sentence him to a lifetime of grappling with that horror.

God, he'd hidden so much of his past from her, a past murky, half-spoken, all of it covered by the pretext that he was trying to protect their relationship from the office. It tired Ames, despite erasure having become a second nature mode of dealing with his past.

In his office now, Katrina scoots forward in her chair and takes his hand. "Ames, help me," she says softly. "What do you want to do? I'm not asking you to decide anything for me. I surprised myself by finding out I'm excited. I feel vulnerable saying that, so please, give me some sense of what this means for you."

She touches her stomach again. The baby-yet-not-yet-a-baby beneath her hand. He remembers hearing that a fetal pulse is detectable at four weeks. He remembers that she has miscarried before. The quiet pain of that. It hurts to think about what she might be going through. "You told me you were sterile and now I'm pregnant," she says. "Now the only thing you have to tell me after my doctor's confirmation—that *you* asked for—is that your testicles are atrophied? This is not how most men react to finding out they are a potential father."

Father. Spoken from the *mother.* She lets go of his hand, and picks up her manila folder, then examines the papers herself now, avoiding eye contact as she goes on.

"This is definitely not how I'd expect you to act if you truly believed it wasn't possible. Happiness, fear, joy, anger, whatever. But your level of surprise is like if we got dinner reservations somewhere you thought you couldn't get on short notice. Can you explain to me what is happening in your head?"

Ames inhales. Waits. Exhales now. She's waiting. Expecting him to say something, do something. That's who he is now, he reminds himself, someone who makes decisions, who doesn't let life just act upon him. Wasn't that the big lesson of transition, of detransition? That you'll never know all the angles, that delay is a form of hiding from reality. That you just figure out what you want and do it? And maybe, if you don't know what you want, you just do something anyway, and everything will change, and then maybe that will reveal what you really want.

So do something.

And maybe he couldn't have picked a better spot than his office to tell her—he'd always thought it would happen over dinner at some place where they'd be stuck discussing it. But in view of the office kitchenette? At work? This is the one place where she couldn't freak out, where she'd have to at least feign chillness.

His silence draws out. Finally, Katrina makes a gesture with her hand, flipping up her palm, like, *What?*

Just say it.

So he does. "I was told that I was sterile by the doctor who gave me estrogen. I injected estrogen and took testosterone-blockers for about six years, when I lived as a transsexual woman. He told me I'd be permanently sterile after six months. So, like, given my past as a woman, fatherhood is a lot for me to handle emotionally."

"I'm sorry, you lived as a what?" Expression drains from her face.

"I was a transsexual woman. That's why I thought I was sterile." He reaches out to her shoulder, to steady her. He's about to ask if he can tell her everything.

A quick jerk of her arm out from under his touch, and her file of vasectomy reports and the pregnancy test flies at his face. Instinct bobs him a quick step to the side. The manila folder glances against his shoulder, opens, and printouts scatter.

He wants to soothe her, to try to touch her again—but she nimbly hops to her feet. "I can't believe this. I feel, god, I feel—" She can't seem to speak, and instead brings her hands to her collarbone as if to push out the words that have gotten caught. "*Deceived!* You deceived me. Why would you do this to me?"

He has enough experience with coming out to know that insisting he wasn't *doing* anything to her would only escalate the moment. Instead, he fights an impulse to stoop and gather the printouts back into their folder. The Reddit forum printouts now seem more glaring, more deviant than if she had tossed all five months' worth of their selfies and sexts. Still, he doesn't move. She's standing with one shoulder forward now, like a boxer, and although it'd be completely out of character, he's not sure that if he leans down, she won't pop him in the eye. But then, abruptly, she startles, and whirls.

Josh, from the biz dev department, stares at them through the glass partition. When Katrina catches him gawking, he leans toward the kitchenette and snatches an apple from the wire basket hanging by the door. But he can't help himself, and turns back to regard the office diorama through the glass. He gives Ames a quick *yikes, bro* face. Katrina stares at Josh. She's visibly upset, her in-control-boss demeanor still largely disassembled.

"Hello, Josh," Katrina says curtly through the glass. Josh is so enthralled by the scene that he doesn't seem to notice a break of the fourth wall. Decisively, she takes two steps, ignoring the scattered printouts, and opens the door. From the hallway, she spins and glares at Ames. "Can you please pick up that file I dropped"—she points at the papers scattered on the floor—"and bring it by my office in about an hour? I'm late for a call right now. But we can discuss this further then."

"Of course," Ames says. "Can't wait."

Ames stoops to gather the papers. Josh waits until Katrina has rounded the hallway corner, leans in the door left wide open by her exit, tosses the apple in the air, catches it, and smirks down at Ames. "Lover's spat?" Josh asks.

"Your fountain of youth doesn't seem to have run dry yet," observes Ames, sneaking a look at Reese's face as they move into a shady eddy in the slowly drifting current of idlers taking in the April sun of Prospect Park.

She looks to him much as she had in her twenties. In fact, she's softer even—in her lavender-and-white-checked dress, she flaunts that pear shape that women's magazines identify as a body type one must dress carefully to flatteringly de-emphasize, but that Reese always not-so-quietly prized as a marker of uncommon passibility.

His own period of softly estrogenated vampire skin had slowed the onset of cracks and furrows, but when his skin roughened again and the stubble poked through once more, a few gray scouts had camped among the darker hairs. He had carefully shaved them this morning. Both as a man hiding any signs of aging before he sees an ex for the first time in years, and confusingly, out of a dormant sense of competitiveness, an urge to show himself off as still a beauty.

"Your own estrogen levels seem to have run low," Reese says, but without much venom, like she's too tired for niceties, rather than really trying to hurt him.

"I'm told my crow's feet are dashing."

Reese sighs. "I don't want to talk about how you look, Amy. I'm not going to do that."

"Of course. That's fair." He ignores the "Amy" part. The name doesn't offend him, it's just a name no one says anymore. "I just wanted you to know you look great."

Reese shrugs, then licks the edge of the ice cream sandwich he had brought her.

Her disinterest surprises him. He had figured on the compliment mattering to her.

"Hey," he says, affecting a light tone, "I'm putting myself out there, admitting how great you look."

She gives him a look like he's just stepped off a spaceship. "Oh," she says finally, "I get it. You were giving me that compliment as a guy. You're used to women acknowledging compliments like you're a guy."

It's true. His compliments tend to have, at a minimum, the effect of being noticed.

She performs a gruesome parody of batting her lashes and clutching her heart. "My stars! Lil ol' me?"

"All right, Reese."

"You're lucky I even agreed to come here. You're not getting a boy-crazy teenager on top of it."

"I can see that."

They had first met at a picnic here. A trans lady picnic. He still had his apartment near the north side of Prospect Park. The one they had lived in together. Over time his memories with Reese in the park had been replaced by new ones. The places where he jogged, where he read by the pond, or watched birds—hoping for one of the red-tailed hawks that nested there, often settling for an escaped songbird, or, if hard-pressed, a swan. But seeing Reese reframes everything, conjures up the past.

He can't quite figure out if she suggested meeting him here as a tactical move. Something to throw off his confidence. He can feel the lack of their prior intimacy—though whether or not that absent closeness is forever gone or like a child playing hide-and-go-seek, he's not quite sure.

The rusty hinge of a grackle sounds from the trees overhead. He's about to apologize, to say that he made a mistake and go home, when she offers him the ice cream sandwich. For the first time all afternoon, she lowers her guard, with something like a smile. "Look," she says. "I played along a little. I waited with those other women and let you buy me ice cream like we were just another hetero couple out on our hetero Sunday date with the boringly hetero idea to go to the park. Now have some ice cream, I don't want to eat all of it."

He takes a bite, and she pulls it back.

"One thing I'll tell you, though," she says. "You move differently than before."

"Move differently?"

"Yeah, you were always graceful, but you used to be so careful to swing your hips. You were a languid boy, who learned to move like a woman, who then learned to move like a boy again, but without wiping your hard drive each time. You've got all these glitches in the way you move. I was watching you in the ice cream line—you slither."

"Wow, Reese, just wow."

"No! It's charismatic. Remember how Johnny Depp pretended to be a drunk Keith Richards pretending to be a fey pirate? You can't help but be a little drawn in, like: What's going on with that one?" She smiles at him and takes a lick of ice cream, mock innocent.

"I forget what it's like being around trans women," he admits. "That for once, I'm not the only one constantly analyzing the gender dynamics of every situation to play my role."

"Welcome back," she says, seeming considerably cheered. "You must have also forgotten that I taught you everything you know."

"Please. The student surpassed the master long ago."

"Girl, you wish."

It's like coming home, that quick "girl." Something warmer and sweeter than the spring sun heating his neck and the ice cream lingering on his tongue. It's scary-seductive, emphasis on scary. Start looking for that kind of comfort and he's bound to make a fool of himself.

The temptation to beg for inclusion pulled at him every time he spotted a trans woman on the street, on the train. A stab of need for recognition by her. Most apostates must feel similar, whether Amish, Muslim, ex-gay, whatever.

Back when he lived as a trans woman, hardly anyone spoke about detransition. It was treated as the purview of conversion therapists and tabloid headlines: *He Was a Man, Then a Woman, Then Back to a Man!* The topic of detransition was boring—the reasons for it were never complex: Life as a trans woman was difficult and so people gave up. Even worse, to discuss the possibility of detransition gave hope to the lunacy of bigots who wished that trans women would simply detransition (i.e., cease to exist in any kind of visible, and hence meaningful, way).

He went two years as a woman before he met a truly detransitioned person. Amy was at a queer dance party with Reese and six other trans women. Defensively, they'd claimed a small corner of the room—a section then promptly quarantined for disinterest by the gays and trans mascs and cis women. So once again, the conversation among the trans women was the same as it always was at queer dance parties: figuring out new ways to complain how "We look fucking hot. Why is everyone ignoring us?" It was a topic that, as the drinks lowered inhibitions and standards, gave way to pairing off and hooking up with each other. Except at that particular dance, halfway through the monologues about being ignored, Amy couldn't help but notice that they actually weren't being ignored.

A plump man in his early thirties with a week-old beard had leaned in, and was laughing and shaking his head knowingly. Amy waited for someone to say, "Fuck off, chaser." But no one made eye contact with him. Instead, they made space for him with an air of resigned indulgence. It was as if he were an apparition whom they all could see but no one wanted to acknowledge—not because the haunting frightened them, but because the ghost had a tendency to interpret any attention paid to him as an invitation to once again repeat the embarrassing story of how he'd died practicing auto-erotic asphyxiation.

Two obviously straight girls who had clearly dressed up in fishnets for the queer party and were about a decade or so younger than the man, brought him a drink. Yaz, one of the trans women, let her interest flick briefly toward them, but pulled it away when she saw to whom they delivered the drink: an untouchable so pitiable and contagious that even the giddy proximate cleavage of overeager twenty-year-olds had been marked verboten.

Finally Amy pulled Reese aside. "Who is that dude?"

Reese waved her hand. "Ugh."

"No, tell me. Who?"

"I guess he calls himself William now. He detransitioned but still shows up to hang out with trans women occasionally."

"Really?" Amy couldn't hide her curiosity.

"Yeah. I guess he still shows up to group therapy and stuff. He's . . ." Reese couldn't find the word. "It's just sad."

When William went outside, Amy slunk away to follow him a few moments later. She found him half a block away, smoking a cigarette. "You're William?" she asked.

William was quite drunk. Too drunk to speak in grammatical sentences. But his face lit up at her attention in a way that hurt Amy to examine directly. She watched his cigarette instead of his face. Tried not to notice the soft and pupal quality to his body. Here's what Amy got from the conversation: He'd lived as a trans woman for seven years. But it was too hard. Too hard. He didn't pass. He wanted to die. He was still a trans woman. Everybody saw it, no matter what he did, but since he wouldn't say so, they couldn't either. He had a good job now. Medical supply distribution. He lived on Staten Island with those two young girls. He drove them to the party tonight and helped them get dressed. He didn't touch them, don't worry. He just liked being one of the girls. The cigarette looped in his hands, inscribing arcs of red in the night as he talked. Amy focused on the tip as if it were writing secret messages just for her. The more he spoke, the more Amy understood the polite, unsettling disdain the other trans women had shown him. She wanted to be anywhere but standing there listening to him. Pity teetered on the precipice of disgust.

When Amy detransitioned herself, she promised never to let anyone see her as she had seen William that night. Never to pant for inclusion from trans women. Ames wanted no pity and rejected their disgust. But despite Ames's rigid need for dignity, for all the careful lines he drew to respect the differences in how he lived and how trans women lived, they called to him in a siren song. Whenever a girl passed, the William inside of him begged to be let free, to run toward her pleading pathetically to be noticed, to bask in every moment of her icked-out attention. The obvious answer to keeping other girls' pity and disgust at bay had been the hardest—the addict's moment of clarity: Cut off those girls cold turkey. Because a single indulgence, and you're William.

The past is past to everyone but ghosts.

Except now, hear the whispered call, feel that ache: *Girl, you wish.*

A temporary chain-link fence rises behind the bench on which they sit in the park, casting fish-scale shadows on Reese's shoulders and face. "Okay, Daddy-O, so you got some woman pregnant," Reese says. "I'm still waiting for what that has to do with me."

The "Daddy-O" indicates half his work of explanation is done: The insult would have no bite if she thought he had come to terms with fatherhood.

"Come on, Reese. Just be civil."

"Daddy," Reese says. "You might as well get used to hearing it."

"Not if you'd listen instead of taking shots at me!"

Reese pulls back. "What do I have to do with it? So far as I can tell, I'm not taking shots at you. I'm defending myself from whatever you called me here to rub in my face."

"You have everything to do with it!" Ames's voice rises into an exasperated near-shout so that a couple of passing college girls, maybe a little tipsy, stare at him, then make wide eyes at each other and glance at Reese like: *You poor woman.* This is how Reese has always fought with him. Preemptive defense. Ames puts his hands on his lap, with the palms facing up. A few months ago, he'd seen an interview with the actress Winona Ryder in which she said that when she wanted to appear unthreatening in her films, she often sat with her hands folded palms up on her lap, because this communicated openness and vulnerability, a gesture that Ryder had credited for her reputation as delicate. Ames has been trying out the gesture ever since, in an attempt to defuse arguments, especially ones where maleness comes across as threatening. Carefully and quietly, he says, "I'm trying to tell you that I want you to consider being a mother to this baby."

Last week, after Katrina showed him the pregnancy test, he went home and lay in bed like a morose sea lion, moving only to scan through, yet again, Katrina's only social media account—Instagram. After gazing at Katrina's face for an hour, he pulled up Reese's account, as was his habit when lonely or distressed, a habit he'd never quite been able to break. If he went far enough down in her feed, there were pictures of her from when they lived together—all the pictures with him were erased of course, but in many others, he knew that he was standing just off frame. Looking at a shot of her wearing bunny ears from an Easter morning in their apartment, he tried to predict her scoffing reply were he to tell her that he was a father. In that exercise, he was surprised to brush, for the first time in hours, against a feeling like hope. It had only ever been through her, with her, that he could imagine parenthood. Why not again? Reese—the trans woman from whom he'd learned about womanhood—would see his fatherhood and dismiss it. To her, he would always be a woman. By borrowing her vantage, he could almost see himself as a parent: Perhaps one way to tolerate being a father would be to have her constant presence assuring him that he was actually not one. This possibility dovetailed with what he wanted anyway: to be family with Reese once more, in some way. So why not in parenthood? Was it such a wild proposal to contemplate? Were Reese to help raise the child too, everyone would get what they wanted. Katrina would have a commitment to family from her lover, Reese would get a baby, and he, well, he'd get to live up to what they both hoped he could be by being what he already was: a woman but not, a father but not.

"What? You want me to consider being a mother to this baby?" Reese does not have her palms facing up. "That doesn't even make sense."

"Yes it does. Listen to me." But Ames has not fully convinced himself that his plan makes sense either, that he isn't speaking out of a deluded panic. That the game pieces for Katrina and Reese that he has been pushing around his mental chessboard bear only dubious relation to the movements possible by the actual Katrina and Reese.

He laid it out. Katrina wanted him to be a father. If Ames could not, in fact, be a father, then Katrina did not relish the idea of being a single parent, and would schedule an abortion. Ames, for his part, wanted to stay with Katrina, and he could envision himself becoming a parent, but not a father. He knew, however, that Katrina didn't have the queer background to allow for that distinction, and that despite all his best intentions, she would default to the assumptions inherent in a man and a woman raising a child together. Unless he could find a way to escape the gravity of the nuclear family, no matter what he called himself, he'd end up a father. He didn't need to explain this to Reese. She knew that no matter how you self-identify ultimately, chances are that you succumb to becoming what the world treats you as. "That's where you come in," Ames says, allowing for few pauses so that Reese couldn't interrupt him until he got it all out. "I want you to raise a baby with me, and Katrina. With three of us, it'll be confusing enough to break the family thing. Katrina won't know how to see me as anything but a father, but you will; and speaking from experience, your vision, your way of seeing things is infective. Together, maybe we could be a family that works."

Reese says nothing.

"Think about it, Reese. You could be a mother. You could raise a child. Like we always wanted."

"I'm going to get up and leave," Reese says finally. "You've lost it. I thought I couldn't be shocked by your dumbass transformations anymore, but even I couldn't have predicted that you'd come back to me proposing to become a bigamist. What the actual fuck." But she doesn't get up and leave. She doesn't move at all. He catches his breath, waiting for her to say no, to say that she'd never raise a kid with him, to close the door on the best offer he'd ever have to put on the table. If she wouldn't accept motherhood from him, she'd never accept anything.

"Is that how little you think of me?" Reese continues after a minute. "That I'd accept some second-rate motherhood? And meanwhile, why the fuck would this other woman carry a baby for a transsexual and an ex-transsexual. Who is this woman? What's wrong with her?"

"Nothing is wrong with her. I don't even know if she'll be open to the idea. I haven't proposed it."

"Oh my god, you came to me first? You absolute psychopath."

"She can say no! You can say no!"

"Who is she?"

And so Ames gives the particulars, the way you might introduce yourself to a new acquaintance: your work, where you're from and if you're a New Yorker, your neighborhood, and maybe, if your sangfroid is really pumping, your age. For Katrina, Ames reports these variables as: his boss at the ad agency; she's from Vermont but has lived in New York since college; she's got a two-bedroom in Brooklyn, and she's thirty-nine; she had a miscarriage before. But having repeated these facts, Ames feels like he hasn't said anything important, anything that captures Katrina at all, or why he thinks she'd share raising a baby.

A dog bounds toward Reese, interrupting his explanation. Reese gives the dog a pet and the dog's owner apologizes. In refocusing on what he had been about to say, Ames attempts to dispel from his mind the slivers of moments, opinions, and impressions particular to his intimacy with Katrina that obscure the bold plain structures of her, in order to describe her as a dispassionate stranger might see her.

"When I first met Katrina," he says, "she seemed kind of basic to me. Maybe it was because she was my boss and so that was part of her professional distance. But as I got to know her, I came to see her basicness as a disguise, or a defense mechanism. But not something

conniving or intentional. It's more like she's layered all this weird-
ness together in her life experiences, from growing up in Vermont,
then leaving her husband, and just a fundamentally idiosyncratic
personality; and then, as though she's shy about it and doesn't want
anyone to notice, she'll cover that with being a foodie and doing
Pilates or whatever. But underneath, she's wild. Not at all conventional. She might go for this."

"What's she look like? I want to picture her," Reese says.

He considers pulling out his phone to show her a photo, but he
doesn't really want to get into a moment where Reese is comparing
herself or evaluating the looks of another woman. "She's average
height, kind of delicate. Really cute toes."

"You perv! That doesn't help me see her. Is she a blonde? You
always liked blondes."

"No, straight brown hair. She's mixed-race, actually. Her mom
is Chinese and her dad is Jewish. But she got her dad's last name,
Petrajelik, and freckles all across her nose, so she passes as white
with white people. In Vermont, she grew up with only white kids
around, so she says it was a shock when she went to Amherst and
other Asian kids immediately recognized her as Asian."

Reese laughs. Of course that would be the case. Same story, different minority: No matter how easily she passed as cis among the
cis, passing as cis among other trans women never happened—they
had trained their entire lives to see signs of transness, and hope
alone dictated that they would detect those signs in Reese. "Great,
she and I already have something in common," Reese says. "We're
both *almost* cis white ladies."

Ames had had more than a couple of conversations with Katrina
about race and Katrina always expressed a sense of dismay about
her passing. "Yeah, you two both pass. But I don't know if she's as
aspirational about it as you are. Almost the opposite: I gather she
feels something lost by her passing as a white lady."

"She grew up entirely in Vermont?"

"Yeah. But not just Vermont, like, rural, back-to-the-land Vermont. They didn't even have a TV until she was a teenager."

"Primeval."

"She loves pop culture, the way kids whose parents didn't let them have sugar love candy." Katrina's stories from her early childhood struck Ames as cribbed from a cautionary post-hippie novel. The kind of story where idealistic types end up starving out on a commune somewhere, flower crowns wilting to reveal a grim human nature hidden beneath.

In first-generation style, Katrina's mother, Maya, had staged a twofold rebellion against her immigrant parents. First, Maya insisted upon becoming an artist, and second she met in an art history class, and later insisted upon marrying, a Jewish kid from Brooklyn named Isaac. Before college, Isaac's Zionist parents sent him to live on a kibbutz in Israel for a year. At eighteen, he volunteered for the Israeli military service, which nearly lost him his U.S. citizenship. Within the year, he found himself participating in the incursions into Lebanon that came to be known as the 1978 Operation Litani, a participation which, to his parents' great dismay, disillusioned him to Zionism and, in the process, religion in general.

He returned home with signs of what might now be called PTSD and convinced that his stint in the promised land made him some kind of farmer. This conviction remained with him throughout his romance with Maya, through his dropping out of college to elope with her, until at last, he spent an inheritance from his maternal grandmother on a tract of land in Vermont. At that point, as close to being a farmer as he'd ever been, he moved his newly pregnant wife away from her disapproving family to a drafty farmhouse on twenty acres of granite hills not far from the border with New Hampshire, promising to convert the back porch into a light-filled art studio for her work.

After a couple of poor seasons trying to raise vegetables and sell them to restaurants and farmer's markets, Isaac met a man who introduced him to a Danish system of raising mink for fur. So for the majority of her childhood, Katrina lived on a mink farm, where her daily chores included feeding a mixture of pureed meat and dried fish to hundreds of slinky river predators stacked in twenty-four-by-forty-eight-inch cages.

"Fur is really so gross," Reese says. "I'm lucky I could never afford a fur coat, because that kind of raw barbarism is a little bit sexy. I wouldn't be able to resist flaunting it."

"Yeah," Ames agrees. "She has a picture on Facebook, from like eighth grade, where she skinned a mink in front of the class as her science project. The student newspaper took the photo. It's like, of a pretty, gawky girl smiling in front of a pile of red gore."

"Horrifying," says Reese happily. "No wonder she pretends to be norm-core now."

Ames's favorite story from Katrina's childhood was the one where a young black bear broke through a screen window and into their house while the family was out. The bear crashed around the kitchen, broke two bottles of red wine, then trod through the resulting wine puddle, leaving red paw prints all over the seventies white carpet and cream-colored couch. Isaac came home and, enraged at the property damage, charged around the house brandishing a fire poker, convinced that he had the skills to engage a bear in combat. Maya, by contrast, arrived home carrying Katrina in one of those toddler back-slings and clapped her hands in delight.

Mink pelts were never as lucrative as Isaac had been promised by mink breeders, and so the couple faced dire finances at times throughout Katrina's childhood. Within two weeks, Maya had sold the paw-printed couch to some rich New Yorkers with a nearby ski lodge, who displayed it in a position of honor, the perfect conversation piece for their friends to admire. In fact, the couch sale was so lucrative that Maya forged a bear paw, poured out another bottle of red wine, and embellished the bear's paw route to include two other chairs that she went on to sell.

"Huh," says Reese. "When I tortured myself thinking about

what women you'd love instead of me, a rural Jewish Chinese mink farmer was not what I came up with. My stereotyping has failed me."

"I'm not sure she's so happy I've picked her either."

"So why does she put up with you, may I ask?"

"My rugged masculine good looks, obviously."

Reese scoffs. He's still too pretty by half; the once rhinoplasty-perfect nose now broken but still delicate, and those light blue eyes that, in old photos, would have come out empty-white, one of those colors that required photographic technology to evolve before it could be captured on film.

"Is she queer at all, this woman?"

Ames had thought a fair amount about this. "I don't think she appreciates queerness so much as she came to feel ambivalent about heterosexuality. I know those two aren't the same thing. She's attracted to masculine bodies, of that I'm sure." He flicks his wrist in a semi-ironic indication of his own now-curve-depleted body as evidence. "Although perhaps not men as a class. A lot of what she liked about me, she says, is how different I am from the other men she's dated. I think what she might be attracted to is my gender, the traces of queerness about me—with me she gets queerness without ever having to name it or dredge up any attraction to women. But now that she knows I was once a transsexual, she acts like it's the only reason I am how I am. Everything she liked about me before is suddenly fraught. She's not taking it well."

And it's true, she hasn't been. She declines his calls, and speaks to him only enough to keep up appearances at work. A few days after he told her, he caught her staring at him across a conference table, her eyes almost unfocused, the way one stares to make sense of an optical illusion. He recognized what she was doing: She was making him into a woman in her mind, an exercise that he'd done countless times himself but in reverse—the ugly involuntary method by which his hateful vision broke a trans woman's face down into component parts, then remodeled them in the brain to strip away the apparent feminization and see what she had looked like before transition. His brain was an asshole, because the result of this exercise was to triple his insecurity. Given how easily and involuntarily he did it, even while aware of the high fucked-up quotient, he imagined how frequently other people without his sensitivity had done it to him.

He guessed that his take on Katrina's queerness was one that would predispose Reese to at least not hate Katrina. The mention of motherhood would have softened Reese up, and now he finished her off with secret moments of weird gender feels or confused faggotry: Reese's bread and butter.

"I get it," Reese says when he finishes. "So everything is upside down for her, right? Post-divorce, now she's pregnant. She's kind of a weirdo, and she's unsure about what she wants. She's questioning herself. And so you're thinking she might just let you invite another woman to raise your baby with her?"

"Don't make me sound so sinister," Ames responds. But he has presented the argument with a sinister cast in an appeal to Reese's sensibilities. It hurts less to discuss a baby that she would desperately want to love and raise in the same way that Cruella De Vil discusses puppies.

"Please. You come up with the most fucked-up shit," Reese says. "You are so weird and devious, even when you were doing that Martha Stewart thing you did with me, and definitely while you're doing this fake cis thing. But I get why you think it will work. You pitch her on the idea while she's confused and trying to figure out a new way of seeing the world. Isn't that right? Isn't that your plan?"

"No! I actually want to do this right. Be good to her. I think this gives her every option— an extra option, even. If she wants to raise a baby on her own, I'll pay child support and do what I can. If she wants an abortion, obviously I will support that. And finally, if she wants me as a father, I will say yes, and then propose that you enter our lives."

"Ah," says Reese. "Once again, Reese is your plan C."

"I'm doing my best here, Reese. I can't force her to do anything. I don't even want to do that. The thing I am totally against, however, is the outcome where she gets an abortion, then she hates me, while you go on hating me too. The everyone-hates-me option, which, frankly, is looking the most likely. I want to avoid that."

Reese made a scoffing noise. "That's only the worst outcome for you. Maybe for us, being free of you would be ideal."

"And then you'll pass up yet another chance to be a mother."

Reese flinches slightly and doesn't respond.

"Reese," Ames continues, "I'm sorry I can't promise anything. But I'm asking you to consider an option where you're a mother."

"I'm here. I'm entertaining you, even if this is so messed up. But now"—Reese puts two fingers on his shirt—"I have questions. Tell the truth. Do you love her?"

"I want good things for her. I for sure don't want to hurt her."

"Answer my question, Amy."

"Yes. I love her. We don't say the word 'love' to each other. But I love her." He can't seem to make eye contact, and instead peers upward at the breeze rustling through the leaves above.

"Second question. Do you still love me?"

This was maximum Reese. Asking such a thing at the moment when she had the ultimate advantage—when he'd just laid out his feelings for another woman. "Yes and no. Some days I still love you and some days I don't."

Reese waited, sensing there was more. So he let her have as much of the truth as he could bear. "But the days I don't love you . . . I have to work hard to make those days happen. The days I do require nothing of me. You were the most important person in my life for so long, and then . . . then everything went wrong and we just disappeared to each other. When I think about raising this child with you, well, it feels like a kind of redemption. Romantically, fuck, who knows if we would ever be right for each other again? It all fell apart so badly that I hesitate to even hope for that. But if we weren't meant to be lovers, it doesn't mean that we weren't meant to be family. Every single time I remember the state of things between us, I want to cry. I thought it would fade, but it hasn't; it's just changed. If we don't try again, it's like our time together . . . Not only did it end, it was like it never was."

"You're the one who disappeared, Amy. Look at yourself."

He rushes on, over her comment, afraid to lose the moment. "But that's why I'm trying to see this as an opportunity. Right? What if we could make those years together into something new? All of our past could be the groundwork for something lasting."

Reese puffs up her cheeks and blows out a little *pfft*. She shakes her head, almost in wonder, and then an abrupt grin cracks her face. "You know what, Amy? I think the best way to get back at you is to say yes to this offer, and then watch you struggle to figure it all out from a front-row seat. So fuck you, my love. Yes, I will consider it."

"Consider it."

"Yes, go ask this other woman, Katrina, to split her unborn child with a transsexual. I fully expect that she will murder you for the suggestion, for which I will take a portion of the credit without having to risk jail. If you are still alive in a week, we'll take it from there."

Ames grips his own hands tightly. "So you accept?"

"I already said yes." Her voice betrays too much sincerity, and she worries that Ames can hear the naked hope that has already entangled her. He says nothing more, so she smacks him on the thigh, laughs a short nervous laugh, and then puts her face in her palm and mumbles, mostly to herself, "Actually *this* might be the most trans way of getting me pregnant."

CHAPTER TWO

Eight years before conception

REESE WAS TWENTY-SIX the first time a man hit her—as a man will sometimes hit a woman: not to injure her, necessarily, but to show her something. The blow, an open-handed hook, caught her as she opened her mouth to insult him. She hadn't seen his hand coming. Her head jerked back. Her vision wavered. Surprise turned to pain, which in turn surprised her with its force. "Really?" she asked quietly.

He coiled his muscles tight again, as if to show her that yes, really. If she had it all to do over, she would have spat at him. But her body, which did not like pain, betrayed her, and without thinking, she flinched and blurted out, "I'm sorry." Satisfied, his shoulders dropped.

Copper trickled thinly from a split lip into the cracks between her teeth. She probed the edges of the cut with her tongue, while her hands hung motionless at her sides, the stillness of an animal turned statue before a predator.

Somewhere distant from her traitorous body, a covert part of her mind slipped away to calculate her advantage. Already she saw the doubt gathering across his face, the regret and worry that he'd hit her too hard. Already, in the cool distance, she saw how this would play out: She would make him suffer for this. She'd chip away at his self-image of a calm, assured, stoic man, ever in control of his will, unable to be goaded. She'd make him guilty, she'd make him doubt, she'd hint at abuse. When the animal part of her body had calmed itself, when the pain had turned to memory, she supposed she'd finger the bruise, almost voluptuously, her trophy from a grim victory. His name was Stanley, and he was a rich man in his late thirties who didn't like dogs. That he didn't like dogs was one of the things Reese decided was important about his character. When she told her friend Iris his name, Iris said that there was no such thing as a good Stanley. That the name is a curse that parents place upon a son to ensure the boy grows up to become a douche. Reese knew her Stanley was a douche. Reese desired him, but she wouldn't say that she liked him. She liked his jealousy, his controlling behavior, the way he told her how to dress. She liked seeing herself through his eyes: vulnerable, fragile, prone to the most exasperatingly feminine qualities—he made fun of her for being obsessed with her looks, for flightiness, dreaminess, and her highly subjective and associative takes on the workings of the world. She liked how he called her a whore, then bought her expensive gifts. Rub his leg, ask for a new dress, get called a bimbo, go shopping for the dress. She liked how infatuated with her he had become, and how much he resented his own infatuation. The more he demeaned her, she knew, the more she'd hooked him. And so goading him into anger took on an unctuous, dangerous pleasure. Her friends hated him.

Only Iris, she of the gorgeous blond hair and the party habit, who frequently disappeared into two- or three-day meth-fueled sex benders, really understood why Reese kept digging in deeper with Stanley. "I want to drive men crazy," Iris said in her customary arch manner. "I want men to suffer. I want a man to love me so much he murders me. I want to die because I'm loved too much for him to tolerate my existence."

Reese didn't want to die. Compared to Iris, Reese felt like she was only playing at this sort of psychodrama—Fisher Price: My First Abusive Man. Whereas Iris *only* had time for abusive men. Iris had a doll's eyes and a practiced Marilyn Monroe giggle. She'd been an English major at Brown before she had transitioned, but refused to read any books afterward, and instead presented vacant ambitions in which she could remain an object: get discovered and be a movie star, become a Lana Del Rey song personified. In the postmeth lows, she spoke in other images, laced with serotonin-depleted terror and an almost prideful insistence on describing her own actions in the passive voice: *being pimped; having my pussy pledged; spending days in addled semi-captivity among faceless men who made me addicted, who owned me, who fucked me limp, whose lives depend on my body.*

The dreamy way that Iris talked about what should have been horror made Reese jealous. Before Stanley, Reese's own sex games only flirted with possession, and alone with her Hitachi, images from Iris's stories kept making cameos in her fantasies. Hands on her throat. Slaps to her face. Fight leaving her body. To Iris, though, Reese said little, other than "whoa." Once, Reese asked Iris if she needed help, to get away from those men. In response, Iris grimaced and said, "It's not like that." And for once, Reese, the transsexual who hadn't gone to college, much less Brown, was embarrassed by her sensibilities, as she clutched her pearls, primly imagining the sensationalism of an SVU episode featuring sex trafficking instead of whatever Iris actually got, emotionally or otherwise, from the men with whom she disappeared. It was the same tone of uninformed concern that older cis people used with Reese when they discovered she was a transsexual: *Oh dear, your life must really not be okay.* The response always surprised them: *I chose this. I want it. It makes me feel right.* Whatever Iris was getting, Iris got it because she found in it something she wanted and Iris had shared it with Reese, because she had sensed that lurking in an unspoken place Reese craved something kindred. The least Reese could do was to be honest, to not pretend like she didn't understand the chaos that separated what can be wanted and what can be said.

Consider for a moment Reese's own damage: She met Stanley on a fetish site with the word "tranny" in its name. During that period of her life, Reese only ever dated on fetish sites. She disdained the trans girls who disdained tranny chasers. It's stupid to rule out every single man who has come to the understanding that he desires your body. It's a mark of prudish inexperience to think that being fetishized and objectified isn't the hottest thing going in the bedroom.

Reese's dating practice prescribed that the only chasers you had to avoid were the crypto-trans women, the ones who want to be women but are too closeted to handle it, and so they live their fantasies through you. You can feel it when you're with a crypto-trans. A crypto-trans has to evacuate you, your personhood, to use you, to fantasize that he is you getting fucked even as he fucks you. You're just a body for him to live through vicariously. It's the most alienating thing in the world. It's like being psychically worn. Like you're a glove. Reese fled at the first sign of a crypto-trans. She wished they'd just become ladies and stop being so weird.

But every other chaser? Why bother convincing clueless, gunshy boys on OkCupid of the sexiness of a girl with a cock when there are thousands of men out there who already know it, and among whom you get to have your pick? Want a movie star? You can have one (albeit a B-lister if you're willing to satisfy a guy's curiosity about bottoming for a transsexual, otherwise a C-lister). Want a tech scion to show you his yacht? Great! The ones with powerboats are best, guys with sailboats will make you pull random ropes, and to imagine yourself as a cool Jackie O is one aspirational self-delusion too far. Want a walking Bruce Weber photograph with washboard abs cut so deep it looks like he's constantly side-lit? Take a couple of male models and save one for later. The only thing you can't have is a decent guy who will take you home for Thanksgiving dinner, but you're not going to get that off a non-fetish site either, so at least have the good sex.

How many girls did Reese know who, to prove to themselves that they could be just like every other woman, found themselves sifting through thousands of men on some straight dating site, looking for the non-horrible ones—a task that even cis women find awful? And then, how many times had Reese heard about these girls who wasted hours, days, weeks, months trying to find one of the non-horrible ones who would be willing to give a trans woman a try, only to finally end up in his bedroom, standing exposed with only a stupid lacy lingerie set for armor, as he sized up the new-to-him proportions of slender hips to wider shoulders, and nervously muttered that it's not for him?

No way. That shit is way more traumatic than running into any chaser. Go to a fetish site for men who already know they want a trans girl, and select a decent one from among the many begging for you. In matters of the heart, Reese had one firm maxim: You don't get to choose who you fuck, you get to choose from among those who want to fuck you.

She found Stanley on the most embarrassing of her many embarrassing fetish sites—a site that hadn't updated its technology, much less its design, since the era of Web 1.0, but on which she reliably pulled all sorts of guys who didn't know enough about the queer world to look elsewhere for the kind of submissive trans girls they'd seen in porn but never in the bars they frequented.

On their first date, he showed off by taking her to a Jean-Georges restaurant. He picked out a bottle of French Bordeaux from a separate section of the menu, where the prices were so high that they were vaguely shameful and had to be tucked in at the end, like the ads for dominatrices in the back pages of free weeklies.

After an appropriate period of chitchat, she asked her standard opening question: "So tell me about your previous experience with trans girls."

"I've always liked trans girls, but my experience has just been escorts," he replied, then paused. "I've had ongoing things with escorts, but in the end, those always made me feel bad."

"Because you don't like paying for sex?"

He blinked. "No, I don't mind paying for sex." Then without affect, so she couldn't tell if it was a joke, he added, "What do you think this dinner is?"

Without seeming to register her aghast face, he continued, "The problem for me with trans escorts is that they all want vaginas. Most of the ones I met were doing it to make money until they could get one. It made me feel bad. I want to see that little bulge, and they all

wanted to get rid of it. That's why I went to that site. I figured anyone calling themselves a sissy or tranny had probably come to terms
with her cock." He broke a piece of bread with his hands and popped
it into his mouth.

Reese continued to stare, unable to formulate a response. He
said, "Come on, you asked me a blunt question about my sexual
past and sexuality. I gave you a blunt answer. It's your turn. Don't
act demure now. Do you want a vagina?"

He had blue eyes in a big bland face, shaggy hair, and was dressed
like he planned to be photographed for a lifestyle magazine for
wealthy understated men interested in bird-watching or some other
non-vigorous outdoor activity, in a waxed canvas Barbour jacket
with many pockets and a heavily cabled turtleneck. When they met
on the street, she joked that she was expecting a Wall Street guy in
a suit. "Those are the sellers. The bankers. Guys who want money,"
he said dismissively. "I represent the buyers. The guys who already
have money. I could show up to work in my swim trunks." Even
Reese knew enough about finance to recognize this as a suspect
oversimplification, but it sounded so much like a line from *Glen-
garry Glen Ross* that Reese merely said, "Wow." And even she was
unsure if that wow was because he had impressed her with his confidence or because she had never heard such a clichéd performance
delivered with so little irony so soon after an introduction.

"I sometimes want bottom surgery," Reese said. "When I turned
eighteen, I got some money that my grandmother left for me. It was
about two-thirds of what I needed to go to Thailand and get one.
Instead I spent it on a road trip with a boyfriend and moving to New
York. I got a job here in a daycare, then as a server, and I figured
that it'd be years before I could afford surgery working as a waitress, so I've worked to get comfortable with the idea that I have a
penis, but that it's a woman's penis. I'm pretty much there, mentally.
It helps that I grew up watching trans porn. I watched way more
trans girls getting fucked than cis women, so I think I internalized

the idea of trans women with cocks as the hottest, most feminine women out there."

"I like that," Stanley said, and grinned for the first time. "I could see you as a hot Jersey housewife. I want to put you in a pair of yoga pants, tight enough that you can't hide your cock."

Reese really liked wearing yoga pants, but his interest in her penis so early in the date meant that she wasn't yet going to give him the satisfaction of saying so. She wondered if he'd somehow gotten confused. She'd clearly stated that she was a strict bottom on the fetish site. "You know I don't top, right?"

"What? Of course not. I don't want that."

"Okay, well you had so much interest in my junk."

"I'm interested in everything decorative on a woman."

Referring to Reese's genitals as purely decorative was an objectively asshole thing to say. But instead of being offended, she was turned on.

The waiter stopped by the table at this moment to refill Reese's wineglass, and Reese inadvertently blushed, unsure what he had heard. Meanwhile Stanley was saying, "I like dressing up women. Controlling them. It's never role-play." The waiter set down the bottle and departed with a maximum of discretion.

"Wait, what's not role-play?" Reese asked.

He looked at her sharply. "You need to listen better. The whole dominant thing. That's just who I naturally am. I don't need protocols, or bullshit like that. I want the subjugation to be real. But the only politically acceptable way to subjugate women is financially. Because women want that subjugation themselves. One thing I liked about those trans escorts was how easily I bought them."

She had long since discovered that most talk about owning her turned her stomach liquid with desire. But at that moment, she had four hundred dollars in her bank account—cracks webbed her phone screen, she needed a plane ticket to see her mother, and just as the items she needed weren't sexy, the idea of trading subservience for them wasn't that sexy either. It wasn't her fault that people paid finance douches millions and no one wanted to hire an uneducated transsexual. She had a funny-'cause-it's-true joke that she liked to ask whenever she met a new trans girl. *So which of the three transsexual jobs do you do? Computer programmer, aesthetician, or prostitute?* Reese always hoped the answer would be prostitute, because prostitutes were the ones with a good sense of humor.

"Subjugation is fun in bed," Reese snapped back at Stanley. "Women don't want that anywhere else, especially not poor trans girls who don't have any choice." He darkened and told her to sit up straight, that she had bad posture. She did as he said, feeling self-conscious and humiliated—but not in a fun way—and resolved to order only a salad, since this date would clearly be their last. She couldn't afford to split the meal, but she wanted to make a show of non-obligation.

When the food came, he criticized her use of utensils. "You don't come to a nice restaurant and then eat like a slob. Didn't anyone teach you?" He held his fork in his left hand tines down. "See? Like this."

"I know how to eat. I work as a waitress."

"Nowhere I'd want to eat."

She glared at him. But when she tried to use her fork tines down, she couldn't manage it. Not because she couldn't eat that way, but because he had intended to humiliate her, and had succeeded, which threw off her coordination. In trying to pick up a piece of flaking salmon from her salad, she shredded it into tiny bits too small to be speared on the tines. She blushed, set down the utensils, and took a sip of water. "Oh, just eat your normal way. This is embarrassing to watch," Stanley said. "But you need to practice your etiquette. Unless you want me to cut your food for you and you can use a spoon?" Having sufficiently humbled her, he grew friendlier, conspicuously popping chunks of steak into his mouth, speared tines down.

On the way out, he wrapped a sudden arm around her and gave the side of her face a bizarre kiss, closer to a nuzzle than anything else, and then pressed a fifty on her, saying, "It's late, take a taxi." Reese hesitated, then pocketed the fifty, waited until the car he'd ordered arrived to take him home, and then walked to the train. No way was she wasting fifty bucks on what could be a $2.25 subway fare, with only one transfer on the way.

The next morning, she woke up to an Amazon gift certificate for five hundred dollars delivered to the email account she used for fetish site communiqués. He'd sent it with a note. *I saw you didn't get a car home, even though I gave you money for one. I wasn't paying for the pleasure of your company, but since that seems to be what you want from me (despite your little outburst to the contrary) I've sent you what I think you're worth. Use it to buy some yoga pants to please me, and do whatever you wish with the rest.*

She entered the code into Amazon, and considered doing as she had done with the fifty, buying the cheapest pair of yoga pants that she could find so that she could pocket the rest. But looking at her options, she decided, fuck it, when unexpected yoga pants come your way, go full Lululemon. She hit the Purchase button, and said aloud, "I hate him." But, considering it didn't even cross her mind not to buy yoga pants at all, the heat that came over her wasn't only from hate.

She replied with a screenshot of the receipt and he wrote back an hour later. *God, that was so easy. I didn't even have to work to make you into a whore.*

I haven't fucked you yet, asshole, she wrote back.

He replied with a second Amazon gift card for the same amount, along with an OpenTable reservation for seven-thirty P.M. that Friday to a steak house, and the instructions: *Wear those yoga pants. Don't tuck.*

"I fucking hate him," Reese said aloud again, as she dutifully scheduled the date on her calendar. As she shaved her legs in her cramped tub before the date, she reached down and idly rubbed her shaving cream–covered clit, and said it again.

· · ·

If there is such a thing as a hate-fuck, theirs was a hate-courtship, with plenty of hate-foreplay. One week, in the midst of a January cold snap, he rented her a room at the Ritz-Carlton Battery Park, near his office. Once he had installed her in the room, he took away her clothes, leaving her only a one-piece swimsuit and the hotel bathrobes, so that she'd freeze if she left. She spent four days looking out at the frigid Hudson River, living off room service and waiting for him to stop by during his breaks to fuck her (or depending on his time constraints, to hold her face into a pillow with one hand, and jerk off onto her back with the other), turned on and resentful the whole time. At night, she invited friends to the room, and they drank bottles of wine on his room service tab, but she followed the rules, and didn't ask to be brought anything else to wear.

Stanley had a wife, because of course he did. But the wife hospitalized herself for depression at about the time that Reese was willingly trapped in concubinage at the Ritz. This hospitalization—or specifically, her subsequent inpatient treatment for it—precipitated a series of conversations between the wife and Stanley about life goals, followed by a sudden separation. In lieu of a long divorce settlement, he promised his ex-wife a sum sufficient to buy a house in Portland, where her sister lived. Within a few weeks the wife had embarked along the Oregon Trail. Stanley told Reese he'd be pushing harder on riskier investments to make up for that unforeseen financial expense. Accordingly, he also told Reese that she should move into his apartment with him, as he didn't want to pay her rent any more—something he'd been doing since their third week together.

As a child in Madison, Wisconsin, Reese had badly wanted a best friend, someone who was yours and you were his. Her early childhood was one of serial BFF-monogamy until sometime in mid-puberty, when the other boys around were made to know—in the form of shunning—that being paired as a best friend with someone so feminine pointed toward a clear and uncool faggotry. Later Reese re-narrativized the childhood urge. She hadn't wanted a charming, reliable boy for a best friend; she had wanted a charming, reliable boy for a sexual, romantic, and life companion, and simply framed that as "friend," the only word available to her. She'd found charming plenty of times, but reliable hadn't come her way. So she found a certain comfort in Stanley's possessiveness, his assumption that she was his to install in an apartment as one installs a new sink. His controlling behavior confirmed how badly he wanted her. Anyone who needed her so close, who assumed the right to know where she was at all times, whom she saw, what she wore, was someone who wasn't going away, someone who could be counted upon, not just despite her trans-ness, but for it. This time she felt she'd found reliable, if not charming.

Which is how, in accepting a fifty on the way out of a restaurant from a guy she had been telling herself looked like a tool who bought scalped tickets to Burning Man, Reese found herself looking at an empty walk-in closet in Stanley's bedroom. It was thirty-five square feet of recessed-halogen-lit floor that amounted to all the physical space in the world over which she held complete dominion—and even that space really belonged to Stanley. She stared at the empty hangers and thought about how she really had to get better at fighting back, because she had lost not just the upper hand in this battle of a relationship, but all her other limbs as well. As she thought such things, he pointed to a mirror he had recently hung on the back of the closet door and said, "And now, you can spend hours staring at your own reflection, like the parakeet you are."

Despite hate-fucks that led to a hate-courtship that built into a hate-relationship, six months passed before Stanley finally hit Reese and split her lip. The question of motive gets dicey, however. Why that moment, and not so many others?

Even a mediocre lawyer could establish certain basic facts: Stanley bought Reese a particular pair of expensive designer boots, and she, knowing it would anger him, exchanged them for a pair she preferred. Then, in an attempt to deceive him, she purchased a pair of cheap knockoffs that resembled the original pair, which she endeavored to pass off as the authentic item. Whereupon Stanley immediately recognized the forgery and took her attempted deception as an insult. How dumb did she think he was that he wouldn't notice the difference between some ordered-online-and-sent-from-China ill-fitting glorified socks, and the eight-hundred-dollar Stuart Weitzman signature suede Lowland above-the-knee boots that he had personally picked out and bought for her? It wasn't bad enough that she exchanged his present? Then she went and faked like she hadn't, like she thought he was too stupid to know what he'd held in his hand? No. Fuck that. Slap the bitch.

But in the way relationships get twisted, in how lovers—or rather, combatants—develop their own private language of aggression, the Boots Incident was even more complicated than it seemed. In truth, Stanley already knew that Reese would hate the boots when he picked them out. He bought them for that exact reason—to spend money on a luxury designer item that she could never afford on her own, but that she also couldn't enjoy, in order to see the conflict that such a purchase would raise in her. He bought the boots to demonstrate for her a simple calculation of power: She enjoyed living in style, but her dependence on him for that style made him the final arbiter of what she put on her body.

As a set of objects, the boots were beautiful: finely stitched in a soft suede the same gray shade as a manatee's hide, lined with satin, and set on a carefully molded rubber sole, with little *SW*s imprinted on the bottom, so that as you walk the earth, your steps imprint the designer's initials. But once snugly up a pair of legs, the boots took on a second, more socially fraught function. With their incomprehensible combination of thigh-high length and flat soles, they seemed designed to allow for impossible models to flaunt how their legs refused to end—even in what might have passed for the slouchy bottom half of an elephant costume. Reese's legs, by contrast to a supermodel's, would take only a short, truncated journey in those boots, a brief trip that would come to a definitive end in the cul-desac of bodily dysphoria. Gigi Hadid wore high flat boots like this, but the squattest of lucha libre wrestlers did too. Stanley knew which of the two Reese's cruel dysmorphia would reflect back to her from her parakeet mirror.

Yet again, knowing Reese for a brand whore, Stanley expected she would still attempt to wear such expensive boots. However! In a climactic twist that Stanley had not expected, Reese returned the insult.

In her own passive-aggressive calculus, Reese never meant for Stanley to be deceived when she bought the knockoffs. She meant for him to easily recognize the difference between the designer boots and the poor imitations. She meant to show him that he was just as disposable to her as she was to him, that she had him figured out, and if he fucked with her in any way that she didn't find, at minimum, sexy and fun, she'd take his money and lie to his face. This unexpected declaration of her power, which they both understood to be communicated as an insult according to the rules of their ritualized unfriendliness, is why he slapped her.

But in ways that both of them felt but neither could fully admit, the entire saga of the boots that led to the slap was a form of pageantry. Beneath it lay Reese's own sense of womanhood. The reason Stanley hit Reese reversed everything both of them wanted to be true: Stanley hit Reese because she wanted him to hit her.

Reese wanted to end their games, to get hit in a way that would affirm, once and for all, what she wanted to feel about her womanhood: her delicacy, her helplessness, her infuriating attractiveness. After all, *Every woman adores a Fascist.* Reese spent a lifetime observing cis women confirm their genders through male violence. Watch any movie on the Lifetime channel. Go to any schoolyard. Or just watch your local heterosexuals drinking in a bar. Hear women define themselves through pain, or rage against the assumption that they do, which still places pain front and center. Hear the strange sense of satisfaction when they talk about the men who have hurt them—the unspoken subtext of it being *because I am a woman.*

The quiet dignity of saying *ow* anytime a man gets a little rough—asserting that you are a woman, and thus delicate and capable of sustaining harm. A girl could be twice the size of the man—that little *ow* reminds him that he is a man, she is a woman. Once, Reese's friend Catherine was walking home drunk with her boyfriend when he tried to flirt with her by pushing her into a bush. She bounced back out of that bush like an enraged wolverine: spitting, scratching, fighting. For the rest of her relationship with him, he would say, "Careful, Catherine is *aggressive*," and Catherine would wince, understanding her womanhood was on the line every time. A good woman, she heard in the subtext, would have stayed in the bush and cried. If only some man would push Reese into a bush, she'd know what to do.

Anyone who had shared a hotel room wall with Reese and Stanley could attest that Stanley had laid hands on Reese before. He took his belt to her ass on their second date and told her he wouldn't stop until she cried—tears fell after six strokes, she sobbed after eight, and twenty minutes later she shuddered her way to a tectonic orgasm.

A few years back, Reese might have thought their play extremely racy, titillating, and far beyond the sexual ken of most women—she thought of the desire for violence in sex as some kind of resulting damage from being trans. Then, at around age twenty-three, she watched the Catherine Deneuve film, *Belle de Jour,* and recognized her own sexuality in the upper-crust Belle's secret desire to be mistreated and abused as a whore. Which meant that the strain of masochism that ran through her sexuality was only as racy as a fifty-year-old film that shared a marquee with romances starring Doris Day. Everything about Reese's sexuality, she realized, was banal. Sex at the edge of abuse is banal. And when it comes to gender, consent makes it all pretend, which left consensual violence lacking real value in Reese's tally of gender affirmation.

In old books she had read, Reese remembered women saying that if your husband doesn't beat you, he doesn't love you, a notion that horrified the feminist in Reese but fit with a perfect logic in one of the dark crevices of her heart. And yeah, liberal feminists— especially the trans-hating variety—would have a field day with her. She supposed that they would accuse her of misogyny, of being a secret man, a Trojan horse in slutty lingerie who sought to recapitulate under the guise of womanhood all the abusive tropes that they, in the second wave, had sought to put in the past. But you know what? She didn't make the rules of womanhood; like any other girl, she had inherited them. Why should the burden be on her to uphold impeccable feminist politics that barely served her? *The New York Times* regularly published op-eds by famous feminists who pointedly ruled her out as a woman. Let them. She'd be over here, getting knocked around, each blow a minor illustration of her place in a world that did its gendering work no matter what you called it. So yeah, Stanley, bring it on. Hit Reese. Show her what it means to be a lady.

For years, Reese had a rule: Don't date other trans women. It was a hypocritical rule. Had anyone else ever ruled her as ineligible for dating on account of her gender, she'd have cried transphobia. But in her own secret heart, the idea of dating another trans woman repelled her. She understood but did not want to admit that the repulsion spoke to her own self-disgust. Instead, she explained it to herself by saying that she was hetero in the etymological sense: attracted to difference. It didn't really matter what the difference was—although usually it was maleness to her femaleness, because men knew how to make her feel feminine, and feeling feminine turned her on; but she supposed she'd be open to other different types who could do the same. However, never someone just like her. No one should be that vulnerable to another.

With another trans woman, she imagined she knew the exact locations of all the seams; she could unstitch them with a simple snip, and vice versa. But god, Reese couldn't take her eyes off the baby trans sitting there with Felicity. She stared in a way that risked costing her all her veteran trans aloof cool. She stared like the most blatant of repressed chasers. She couldn't help herself. It was like the concept of space warped so that her every line of sight could only lead straight to this girl's face. Her only reprieve from overt lechery was her history. None of the dykes at that monthly trans lady picnic would suspect her of creepiness; a handful of them had tried it with her, and although she hadn't explicitly articulated her rule, the other women had intuited its general outline and word got around.

Still, the sight of this girl caused her to bathe in a fragrant soup of her own pheromones. She knew why too. It was something even more taboo and transphobic to cop to than her rule, something she was never supposed to say, because what she saw when she looked at that girl was maybe a boy. Albeit, a specific boy. This girl looked exactly like Sebastian. Same frozen-pond eyes, same sharp cheekbones. Were she to have taken a photo of this girl and posted it online, Facebook's facial recognition algorithms would have mis-tagged it as either Sebastian or someone's Siberian husky. Maybe this girl was a little smaller and slimmer than Sebastian, but as Reese watched her talk, she noted half of Sebastian's gestures, and three-quarters of his expressions.

Little conical mushrooms polka-dotted the expanse of grass that lay between Reese and the girl, distant enough that Reese couldn't hear the girl's voice, but her brain filled in Sebastian's looping Norwegian accent.

From beside her, Iris said, "Another year on hormones and she's going to be really pretty." She had noted Reese's silence and followed her gaze. "Should we be threatened?" The girl wore a pair of tight gray pants, calf-height harness-style motorcycle boots, and a long oversized boiled-wool jacket: the uniform of some 1930s European military officer with a flair for androgyny. It was a hard outfit to wear and the girl wore it well, although Reese couldn't tell if the style mix-and-match reflected excellent fashion or such an early stage in transition that the girl didn't yet have a fully feminine wardrobe to pull from.

Neither Iris nor Reese had been to a trans lady picnic in a while. Both had soured on advising just-transitioning girls on the process, or putting up with their dramatics, hookups, and general "woe is me." But Reese had been looking for an unimpeachable reason to avoid Stanley for a few hours on a Saturday, and Iris had been in a low for about a week and wanted to go somewhere where she'd be looked upon with adulation, which the baby transes happily provided whenever she could bring herself to be friendly instead of hanging around the edges making bitchy comments with Reese.

Both Iris and Reese had a sense of themselves as trans elders; despite only being in their late twenties, they were, in trans age, much older than even that trio of just-out forty-somethings sitting together on a checkered blanket, who self-consciously checked their reflections in their phones with a paradoxically unselfconscious lack of discretion.

"Stop staring at her," Iris said when Reese didn't reply. "Everyone's going to know you're jealous."

"It's so much worse than jealous. I'm having a weird crush. It's really embarrassing," Reese said, still staring.

"Ha ha, def," Iris said, without laughing. Iris texted so much that her speech had come to unironically resemble SMS messages. "Stanley will love that."

Reese didn't want to think about Stanley right then. "I wish I was threatened or jealous. It's so much easier to be jealous of another trans girl than attracted to her. Don't you think?" asked Reese. "At least jealousy is the kind of personality flaw you can work on."

"Girl!" said Iris.

But beneath that performance for Iris, the kind of talk that Reese could run on autopilot, Reese's thoughts were strange and stupidly hopeful. She'd gotten what she needed from Stanley. She'd proven to herself, to the world, that she could be a good little girlfriend. She needed to move on. *I'm going to fall in love with that girl,* Reese decided abruptly, and it felt oddly true.

· · ·

Sebastian had been a tall Norwegian foreign exchange student with a head of wild blond hair and a long body and swimmer's shoulders, which he had gotten, naturally, from swimming. Specifically, Sebastian had been on the University of Oslo's champion relay team, but had been issued a year's suspension from Norwegian competitive swimming after he'd tested positive for drug use after a Christina Aguilera concert. The gender norms in all cultures are different: In Scandinavian culture it is apparently okay for a hetero young man to be quite into Christina Aguilera.

A girl he knew who worked for the promoters told him which bar Xtina and her entourage were heading to after the show, and there he met one of her dancers—a tall American named Tiff who spoke with a Texan accent that Sebastian found both intoxicating and difficult to understand. Tiff seemed weary with tour life and wanted to see the city. To impress her, Sebastian and a friend offered to build her a bonfire in a nearby snow-filled industrial park along the docks, so that she could both stay warm and see the sea. To impress her further, they got another friend to bring cocaine. When the police arrived, unsurprisingly drawn to a two-meter bonfire in the empty lots along the water, they'd all been detained— but the officers seemed not to want the hassle of it all and so they were let go. The next day, and not coincidentally, everyone on Sebastian's swim team was subjected to a drug test. His came up positive for both marijuana and cocaine.

Were he to leave school officially, he'd be required to complete the mandatory nine-month army service—most likely guarding the far northern Russian border, which his older brother had told him consisted of bored boys shooting the occasional tank round at stray reindeer every twenty-three-hour Arctic night after twenty-three-hour Arctic night. Rather than Sebastian spend a winter making Jackson Pollocks out of ruminants, his swim coach found him a semester abroad program at the University of Wisconsin, where he could train with one of the better teams in the States and come back a faster swimmer than when he left.

Patty, another waitress at the Madison diner where Reese worked, brought Sebastian in. The place was a kitschy Midwest diner, a necessary stop during campaign seasons, where presidential aspirants ate real middle-American pie for photo ops. In a presidential off-season, Sebastian stood out among the diner's clientele. He wore a nutria fur coat and a sweatband, which, it still being a warm day in September, was perhaps the only thing he could have worn louder and more gauche than his own beauty. Between the outfit and the accent, Reese could not figure out whether he was gay. The first thing he said to her was "Your pants are stupid," which settled that he was an asshole, but could have gone either way on the gay question.

Under the short waitress apron in which she kept a notepad, she had on a pair of tight jeans dyed a faux snakeskin pattern that she thought created a curve-enhancing optical effect.

"Your hair is stupid," she shot back without thinking, then floundered, ". . . mullet-head."

"What's a mullet?" he asked.

"What's on your head."

"Hmm." He turned to Patty, and pulled a low-budget digital game with an LCD screen from the giant pocket on the jacket. "Come on, let's keep playing." He pronounced both the *P* and the *L* distinctly, so you could hear the puff of the *puh* and the light flick of his tongue against the back of his upper teeth in *lay*. (A year or so later, working as a waitress in Manhattan, Reese discovered the contours of her own Wisconsin accent after repeatedly asking patrons if they'd like orange *jews*.)

To Reese's dismay, Sebastian came back to the diner the next day, without Patty, and sat at one of Reese's tables.

"What's the best sweet?" he asked Reese.

"I don't know. Maybe key lime pie," she suggested.

He ordered two key lime pie slices, and when she set down the two plates before him, he pushed one across the table and commanded, "Eat with me."

"I'm working," she said.

"There's almost no one in here," he replied. "And I am trying to apologize."

Her pants were not stupid, he explained, they were beautiful, and some girls were so beautiful that they made him angry and she was one of these girls, and yesterday he was baked out of his mind, so he directed his anger at her pants. "Sometimes," he confessed, "I pass by a girl, and she is so beautiful, I just shout 'fuck.'"

She was so surprised she sat down with him. "Oh! Well, that explains why people have been shouting 'fuck' at me. I figured it was for something else."

"Because you used to be a boy, yeah?"

Immediately she stood back up, her own "fuck" ready on her tongue.

"I like that," he said mildly, as though he hadn't noticed how she sprang to her feet. "My first was someone like you. Older though. I was fifteen, she was twenty-seven."

"That's illegal."

"It's different in Norway. And anyway, I have always been tall and I told her I was twenty."

"We aren't in Norway."

"I know," he said. "I just bought a Chrysler LeBaron." He stabbed his key lime pie with the tines of a fork to emphasize his point.

The complete lack of segue threw her. "A what?"

"A Chrysler LeBaron." He aimed a whipped cream–covered fork out the window. Parked in front of the diner sat an early-nineties-era red Chrysler LeBaron convertible with the top down. "It is not a very good car, everyone tells me, but it looks like such an American car—like what I saw on television in Kristiansand growing up—and it was so cheap. I could never have a car like that in Norway."

She stared at the car, at a complete loss. She didn't have a car, but even if someone offered her a LeBaron, she wasn't sure she'd want it.

"Will you come for a ride with me?" Suddenly, he was boyish, his face animated, and Reese had a moment to contemplate how charm and charisma had something to do with how someone speaks, the patterns and pauses, and how an accent can suddenly amplify that. "Say yes, please"—again the strange *P* to *L* shift that Reese had already noticed—"I have a red American convertible and I need a pretty American girl in the front seat."

She nodded without quite thinking of what she was agreeing to, just happy to be in the pretty-American-girl category. "After work, though. At seven."

She sat in that same seat two weeks later, as he drove the LeBaron west, across the pastel Badlands of South Dakota. He hadn't liked the rules of the Wisconsin swim team any better than he'd liked the rules of the University of Oslo team, and he found Madison as stultifying as the prospect of forever nights at the Russian border.

She'd been blowing him since the first date, but only took her panties off in front of him at a motel outside Wall, home of Wall Drug, because she had already convinced herself that she was in love with him, and so she had to do it sooner or later. He did not go down on her in return. In the darkness afterward, his arms wrapped around her, big spoon style, she allowed herself one quiet sob at her own weakness when listening to the boring older transsexuals in her support group. They'd advised her to wait on surgery at a time when she had half planned a trip to Thailand to buy herself a pussy with the money her grandma had left her for college—to which she had also not gone. Listening to Sebastian's slow breathing near her ear, with his one inert hand coming from beneath her body to softly hold her breast and the other resting on the widest part of her hips, she would have so much rather had a pussy than the slowly dwindling balance in her bank account.

By the time they'd seen California and headed back East, overshooting Wisconsin to arrive in New York City, she'd put aside her doubts and cultivated the fantasy of life with him. She would be his wife. In Norway, a man could marry a transgender woman, who would be recognized as a woman as long as she had been, as the website Sebastian showed her had translated it, "irreversibly sterilized." But Reese had also almost run out of money, and news that Sebastian's swimming stipend had been canceled arrived by email when they were somewhere in Pennsylvania. In New York, they crashed in Astoria with some trans girls she knew from LiveJournal. Their second day in New York, Sebastian sold the LeBaron on Craigslist to pay for a ticket back to Norway.

His plans were vague. He'd sort out his military-service problem then send money for her to fly to Oslo. "It won't be more than three months," he calculated. He told her to get a job as a waitress again. She got a job nine days and twenty-six applications later, in the East Village, an hour's commute by subway from the couch in Astoria for which she had begun to pay rent to the other trans girls to sleep upon. The restaurant wanted her for one shift a week. But a waitress there knew the manager at a gym opening up in Chelsea that needed people to run the in-gym daycare.

She applied to the job stealth, the first time she had professionally hidden her trans identity. But she wanted no trans panic when it came to her and children. She got the job without incident. Thus, starting at five A.M. the following Monday, Reese found herself sitting in a playroom done up in bright primary colors, replete with games, a foam castle with a ball pit, a corner for art, and all manner of toys. Ambient music from *Sesame Street* played from hidden speakers. All day long, the count, that purple, vampiric muppet who suffered from a nearly sexual obsession with positive integers, sang of his love—"ONE! Heh-eh-eh-eh, TWO! Heh-eh-eh-eh!"—as mothers came in and handed Reese their children for an hour or two, while they took a spin class or ran on the treadmill. In the corners of the room, cameras surveilled and broadcast everything that occurred there to closed-circuit channels, which the mothers could watch from various angles on channels one and two of the LCD screens mounted to the workout equipment.

The second week, two mothers who were friends came in simultaneously, each handing Reese a six-month-old infant, a diaper bag, and a bottle of breast milk. "If she starts to cry," each mother said of her respective daughter, "just give her the bottle." Before this moment, the youngest children brought into the daycare had been toddlers, and now, suddenly, Reese found herself entrusted with two infants. Neither mother appeared to doubt Reese's credentials— a young woman in childcare? Such a luxe gym must have checked out her background, right? Great, here's a baby!

Reese experienced a moment of initial panic when she forgot which bottle of breast milk went with which tiny girl. She pictured the mothers watching her on the surveillance feed while they sweated on their ellipticals. Then something clicked. The tiny soft bodies in her arms, the way they giggled and cooed, triggered some sort of deep oxytocin-laced trance in Reese. She felt she knew instinctively what to do, knew just how much of the breast milk to give each girl so that she didn't get sick, knew when they needed to be burped, knew when each needed to be picked up and held, when each could be settled back into her baby carrier. The mothers returned to their daughters sleeping and fed. They gushed that Reese had natural mothering instincts, and together began asking at the front desk for Reese's schedule, planning their workouts to correspond with her shifts, then telling other young mothers about the tall maternal brunette. Within a few weeks, Reese was overwhelmed with children during her shifts, and offers to babysit in her free time, so that management was faced with either hiring a second employee during her shifts or changing the policy to no longer disclose her schedule.

At the end of three months in New York, Reese had an evil genie's facsimile of her dream life: surrounded by children, with a man who promised to take care of her. Only the children were not her own, and her man lived an ocean away and rarely called her anymore.

When she and Sebastian did talk, he was often drunk. Increasingly panicked, she held back the need to ask about the plane ticket, about the plan, about his love. When she finally blurted something out, on a low-quality VoIP call from some third-rate bodega calling card, it came out resentful, half-formed, and not at all the first move in the meticulous chess match she'd planned to get him back on track. "You're never going to fly me to Norway, are you?"

"I have a theory," he responded.

"What are you talking about?"

"I have a theory," he said again, then went on when she didn't speak. "My theory is that the only thing I enjoy doing is destroying my own innocence. I have no more innocence to destroy with you."

She had, after only three months of dealing with young men in New York, come to recognize the grandiloquence of a man in love with himself, the hero of his own private movie—and Sebastian's movie included a dalliance with a transsexual, to establish his libertine character. "What the fuck does that mean? Am I supposed to find that some kind of tragedy?"

"It means I can't fly you to Oslo."

She knew it was coming. But still the pressure inside her chest made it hard to breathe, and when she finally spoke it was because something inside her had broken. "I waited for you," she said into the crackling VoIP line. "You promised me."

"My promises are no good." He sounded sad about it. "I want a family someday. I don't think you can give me one." How cruel to be accused of lacking the one thing she most desperately wanted, a thing she felt sure he could easily give her. She let out a low moan, but then, even in her incipient grief, hated how low the pitch sounded and cut herself short. She needed an unguarded moment, a moment of actual pain. But instead, fear of a non-passing voice shocked her into doing what she always did: Push down her feelings. Get cold.

"We can fix this," she said as evenly as she could. "I know we can. I love you. You love me. Just tell me what you need."

"No," he said. "I just . . . you're not a forever person."

She knew that in only a few moments the guillotine of sadness would slam down upon her, severing her from her pride, and anything that might keep back despair. She would beg, she would cry. But it hadn't yet come down. The sentence had not been executed, and her sense of pride, in its last moments, remained defiant—say anything, no matter how stupid, don't go down crying. "I guess I shouldn't have taken off my panties," she spat out, then hung up, and waited for the agony of heartbreak to hit as she considered the thousand other more biting or pleading ways she could have said goodbye.

The trans lady picnic occupied a clearing atop a hill across from the Picnic House in Prospect Park. Reese had to admire how, in the way that trans women can be ever and subconsciously vigilant, the picnic's organizers had chosen a militarily advantageous hill, the kind of hill a general would have chosen to make a stand: wooded on three sides, with a view of the grassy fields below as well as every path by which a pedestrian could approach. Arrivals to the picnic were spotted and identified among the drifting weekend crowds of Park Slope parents long before they had summited. No one would be sneaking up to surprise the transsexual women. Which is not to say that the passersby were not themselves surprised. Among many other instances, Reese saw it in the body language of a pair of teenagers ambling by. The moment the two boys glanced up the sloped lawns to the group of women sprawled on blankets passing Tupperware back and forth, their teenage figures suddenly huddled into each other to confirm and broke apart with a laugh.

When Reese turned back from the teenagers, she found Sebastian As a Girl watching her. A jolt ran through Reese. In the intervening years, she'd downgraded Sebastian from real love to a teenage affair, and her own feelings from tragic to immature. But the near-familiar face planted doubts about that revision, the lingering suggestion that she'd downgraded defensively to spare herself. Sebastian As a Girl held Reese's gaze for a beat or two, the almost-known features wobbling from an uncertain frown into a friendly, even smile, a slight nod, before she turned back to other women beside her. Iris tapped Reese's knee, drawing her attention.

"I know Felicity," Iris indicated with a nod toward the pretty Latina girl who had somehow skateboarded there in a dazzlingly white dress and was just then making Sebastian As a Girl laugh. "Wanna go over and talk? Get an introduction?"

"No, of course not," Reese replied. "I've lost control of my heterosexuality, not my dignity."

Iris snorts. "As if you have dignity. You had to sneak out of Daddy's house today."

Reese thought it was natural that she didn't bring Stanley to queer parties or spaces for what seemed to her complicated but obvious subcultural reasons. She was afraid of the things he might say, his big body and L. L. Bean–style among the sea of queer, cutoff black jeans; the way he'd take up space, make decrees, and just generally be *triggering*. Even if he kept his mouth shut, something he'd never shown much interest in doing, it'd be like bringing a water buffalo to a suburban pool party. Yes, that water buffalo might just be standing in the shallow end, gnawing happily on cud. But, still, no one was about to cannonball into the pool and splash around.

Reese turned back to Iris, who blew smoke over her shoulder and held her cigarette in her particular way, arm almost straight, two fingers outstretched, as though she hoped to pass it to someone else. "Let's cut temptation off at the root," Reese said. "Let's get out of this stupid park and go to some straight bar. Somewhere where we can get high on the ambient testosterone."

"What, like a bowling alley?"

"C'mon. Pick a spot, I don't care."

"Okay," Iris agreed. But rather than make any move to pack up, Iris rose and sauntered over to Felicity. She bent to kiss her hellos, to hold out one hand in a light touch while her other kept her cigarette at a distance, but every time she could get away with it, she flashed a discreet but malevolent grin at Reese. Iris had a fifth gear of charm that she rarely bothered to engage, which she only ever shifted into to make trouble. "Reese, Reese," Iris called after a minute, like a hostess at a fifties dinner party. "Come over here, there's someone you just *have* to meet."

Felicity and Sebastian As a Girl watched as Reese stood, so that she had no moment to collect herself, straighten her clothes, pat her hair, or basically do anything but walk over to their little cluster as nonchalantly as possible to say "hey," like the worst kind of bore, because what else was there to say after you made that kind of painfully laborious entrance? She couldn't even stab Iris in the heart, because although at least that would have been more interesting, it might have made for a bad first impression.

Felicity, whom Reese had met a few times before, greeted her with a lazy "Hey, girl," which Reese returned before sticking out a limp but not too limp hand to Sebastian As a Girl. "Reese," she said.

"Amy," said Amy, and gave Reese's hand a light tug. "Sit with us."

Reese scooped her skirt beneath her and sat beside Amy. The women on the blanket were playing a casual game, one of those conversational exercises that fritter away time among acquaintances with whom you want to give the impression of high-spirited openness, but with whom you can only risk it obliquely. The rules: Pick three items from your local CVS that would most upset the checkout clerk when rung up at the counter.

A sample from that conversation:

"A dog collar, those long balloons that you twist into animals at children's parties, and a tub of Vaseline."

"Sudafed, a kitchen knife, and some twine."

"Condoms, a shovel, and a Styrofoam cooler."

"They don't sell shovels at CVS."

"Yes they do!"

"Where are you from? Like Montana? They don't in New York City."

"A trowel then, one of those little shovels?"

"No."

"Fine, then I'll walk in carrying a shovel, and buy those other two things."

"That's not in the rules. If you're allowed to bring things in, there's stuff way more disturbing than a shovel."

When the game came around to Amy, she said, "I think we aren't really taking advantage of the rules. Like, everything you all said hints at sex or murder, which, yeah, is upsetting in a generalized scandalous way. But I think if you can trigger someone to make them sad about their own life, it's way more upsetting. I'd find the checkout person who looks the most tired and lonely, and then I'd buy a huge tub of chocolate-chip cookie dough ice cream, a bottle of diet pills, and whatever women's magazine has the saddest headline, like: *How to Get a Job that Isn't Degrading,* or *How to Not Still Be Alone Years After Heartbreak,* or *Orgasms! Will You Ever Have One?* You'd have to pick the right clerk, but if you did, it'd be devastating."

Oh yes, Reese thought, *this girl is for me.*

When the conversation turned to a cadre of literary-type punk girls in whom Reese had zero interest, she allowed her attention to drift. When she tuned back in, Amy was pointing to a cluster of buildings to the south that rose visibly above the rim of green encircling the field. She lived in one of those buildings. Reese didn't bother to ask what Amy did. She already knew the equation: white young trans woman plus apartment right beside the park equaled job in tech.

Reese barely paid attention to Amy's actual words. She had the same mannerisms as Sebastian, but her voice, the way she used it, was flat and Midwestern with none of Sebastian's charismatic pauses and accented flourishes. The phantom of Sebastian disappeared from her as she spoke and rubber-banded back when she went silent. Then, suddenly, the conversation split. Iris and Felicity got up, hunting to see who might have brought beer in a backpack, and Amy and Reese sat alone.

"I saw you looking at me," Amy said—boldly, in Reese's opinion. "You look familiar, have we met before? Maybe we know each other from online?"

"No," said Reese, not thinking before she spoke. "I would have remembered."

Amy smiled, unsure if she'd been offered a compliment.

"You look spookily like someone I used to know," Reese said.

"Who was she?" Amy asked. And suddenly the trap that Reese had inadvertently set for herself sprung. There was no way to admit that she had been thinking of a boy. Such admissions will scar a baby trans. *Fuck it,* Reese thought. *I'll flirt my way out of this one; it's what I want anyway.* "An old lover," Reese said, and looked hard at Amy, whose backlit face remained slightly shadowed with her hair haloed. "One of my best."

Amy laughed lightly, then squinted at Reese to see if she had been teased. Reese indicated nothing, simply held her gaze. "All right," Amy said after a moment, with a slight nod, as if affirming an offer. "Good."

All week they texted each other and it was breathplay—a tiny suffocation veering toward death between every blip of dopamine-bestowing communication. On a night that Stanley had gone to dinner with his friends, and Reese knew he'd be out for hours, she invited Amy over. Reese ignored Amy's questioning eyes, which cast about the lush masculine apartment, and just led her to Stanley's bed, stripped her bare to finger and toy her until she came.

Afterward, Amy observed, "You have a working fireplace in your apartment?" Reese understood that Amy was asking a question she couldn't bring herself to say directly.

"He pays for everything."

"He?"

"My boyfriend. Or whatever he is."

"If he's not your boyfriend, what is he?"

"Mostly an asshole."

Amy laughed, assuming that Reese's insult had been affection-

ate; careful to maintain a tactful distance between her own hopes
and the primacy she assumed Reese still gave to her boyfriend in
matters of love. But Reese betrayed no humor.

Amy caught her laugh, suddenly protective. "He's an asshole?"

"Unquestionably so."

"Why don't you leave?"

Reese shrugged. She had half affected a world-weary attitude
about Stanley to impress Amy, but at the question, the weariness
congealed into a real emotion. "And go where?"

In one of those wild leaps that come only at the outset of a devastating crush, Amy blurted out: "Come live with me!"

Reese turned, cocked her head to the side, then reached out to tip
Amy's chin toward her. "You want to U-Haul already? You really
are a lesbian, huh?"

Amy and three of her friends, all women, handled the move with
the military precision of a hostage extraction. They waited until
Stanley went to work, arrived in a rented truck, and moved Reese's
belongings out of the closet in Stanley's apartment and into Amy's
place by noon. Reese and Amy had already eaten two meals together in their new home before Stanley even learned of his own
reacquaintance with bachelorhood.

Reese stole Stanley's blender when she left. She told herself that
both she and he deserved it. That small theft turned out to be the
grievance on which he litigated his subsequent stream of enraged
voicemails, texts, and emails: her greed, how spoiled she was, the
way she used people, broke them down, and ultimately stole their
small appliances.

Then the messages stopped. Even a few years after the financial
crash, the occasional aftershock reverberated to collapse yet another firm. This time it was Stanley's.

CHAPTER THREE

Six weeks after conception

WAVES BOOM AGAINST the breakwater along Lake Shore Drive, beneath the Chicago skyline. They bounce back from the vertical concrete seawall into the oncoming sets, rolling under and over the newcomers, violently hoisting each other aloft then dropping apart diminished. Even from inside the taxi, with the windows rolled up, Ames can smell the water, can sense the ionized air that jolts him into a pleasant alertness, as happens near water-falls, or just after a sudden, hard downpour. Bikers weave to avoid the spray, which gets caught by the wind and carried over the lake path. Two windsurfers rip across the flat inner breakwater at Navy Pier, bracing their weight so hard against the gusts that they've pulled back the sails, closer to parallel with than perpendicular to the horizon. One of them carves toward the channel entrance, where the steeper whitecaps come in, catches the first big crest, and launches twelve feet into the air, hanging for a moment like a kite. Ames is so surprised and impressed by the maneuver that he cries out and grabs Katrina's arm, forgetting that, for the past week, every conversation that does not stick tightly to questions of their work has ended in uneasy sadness or recriminations.

"Sorry," he says, his hand retreating. "Did you see that, though? That guy was using his sail like a wing when he jumped off the wave."

Katrina refuses to direct her attention toward the lakefront, and the full bore of her distress is recalled to him. He exhales slowly through his nose.

At Michigan Avenue, the taxi pulls off the drive and shoves its way along Chicago's best rendition of glitz. Their clients have chosen some bistro off the Magnificent Mile that bills its food as "Wisconsin cuisine," a nouveau supper-club concept that only makes sense as the kind of food Chicagoans would decide New Yorkers need more of. Ames grew up in the Midwest, among the casseroles of St. Paul, which was why, he supposed, he didn't have much tolerance for Midwestern *aw-shucks*. Out here, people acted like you were putting on airs if you majored in art history before you went to business school, much less changed your name and started shooting estrogen. The resentful Midwestern inferiority complex. The last time he'd seen his aunt, nearly a decade ago, he'd offered her French press coffee, and she'd sniffed that Folgers was good enough for her. She didn't need anything delicate and foreign. "Good," he told her, "because this will be dumping boiling water on grounds and waiting five minutes." Then he transitioned and they hadn't spoken since. In his aunt's schema, changing one's gender might rank as even more snooty than French press coffee.

Now the taxi idles in traffic by Water Tower Place. Ames risks a glance at Katrina, who is gazing at the giant billboards of women in Victoria's Secret.

"I'm glad we're getting to have dinner together," Ames says inanely, as though by going with him to a business dinner, she'd agreed to a date.

"You made the travel arrangements," Katrina notes.

"I mean, I know it's for work, but I still love traveling with you. Remember when we made that weekend trip to Montreal?" They had spent almost the entire weekend in bed together.

"Yes," Katrina agrees. "You got me there under false pretenses." The taxi driver took a peek at him in the rearview mirror.

For a moment, Ames casts about for something truly awful to say to her, but he can't think of anything and the urge subsides. She doesn't deserve it. The past week without her closeness has illuminated for him just how much he has come to need it, how big a place she's come to occupy in his emotional habits. At work, he's spent the past several days maneuvering to spend time with her in situations that cannot devolve into demands that he make a decision about the pregnancy.

His efforts had been assisted by their current project, another one of her weird marketing ideas: creating a nineties retro Giga Pet app for a pet insurance company. Because what would get pet owners more alarmed about their pet's health than gaming out for them the many horrible ways that Fluffy might succumb? They'd have to hire out of house for programmers to create the app, at considerable cost, so Katrina and Ames came to Chicago to convince the clients to sign on to a simpler approach that could be done in-house, and thus add profits to the project.

Ames had worked stupidly hard to set up the deal, which culminated in this trip. In his free time, to avoid getting lost in his own thoughts, he'd spent almost every waking minute digesting the intricacies of the pet insurance market, understanding the clients in the online pet arena, and charming his counterparts in the client's marketing department—all for a chance to show Katrina that he was a reliable person who could protect her reputation and interests, which in turn, he hoped would create a situation in which he'd have an opportune moment to propose his plans for the pregnancy.

At dinner with the clients, she surprises him by ordering two bottles of champagne. She commences to fill and empty her glass much more rapidly than he has ever seen her drink, chirping happily that progress on the deal needed celebrating. Two glasses down and Katrina's cheeks and ears have flushed, her quick eyes taking on a shine.

She's talking to the clients—the pet insurer's marketing strategist and the assistant chief of business development—with more animation than Ames has seen all week. The men, speaking almost in tandem, like a stage act, explain how they live in a suburb called Naperville. They live in the same neighborhood, with kids who go to the same school, and wives who were friends first—one of them even hired the other.

"Oh, that's cute," Katrina says. "I bet you two carpool." The men consider this, and Biz Dev tentatively agrees—yes, perhaps it is indeed cute. To Ames, Katrina's out-of-character theatrical enthusiasm, like her champagne order, demonstrates an attempt to cover for emotional distress beyond what he'd expected—she seems on the edge of some wild action—but neither man notices. Instead they marvel at the fun side that this previously all-business lady has unlocked from her safe and brought to dinner. She avoids Ames's eye contact, and when he manages to catch hers, the brown of her eyes shines back deep and glassy rather than with the customary shrewdness he expects from her glance.

The appetizers arrive: various fried breaded things, and a plate of cheeses, on top of which sits a pile of fresh cheese curds. The waiter, with the same gravitas that he names the Norwegian *brunost,* announces the curds are "squeaky cheese," clarifying that they will squeak when you bite them.

Katrina pops a few curds of squeaky cheese into her mouth and chews with her mouth open, biting into the curds with her molars. "Oh, can you hear that?" she asks. Biz Dev leans close to her face to listen. "I can!" he says, with more amazement than Ames feels is required for listening to someone else chew food. "Can you hear it when I do it too?"

Ames might have thought she was doing impressions of a drunken hostess desperately willing her party to be fun, had he not made a face at her and seen in response a private look of near anguish cross hers. A moment later, she covers for it. "Listen, Ames! Listen to him chew!" she suggests. Ames obliges and bends in toward Marketing's mouth. The man bites down. Out comes the little flatulent squeak. "Yep," agrees Ames, "it squeaks!"

Ames tries to bring up the pros and cons of flash-based programming for the Web version of the app, but Katrina keeps interrupting by asking personal questions of the men. Finally, Ames gives up and attempts some small talk with Biz Dev about where Ames had grown up, how his grandparents had actually gone to supper clubs in upper Wisconsin—a similar culinary experience entirely in brown: meat and potatoes and gravy and beige carpeting and instant coffee and grease-darkened oak tables.

When the waiter passes by, Katrina orders a bottle of wine. "Whatever is good and white," she instructs. It arrives and another glassful disappears—he's so taken aback by her performance that it's only when the food arrives that he wonders if the drinking is a sign meant for him to interpret. The pregnant woman downing alcohol. Even Biz Dev is beginning to notice that the rate of wine consumption has gotten awfully high for a dinner like this. He puts his hand over his glass when the waiter tries to refill it.

"Oh, yes, well, I should probably stop," Katrina says, waving her hand lazily, signaling the waiter to top her up. She's pretty drunk by now, eyes bright, cheeks flushed, just beginning to teeter on sloppy. "But Ames is in charge of travel, so he'll see that I make it home okay."

"Still," Ames says diplomatically, "you don't want to be hungover tomorrow."

"How the fuck do you know what I want?"

The fun-loving hostess pulls off her mask. Behind it is Katrina herself, looking straight at Ames for the first time tonight with her usual fierceness, unable to hide her sudden fury. Biz Dev and Marketing both find something to examine in the food on their plates. Katrina points a cream sauce–covered spoon at Ames, but addresses everyone else. "He forgets that I'm his boss."

Ames makes a *what-the-fuck!* face. This is her project, her reputation as the firm's weird genius who pulls off unlikely deals that she's in the process of exploding. She's mostly hurting herself.

Obviously choosing words with care, Marketing says, "Ames has been just super on this project."

"Just super," Biz Dev chimes in. "I didn't think anyone could understand the pet insurance sector so fast, and then actually be funny about it."

"Yeah, we're really about it."

"Yes," says Katrina. "Ames is quite the charmer. I'm constantly surprised at just how *varied* his life has been. He seems to have a way with *all sorts of interesting people*." Her delivery buzzes with malice. "He has the most *unusual* past."

Ames wants to kick her under the table, but she's sitting too far away. He suddenly realizes that she is very drunk in addition to being very upset. He's done this himself at times when the pressure of discomfort at some social event valves over into some increasingly recursive internal monologue, until he is ready to lash out at everyone near him.

But the men don't take the bait on Ames's past. They are interesting men themselves.

"Charmed me," says Biz Dev.

"Ditto," agrees Marketing.

"I wonder," says Katrina.

"Okay," says Ames, striving to end this moment. "What about dessert?"

"Transsexuals," Katrina says, ignoring him.

Ames sighs, and runs a finger down the bridge of his nose, where it had once been broken. "You're going to do this? Now?"

"Pardon?" asks Marketing.

"Transsexuals," repeats Katrina. "Ames has a *history* with *transsexuality*."

Biz Dev can't help himself. "You like transsexuals?"

Unbidden, Ames pictures Reese as she had been when they lived together, as she had been when she thought herself unwatched in their shared apartment—her eyeliner wings smudged at the end of the day, wisps of hair along the sides of her face escaping a now-loosened ponytail, her public-facing dancer's posture lowering into a slouch after she's locked the front door and slumped down on the couch. "Yeah," agrees Ames, and he wipes his mouth with a napkin. "I like transsexuals." A challenge sits at the edge of his voice.

"No," says Katrina. "That's not what I'm saying, I'm saying that—"

Water spills as Marketing sets down his glass of water with a clunk, and Ames flinches. Ames is willing himself to recede from the scene, but maybe not fast enough. He's angry, not sure he can handle even the mildest slur about trans women from these guys. "Now, look," Marketing says, addressing no one in particular. "I've been married fifteen years and no one has ever asked me about my wife's genitals. Any man who does can expect a punch in the mouth, and I'd expect Ames to do the same for whatever woman he loves." He ends this declaration with a masculine nod.

Ames, his fingers tight on a balled up napkin, has prepared himself for an entirely different statement. He needs a moment to key in to the present, a moment to sort the various implications through which to refract the man's meaning. What Ames would have given, for years, to have heard a straight cis middle-class man compare a trans woman to *his own wife*, much less in order to defend the trans woman. Now, much too late, one such man has appeared just in time to hurt another woman Ames cares about. This man meets Ames's eye in man-to-man acknowledgment: *The women we love are sacred and we will defend them*. Across the table, Katrina shifts in her chair, and Ames catches a waver to her face. A part of her must understand that that moment between men excludes her, will always exclude her—but worse, a part of her must also see that in that moment, she is not the woman whom Ames, or anyone else, has positioned as eligible for protective love.

"You're not hearing what I'm saying," she suddenly interjects. "I'm saying that your good buddy Ames here used to be a fucking transsexual."

Reese knows that Ames has gone to Chicago with Katrina. He told Reese that he'd talk to Katrina about his plan, the one that Reese agreed to, sometime while on this business trip. She keeps checking her phone, and still she hasn't heard anything from him. The stress of it is getting to her, and the more time that goes by the more implausible it seems. Is sharing motherhood really what she wants? Or is she so desperate that she'll take any scrap thrown her way? And if that's the case, it seems to Reese unlikely that an apparently successful cis woman would settle for so little. To distract herself, Reese has been seeing a lot of her cowboy.

But predictably, tonight, her cowboy called to postpone their date. On a last-minute whim, Reese decided to go see her friend Thalia's weekly set at Dynamite, one of several North Brooklyn queer dive bars run by the same shady family of straight people. Thalia was a former drag queen turned transsexual, one of the earliest converts in the Great Drag Enlightenment, when a significant quorum of Brooklyn's queens came out as trans, began to inject estrogen, and renounced their gay past, the consequences of which miffed them into misandry, as the desperately cute twinks who used to sleep with them no longer would. Thalia runs a set called *Anger Management,* in which she plays tropical dubstep to keep everyone chill, then undercuts her chill vibes with hourly advice sessions in which she solicits Ann Landers—style questions from the various twinks who form her now sexually unavailable fan base, then berates them for their stupidity in profound and profane harangues. It was reliably the most entertaining way for Reese to spend a Tuesday night.

Tonight, one of the twinks asks about sharing chores in a relationship—the twink has found that in his relationship with a masc dom, he is doing much more household work, so can he employ feminist arguments for a more equitable share in the domestic labor? To which Thalia responds that no, he is a little bitch, and in the midst of a shortage of actual true-to-god dom tops, he had best start scrubbing if he wants to keep his man happy. However, Thalia adds, the whole premise of the question ought to be rejected, because there is no such thing as a pure masc top—everyone will eventually want something in their butt, because that is the nature of having a butt—when the moment comes that things get equitable in bed, so should they be in domestic labor. The twinks giggle happily, but Thalia rebukes them, and demands they give her quarters for her own laundry, because her parents have cut off her money as a consequence for yelling at them on the phone. For emphasis, she shakes her tip bucket from the pedestal/deejay booth from which she reigns, then segues into one of her favorite themes: her parents. Her parents are good, long-suffering people, she tells the assembled twinks, and these good, long-suffering people still support her at age twenty-nine, because she is a spoiled brat who has never had a job—a weekly show at a queer bar doesn't count—which is an embarrassment to her. And what does she do to repay her parents for their generosity? She spits the words into the mic so acerbically that it pops with her consonants, then pauses a second before answering her own question in a mock outraged oration. She changed her gender! Just to stymie and confuse them! And now she yells at them on the phone and hangs up on them if they misgender her! That's what they get for supporting a child with artistic tendencies! But what else did they expect? Did they think they could just let their child wear capri pants and that there would be no consequences?

"And do you know the worst part?" Thalia demands of her twinks. "The worst part is that most parents get to one day have a moment of comeuppance, when their kids become parents, and then those kids reassess their own childhood with a parent's eyes and regretfully admit that *Dad knew best all along. And Mommy was so generous! So kind! And also beautiful and young!*"

"But not my parents," Thalia concludes with a cackle. "Because with all the hormones, now I'm sterile! I stole that comeuppance from them!"

The cute boys in cutoff shorts lined up along the bar laugh. Thalia theatrically narrows her eyes at them. "What are you all laughing at? If you're here listening to me," she admonishes, "it probably means you're *also* a disappointment to your parents! If you like my shtick, and you didn't just wander in off the street, there is a high probability that you are *also* a degenerate who will never give your parents a grandchild." Thalia spits out her gum in a pique, then continues on to the next question unabated.

Thalia had given Reese a drink ticket and Reese laughs happily along with the rants, sipping on the free Corona. Reese sort of loves Thalia's parents, or at least, Thalia's version of them. She empathizes with them. They make all the classic parents-of-a-trans mistakes, but unlike Reese's own parents, they seem to truly and deeply love their child, as baffling and confusing as they find her. Reese can relate: Thalia is deeply lovable and talented and spoiled and capable of inexplicable rage—which makes her one of the most compelling girls Reese knows. Thalia also happens to be one of the most talented musicians in the city, though she prima-donna-ishly refuses almost all offers to perform—her parents' largesse allows her to avoid the grind of petty performances, which lesser musicians accept primarily in order to eat and secondarily to build up a following. Still, although Thalia performs only rarely, half of her twink followers are fans of her music who settle for seeing her yell at them in a dive bar because it is the closest thing available to hearing her sing.

Thalia's talents only explain a part of Reese's deep affection for her. Reese knows a lot of talented people—half the trans women in Brooklyn live in a state of perpetual pre-celebrity, awaiting a well-deserved recognition that will never come. No, more than simply finding Thalia compelling, Reese secretly and proudly thinks of Thalia as her trans daughter. Reese shares this with almost no one, because she'd be mortified to take public credit for how remarkably level Thalia has turned out to be, even though in her own mind, she deserves a healthy share of that credit.

Reese met Thalia in the first months of Thalia's transition, just as Thalia entered the full bloom of the second puberty, just as the changes in her body began to show, just as every evening the momentous pendulum of estrogenatic moods swung to despair, just as Thalia burst into the period of transition when she cried at the moon, and broke mirrors in self-loathing, and fell in love—real and present love—for the first time. How many nights had Reese sat down with Thalia to offer her counsel, both stern and loving, as

Thalia writhed like a turtle who'd lost its shell, its soft unarmored flesh abraded by the newly felt humiliations of life as a transsexual? How many times had Reese gone over to Thalia's apartment and held her when she cried, and tried to give her advice without telling her how to act or patronizing her or creating a hierarchy in their friendship, because as much as Reese wanted to shake Thalia and tell her to grow the fuck up, she admired Thalia, and all the skills and dreams that she harbored—those same dreams and hopes that Reese herself had given up. Isn't that the most motherly thing of all? To hope your daughter has the chances that you never gave yourself—or that you were never given?

Mother-daughter relationships among drag queens or gay men have a long lineage as a New York City phenomenon, as every queer to have reverently watched *Paris Is Burning* will gladly inform you. Reese knows the mother role still holds sway with the black and Latina girls adjacent to the ballroom world—girls whose families reject them young and early, who need guidance and love and firm talking-tos on occasion. That's not how it is with the white girls Reese knows, though. Those girls, unlike the teenagers seeking family in the ballroom scene, often haven't yet lost their sense of entitlement, and won't stand to be told what to do, won't accept an explicit hierarchy of mother-daughter, especially not from some tranny only slightly their elder whose own mistakes layer and squish on each other like a melting cake. Reese has raised a few trans daughters over the years, and all of the mothering has been tacit: The girls need it, yearn for it, but won't accept it if they realize what it is. And Reese, for as much as she complained about these ungrateful girls, needed them too—craved the chance to nurture someone, to care and soothe them with her softest, most selfless love.

Of course, her first trans daughter—Ames—had also been her lesbian lover. Amy. A daughter whom Reese had raised to love Reese well as a wife, with all the strange dynamics in power that entails, the dynamics that are so confusingly sexy and painful and satisfying and awkward that the rest of society has an incest taboo to avoid them. When her daughter/lover detransitioned into her son, he weirdly put her through all the stages of anger, rage, and betrayal that Reese had heard from countless other parents when their daughters transitioned for the first time. So was it any wonder that when Ames popped back in her life, he did so with the intention of making her a mother? Reese had caught Amy so young in her womanhood, in early pliancy, and motherhood had always been a code to their love. Not just two women in love, but mother and daughter.

Thalia sways slightly on her DJ pedestal. A little dance that both mocks and gives in to the cheesy chill of the vapor-wave song she's just put on.

All Reese's children, and here she is, still alone.

How can Reese not feel kinship with Thalia's parents? These nice middle-class people—he a doctor and she a teacher—who ache with worry for their daughter and who have no idea Reese exists? Who can't know there is a shadow mother, plotting and worrying alongside them? She wants to hug Thalia's parents. To tell them it will be okay.

Suddenly Reese has to get out of the bar. She has the awful fear that she might begin to cry—pity from the early-twenties trans girls among whom she sits would be the final mortification. Grabbing her purse, she slips out. No one notices. Behind her, Thalia, charismatic as always, tosses back at the audience the slips of papers on which they have written their questions, then slides up the volume on another breezy dubstep mix in a show of huffiness that may or may not all be part of the act.

On the sidewalk outside the bar, Reese attempts to bum a cigarette from a handsome guy who looks to her like a slightly femme Vin Diesel, but who doesn't register her until she speaks directly to him, because he's fixated on two slim boys leaning against each other in the doorway. Distracted, he gives her a cigarette, and then coming to himself, chivalrously lights it for her.

"That's my daughter in there," Reese tells Femme Vin Diesel.

He peers through the darkened glass windows at Thalia, then back at Reese. "You must be very proud," he says gamely.

The two slim boys move back inside and Femme Vin Diesel glances at them with an expression of loss, unsure how he has committed himself to a supporting part in some transsexual neurotic-mother role-play.

"Go with your friends," Reese tells him. She angles a stream of smoke out the side of her mouth, and waves the cigarette cherry in the direction where they've slipped away. He nods gratefully and steps lightly after them.

A few moments later, Thalia comes out. "Oh my god, I had to escape the baby transes in there. One of them was complaining about how a cis woman *looked* at her today at the store. That's how wounded she is, she can't take being *looked at*. Two eyes appraising her is *trauma*. I can't take it." Such is the explosion of girls transitioning in and around the Brooklyn drag world, and so devoid are these girls of their own trans history, that Thalia, having been on hormones not quite two years, has found herself forcibly placed in a maternal role. Her tone evinces a teenage mother's exasperation with children, having just been one herself. Without asking, Thalia takes the cigarette from between Reese's fingers and puffs hard.

Reese laughs. "This is the moment."

"What is the moment?"

"The moment you just said your mother would never get. When a daughter finally has kids of her own and begins to understand that her mother knew best all along."

Thalia exhales and hands the cigarette back to Reese, who declines it. "Don't be smug about it," Thalia says. "Maternal smugness is very annoying. Remind me to tell that to my mother next time I call her." She lifts the sole of her shoe behind her, twists herself with easy balance to stub out the cigarette on it, and flicks the filter into the gutter. Her lashes curve luxuriously around her eyes even when she doesn't wear mascara, and tonight, she's worn the mascara thickly, making the amber irises appear bright and unearthly by contrast, illuminated as they are by the orange light of the sodium-vapor streetlamps. Many people think a trans woman's deepest desire is to live in her true gender, but actually it is to always stand in good lighting. Normally that means avoiding the unflattering orangey glare of streetlights. Yet Thalia, with her dark curls and smooth skin, stands resplendent as a Greek pop star in the fiery hues.

In Reese's memories of childhood, night had a different blue-black tone than in her adult life. And, in fact, she later learned when she returned to visit Madison after a long hiatus, this change in the color of night was not an illusion of time and remembrance but a historical fact. Like most American cities, Madison, Wisconsin, had replaced the blue-white lighting of incandescent and mercury-vapor streetlamps with the orange of sodium-vapor. This not only required less energy to run but, because a trick of the human eye perceives orange light to be brighter and thus more revealing than the same lumens of white-blue light, cities installed sodium-vapor in the "super-predator"-panicked nineties as a method to deter street crime. As though one would comfortably rape and murder and steal in the privacy of blue light, but would hew to a life of church going and clean language if illuminated by the eerie public gaze of yellow-orange sodium-vapor lamps. In the pictures of Reese's early childhood, cities shone as stars, but now they burned a combustion-orange glow heavenward, flames licking the firmament as whole cities engulfed themselves in nocturnal conflagration, eternally incinerating, blazing, scorching everybody caught within their scaffolds of kindling. And at the center, her daughter, Thalia, queen of fire.

"I think I need my shot," Reese tells Thalia. "I'm feeling very grandiose and morose and old. That's always a sign that I'm hormonal. I was thinking that night is a different color than it used to be."

"I have to change songs," Thalia says, taking Reese lightly by the arm. "Stop being weird and come back inside."

And this, Reese reflects, is the other reason to be a mother—in whatever fashion motherhood comes your way—so when you're old and alone and feeling sorry for yourself, your daughter will roll her eyes at your theatrics and bring you in from the cold.

After the disaster of their dinner with Biz Dev and Marketing, Ames puts a drunk Katrina into a cab and, despite her protests, gets in after her. "I'm not leaving you alone. No matter what you say to or about me," he insists. His reasons for staying with her were twofold: wanting to make sure she was safe and because the driver seemed skeptical about having a drunk woman in his car without a chaperone. Now Katrina slumps against the window, holding her head.

"I'm not that into pet insurance anyway," Ames says finally, into Katrina's silence.

Katrina doesn't change position.

The car travels slowly, block by block through traffic. Tourists and a few groups of teenagers Frogger their way across the streets. "Did you drink like that to punish me or the baby?" Ames asks as the car pulls back onto Lake Shore Drive.

Katrina pulls her head up from a loll. If there wasn't all the road noise, Ames guesses he'd hear the whirring of a mind calculating the most damaging insult. But instead, she pulls her thin jacket closer and starts to softly cry. "I don't know," she chokes out after a minute or so. "I didn't mean to out you. I don't want to hurt you either. I don't know what I'm doing. You were supposed to care about me. I wasn't supposed to be alone."

The volatility of this mood change wrong-foots him. The delicacy of her frame shows in her coat, the fabric hangs loosely from heaving shoulders only moderately wider than his forearm is long. "No, Katrina," he protests, but it's a weak protest. "I'm not sure what to do either. I mean, I'm trying to come up with a plan."

"Why do you need a plan? Why can't you just love me, and be who I thought you were?"

"I am who you thought I was. Everything I did—it's my past that made me like that."

"No." She rubs her eyes hard and the mascara she put on for dinner smudges. "I thought I knew you, but I don't. I trusted you. I opened up to you and told you about myself. I told you how vulnerable I've been. But you didn't do the same. You could have told me at any time. But instead you *betrayed* me. You hid yourself from me. And only now that I'm pregnant, when you can't lie anymore, for your own sake, are you willing to tell me the truth."

She wipes her face and shakes her head, as if she's heard something she doesn't like. "I blame myself. I still want to hear you try."

"What do you mean?"

She stares at him, then at the seat in front of her. "I broke so many rules—my own, and bigger ones. I hooked up with someone who *works* for me. I told myself it would be fine because we had something so special. I was swept up in it. But it turns out, I was deluding myself. I don't know you. I don't know you at all. The person I thought you were, not only would he have actually shared his past, but he sure as fuck wouldn't have left me dangling for a week."

"I'm trying."

But she shakes her head. "I'm divorced. I'm pregnant. I'm thirty-nine. You know that doctors call pregnancies over the age of thirty-five 'geriatric pregnancies'? I have to make one of the biggest decisions for my future, and I'm a mess, and I don't trust myself, and I can't even learn from my mistakes— Because you know what the worst part is?"

"We don't have to focus on the worst part," Ames tells her.

"The worst part," she continues, ignoring him, "the worst part is that I miss you." Her lower lip is extruding, she's trying to hold back any show of emotion, and failing. "That's how bad my judgment is! Even now, I miss you enough that I just want you to lie to me! I want you to tell me it's okay, that you'll love me, that you *want* to be a dad in my life. But I know that'd be a lie. If you lied about something so fundamental before and treated me so cruelly because of your own shit—how could it not be a lie?"

He puts out a hand. "I don't know. I am desperate too. What can I do?"

"Nothing."

He shakes his head. "Let's start small. What if I promise to tell you everything you'd ever want to know?"

She looks at his open palm. A moment passes. The shadows rotate like a second hand with every streetlight that passes. The whir of tires hiccup regularly over the tarred repairs of the Chicago streets. Tentatively, she presses her forefinger into the center of his palm, and his hand curls around it. "I'd tell you that you're still probably lying, but that I want to hear it."

"Come here," he says, pulling on her hand. "Come here, please. Sit in the middle seat and lean on me instead of the window." She hesitates, then fumbles with her free hand to unlatch her seatbelt, slides into the middle seat, where he circles his arm around her shoulders, pulls her in.

He wakes up in her bed, his nose inches from a lock of glossy hair that had trailed off her pillow to violate the imaginary DMZ he'd unilaterally marked down the center of the bed. Four empty plastic water bottles, the complimentary contents of which she'd chugged to stave off the hangover, lay scattered on her nightstand and she's snoring cutely. Quietly, he slips back the sheets, walks down the hall to his own room, and collects the four water bottles the hotel had allotted for his room.

She's peering at him groggily when he returns to set them down beside the empties.

"More water for you," he says.

"Fuck." She sits up and puts a hand to the back of her neck, then fumbles through the empty bottles to check the time on her phone. "Oh fuck. Oh fuck-fuck. Last night was a mess. I'm so sorry, Ames."

"Yeah, it was."

"We've got a meeting with them Thursday. Think we can fix it before then?"

"I don't know. You outed me to them. What's there to fix?"

Katrina scrunches her nose. "Yeah, but those guys were on your side."

He sits on the bed next to her. Quietly he says, "Abby is the project manager for them. And Josh is dealing with the contract. If they tell either of those two what you said. Well"—he pauses—"you effectively told the whole company last night that I used to be a transsexual."

Katrina's face goes slack. "Oh god. Oh fuck. Those guys probably won't tell, right? I mean, why would they?"

Ames shrugs. "Who knows what they'll do?" He wants to add that she really fucked him over, but she seems to know.

Katrina groans. "We can deal with this, Ames. I'm sure we can."

"Maybe. Maybe not. But maybe it's okay in the long run. Maybe we're even now."

Even in hungover remorse, she's not quite having it, and looks up at him from under a curtain of hair. "I feel awful, but I don't know if comparing our crimes is a road you want to go down."

"Well, what then? What's next?"

She winces. "Coffee and breakfast. Then we strategize. We've got a day before we meet with them again."

"I meant about us. Not just about work. What are we going to do about us?" He puts his hand over where he guesses hers is under the covers and gets a wrist. "Do you still want me to explain everything? That was the plan last night. I want to show you I can let you in."

She grimaces, then says, "More water."

He takes his hand off her wrist to hand her another bottle. She drinks half of it in a go, then wipes her mouth. "Yeah, we'll do that too. But not until after food and caffeine."

They sit at Oak Street Beach after breakfast. The wind has

changed direction since the previous evening, a warmer summerish breeze from the south that has pacified the previous night's chop. The air smells totally different. Katrina is caught in the stupor of her hangover. The time strikes him as good as any to tell her about transition. She regards him flatly, emotions ironed out of her affect by the weight of her headache. He tells her about cross-dressing as a kid. About trying to make it a part-time thing. About how his parents hadn't spoken to him for a year when he finally went on hormones. How meek he had felt as a trans woman. The exhaustion of knowing you're vulnerable. Of seeing bizarre and nonsensical creatures on television and realizing that they were your reflection, as seen through the fun-house mirror of the world's impressions of trans women. He tells her of the courage it took him, every day, just to go to the corner store—the preparations just to leave the house: put on your makeup, keep your shoulders back, walk with an imaginary book on your head, your hips under your spine but still swaying, and keep that emotional armor tight and polished. The cold stab of fear that hit when something tiny happened—say, a teenage boy follows you home from the store, and says appreciatively, "Hey, baby, where were you made?" A weird compliment of a catcall that hints how close the boy has come to the edge of figuring something true—but if you speak, he'll hear the real answer in the timbre of your voice. And then you fear the boy will get ashamed and then violent.

This recitation of facts and memories, though they seem to captivate Katrina, has so far been totally unsatisfactory to Ames; he's barely begun to skirt the contradiction of knowing he's trans, yet having detransitioned. It's like trying to explain one's childhood in a matter of minutes. Everything sounds cliché. Everything gets boiled down to types.

He's relieved when she makes a slight conversational detour away from his own story. She's suggested, in the way that naive cis people do, with a hint of self-congratulation at their own broadmindedness, that it seems like trans people are starting to be everywhere, that maybe gender doesn't matter that much. In his reply, he can't help but let loose an old defensiveness on this topic. "I think it's the opposite," he says too sharply. "The whole reason transsexuals transition is because gender matters so incredibly much."

"Does it matter to you like that still?" she asks.

"Yeah," he admits. "This fatherhood thing is proving that I think it'll always matter to me."

"So even though you detransitioned, you still consider yourself transgender?" Her question isn't cruel; it's fact-gathering. She has recognized an important data point.

"I don't think it's something you outgrow."

She peers at him, squinting a little in the sunlight. "Why did you detransition, then?"

He scoops up a handful of sand, feels it run through his fingers. "Do you want the cold facts or the abstract reason?"

"The cold facts."

"Two things happened that were related. I convinced myself that I couldn't protect and satisfy the girl I loved, also a trans woman, while being trans myself. The other thing that happened was that I got beaten on the street and no one helped me. It was the last straw. Living as a trans woman just seemed too fucking hard after that."

"In New York?"

"Brooklyn. But not what that makes it sound like. It was a rich white guy who did it. In Williamsburg. He wore khakis. His getaway car was an Audi SUV."

Katrina gave him a once-over, as though looking for wounds or evidence, as if he were saying it had just happened. "So you got sick of being trans?"

"I got sick of *living* as trans. I got to a point where I thought I didn't need to put up with the bullshit of gender in order to satisfy my sense of myself. I *am* trans, but I don't need to *do* trans."

Ames could run through this routine without even thinking about it. How many times had he tried to explain his detransition to other trans women? Tried to assuage the sense of betrayal that their wariness obviously communicated?

In Ames's formulation, trans women knew what trans women were, they knew how to *be*, but they didn't know how to *do*. All the intra-trans fights online, all the arguments with cis people: All of it was just to define what it meant to *be* a trans woman; to say what she *was*. But when you're a trans woman, there's almost nothing out there on how to actually live.

In his last year of living as a woman—the year in which Ames stopped being so angry with how cis people treated trans people and he started growing sad and contemplative about how trans women treat each other—he came up with a private, not-particularly-catchy term for the trans women of his cohort, the ones who began transition in the early 2010s. He called them juvenile elephants. Nowadays, Ames didn't really feel that he had the right to say anything much about trans women, but if you had asked him that year, he would have told you about juvenile elephants.

In 2002, park rangers in the Hluhluwe Imfolozi Game Reserve in South Africa hunted down and shot a gang of three juvenile elephants that had made a sport of chasing, raping, and killing rhinoceroses. The elephant gang raped and murdered sixty-three rhinos before the park rangers caught up with them. In Sierra Leone, another herd of elephants razed a village of three hundred, flattening the mud-and-wattle homes, and killing an elderly woman who attempted to chase them away. A young elephant in that pack, barely full-grown, pinned the woman to the ground with a knee, and slowly gored his tusk through her chest with malicious precision. Toward the end of the civil war in Northern Uganda, Karamojong villagers began to leave out poison-laced elephant snacks, to retaliate against raids by the legally protected elephants of nearby Kidepo Park, who smashed the homes in the adjacent villages to get drunk on the fermenting fruit the Karamojong used to brew wine. Perhaps the villagers needn't have bothered. Since the midnineties, ninety percent of male elephant deaths in South African game parks could be attributed to murder by other roving gangs of pachydermicidal elephants, a fifteen hundred percent increase in elephant-on-elephant violence over previous decades.

Ames learned all this in an essay titled "Elephant Breakdown," published in the science journal *Nature,* in which a group of leading elephant behaviorists argued that the abnormal quality and frequency of elephant attacks and violence could no longer be understood through the long-standing reasoning that suggested high levels of testosterone in young males or competition for scant land and resources. No, the behaviorists argued, the younger generation of elephants suffered from a form of chronic stress, a species-wide trauma that has led to a total and ongoing breakdown of elephant culture.

The cause is simple: Throughout their long history, elephants have lived in intricately ordered social structures. Young elephants learned their place and healthy behavior in concentric societal rings of caregivers—birth mother, aunts, grandmothers, friends—relationships that might last a lifetime: seventy years or more. Unless orphaned, young elephants stay within fifteen feet of their mothers for the first eight years of their lives. When an elephant dies, her family members grieve and ritually mourn. The bereaved conduct weeklong vigils by the body, covering it with brush and rubbing their trunks along the teeth of the lower jaw of the carcass, a gesture of greeting among live elephants.

This millennial generation of elephants is an orphan generation. In the last few decades, humans have murdered, mutilated, or displaced an entire generation of older elephants who might have bestowed upon this generation the familial, societal, and emotional skills required to handle one's individual fifteen thousand pounds of muscle and bone, through which courses intolerable memories of pain, trauma, and grief.

When the park rangers in South Africa finally caught and shot the three elephants responsible for the rhino assaults in the park, researchers examined the corpses and determined that all three perpetrators had been transported by wardens to the game reserve some years earlier. All three had been adolescent males, originally found as juveniles chained to the bodies of their dead and dying relatives—a practice that poachers commonly employ so that the park rangers can find and handle the young ones, much as fishermen toss back young fish. Once transported to a new locale, a savannah free of any elders, the three traumatized elephants found each other, bonded in mutual sorrow and grief, and wreaked their vengeance on each other and the world.

Ames, having explained the condition of juvenile elephants, drew this metaphor: Trans women are juvenile elephants. We are much stronger and more powerful than we understand. We are fifteen thousand pounds of muscle and bone forged from rage and trauma, armed with ivory spears and faces unique in nature, living in grasslands where any of the ubiquitous humans may or may not be a poacher. With our strength, we can destroy each other with ease. But we are a lost generation. We have no elders, no stable groups, no one to teach us to countenance pain. No matriarchs to tell the young girls to knock it off or show off their own long lives lived happily and well. Those older generations of trans women died of HIV, poverty, suicide, repression, or disappeared to pathologized medicalization and stealth lives—and that's if they were lucky enough to be white. They left behind only scattered exhausted voices to tell the angry lost young when and how the pain might end—to tell us what will be lost when we lash out with our considerable strength, or use the fragile shards of what remain of our social networks to ostracize, punish, and retaliate against those who behave in a traumatized manner.

"And so we become what we have seen. How could we know not to? Have you seen many orphaned juvenile elephants behaving otherwise?"

· · ·

Katrina puts her hand under the little waterfall of sand that cascades down between his fingers. "I realize my knowledge about trans people is largely just the detritus that floats around the zeitgeist. But like, I got into *RuPaul's Drag Race* for a couple of seasons. And on those, they're constantly talking about mothers, and calling each other mothers. Like, just at a casual distance, I guess I thought of mother roles as part of trans culture."

Ames hadn't expected Katrina to question him on his own trans knowledge. He'd forgotten how much the culture had changed even in the few years since he detransitioned. Caitlyn Jenner and La-verne Cox on the covers of magazines, straight people talking about *Drag Race* the way they used to talk about *Survivor*. And of course, trans motherhood had always been Reese's particular obsession. But he doesn't yet want to start talking about Reese to Katrina. "Yeah," he admits. "On *RuPaul,* those are brown girls talking. Same for trans women of color. They had mother relationships."

Katrina laughs. "Wait, I ignored your self-pity about how it sucked to be a woman, but now you're saying you feel sorry for yourself 'cause you were a white girl?"

On matters of race, Ames feigned a casualness at odds with his actual tendencies to avoid the topic. Of Katrina's two races, he sub-consciously found himself often appealing to the white one, and at times over the course of their relationship, she had recalled for him that he was not, in fact, speaking to a white person just like himself. In those moments, as now, a wash of defensiveness lapped at the edge of his emotions.

Usually the elephant story really buttered people up. When he speaks again it is without any plan. "Yeah. I have the bad habit of saying trans women when I mean white trans women, which is how you can tell I *was* a white trans woman; it's endemic among white trans women. I'm not saying it's harder for white girls at all. I'm say-ing that the white girls I knew—the generation that I transitioned into, the milieu that basically invented screaming online—were a tribe of motherless women without survival or social skills, prone to destruction, suicide, and romanticizing their own abjection. I'm saying that no matter whatever sloganistic squishy ideology I might have pretended to adhere to, deep down I was ashamed to be one of them, and ashamed of the thwarted life I led. Even the white women who survived and managed to mature didn't want to deal with mothering all that, and immature white girls were too angry and self-righteous to accept mothering anyway. God knows that all the brown trans women I knew were careful to call themselves trans women of color and not just trans women—and I don't blame them for emphasizing the distinction. I suppose that the black and brown mothers out there might take offense to my including their daughters among the orphaned elephants."

Katrina shrugs and addresses the understatement with another understatement, "Yeah, probably." But beyond that she only asks, "So what did you do?"

"I stopped being an elephant. I became something else."

She still holds a handful of sand, seeming to have forgotten about it, squinting one eye at Ames in the sunlight. "But elephants can't stop being elephants. Or more to the point, women can't just stop being women. I can't stop being a woman just because it's hard—not that I would even if I could."

"I know. That's my problem."

"So do you think about re-transitioning?"

"Would you put a traumatized juvenile elephant back where the poachers killed her mother?"

She tosses the sand aside, but little dry brown burrs in the sand cling to the edge of her sleeve. "Shouldn't the correct answer be that those elephants eventually grow up and just chill the fuck out?"

"Yeah. At some point juvenile elephants become adult elephants. Then, eventually, they have their own kids, and hopefully, they treat those kids right and they get to reconstruct the matriarchy."

Something clicks for Katrina, she pulls her hands close to her, defensively. "Is this your way of talking about the pregnancy?"

He sighs. "Yeah. It's hard for me. I've got some fear going on. I talk obliquely when I'm scared."

Charcoal smoke passes on the breeze. Two men debate in Spanish the optimal way to set a small hibachi grill into the rocks of the breakwater, while their families play soccer on the grass alongside the boulders. Down on the beach ripples lap against the shore and a couple introduces their child to the water's edge. The woman wears a red one-piece. She leans over her daughter, pointing out little freshwater shells and seaweed. The child wears a white hat to shield her from the sun. A man stands protectively off to the side, poised to leap into action, should anything approach from either lake or shore to threaten his wife or child. The scene could be B-roll footage for wholesome family time. It's too much for Ames, like the world has chosen to mock him at that moment.

After moments of silence Katrina begins, apropos of little. "My friend Diana and I were talking. You met her last year at the NYF Advertising dinner. She's baby-crazy and trying to make some choices. We were saying that it seems like all of our mutual friends who got pregnant act like they got sure of everything in pregnancy. That nature just makes that surety happen. You don't actually have to decide things. Instead you get some kind of biological mama bear instinct that shows you the way. I don't feel that way. My mama instinct hasn't kicked in. I don't know what to do."

She laughs, not happily; she stares too intently at the flower gardens in the middle distance, blinking back emotion.

He wets his lips, pauses, and says, "What are you thinking about doing?"

Katrina throws her palms up, helplessly. "I've been waiting for you to give me some input. But since you can't do that, I have to consider ending the pregnancy. It's not like it sounds like you're going to be a father. Or whatever."

"No."

"No?"

"No, don't end the pregnancy." He's fumbling with his words, trying to pull up some semblance of bravery. "This is what I'm say-ing. You don't have to be a single mom. I don't know if I can be a father—but like, I can be a parent."

Katrina drops the stone she'd been fidgeting with. She gives a hard stare. "What's the distinction?"

He still can't quite find the courage to tell her what he'd offered Reese. His own weaseling shames him, and he sits up straight, as if a physical backbone has some connection to a metaphorical one. "No, but like, I think if I'm going to do this, I need to be back in the trans community or at least have other trans people involved. I need to be with people who understand where I've been."

"What are you talking about?"

Ames cocks his head in involuntary sheepishness. "Well, I talked to Reese."

"Who?"

"Remember that girl I told you about earlier? Reese? My ex? When I used to complain about not knowing how to live she just scoffed at me and said, 'I'm going to live and do like millions of women before me: I'm going to be a mother.' Our plan had been to become parents. To raise a child. I think if she was part of raising our child, I could do it."

"As our baby's godmother or something? I don't think I'd have a problem with that."

"Well, I was thinking of a role closer than that. Like another mother or something."

Katrina holds her breath, the way one does when contemplating the water below from a high dive. There's a lot roiling just behind that stillness, but Ames can't read it, so he just goes on, letting his words tumble out. "I believe she will love a child more fiercely than anyone else I've ever met. It'll be hard, because she's trans and I'm . . ." He searches for the word, and abandons it, "I'm as you know I am—but she's the type to turn hardship into hardness, like a shield for people she loves. That baby will be safer with her than at the center of a fortress. And I think we could do it with her—

parent, I mean. I've been trying to feel what I want, and I want to be with you, Katrina. I'm afraid if you end the pregnancy, it'll end our relationship with it. So I want to be a parent with you. And with Reese, I could be a parent without being seen as a father. Maybe only with her."

Katrina blinks. Wisps of hair have freed themselves from her ponytail and tremble in the light breeze. She swallows before speaking. "You're, like, actually crazy." Her tone borders on shock. "Like a sociopath or something. No one could believe you'd ask that. No one *will* believe it." She doesn't sound angry. She sounds as if she's speaking to herself.

"Just think about it."

"What am I, some kind of walking uterus to you? Have you seen pregnant women? Do you think I would choose to go through that just to play a part in giving a baby to your ex-lover? Do you have any respect for my body? Do you value me at all?"

Ames tries to calm down, reminding himself how much he really cares about her. "Katrina. Please understand I mean this: I will support you however I can. But you're not being exploited here. You actually do have the power. You say no, that's a no. You tell me what to do, and I'll do it. But you've asked me for honesty all week—to tell you what I really think would work, and now I have."

Katrina stares at him in a strange wonder. Then with a sudden gesture of her hand she waves back the wonder, tucks away the moment the way you pocket the business card of someone you're sure you'll never call.

At just that moment, Ames's phone rings. It's Biz Dev.

He tilts the screen so she can see. "Take it?" he asks her.

"Yeah, you better."

On Thursday, the pet insurance representatives sign a contract to add Web functionality to the app. No one mentions Katrina's dinner behavior or drunken revelation. Only once does Ames catch Biz Dev scrutinizing him. On a break, Katrina says to him, "Maybe it will be fine? Maybe they just thought I was drunk." To Ames it feels like wishful thinking, but too many other things crowd out his attention, so he agrees, and slowly begins to indulge in that same line of thought. *It will be fine. Those guys don't care, right? And so what if they do?*

On the plane ride home, they fly business, sitting beside each other. Katrina rubs his arm in a friendly, distracted way that he can't make sense of, so he pats her hand in an avuncular manner that immediately dismays him. At LaGuardia, when he asks if she wants to share a cab, she declines. "I need some space. I need you to give me some time to myself. I'll call when I feel like talking again."

It is Monday when she approaches him again, by calling him into her office. The weekend of silence has been agony. She doesn't sit behind her desk. Instead, she closes the door, and perches in a chair beside him. "Ames, I thought about it all and—" Katrina begins, but the solemnness of the moment, the sense of portent, is broken, because a strand of her hair has slipped and gotten to her lip gloss.

"Ugh," she says. "This is what I get for freshening my makeup before you came in. Backfire!" She's visibly nervous, and picks the hair free and tucks it behind her ear. "Anyway, what I was going to say is that I told my mom."

"You told her everything?"

"Yeah, I mean, I couldn't tell my friends, and I couldn't be alone with it anymore."

Ames nods. Then, in a way that even the pregnancy test or the conversation with Reese had not, the pregnancy becomes real to him. It is no longer their secret. It is no longer just theirs or with the people with whom he had shared it. It was one step further to being public. A known fact. Collective knowledge. He had *fathered* a child.

"My mom is someone who I know for sure is on my side, even if I was really afraid of her judgment," Katrina says. "I was expecting her to tell me to run away from you. I guess I even wanted that.

Someone to make you the villain so I didn't have to. But you know what? She wasn't even that judgy. Who knew? Turns out Mom has some wisdom about mothering."

Ames hadn't even considered that Katrina might tell her mother. Because he had gone so long without telling his own mother anything, he had forgotten such an act was possible, much less permissible. But of course Katrina had told her mother. Several times in the past, he had been on the couch, just out of view of her phone's camera, when she chatted on video with her mother. And he had heard, firsthand, the conversation between two women on such familiar terms with each other's lives that they spoke in near code: nicknames, allusions, inside jokes.

Sometime when Katrina was in college, Ames knew, her father had fallen off a ladder. The fall resulted in a traumatic brain injury. He spent three weeks in a coma, then awoke an angrier, more impulsive man. Maya nursed him through a year that Katrina winced to describe, then left him, though the two never officially divorced. In singledom, Maya bloomed, moving to the Bay Area, where in the first housing bubble, she built a niche as an interior designer providing, as with the bear-print couch, unexpected home décor touches. Her reputation survived the crash, and as tech millionaires bought up and down the bay, her name made its way to one of the prominent Mrs. Googles, who wanted to remodel her vacation home in Montana. After that job, Maya had all the work she could take. When she called Katrina, it was usually on the pretext of showing her some item she'd found, asking her daughter if maybe this time it was too weird, if she'd gone too far. On the first phone call Ames overheard, it was a set of antique dresses, which Maya had repurposed as wall hangings, and he was so curious as to how exactly this was to work that he nearly blundered into the line of the camera's sight and revealed himself as an incorrigible eavesdropper.

Katrina's hair has gotten caught in her lip gloss again. This time, she pulls an elastic from her wrist and ties her hair back, as she continues to speak. Katrina has only met her grandmother once, she tells him. Her grandma had never grown comfortable speaking intimately in English. She was not pleased to have a granddaughter who looked more like the American parent and spoke only like that American parent. "I don't know what she said to my mom," Katrina says, "that one time we visited, but I know it was a short visit."

When Katrina told her mother she was pregnant this past weekend, Maya had begun to cry, and at first Katrina thought that Maya was upset with Katrina's situation. But that was not it. Maya was crying because she couldn't help recalling the things her own mother had said to her when Maya herself had become pregnant with Katrina. Maya's unborn child with this suspicious man, Isaac, Maya's mother had intimated, would not be welcomed into the family. The coldness and distaste that Maya's mother had shown for Isaac would be shown as well to his child.

"You know, my mom has never pressured me about having children," Katrina says. "But on the phone this time, she said she wanted to be a grandma. That she has always felt guilty about how much I missed out on by not having a grandmother, and how often she fantasized about being the good grandmother that I never had. I didn't realize she had wanted it that badly. I'm impressed that she only badgered me a little about it all through my marriage with Danny."

"I'm sorry," Ames says.

"Actually, my mom was crying on the phone, and then I started crying too. And we were both crying about the same thing—that I did and didn't have a grandma."

Ames nods. He had a grandma, who was fine, he guessed. His family was a chain he'd voluntarily decoupled from in order to breathe, so he couldn't quite relate—but now wasn't the time to say that.

"I thought about what you were saying about redemption, and I realized that I felt the same thing. That I had a chance to connect my mother to my child, to relink the maternal line that my birth broke."

Ames couldn't help but sit up abruptly, suddenly wildly alert. "So you're going to keep the baby?"

"Well, that's the thing. I was talking to my mom. About you and what you proposed. About this woman, Reese. About my career, and my finances, and my time commitments, and what I want in a relationship, and well, so much. We were talking for hours, listening to each other—and you know what she said?"

Katrina doesn't wait for Ames to ask but pushes on. "This is going to sound crazy, but somehow, even though I'm nearly forty, when my mom approves of something, it makes it seem possible, like, not rebellious. You know? Like, when you want to do something wild as a teenager, and you realize your mom also thinks it's cool, suddenly it's like, doable?"

"Katrina," Ames cuts in and puts his hand on his sternum to settle himself. He thinks he sees where Katrina is headed, and can't tell if his sudden anxiety would be better alleviated if he were right or if he were wrong about his suspicion. "I know you're really good at dramatic presentations, but please, the suspense is killing me."

"My mom, well, after we talked about everything, she was like, 'The one thing I learned raising you—through successes and failures—is that the best way to be a mother is to do so with as many other moms around as possible.' You laid out a number of options for me to choose from, and the thing is, honestly—what if we had them all? I want my career, I want to build and commit with you, and a child is a lovely time-tested way for that. Meanwhile, you want this woman Reese as your family, and she wants a baby and respect and purpose as a mother; and my mom wants to be a grandma; and you and I could be good to a child, I think, and we all want it to be something redemptive."

Ames waits and Katrina angles her glance at him slightly askance. "So," she says, "I'm just asking you what my mom asked, as like, a question to explore . . . But during your time, uh, in the queer world, was it common for people to raise children in a family that is— What do you call it? Something like a triad?"

Chapter Four

Eight years before conception

THE POPPERS HIT. Purple jellyfish expanded and pulsated across the backs of Amy's eyelids. She had just enough time to get her mouth back on Reese's soft cock before her constant interior monologue, that complicated apparatus that processed all the raw signals from her body into a tolerable meaning, for the first time in her life, cut out. Some critical component of consciousness withdrew like the needle lifted from a still-spinning record. No words. No thought. Just raw, unprocessed, open fire hydrants of data that rushed in from Amy's senses. Time became a slippery fish among it.

Fragments of atomized notions began to coagulate. Slips of words formed, as cosmic dust gloms together by its own weak gravity, drawn together into molecules of gas, pressed against other molecules, collectively gravitated pressure growing, until a change: fusion, heat, light—and Amy flared back into an interior language, into words and the possibility of reason. The purple jellyfish descended back into the depths. Her vision cleared. Where was she?

Oh. There: sobbing with Reese's cock in her mouth. Shivering. How long had she been sobbing? She didn't want to sob, she wanted to kiss the pretty dick resting on the pad of her tongue. For the last month, she had been obsessed with Reese; all she wanted to do was get closer and closer to her. It was to the point that the phrase "I just want to eat you up" took on shades of the literal—digestive incorporation being the only act that Amy could imagine getting her closer to Reese than sex. Just an hour before, Amy had watched Reese brush her teeth, her long brown hair hanging loose, and her arm pistoning back and forth so hard as she brushed that her tits waggled side to side under her slinky nightgown. Amy decided it was the sexiest thing she had ever seen, topping each of the fifty other Reese actions she'd decided one after another that day was the sexiest vision ever. The simultaneous emotions of wanting Reese so badly, the happiness of actually having her, and the fear that something might happen to either herself or Reese to ruin it all made her stomach fizz with a virulent form of a crush.

Mixed in with the crush-sickness, stiffening out the saccharine taste, floated a few drops of unease. Amy's trust of Reese was shaky. Or rather, the fact that she didn't fully trust Reese, that she couldn't quite map squarely the Reese she knew onto the Reese about whom she'd heard stories. The expression "suite of personality disorders" had been said to her about Reese by two different people. Amy couldn't say whether the expression had been repeated simply because it was a catchy queer-approved pseudo-psychological way to talk shit or whether the phrase arose independently each time because it apparently described Reese so well. But either way, the general consensus when Amy moved Reese into her apartment a week after meeting was: 1) Yes, that's exactly how Reese operates and 2) Girl, be careful.

The first person to use the expression about Reese had been a trans guy named Ricky, whom Reese had dumped cold when she took up and moved in with Stanley, the rich finance guy Reese had left for Amy.

"I don't know exactly what Reese's diagnosis would be," Ricky told Amy, when she volunteered to help him fix his motorcycle, which mostly consisted of handing him tools; Amy was ideal for the task because she knew enough about engines and tools to play assistant, but she also understood that ogling a trans guy while he fixed his motorcycle was gender-validation time for them both. "But it's got to be a whole suite of personality disorders."

"Come on," Amy chided, "just say you don't like her, don't play armchair psychiatrist."

Ricky hesitated. He'd propped his motorcycle, some sort of a 1970s-era Honda, on its center stand in the middle of the Bushwick sidewalk. Pedestrians stepped over the scattered paneling he'd removed. "Reese has a lot of amazing qualities," Ricky said, "but I'm probably the wrong person to enumerate them 'cause—and it hurts my pride to say this—I was stupid enough to let her casually break my heart. I'm not going to say anything more if you're too wrapped up with her to hear it."

"Please tell me."

"She's so incredibly charming when she wants to be," Ricky said, crouching by the chain, "but she has only a few close friends. That alcoholic, Iris, who I trust less than her, and otherwise, just whoever else is infatuated with her at any given moment. Sociopaths and pathological liars are charming like that. They'll read you, process you, figure out your insecurities, then tell you everything you want to hear because for as long as they desire you, they believe it too. But eventually, it falls apart, and you figure out it isn't true—can you put an eight millimeter socket on the quarter-inch ratchet?"

Amy attached the socket and handed it to him. She noticed that he gripped the chain without regard for the grease getting all over his hands. So masculine. Last time she had seen him he had one of those ironic bowl cuts that queers inexplicably loved. Having worn that cut herself as a little child, Amy couldn't quite shake her infantile associations with that look, the faded memory of sitting in a barber's chair with a balloon-printed bib around her tiny neck, hair falling away from the sides of her head in tufts under the buzzer's drone, while the barber called her "little man" and her mom tutted "Handsome!" Still, she always complimented bowl cuts, because she'd made enthusiastic appreciation of queer style an important part of her social approach, regardless of her actual opinions. Since she'd last seen him, thank god, he had shaved off the bowl and left his hair and stubble the same length, which Amy could compliment with much more genuine gushing.

"Reese doesn't tell you what's true," Ricky concluded. "She tells you what you most need to hear. Stuff that you'd told yourself no one would ever understand about you—she figures it out and tells you. Tells you that the thing about you that you most want to be is exactly what she loves about you. It's fucking intoxicating. It's like drinking validation from some psychoactively seductive source. She loves being that source. She loves being the thing you need so bad. She means it all too, but only for the moment she's directing her charm at you. Like the love and joy you feel on Molly or something, it's real while you feel it, but only for that long."

He grimaced as he pried a bolt loose. "She's not intentionally cruel. That's why I say she's just got, like, personality disorders. And she ends up hurting people, so then she's alone, which makes her lonely enough to do it even more."

Amy didn't know how much to believe. The tendency of lay queers to assign other people psychological pathologies struck her as boring and tautological: A certain person does a thing because that person is the type of person who is compelled to do that thing. No capacity for either change or responsibility or even a consideration of the why, much less the how, of a particular human. Why does the cat torture the injured mouse? Because the cat is a cat—and so shall it be forever. Besides, rumor was, famously stoic Ricky had gotten drunk and then loudly, inconsolably, and theatrically sobbed in the corner of a Hey Queen! party the night he discovered Reese had left him to move in with a finance guy. Maybe he had to pathologize Reese into a sociopathic, manipulative, emotional mastermind in order to explain his own vulnerability to heartbreak.

"Look," Ricky said, reading Amy's skepticism. "Here's a story: One time I slept over at her house. If you know her, you already know she is incapable of hanging up a towel after using it. She left early to meet someone for coffee, so I stayed in bed for a while, then I took a shower, picked up her towel from the floor—she only had one—dried off with it, and carefully folded it in thirds and hung it up over the top of her closet door. Then I left. Three days later we go to her house. And the towel is exactly where I left it. But she's freshly showered and made-up."

"Uh-huh," Amy said. She wasn't sure she was going to believe any story that turned on a towel. But on the other hand, it was true: Reese left all her clothes and towels wherever they fell when she was done with them.

Ricky dropped the ratchet to focus on telling his story. It hit the concrete sidewalk with a clink. He needed to wave his hands around in order to express how much this incident exasperated him. "So I ask her where she got ready, and she gives me a look like I'm crazy and says, 'At home, of course.' So I point to the towel and I was like, 'How did you dry off? That towel hasn't moved in three days.'"

Ricky paused for effect. "She fucking lost it. She doesn't say she has two towels. Or that she air-dried herself. Instead she starts screaming at me like, 'What are you, a towel detective? Did you fucking solve the case of the folded towel?!' It would have been al- most funny, but she was so wild-eyed about it that it was straight-up alarming. Especially because she wasn't trying to be funny, she wanted to demean me. It just devolved into what kind of insecure loser I was, leaving booby-trap towels in her room. Calling me jeal- ous. Asking what kind of man I was who had to know where she was all the time. And I— You know, I just backed down, because what am I going to do, make my last stand over a towel? And as a result, I never really asked where she was that night. Or if she was gone for three days, or just one night. But I was dying inside, be- cause it's one thing to be like, okay, she's seeing someone else. But the way she does it, it's like she's furtively hiding another life that you aren't allowed access to. And here's why it's poison: On one hand, she has this incredible ability to sense what you desperately need to hear, to see your insecurities and placate them. On the other hand, she's secretive and she lies. So it feels like the things she told me that felt so good are lies. That, in reality, everything I fear about myself is correct. It's murder on your self-esteem. You doubt your- self. You end up feeling way worse about yourself when she leaves.

"You know what the worst part is?" he continued. "I finally put together a conjecture: Whose towel was she probably actually using? That finance douchebag! Who was secretly paying for the apartment! Which she also hid from me! A guy who is jealous and has to know where she is all the time! The kind of guy she demeaned me for being is what she really wanted all along!" At this last statement, his hands flapped around like wounded seagulls. He inhaled, calmed himself, and picked up the dropped ratchet. "I'm telling you: personality disorders!"

His assessment had been echoed even by those who'd never crushed out on Reese. Ingrid, one of the trans girls who'd been around Brooklyn at least as long as Reese, had said in half admiration and half condemnation, "Reese is the only trans girl in this city whose incessant drama really has almost nothing to do with the fact that she's trans. Her drama is just what she makes for herself as a woman."

Two weeks later, Amy lay crumpled in bed, having inhaled poppers for the first time, and decided that nothing felt as good as being vulnerable to Reese, so fuck whatever everyone else said. Might as well enhance that vulnerability with chemicals, and Reese had whispered to Amy that the poppers would make her helpless, docile, and pliable. Amy's whole problem pre-transition had been a complete inability to ever let anyone far enough past her defenses to glimpse any vulnerability. She'd always shut down or dissociated first in order to avoid it. If Reese had some magical ability to see what Amy most craved, to see past her crust of armor to what that tender, mewling inner self most wanted—then please, oh, please, bring it on.

Amy hadn't expected to have such a strong crush—only in movies did people fall for each other in a matter of weeks or days, and even in movies only the most sentimental characters could believably do so. So when it happened to her, she wasn't ready for it. For the past year and a half, peering into her future provided her with only the haziest of views, a gray mist in which the barest outlines of events began to reveal themselves only one to two months away. Transition had been the first of a number of unthinkables. Other unthinkables had been her long-term girlfriend breaking up with her, her parents refusing to speak with her, the shattering of her own confidence. She'd lied to herself about her own gender for so long and lied so deeply, how could she have any faith in her own convictions?

"Whoa, babe, whoa, whoa." Reese's voice came gently. "Take it easy, sweetie. What's the matter?" Her hand on Amy's shoulder gently pushed Amy away, and still uncoordinated, Amy tumbled back like a rice sack into the scrum of blankets, one leg falling off the mattress. Amy's vision came to rest on the *Attack of the 50 Foot Woman* poster that Reese cut into three strips and hung like a trip-tych by the now-darkened window. Amy didn't like the poster at all, but that came with a certain pleasure—a perverse stab of joy wak-ing up every morning to the sight of stupid kitsch in what had be-fore been her intentionally sparsely decorated bedroom—because it meant she no longer inhabited it alone.

Post-poppers, Amy couldn't stop crying or shivering. Couldn't explain that everything was fine. She only managed to say "Oooh-wee," and weakly held out her hand, trying to signal that every-thing was fine. Her teeth clattered, and Reese leaned over, pressed her body weight down on Amy, and wrapped the comforter around them both. Reese's amused voice showed only a touch of concern as she murmured, "Baby, what just happened?"

Only twenty minutes later had Amy returned sufficiently to her-self to begin to explain. Amy had made a seat with four pillows: Reese's two and her two. She could tell her pillows and Reese's pil-lows apart because she couldn't seem to get Reese to stop sleeping in her makeup, so two of the four pillowcases, once a bright solid yel-low, now had squiggly patterns, single eyeliner wings pointing off in haphazard directions among the centipede footprints of mascara-drenched lashes. Taylor Swift played from Reese's laptop.

"God, those poppers made me so dumb," Amy ventured.

"Of course," countered Reese, who snapped shut her laptop now that Amy no longer appeared aphasic. "Poppers are supposed to make you dumb. A dumb little slut with zero inhibitions—just how I like you." Reese hesitated. This was perhaps too direct. For as much as Amy was able to say that she was in love to the point of sickness—their sex had not been good. It had been tentative, quiet—both intense and mild. Penetration was aborted in favor of oral, or even more frequently, mutual masturbation—the more sex became like cybersex or camming, only in person, the more comfortable Amy seemed. Reese surmised that the majority of sexual situations in which Amy had genuinely felt at ease had occurred within easy reach of an Off switch.

Reese had been trying to get Amy to loosen up, to begin to curb Amy's habitual shutdown at the prospect of sex—to keep Amy present, and in the body Amy had spent a lifetime learning to avoid acknowledging. But it was a tightrope walk: Tell Amy what to do too forcefully, and her shame at the prospect that she was not great at sex would make her dissociate, but leave her to her own devices and patterns, and she'd dissociate from the start. Telling her what was cute might have been too much, so Reese added, "But poppers are not supposed to make you shiver and cry. I want you helpless, but not that kind of helpless."

Amy nodded. "I'm not sure why I shivered. Maybe my blood pressure dropped too much." Amy'd seen signs at Callen-Lorde warning against the use of poppers while on Viagra because both caused drops in blood pressure. She hadn't taken Viagra, but she had uncommonly low blood pressure, a consequence of her spiro, the testosterone blocker she took every morning in two round 100 mg pills that looked and tasted like breath mints made from corpses.

Reese said gently, "But, baby, why did you start crying?"

Amy tried out an explanation. "The poppers made me dumb," she said. "That was the problem and what was so good. So dumb I had to be present."

The first year of transition, Amy discovered, was about learning how much you've lied to yourself. How unreliable your own self-assessments were and how little the sense of self from your past could be put to good use in transition. The awful part was watching what therapy called "your coping mechanisms" flame out. There was a moment in which you could catch a glimpse of how scared you'd been and the degree of pain in which you'd been living as a boy, before that pain and fear actually hit you and shredded you. The same way in which 1950s films captured men in early atomic bomb tests watching the flash and mushroom cloud rise, marveling at the Shiva-esque destruction for just a split second before the shockwave and heat sent their searing bodies flying backward, along with the camera recording those bodies, and after which nothing could be seen, only felt.

And then you developed new coping mechanisms, new language, new walls to keep yourself safe. The problem with the poppers was that they made Amy too dumb to keep all that cognitive machinery going. It all ground to a halt, and instead of the new lies, she fell into direct contact with a raw fact: She was a girl in love with a girl. It was overwhelming. It was all she had ever hoped for.

To say that Amy had never before had sex as a woman was the kind of thing that trans activists would take issue with. Feel free to peruse the Tumblr-Twitter industrial complex for all the ways that "trans women have always been women"—even before they transitioned. But for Amy it was the first time she saw herself fucking as a woman without laying a psychic veil over whatever sexual scene was occurring; the first time it just *was* rather than something that, with effort, she could manage to see. It was the first time she had been present as the woman she so obviously had been all along, a woman who required no effort to be present, and who connected directly with Reese.

So often when she had sex, she allocated the majority of her mental capacity to managing her own impression of herself as she fucked, with a secondary concern being her partner's impression of her. This allocation left little mental energy for actually desiring her partner, much less vocalizing or displaying that desire. Which, she knew, did not make her a good lover. It made her a bad lover, and this was, in fact, her impression of her own sexual prowess: disappointing, tepid, with occasional flashes of mediocrity.

The exception to this was the men she slept with back when she was a cross-dresser and called herself a sissy. She did not care about those men, was not attracted to men, and so didn't care what their impressions were—they were simply another feminizing accessory, albeit a difficult and unwieldy accessory. But when deployed right, they were even better than a corset for making a girl feel dainty. Their job was to provide lots of masculine contrast to her girliness, a task they set about diligently, because most of them were straight-identified, married, and therefore invested in getting to enjoy her body while avoiding any thought that allowed them to ponder why the thing that made their cocks hard was a hard cock on a girl. The whole object of these encounters—and the men acted reciprocally— involved ignoring the man's needs in order to instead focus on herself and what kind of person she must be that a man was using her for his own sexual enjoyment, even as she ignored the particular man and his particular need.

Amy lost her virginity when she was fifteen to a seventeen-year-old cougar named Delia. Delia was punk, with piecey bleached and waxed hair and threadbare vintage shirts that advertised intentionally uncool brands—*Pepsi! Taste of a New Generation*—an overall gestalt that read to the adults in their lives as "troubled." Delia had been in and out of hospitals with an eating disorder, had tried both coke and heroin, and the rumor at school was that she had done anal after a rave with a twenty-eight-year-old. Whether or not that was true, she always made out with other girls at parties. Three weeks after Delia and Amy slept together for their one time, Delia's parents mortgaged their house to send her to one of those military detox schools in the middle of the desert, where semi-professional guards locked kids in their rooms or left them in the middle of the wilderness. Amy never saw Delia again after that.

The afternoon she lost her virginity, she was not supposed to be with Delia. Instead, she was supposed to be going home, putting on a decent collared shirt, and returning to school for an awards ceremony for her baseball team. Her team had come in sixteenth in the state, a feat that sounded solidly unimpressive, but because her school was a fraction of the size of the giant baseball breeding farms in the rural areas of Minnesota, had become something of a miracle story. Amy, in her own miracle, ended up stealing the most bases in the league that season, a feat she accomplished by leaning into pitches, getting hit, and taking a free base, then stealing her way around like a twitchy squirrel. Bruises brindled her left arm and torso from March until June.

On the bus home after school the day of the baseball awards, Delia traced the stitching on Amy's jeans with her finger and said, "My parents aren't home." Which was how Amy's own parents ended up sitting together at a baseball awards ceremony, increasingly embarrassed, as the coach repeatedly called out the name of their always-baffling teenager to come receive a plaque while other parents stared at them questioningly.

At that moment, the teenager in question was eating pussy. Something she'd never before done. She'd fingered a girl once, a girl who, to show she wasn't a slut, unbuttoned only the top button of her button-fly jeans, leaving Amy little room to actually maneuver or learn anything in the space between denim and body. When Amy went in for a kiss and got an ear, the girl began to giggle, and Amy was relieved to withdraw her hand; she'd been terrified and ashamed that she was doing everything wrong. That her inept and cramped fumbling would make obvious to the girl what Amy already knew: that there was something wrong with her masculinity. That she was flawed in deep and terrible ways as a boy, and worse, that anything to do with socially expected sex would cause these flaws to reveal

themselves. The only consolation came from the young adult au-
thors she'd read, the books for girls that she'd taken from her sister
and read in secret, where the common theme involved the anxious
awfulness of teenage sex. In light of these stories—except for the
blustery eagerness to partake in sex that all the boys were supposed
to have, an eagerness she barely registered in herself except as a social
rite that was dangerous not to perform—she could almost convince
herself she was normal.

Why had she gone home with Delia? She knew her parents
would be furious that she had skipped the awards. They had been so
grateful that she'd finally given them something proper—a son
who was good at baseball—of which to be proud as parents. And
then she'd stolen that from them. And why? So she could tentatively go down on Delia. She had her face close to Delia's vagina,
her body tense, like a cat attempting to sniff a candle's flame, ready
to pull away at any sign of pain from this apparition. And yet, still,
why?

Did she want Delia's vagina? Did she want to taste it? That was
what she was supposed to want. How many boys had she heard describe the taste of pussy? She opened her eyes and looked at it. She
didn't know what was what or where. Stupid. How stupid she was.
And above her, Delia waited, with her own eyes shut. Then Delia
craned her neck forward and peered at Amy. "How are you doing
down there?"

"Fine," Amy said. How incredibly stupid. *Fine!* The least com-
mittal, most unsexy word you could say. "Fine" was what you said
when someone asked you how you were, and you didn't want to talk
about it. She might as well have said, "I am confused and ashamed."

To counter for her shame, she began to lick, hoping to convince
Delia of the eagerness she was supposed to have. Maybe this was
how you did it.

"Higher up," Delia said from above.

"What?"

"Use your tongue higher." Delia had her eyes shut again, frowning like she was concentrating hard on some thought. Amy cringed. It was awful how much she didn't know.

Amy tried again, and after a moment Delia stopped her. "Look," said Delia, as she spread her labia with two fingers, "this is my clit." Amy nodded, but a second later, she realized she'd been too ashamed at having needed the instruction and hadn't paid attention. She'd focused instead on examining Delia's face for mockery or derision. *This is not a big deal,* she told herself. *It is your first time. Delia knows that. She can't expect you to be good.*

"Is it good?" she asked Delia.

"Yes," said Delia flatly, in a way that Amy knew was a lie. What else could Delia say?

"Good," Amy said. "I like it too." Two lies.

The only thing worse would be if Delia faked an orgasm. Amy had seen an episode of *Sex and the City* where the four women talked about inadequate men they'd had to fake it for. Delia's leg twitched as if in involuntary pleasure, and Amy, to punish herself, thought: *Fake.*

How long did it go on for? Until Amy felt Delia gently touch her hair, which was short, fuzzily growing out from a buzz cut she'd impulsively given herself one night.

"Let's take a break," Delia said. "Maybe just have sex. I like sex best."

"Okay," said Amy. She pushed herself up and tucked her legs under her to look around the room. A girl's room, more feminine than Delia's punk aesthetic might have indicated. Lavender accent wall that Delia said she had painted herself. Nail polish lined up along the windowsill under diaphanous sea-green curtains wafting inward on a breeze. Amy loved getting girls to paint her nails. It happened less and less, though—in middle school, girls loved to paint the boys' nails. By high school, they mostly didn't give a fuck what boys did with their nails. Clothes were piled up beside the bed, with a pleasantly faint odor of Delia, a scent that Amy previously hadn't known was the odor of Delia, until she smelled the clothes, and then it clicked. Next to the bed was a copy of *Prozac Nation*. Amy reached for it. She had never read the book, but she had gathered that this was a book you were supposed to make fun of. A lot of Amy's cultural touchstones in high school were like that: things to which she was ignorant or indifferent, but about which she opined her received wisdom. She didn't make fun of the book, though. On the bed, Delia looked so frail and so beautiful beneath the sheets— she wanted Delia to hold her, or she wanted to hold Delia. She did not feel sexual. Once, on the bus home, Delia told Amy that she'd lost so much fat from her bulimia that her body grew a layer of soft down to stay warm and compensate for the lack of fat insulation. She didn't know how to help, but she liked how Delia had gotten in the habit of confiding in her. Delia had asked her if she could keep secrets, and for once, true to her word, Amy repeated nothing that Delia had told her.

But looking over Delia's body, half-illuminated by sunlight, with blocks of color from a small stained-glass charm suction-cupped to the window, Delia's skin just looked soft and bare. Over the winter, when no one could see and it was acceptable to wear windbreaker pants to practice, Amy had shaved her legs and gotten terrible razor burn that turned into acne as seemingly each hair on the backs of her thighs inflamed itself into a pimple. It was bad enough that it hurt to sit down. How did girls like Delia avoid that?

"It's good," said Delia, of the book. "I'm angry about the same things as her."

"Should I read it?"

Delia scoffed. "I don't think it'd be your thing."

What was Amy's thing? Pop-punk and baseball? That's what people thought. Amy had pierced her ears over the winter, but her coach made her take the studs out. When her mom saw the little studs, she called Amy a dork. She didn't think her mom was using the word "dork" correctly, and that probably the word her mom was looking for but didn't know was "poseur." Still, getting called a dork hurt her feelings, because she understood what her mom meant, and if even her mom could see it, the other kids absolutely could too.

"Do you have condoms?" Amy asked. She had never worn a condom.

"No, I'm on the pill. One of the few things my parents and I agree on."

Amy nodded, and Delia smiled and cocked her head to the side. "Take off your boxers." Amy did as she was told. She was not hard. She didn't know if her penis was good. Besides size, she didn't even know all the other ways it might not be good. Probably it wasn't, and she fought the urge to cover herself with a sheet.

"Come here," Delia said, and Amy cuddled up close to her. Delia's hand touched her. Amy was desperate to get hard. She began to concoct a fantasy. Something that fit with what was happening, but wasn't actually what was happening. She was Delia's pet. Her owner wanted her to get hard, and she didn't want to disappoint. It would happen whether she wanted it to or not. Her owner thought she was pretty. She looked at one of the bras laying on the floor and told herself, *That's my bra, she took it off of me.*

"Oh, you like that," Delia said. Amy was hard.

"Yeah," Amy whispered, afraid that the intrusion of reality might disperse the fantasy that let her get hard.

"You ready?" Delia asked.

"Yeah."

Delia threw off the sheets, lay on her back. She guided Amy in. The first thoughts Amy had were of warmth.

"Slow at first," Delia said. She had a half smile. It was too much. Too close to being laughed at. Amy shut her eyes and focused. But she could feel the sexual charge leaving her. She pulled the fantasy back up: She wasn't really fucking Delia. Delia was fucking her. She belonged to Delia. She was Delia's girl.

"Yeah," Amy said, and Delia made a noise like an affirmation.

What did she wish Delia would say to her? Maybe something like *you're mine.*

"You're mine," she whispered to Delia.

Delia's eyes widened in surprise and she pulled Amy closer.

Delia liked it, Amy realized. Delia liked what Amy liked.

What else did Amy want to hear? She submerged back into the fantasy, like sinking into a pool. She was in Delia's room. Delia was fucking her. Delia was grabbing her body. Telling her she was a hot little thing. And Amy was grabbing Delia's body. Was fucking her. She tried to call Delia a hot little thing, but the words choked in her. "So hot," she grunted. And back into the fantasy: Delia was calling her a slut, had a hand on her neck.

Could she do that? "I wanna make you my slut," Amy said.

Delia looked up at her quizzically. "You like talking dirty," Delia stated.

"Do you like it?"

Delia grinned. "Yeah."

Amy grabbed Delia's hair. Pulled her around. "Can we do doggy?" Amy asked.

"Yeah," said Delia, and pushed Amy off, turned over. And then Amy was back in. Both into Delia and into the fantasy. In two places at once. Amy wanted her ass grabbed. She grabbed Delia's ass. Delia moaned. She pictured Delia pinching her nipples, and reached around and pinched Delia's tiny breasts. And then, without warning, Amy was coming. Not in the room with Delia, but in another similar room, where Delia was spanking her, where she was Delia's little slut, where Delia had her captive, where she was Delia's good girl, forever and ever.

And then again, she was back in Delia's actual room. She'd collapsed on top of Delia. "Wow," said Delia, and it sounded genuine. Slowly she pulled herself off of Delia and Delia flipped over, and she nestled under Delia's arm. Amazingly, Amy had the sense that she had done a good job, that she was a good lover. Wherever she had gone, Delia hadn't noticed. And maybe that was how you have sex.

Later, much later, she would learn the word for this: dissociation. She'd figured she had just been fantasizing. The word "dissociate"

sounded pathologizing to her at first—why should she be accused
of dissociating when normal people get to call it fantasizing, and
talk about how fantasy just made their sex better and better? But
pathology felt more and more apt the more sex she had. It took her
a while to understand the cyclical loneliness of disappearing in dissociation during sex. That people have sex for a shared joy that
keeps an existential loneliness at bay, so when she disappeared inside of herself, her more experienced partners sensed that absence
and her disappearance hurt them. Since she dreaded hurting those
she most wanted to connect with, she grew to dread and avoid sex
with specifically those most-liked people. And of course, clearly
dreading having to have sex with a person only hurt that person
more and drove them away—concluding in a final angst in which
the loneliness that had made her want to connect with someone in
the first place returned upon her tenfold with every attempt to have
sex.

In fact, it was Reese who had best named the sex Amy had been
having for most of her life. "You learned how to fuck like a crypto-
trans," Reese said. "Cis women take a long time to realize when
someone's doing it, because they often don't even know the name
for what they're seeing or what it means. Trans women see it right
away. It's how the most awful chasers fuck, because the most awful
chasers are repressed trans themselves. Meaning, most of us have
fucked that way at one time or another."

The worst part came later that night with Delia. Some part of her
performance changed Delia's estimation of her. She wasn't just the
sweet boy Delia could confide in on the bus home. Amy's performance had created a fundamental separation between the two of
them. Something that hadn't existed before. Something animal in
her. A brute who could take a woman. Delia talked to her
differently—like she had more respect for Amy, but also, had to
maintain a careful distance. This was a budding man, after all: powerful, dangerous.

The person outlined by Delia's new deference horrified Amy.

What did she really want from Delia? She wanted to sit on Delia's bed, surrounded by all that girl stuff and get her nails painted. She wanted to be cuddled. The thing Delia seemed to newly admire in her was everything that would lose her what she wanted from Delia. She pictured how the sex would have looked to someone watching: her behind Delia, holding a fistful of Delia's hair, Amy's hairy thighs thrusting away. The image made her sick. A beast whom women were wise to eye warily.

"We can do this again," Delia said, walking Amy to the corner through her backyard, a route that she chose in case her neighbors reported to her parents that they had seen a boy leaving through the front door while they were out. Amy agreed. She had to agree. That was what she was supposed to do. But Delia and Amy never did it again. Amy's parents grounded her for embarrassing them at the baseball awards, and by the time they freed her, Delia's parents had shipped Delia off to Utah or wherever.

Over the next few years, Amy sharpened this mode of dissociative sex, mostly in order to fulfill a social obligation that she felt from both girls and boys. Girls, who wanted to see Amy respond to their beauty, their flirting, in the correct ways. Boys, who wanted to brag about conquests, or more commonly, bond over them. In Amy's late teens, sharing attempted conquests had become the primary and most thrilling activity among boys. The way they got to know and trust each other. The girls were incidental. More than that, they were vaguely disdained in subtle manners by the boys—in college, a girl Amy talked to about her high school years made a strong case for calling this disdain misogyny—because girls frustratingly didn't always conform to the boys' plans. Still, enough of them did for Amy and her friends. And so the important questions were: How many girls would be at the party? Did you see that short girl? Did you get with her? She had nice titties, didn't she? Did you give it to her? No? She left you blue-balled? Sucks, bro. Bitches be cray.

The more Amy went along with this, the more she grew to fear sex. To fear the comedown afterward, when she couldn't dissociate any longer, and had to confront her obvious brutishness. She came to resent the tight cliques of girls who saw how other, dangerous, and terribly male she was. They might have said she was cute, noticed her abs or her pretty-boy face. But she was not to be allowed in among the girls. Amy was disgusted at the way she craved approval through behavior that made her feel like a cosmic joke: an asshole with no self-esteem who wanted to be one of the girls so badly there weren't even the words for it, so she got close in the crudest ways instead. At times the resentment spiked into self-loathing—whole weeks when she either couldn't bear to look at herself in the mirror or didn't want to do anything else. When she watched the girls she knew, a burning jealousy would stab through her. Little things. How they plucked their eyebrows. How they put their hands on each other's arms. Jealous. Jealous. Jealous. So it was easy for her to call girls bitches. To dismiss their concerns, which cruelly could never apply to her. To charm the boys with jokes about the ridiculousness of girls, of femininity in general.

Her school had a tradition, Student Switch Day, where once a year, each student drew another student's name from a hat, then dressed like that student for a day and attended that other student's classes on their schedule. Amy got Mary Anne's name. Mary Anne was full-figured and gorgeous and probably would have been popular had she not loved horses so much. Mary Anne had been in child pageants. A popular rumor about Mary Anne, one that may or may not have had factual basis but nonetheless had staying power: When Mary Anne hit puberty very young, nine or ten, her mother made her eat toilet paper to starve the fat going to her hips and chest. The fiber in the toilet paper would curb Mary Anne's appetite, her mother said. Nevertheless, by fourteen Mary Anne had the biggest breasts at school.

Other girls told Amy to ask Mary Anne to lend her a dress and do her makeup. And Amy longed to ask Mary Anne for that, longed for it so badly it was terrifying. The night she drew Mary Anne's name, Amy stared at herself in a mirror, trying to picture what Mary Anne's eye shadow and mascara could do for her face. But she never asked Mary Anne for anything. Instead she found a triple-F bra at Goodwill, stuffed it, and did nothing else to impersonate Mary Anne.

Amy arrived to school on Switch Day with the bra stuffed under Amy's otherwise everyday clothes. Mary Anne's face fell the second she saw Amy; it was a look of pure hurt, crestfallen with disappointment in what Amy found to imitate in her existence and body. "Why are you so mean?" she asked Amy. And suddenly Amy saw what she had done: a pair of tits. She was saying that's all Mary Anne was. And at that moment, when she might have apologized, might have found the courage to ask Mary Anne for help, to tell her she wanted to understand her better, that she wanted to be like her if only for a day, Jon McNelly came by, pointed at Amy's stuffed bra and said, "Nailed it!" Mary Anne managed a smile with her mouth, but her eyes went wet, and she nodded and said, "I hope you have a good day being me."

Amy considered taking off the bra, abating her cruelty for Mary Anne's sake. But she didn't. She wore it all day. She liked wearing a bra. She liked people commenting on her boobs. That night, she wore the bra again when she jerked off to the fantasy of Mary Anne forcing her to dress up in her clothes, then tossed it in a dumpster on her way to school the next morning.

If that afternoon at Delia's had been Amy's first time having sex with a woman, Patrick had been her first time having sex with a guy. Although whether Patrick was, in fact, a man, Amy later came to doubt.

He was the first maybe-trans person she had ever met. He probably wouldn't have called himself trans. Just a cross-dresser. Which was what Amy called herself at the time. But no one had ever seen her dressed up. Not even on Halloween. She had figured that by the time she got to college and had a lock on her door, she'd spend a

bunch of her time behind it dressed up pretty. But even by her soph-
omore year, she had barely accumulated the basics of a wardrobe.
Her makeup remained in an equally dismal state. She'd had no one
to teach her the art of makeup so she stuck to the three cosmetic
basics whose application was more or less explained by their pack-
aging: lipstick, eyeliner, and mascara.

Her frequent attempts to shop for women's clothes failed more
often than not. She never went into women's boutiques—it'd be
impossible to explain herself in there. Instead, she haunted department stores—Walmarts and Targets—taking circuitous routes
around the edges of Women's Wear, feigning interest in adjacent
kitchen appliances, then snatching something, anything: a swimsuit, a purse, a bra. The whole exercise humiliated her. She looked
like a creep, she knew. But she couldn't be cool. The closer she got
to actually buying clothes, actually browsing in the women's section, the more her blood rushed and her face reddened. The more
her hands shook. There wasn't any way to be casual while holding a
pair of panties and looking like you're at risk of passing out. Because
who did that? What the fuck was wrong with her? And how much
other random shit did she buy attempting to hide those panties? Did
she think the checkout girl wouldn't think a college boy buying a
baby-doll dress was weird if the purchases also included three bags
of chips, some beef jerky, and a folding chair?

She found Patrick in the fall of her second year at college. Forty
miles away. A thirty-six-year-old divorced hotel clerk posting in a
Yahoo group that he wanted someone to dress up with. Just two
guys, dressing up in lingerie, to relax. He undercut his own casual,
no-homo, bro-vibe by adding that he was versatile.

*Nineteen-year-old college student. 5'8" 140 lbs. Do you have lingerie
for me?* It took Amy two hours of deliberation to send that message.
No, but there's a store for cross-dressers where I get mine, Patrick replied. *I'll pick you up from your school if you want and we can go tomorrow.*

Which was how Amy ended up standing on the street in front of her dorm, wearing a hood low over her eyes, as if her pervert tranny intentions could be read plainly on her face by any other passing student who glanced her way.

Picture an anonymous strip mall, veneered in a too-red brick, housing a Subway franchise, a vacuum cleaner store, and sandwiched between the two, a dingy painted sign that read: GLAMOUR BOUTIQUE. Now picture Amy's disappointed face.

With a name like *Glamour Boutique,* she had been naïvely expecting, well, glamour: three-way mirrors, flattering directional lighting, and sleek dresses hung sparingly on brushed metal rails. Instead, racks of clothing cramped the small space. The clothing mostly fell into two categories: frumpy or sexy, like the clientele wanted to either deflect all attention from themselves or wild out in one big skin-revealing splurge. In the back hung black latex and vinyl fetish gear, French maid outfits, schoolgirl ensembles, and frilly sissy party dresses.

At the counter, the clerk, a goth girl with straight black hair and thick winged liner, rang up the purchase of a middle-aged man in golf clothes. The golfer kept his eyes fixed on the middle distance, refusing to make eye contact with anyone, which allowed Amy to examine him surreptitiously. Maybe he told his wife he'd gone golfing. Maybe he'd just finished a round of golf. Either way, a satin corset lay on the counter in front of him.

The goth clerk met Amy's glance briefly, gave a slight nod, then looked away tactfully. After the golfer left, the clerk watched Amy and Patrick without appearing to, her body language communicating that she presumed nothing. But Amy couldn't help imagining what she thought. A tall balding man, and a young slender boy. *She probably thinks I'm the sissy,* Amy thought, and the thought both excited and ashamed her.

Amy paused at a shelf of silicone breast forms. "Let me know if you want to try any," the clerk said. She pointed at a mannequin wearing a bra and forms. "We have a special sheer bra with pockets that can hold them so that you can see the nipples. But you can also wear them in any regular bra."

Instinctively, Amy shook her head. Then she caught herself. "How much are they?" she asked.

"Depends on the cup size. What size are you?"

Amy didn't know how to answer the question. Obviously, she had no breasts.

The girl tried again. "What size bras do you have?"

"I don't know."

"Well, the sizes bigger than D are one-sixty for the forms, the smaller sizes are one-thirty. All the bras are forty."

"Can I see the C-cup?" Amy said.

The girl appraised her. "I'm guessing you're maybe a 34. But I can measure you if you want."

Rarely had Amy wanted something so badly. "No. I mean, yeah. Okay."

In the dressing room, which was a curtain pulled over a closet in the corner, the girl directed Amy to turn around. Amy wasn't sure how, in this moment, she realized the girl was a transsexual. Some combination of aesthetics clicked into place. *I'm getting a bra fitting from a transsexual!* she told herself, not quite believing it. She wanted to ask the girl everything, but even more than that, she wanted to be cool. She didn't want the girl to know what a creep she was. A creep who had jerked off to transsexual porn the night before.

"Yes," the girl said as she wrapped the tape measure around Amy's chest, "You can wear either a thirty-four or a thirty-six. I'd recommend a thirty-four because bras stretch as they wear out."

The girl brought her a thirty-four, with silicone breast forms already in the sheer pockets. The silicone gave off a faint chemical odor, but was pleasingly pliable when squeezed. When the curtain dropped, Amy put it on, and the weight, naturally pulling on her chest, triggered something like an endorphin rush. She gave a little hop, to see them bounce, to feel the weight and movement. A giggle slipped out, like a bubble.

She opened the curtain. "I'm going to buy this," she told the girl. "Can I wear it to try on other clothes?"

"Sure, of course," the girl said. "I'll just take the boxes up to the counter."

From behind her, Patrick gave the thumbs-up. "Looking good," Patrick said, and Amy had the strange urge to cover her fake breasts, her fake nipples strategically visible through the sheer fabric.

Amy had expected Patrick to be something quite different than what he turned out to be. She had imagined someone quite masculine: the stereotypical man-in-a-dress. Some cleft-chinned action hero with blue eyeshadow—Patrick Swayze in *To Wong Foo*. That was the best trans she'd seen on TV. Her other options were *The Silence of the Lambs* or *The Bird Cage* or maybe *The Crying Game*.

She had no reason to think Patrick would have been any of those things. Look at Amy herself: neither comedy nor horror nor tragedy, neither especially masculine nor overtly striving for femme. Just a skinny blond college kid standing on a curb in a red hoodie that repeated washings and wear had faded close to pink; not exactly a macho style, but passably close to indie rock.

When Patrick pulled up, a stab of disappointment came over Amy. Nothing about him struck her as notable: moderately tall, stooped shoulders lost in a knit polo shirt, hair on the top of his head nearly melted away, small neutral eyes peering at her standing on the curb through wire-framed glasses. Even his car: a nineties-era Geo Metro, a car so nondescript she had forgotten the model had ever existed until she saw him in one. She would have thought she might have the wrong guy, except that he rolled down the window and asked, "Tiffany?" The name she'd given him for herself. He hadn't given her his femme name. *I'm just always Patrick,* he'd written.

She got in, and he looked at her cautiously, then slowly drove down the street, leaning forward and concentrating on the road, giving the impression that the passing surroundings were shrouded in mist and appeared to him only a few feet from the end of his nose. They spoke little as Patrick drove through town, as though they might be overheard through the windows of the car. Out in the Berkshires, though, they began to talk.

Patrick worked night shifts at the Red Roof Inn. He didn't like the job, and spoke of it with bewilderment, somehow baffled as to how it had come to be his. He had been the manager at a Blockbuster Video before that, but it had closed. He'd gotten a divorce at the same time, and a judge had ordered him to pay child support for his two daughters, five and seven. "My bitch ex-wife doesn't work, though," he said, and Amy flinched a little. Patrick hadn't previously come anywhere near language so strong.

This guy is such a loser, Amy thought. But the assessment gave her a feeling of security. They occupied worlds and concerns miles apart. No one could tie them together. They would barely understand each other. She had found a truly safe man with whom to dress up.

"Had you heard of the Glamour Boutique before this?" Patrick asked as they came out of the Berkshires and into central Massachusetts. He glanced at her with the same smirk that kids wore when they asked each other about a weed hookup. Amy could see he wanted a particular answer.

"No, should I have?"

"Just wondering if you like the same kind of *stories* I like." He emphasized the word "stories," drawing it out.

"Like what stories?"

"Erotica."

"Yeah." Amy adjusted her seatbelt so she could lean subtly against the door and watch him. "I like erotica."

"Glamour Boutique is the sponsor for the Fictionmania archive. Do you read Fictionmania?"

As if he had physically shown it to her, Amy could picture the

Glamour Boutique ad banner, depicting a line drawing of a Victorian-looking woman lacing up another woman's corset, an ad banner that floated at the bottom of the fictionmania.tv site.

Amy didn't answer. The car banked through a turn on the highway. She had never spoken about what she masturbated to with anyone. The stories of women forcing boys into girlhood. The online archive of Fictionmania stored twenty thousand of these stories, and anonymous writers all across the world added more every day. From the sheer number of stories, Amy understood there had to be thousands of writers, and therefore exponentially more readers, tens or hundreds of thousands of people—an entire literary subculture whose existence required that that subculture itself never be acknowledged. The stories formed a trans samizdat so clandestine that you'd have to be a certain sort of trans to ever think about looking for it in the first place. You must be this trans to ride this ride. The first rule of Fictionmania Club is never talk about Fictionmania Club.

The stories were dangerous. But she knew, from the self-evident existence of the site, that all over the world eyes were eating up the text and penises were spurting at the climaxes of the stories of when the cross-dressers themselves first took dick, or when a former-boy-now-buxom-shemale was humiliated and raped, or when a strong man was feminized against his will. The femininity forced upon the males was the ultimate in degradation and humiliation— and what did that say about her opinion of femininity? Amy hated how much she loved the stories, the orgasms that came as she read them at all hours of the day, sneaking in a story in the twenty minutes between classes, or whole nights spent in a jerk-off marathon, story after story, until reality began to fade. She knew that anyone she knew who discovered it wouldn't understand. They'd just think she hated femininity and equated it with humiliation. She'd be shunned, and deservedly so. For years—until she transitioned, until she met women into rape-play, into servitude and infantilization, women who had eroticized and sexually defanged every unspeakable shame and violation life had thrown at their womanhood—she couldn't actually think of a single argument to counter the undeniable orgasm-certified evidence of her unpardonable misogyny.

Patrick waited for a response. But Amy couldn't seem to find any words. Neither a confirmation nor a denial.

"I'll take that as a yes," Patrick said.

"Yeah," Amy admitted. "I know Fictionmania."

"Which stories do you like?" Patrick asked. Then without waiting for an answer, he continued, "I like the extreme body modifications, when they get given huge boobs. I don't like the stories where they transform through magic. I like the surgery, though. Because it really exists, so I know it might happen to me one day." Patrick's voice took on a note of brightness that Amy hadn't yet heard.

The possibility of anyone choosing to foot the cost of surgically implanting Patrick with enormous breasts struck Amy as no more or less likely than an elf witch casting a spell to give Patrick boobs. But still, Amy knew what he meant. She didn't like the magic either. She liked the stories that were as close to her life as possible. A shy college boy. Domineering older women. What she really liked was when the women made the trans girls have sex with men. When the older women watched and laughed. But there was no way she'd admit that to Patrick.

"I usually choose the *Wedding Dress or Married* category," Amy said. "Weddings are so kinky. I think most non-kinky people just never realize it. Think about it! You put a woman in a special elaborate outfit, and then one man gives her to another man like some kind of BDSM scene, and then they put like a symbolic collar on the woman's finger, and then the man lifts her dress to show everyone there—maybe hundreds of people!—her garter and lingerie. Then he picks her up and takes her away to fuck her while everyone else knows it's happening! It's so dirty. It's like the kinkiest thing I could ever imagine and it actually happens all the time. So I like to think about it happening to me."

She had never said anything like this aloud before. Patrick laughed. And then she laughed.

As she laughed, Patrick did something unexpected. For most of the drive, he'd been leaning forward, peering through the windshield, his hands at two and ten o'clock. But he dropped his left hand and started rubbing his crotch. Amy thought Patrick might just be adjusting, but no, he kept at it. He was playing with himself. He didn't so much as glance at her, just kept going, talking about which of the stories he liked from his favorite category, *Physically Forced or Blackmailed*.

For a moment, Amy felt disgusted. But isn't this what she wanted? Didn't she understand it? Hadn't she wanted to share the sexuality she hid with someone? Anyone? She reached down and rubbed herself too. But she couldn't keep going. The vibe in the car wasn't sexy. She felt like a boy, with a man, but a man she'd judged to be an unattractive loser. Maybe she'd feel differently after they had dressed up.

Glamour Boutique got fun after about a half hour. The clerk introduced herself as Jen. As Amy's jitteriness faded, Jen actually began to help Amy with clothes. The sense of women advising each other on outfits, of her inclusion in that feminine rite, nearly overwhelmed Amy. It was more than she could have hoped for. Wearing the breast forms and bra, she wanted to try on everything—not just the fetish clothes, items she'd only ever seen online—but simple dresses as well. "Always look for the empire waist," Jen encouraged, holding up a yellow dress with a sash under the bust. "Everyone always thinks it's about minimizing the shoulders, but no, it's about the right ratio between shoulders and hips. Empire waists flare out, give you hips."

Amy and Patrick nodded, listening carefully. Patrick had touched Amy a few times now, in ways that Amy wasn't sure how to interpret. Once Patrick held up a dress against Amy's body and said, "This would look nice on you," then ran a hand down Amy's side, pressing the dress against it. A contrail of unease followed Patrick's touch, but she refused to let anything like that ruin the moment. A vague euphoria wafted over Amy. Here they were: a bunch of girls talking clothes. Initially, she glanced at Jen frequently; worried that Jen might be annoyed by their excitement or laughing at them. But no, she judged Jen's friendliness as genuine. It had to be boring to work in a place where you have to carefully avoid eye contact so often, like with that golfer. Maybe hers and Patrick's excitement made them better customers.

Amy had read about transsexuals online. She'd even taken a test—the COGIATI (Combined Gender Identity and Transsexuality Inventory), developed by some transsexual woman and based on DSM psychological models to determine if the test takers were true transsexuals who needed to transition, or merely transgenderists—that is, male fetishists for whom transition would be a tragic mistake. She'd read whatever psychology about trans people she could find at her college library and on the Internet. Most of it was decades old. According to what she'd found online, there were two types of male-to-female transsexuals. Those people who had always been girls, who had played with dolls, were attracted to men, and hated their penises. The second kind, the autogynephiles, were men who got turned on by the idea of themselves as women. These were the fetishistic cross-dressers, who conformed to all sorts of male stereotypes, loved their penises, and got turned on wearing women's clothing. They ought not transition, the psychologists said—they weren't really women, they were fetishists who took their indulgence too far. Amy caught the whiff of moralism in this assessment and understood what it meant. There was something bad and immoral about autogynephilia. In the comments below the psychology articles, a number of trans women irate at this psychology always posted rebuttals. They called the idea of autogynephilia transphobic. They called the psychologists who came up with it chasers.

Amy remembered how one of them patiently explained that the

term "autogynephilia" only works if you don't think trans women are women. If you do, then you immediately see that the majority of women, cis or trans, are all autogynephiles, and that most men would be autoandrophiles—it's not something special about trans women. Of course women are turned on by being women and men turned on by being men! Watch any porn and the sexuality of everyone in it is actually about their own auto-andro/gyne-philia. Listen to them talk. It's all about validating their own gender. *Oh yeah, I'm your little slut . . . yeah, baby, you like this big cock?* And alone on their laptops somewhere: the viewers, turned on to identify with people identifying with their gender.

Other trans women claimed that these psychologists had begun to be discredited, that their research methods were revealed to be the suspect practice of hanging around in bars without Institutional Review Board approval in order to pick up trans women, sleep with them, and later write clinical papers both based upon and obscuring those experiences. But Amy doubted those trans women. No one with expertise cared what the trans women had to say. Who were they to tell psychologists with doctorates—scientists!—that they were wrong? And hadn't it even been a transsexual woman herself who'd written the COGIATI test? Of course a bunch of deranged creeps whose paraphilia revolved around womanhood would claim they're women—crazy people never think they are crazy! Check and mate, sickos!

Amy didn't have to take the test to know her own result: a fetishist, a pervert. But she took it anyhow, a series of bizarre questions about imagining shapes and quantifying empathy. *You are talking with a friend. Outside, far away, somebody is honking their horn regularly and endlessly. It is not very loud, you can just barely hear it in the quiet room. What is your reaction? You meet somebody and they are polite to you, but seem a little distant. They are actually secretly disliking you. How likely are you to know this? You will never, ever be a woman. You must live the rest of your days entirely as a man, and you will only get more masculine with each passing year. There is no way out.*

What is your reaction? You're in a desert walking along when all of a sudden you look down and you see a tortoise. It's crawling toward you. You reach down to flip the tortoise over on its back. The tortoise lies on its back, its belly baking in the hot sun, beating its legs trying to turn itself over, but it can't, not without your help. But you're not helping. Why is that?

Some of the questions made no sense—but others betrayed by their wording a clumsy trend in the conclusions they would formulate. If you had spatial skills and active sexuality you were clearly a fetishistic man, and if you empathized with people and didn't care about sex, you might be that rarest of things: a true transsexual, a woman trapped in a man's body. But Amy wasn't that. The test showed her to be the autogynephilic creep she already assumed she would be.

Jen was obviously a true transsexual. Amy had never met a trans girl in person, and her fascination with Jen bordered on painful. Look at her. She looks like a girl. She sounds like a girl. More than that, Amy thought, she wanted something from Jen. Something like sexual attraction, but shaded differently. Something closer to the thrill she felt when a celebrity passed by. Of a nameless wanting in the direction of that celebrity. The abstract beckoning that celebrities exude. The gravitational pull of their fame that tugged at Amy so that she felt anxious to be close, to be seen, and to be valued. To feel those celebrity eyes move without friction across the smooth surface of a clamoring fandom, then suddenly catch upon her, stop dead, and return her gaze. That moment of mutual recognition, that's the only way to have your existence stamped valid, to transcend the anonymity of mere fan, of inconsequential gawker. Jen's was a noncelebrity celebrity that Amy could feel. A pull that maybe *only* she would feel. Amy kept turning to see where in the store Jen was.

Shockingly, Jen seemed to be having a good time. Moreover, she kept saying things that countered what the COGIATI test said a true transsexual should feel. When Patrick asked about French

maid outfits, Jen clucked in approval. "Back wall," she said, pointing. "But also, we have some sexy ones in boxes in the back that we
never put out because they take up so much space when they're unfolded. It's not the cheap Halloween style, they are the sensual kind
with petticoats that actually fluff." In mock sotto voce she admitted,
"I got one myself. I have a thing for that flouncy feel. My boyfriend
always wants me to tidy up in it for him. But no way. I just wear it
around my apartment for special, uh, *personal time*." She giggled at
the admission and Amy thought that Jen might spontaneously com-
bust from her own incredible and suddenly revealed transcendent
hotness, an attractiveness that had only a tangential relationship to
her appearance.

At one point, Patrick stood on one leg, working a pair of pantyhose up the calf of his other, while Jen stood in front of him with a
French maid outfit at the ready, when the bell above the door
chimed. In walked a pleasant-looking woman, plump with loosely
curled blond hair, and her teenage daughter, who looked healthy,
like maybe she was on the soccer team, an impression that Amy had
because she was wearing casual athletic gear. The two of them were
mid-laugh—perhaps lured into the store by the super-fun-sounding
name—*Glamour Boutique*. What mother and daughter wouldn't
have fun with a little glamour on an outing together?

Alarmed comprehension dawned on the mother's face as she
took in the store. But by then it was too late. Patrick, Amy, and Jen
had all seen her come in. Turning in horror would let everyone
know what she thought of them. No, she would show her daughter
how to play it cool.

Amy's joy in having found a feminine space meant especially for
her dimmed, as the light fades when a heavy cloud crosses the sun,
then winked out completely. The sense of safety that she had spun
over the store vanished. Everything on the racks shrugged off their
previous disguises to reveal themselves as tawdry and desperate.
Inwardly, she disavowed the space. This store did not reflect her.
She did not truly belong there.

Patrick, still only half in his pantyhose, blanched to a beige color and made a fast-walk beeline for the curtains that hid the changing area, stepping on and dragging the half-donned hosiery as he did. Jen winced, still holding the French maid dress. This must have happened to her many times, the panic among customers she'd just coaxed into comfort when civilians wandered into the store.

After a moment, the mother decided on a course of action: She would browse. After all, it was a store and she was allowed to browse, wasn't she? In an attempt to look natural, the mother pawed through the closest rack and bravely held up a top complex with straps and spandex. "Oh, look at this. It's interesting. What do you think?" Despite her bravado, a cringe squeaked into her voice.

"Yes," said her daughter, panicked, without even glancing at it. Her gaze raked the walls, hung thickly with gaffs, breastplates, wigs. Amy saw the store through her eyes: a *Silence of the Lambs*–level display of disembodied female body parts. Worst of all, the red-faced men, one now hiding, the other creepily fingering panties and who knew what else. The specialty panties—*with wider gusset for women of all anatomies!*—that Amy held in her hand and had been examining with curiosity when the bell above the door announced the women's entrance, burned radioactively. She longed to drop them, to throw them away from her, but feared that doing so would attract attention her way, the equivalent of waving a lace-trimmed pink flag. So she stood frozen, apparently transfixed by the panties, hating the image she felt sure she presented. She wanted to apologize.

She couldn't help herself. She stared at the teenage daughter. What was the speed of calculations whirring through that poor girl's mind? How long would her mother fake-browse before they could escape?

"Wigs!" proclaimed the mother, mustering her best cheer. "Fun!"

"Wigs," agreed Jen, setting down the maid's outfit and extending a white hand in a gesture to the wall. "The ones at the bottom are synthetic, at the top are human hair." Like the store itself, Jen had transformed in a moment. Her previous secret celebrity had inverted itself. The polarity on her magnetism had switched: She now repelled rather than attracted. To Amy, Jen's posture now landed with echoes of witches—had she just said "human hair"? Grotesque. As Jen walked back behind the counter into the sunlight streaming through the front window, the witchy aspect grew more pronounced. Amy, who had had Jen's arms around her, fastening a bra in place, before she realized Jen was trans—could no longer see anything but how trans she was, accompanied by revulsion at every feature she identified: lank dark hair, heavy knuckles, gaunt cheeks, traces of last night's makeup darkening the circles beneath her eyes. Fear had poisoned Amy's thoughts. Cruelly and involuntarily, her vision flayed away all the beauty from Jen like sheets of skin peeled from her body.

"We have wig caps, if you want to try one," Jen said.

"Mom. Let's go," said the daughter. The rack of books behind her were illustrated erotica labeled FORCED WOMANHOOD, their covers decorated with drawings of shemales bound and being whipped.

"Yes, okay."

Out darted the daughter, but with the door open, her mother paused. She turned back, her hand resting on the frame. "Your store is fun," she apologized, not just to Jen, but to everyone. She nodded, almost to herself, and a moment later the overhanging bell announced her departure.

Patrick drove too fast on the ride home. The sky had darkened while he and Amy had shopped in the Glamour Boutique. Fat drops of an April storm splatted onto the highway, making the asphalt surface into television static. Amy didn't trust the Geo to stick to the shiny road, slick with oil and rivulets, especially not when Patrick turned off the interstate and onto the windy state highways that cut over the Holyoke Range.

"I'm sorry," Amy said. "I was in a car accident when I was younger, so I get nervous. Can you slow down?" She hadn't actually ever been in a car accident, but it seemed socially easier to blame her unease on herself rather than his driving.

Patrick grunted and lifted his foot slightly from the accelerator. "Roll down the window," he told her. "The fan in this car is broken and I can't see through these windows." When she cracked the window, the sound of tires hissing over the wet pushed in, and droplets sprayed the left side of her face, and with it came the pungent odor of the wet forest, a rich mixture of damp dirt, decay, moss, and sprouting leaves. Amy liked the way rain amplified the mustiest and most comforting smells of the forest, making the forest much more foresty, just how a dog when wet smells so much more doggy.

The smell of the forest appeared to act as aromatherapy for Patrick too. His posture released. He wiped at the window, then leaned back and drove at a reasonably slow speed.

"That was awful," he said into the sound of rain and wind roaring past the cracked window. "Those women coming in."

"No, it was okay," Amy assured Patrick. "I mean, why should we be embarrassed? It's our store." The possessive just slipped in. She wasn't sure how the store became theirs, but the mother had said it too. *Your store*. The store for people like them.

"It wasn't okay," Patrick said.

Amy nodded. He was right. It wasn't okay. She didn't feel at all okay about it. She would do almost anything to never again be looked at the way those women had looked at her. It wasn't that they had even been rude. They had simply *seen* her. *Seen* a true thing in her that she had spent her life making sure never to show to anyone.

Once, when she had been about ten or eleven, her mother had gone on a business trip and come home with gifts for Amy: a pair of fluorescent-blue Rollerblades with neon-yellow ratchet straps, and a t-shirt on which the words FLORIDA KEYS and a picture of a tropical fish had been embroidered in thick thread, rather than screenprinted. The thread on the inside of the shirt was very scratchy.

After about a week of wearing the shirt, Amy had a very good idea. She went to the front porch, where her mother was planting geraniums in the window boxes.

"I love this shirt, it's my favorite," she announced to her mother, "but it is scratchy. It rubs. Can I borrow a bra?"

Her mother continued potting the flowers without turning around. "I'm sorry, can you do what?"

Amy's voice wavered, less confident on her second time asking. She pulled her shirt away from her nipples to illustrate the problem. "The embroidery is scratchy." She had worn her mother's bras in secret, when she was home alone. Now she had an excuse to have a bra of her own. Some of the girls in school were getting them, but she knew she wouldn't without some careful maneuvers on her part.

Then, her mother turned, trowel in hand, and gave Amy a look of irritation. "Just wear another t-shirt under it."

"That will be too hot. A bra would be better."

Her mother set the trowel down with a clunk and gave Amy a strange look. She saw that her son wasn't being stupid. It was the precursor to the look Amy had gotten from the women in the Glamour Boutique.

"That is not something a son asks his mother," her mother said carefully. And in her tone, beneath the impassive way she said it, Amy could feel something harder, a pit of revulsion, pulling tightly in on itself. Her mother had never said anything like that before. She was not the type to categorize behavior into what was and wasn't done.

Amy saw, in a flash, that her mother knew the request had nothing to do with scratched nipples and, worse, it had disturbed her. What seemed like a foolproof ruse had revealed everything.

"Oh!" Amy said. "I forgot! I have that white tank top. I can wear that underneath, and that won't be too hot." She smacked her palm against her forehead. "Of course." Her mother's strange gaze didn't change. Amy walked away with her mother's eyes still on her, and then she avoided her mother for as long as she could. At least until dinner that night.

Now, almost a decade later, Amy finally had her own bra. Not one pilfered from some girl's underwear drawer and stuffed into a backpack at a party. She looked at the bag of her purchases sitting at her feet in Patrick's car. She should have felt happy, but she didn't. Instead, she felt as if she had given in to an urge that ought to be turned away from. As when people shut their eyes in horror at the possibility of an apparition. *Don't even acknowledge it—it'll fuck up everything you know about the world.*

In addition to the bra and breast forms, she had bought a pink dress—empire waist, as Jen had recommended—and a pair of white faux-leather stripper heels, six inches tall and made from cheap plastic, with a thin ankle strap and a two-inch platform. She'd also bought two pairs of panties. All this had been very expensive, nearly three hundred dollars. After those women left, the shopping never got quite as fun as it had been before. Jen seemed more aware of how skittish Amy and Patrick were, and her suggestions were more circumspect. Amy supposed that had those women not come in, she would have bought much more during that brief euphoric mood that made her forget for a short time that women's clothing could be dangerous. She wished that she had at least bought a wig. She'd tried one on and looked terrible. Jen had assured her that makeup would alleviate the resemblance to an eighties rocker, instead of a beautiful woman, that Amy had been shocked to find staring back at her from the store's vanity mirror. The difference between the effect that she had always hoped would occur and the reality of what she'd seen in the store's mirror had so disheartened her that she couldn't bear to try on another. Maybe if the shopping euphoria returned, she'd thought, but it never did.

"I have to be more careful than I was today," Patrick said, breaking Amy's reverie. "I can't let anyone find out about my cross-dressing."

"Me neither," Amy said.

Patrick looked at her. "But you don't have that much to lose. I'm going through a divorce. Anyone sees me and I could lose visitation with my daughters." He swallowed hard. "I used to wear matching panties with my wife—sometimes other stuff. She said it was fun, it was like a sexy game. But I know she has already told her lawyer about it and I think they're going to use it against me."

"Wow. That sucks." Amy only half believed Patrick. Who was this woman who would let him wear panties around her? No. He had to be lying to impress her. Besides, she absolutely had as much to lose as Patrick, maybe more. Patrick was already a loser. She wasn't.

"I can't be seen in a store like that one," Patrick continued. "It could have real consequences."

"But wouldn't anyone going into that store be going to it on purpose?"

"Those women weren't there on purpose!"

Patrick had her there. She didn't know what to say. This was some heavy adult shit. Custody. Divorce. Instead, she changed the subject. "So do you still want to go to your house to dress up, though?" Other than her minuscule dorm room, Amy had nowhere to wear her new outfit. She couldn't bear the idea of donning it all only to strut the two steps that it took to cross her thinly carpeted room, back and forth, like a sad-eyed giraffe at the zoo, endlessly circling her tiny enclosure.

"Yes," Patrick said. "Don't you?"

"Mmhmm, please," said Amy.

For a long time, Amy would remember the day at the Glamour Boutique as erotically charged. But she would remember very little about the sex that she and Patrick had, only that it was not erotic. Eventually, that was how she would come to understand what sex with men was for her. The erotic part lay in the dressing up, the foreplay, the mental switch into a feminine role. And yes, dressing up with men almost always culminated in sex, but a distant faraway sex—one that Amy felt like she hadn't participated in. The sex itself was necessary to break the spell. The orgasm released the tension that had been building and brought you back to yourself. After sex, the spell could dissipate, and she saw herself as she truly was: a boy, lying dazed on his back in a stranger's bed with a dress hiked up to the waist, a string of his own pre-cum on his thigh, and a stranger lifting himself off the bed to sheepishly pull off a reservoir-filled condom.

While Patrick washed himself in the bathroom, Amy got her bearings. Took stock of the action figures lined up along the wall. The shemale porn DVD playing on the TV, which Patrick had stared at insistently and vacantly while he fucked Amy, the way Amy had scrunched shut her eyes and gone far away, taking with her only the sensation of being penetrated, of being filled by cock, of being passive for a lover. It was not Patrick's cock she had taken with her. Or, maybe, in one dimension it was. But in the place Amy had gone, it was Jen from the shop inside of her. The encounter, both real and not, expanded inside Amy's mind, a sequence that moved from that looped memory of Jen fitting Amy for a bra, then to Jen's imagined body, and then, Jen was fucking her, fucking her as a woman; and Amy could feel it, couldn't she? The thrusting inside of her, the hands on her hips and shoulders—feel that? That was Jen fucking her. Yes, it was and would be as long as she clung tight to this faraway place, and in this place she could enjoy herself for once, she could feel everything as it should be.

"I'm coming," Patrick had said, breaking the silence and loosening Amy's grip on the place she had gone, so that it slipped away from her as when you let go of a ledge; and she fell careening back through the wormhole, through time and space, back to Patrick's bed, where she opened her eyes, and saw him on top of her thrusting, then one last hard thrust, with his eyes locked on the television. She didn't say anything. Not like with Delia. No encouragement. No pretending that she had ever been present. Wordlessly, she and

Patrick both understood the rules—rules that she would hence-
forth employ for all sexual encounters with men: Neither of them
would actually be there for the sex. They would take from each
other what they could, each from their own places. They would use
what they could of each other's bodies. But encouragement, or sol-
ace, or care—no, neither of them wanted any of that. Just give me
enough of yourself to put me in touch with the part of me that can
believe I'm a girl, and beyond that, you can go fuck yourself, in
whatever theoretical dimension you need to be in to do that.

"Baby, why are you crying?" Reese had asked. Because some combination of hormones and poppers had made possible the sex that
Amy had given up on. The poppers made her too dumb to flee into
herself, to send herself somewhere. So there she was with Reese.
Not off elsewhere working to see herself as a woman when she lay
on top of a woman, or replacing a man with someone else while he
lay on top of her. She simply was a woman present with a woman. It
felt like some kind of healing, some kind of redemption. And all she
could do was cry.

Later that night, Reese stroked her hair and whispered to her,
"I'm sorry you've been in so much pain for so long."

Any night before that one, Amy would have denied it, would
have told Reese about all the privileges she had, about how lucky
she had been compared to other trans women, how many advantages she'd been granted. How few of the readily nameable traumas
she ever suffered. And without legible traumas to point to, what
would pain make her? At best, a trans version of those Didion-
worshipping bourgeois white girls who subscribed to a Grand Uni-
fied Theory of Female Pain, those minor-wound-dwelling brooders
with no particular difficulties but for an inchoate sense of their own
wronged-ness, a wronged-ness that fell apart when put into words
but nonetheless justified all manner of petulance and self-pity. In
pain? No, not Amy.

That night, however, she gaped at Reese, shocked at how easily

Reese had named what she'd gone through. She remembered Ricky telling her about Reese's uncanny ability to say what you need. Whether she could trust Reese or not, no one had ever said such a thing to her. No one had so casually seen through her hollow stoicism to the accumulated disdain and disgust she harbored within. No one had ever implied that Amy might be wounded or suffering too, least of all Amy. She didn't know she needed that kind of permission until that moment. She opened her mouth to protest, gulped once, and collapsed into tears all over again, sobbing onto Reese's chest at all she had done to herself for years, at the hurt she'd inflicted upon herself and on the people she'd been with, while Reese gripped her and didn't tell her to stop.

CHAPTER FIVE

Seven weeks after conception

O N O N E H A N D , Reese figures that the best strategy might be
to get any crying out of her system *before* she meets Katrina at
the GLAAD Media Awards gala where Ames has contrived for the
two women in his life to first encounter each other. That way, when
Reese is called upon to make a first impression, she will have so
depleted her emotional energy that she'll be incapable of anything
other than somnambulistic agreeableness. Which is why she has
spent the last few minutes unpleasantly blerping out sobs on the
floor of Ames's closet.

Ames had invited her to meet at his apartment and then take a
car together to the awards at the Hilton Midtown. Waiting for him
to get ready, she wandered around the apartment and, indulging a
nostalgic temptation, opened the closet door. The left side of the
closet had once been hers, a fact that was suddenly and viscerally
recalled to her by its faded odor of cedar flakes, wool, detergent,
and old paint, all of which wafted into her face the moment she
opened the door. She swooned backward, the smells forcing her to
relive in her mind the day that she'd moved into Amy's apartment:
how she'd grinned impishly at her lover and swept all of Amy's
hanging clothing to the right, declaring the left side conquered.
She'd been so full of hope that day. So sure that her crush on Amy
meant something new for her.

Today, what? Seven? Eight years later, she crumples under the
force of memory, her face pressed to the polyurethaned bamboo
floorboards. It hurts to remember that first day. It hurts to remember hope like that. It hurts to think that such hope was the naïveté
and stupidity of youth, of a person she would never be again.

She wants to be inured to hope. When it comes, it always disappoints, and unlike in her twenties, now it never comes simply, instead it arrives twisted, with caveats and strings. What was she doing here anyway? Trying to get some cis woman to share her baby with Reese and Reese's detransitioned ex-lover? How sad her life has become that such a ridiculous plan was the best peg on which to hang some kind of hope.

Reese used to say that she was only interested in people who'd had a major failure in life. She believed that one ought to have a singular major failure, in which all of one's hopes were dashed, in order to sprout a life into something interesting, as pruned trees grow baroque and beautiful, because an unpruned tree only grows vertically and predictably, selfishly sucking up as much sunlight as possible.

Only after the breakup with Amy did Reese begin to concede that perhaps Amy had been her own first major failure. She had previously been under the impression that she had failed majorly for most of her life, but in fact, she had simply confused failure with being a transsexual—an outlook in which a state of failure confirmed one's transsexuality, and one's transsexuality confirmed a state of failure. A mistake many of the transsexuals she knew made. Such thinking was static. You had to hope for something in the first place in order to have those hopes dashed.

With Amy, she had hoped. She made her earlier quips about failure because she believed them, but also partly because she thought they made her sound urbane and worldly. She suspected, however, that actual failure had turned her unlovely.

At thirty-four, she feels old.

"What are you doing on the floor?" The floorboards creak as Ames steps out of the bathroom, freshly shaven, wearing a snug linen jacket, his fingers deftly manipulating a Windsor knot with practiced ease. "Are you crying?"

Reese pushes onto her left arm and, looking up, wipes beneath her eyes carefully with the pads of her fingers so as not to disturb her mascara. "No."

"Yes you are! I didn't know what I was hearing. What happened?"

"I smelled the closet. And suddenly I remembered what it was like when we lived together. It made me so sad and nostalgic."

Ames lowers himself into a squat just beside her, resting on his heels. The joints of his knees crack. Tentatively Ames puts a hand on her back on the fabric of her dress. "It happens to me too." Reese draws in a quick sniffle, but otherwise doesn't respond, so he continues. "I read that of our senses, only taste and smell pass directly to the hippocampus, where memory gets stored. Sights, sounds, and touches get converted into thoughts and symbols before they continue on to the memory in the hippocampus. But smell connects directly to memory."

Reese rotates onto a hip, and pushes her back up against the closet wall, gathering the skirts of her dress beneath her. "So you detransitioned into a mansplainer, huh?" she asks.

Ames withdraws his hand. "And you've only gotten sweeter."

Reese frowns, and Ames sees that she might cry again. "I'm just sad and angry," she says in a small voice. She gestures at the West Elm bedroom set that they had picked out together on a fall Saturday five years ago, giggling in the store as they flopped down together on mattresses of memory foam and opened chests of drawers. "This was supposed to be my life. No, it wasn't *supposed* to be. It was."

"It still can be," Ames says. "That's the whole point here. We can still be so important in each other's lives."

Reese shakes her head. "No, we can't go back. Look at you. Everything has changed. Except for maybe how the closet smells."

Two years prior, Katrina and Ames's agency acquired Ketel One Vodka as a client, one of its larger accounts. Because Ketel One—

along with other flagrantly gay brands such as Delta Air Lines and Hyundai—is, and has been for some time, a sponsor of the GLAAD awards gala, the agency has purchased a ten-seat table at the event. Only a few employees wanted to go, so Ames claimed three of the remaining tickets for himself, Reese, and Katrina. His logic, he explained to Reese when he called to invite her, was that the spectacle would offer sufficient distractions to cover any awkwardness arising from their first meeting together.

"Plus Madonna will be there." He dangled the bait. "Sarah Jessica Parker will be there too. Your inner fangirl won't let you miss this."

"My inner fangirl is a cynic," Reese corrected. "But that's just another reason to come."

So here she is now, the glitz of a hotel already putting her in a better mood as she trails Ames up an escalator that deposits her at the entrance to the red carpet. There, a GLAAD volunteer checks a clipboard and directs Ames and Reese toward an area where noncelebrities mill around drinking Ketel One martinis. Reese tries not to take her banishment from the red carpet as an insult. She wears a red satin Marchesa gown that she found marked down to sixty dollars at Beacon's Closet, but which does wonders for her curves. Some tiny part of Reese had indulged in a fantasy that the organizers or media consultants, or someone important, would take one look at her in the Marchesa gown, gasp, and usher her onto the red carpet, whereupon photographers would clamor all over her.

In the noncelebrity area, Reese passes a photo booth in front of a sad little square of red carpet, so that civilians could activate a machine in order to make it look like a photographer had taken a red-carpet photo of them. Reese considers pressing the button for herself and posting the results to her social media, but rules it out: To stage an elaborate selfie on a fake red carpet would be demeaning.

"Katrina says she's by the shampoo table," Ames reads to Reese from a text, then glances up from his phone, perplexed. "Shampoo table? What's a shampoo table?"

"There!" Reese points. A celebrity designer whose features have been pleasingly redrawn with fillers stands before a booth decorated with images of his own face. Two assistants are giving away shampoo to an eager crowd of the noncelebrities. Reese is suddenly covetous, because the bottles look full-sized, not sample-sized. Wait, maybe even family-sized!

"Katrina, this is Reese. Reese, this is Katrina," Ames says to a woman who has peeled away from the crowd.

"Hi," says Katrina, and by way of greeting lifts her chin to indicate the celebrity designer's booth. "Did you get the free shampoo?"

"No! Not yet!" Reese says, and despite herself, she is disarmed.

Katrina hands her a sagging tote bag, heavy with the shampoo, and an additional selection of what looks to be an assortment of lip balms and skin moisturizers. "I grabbed an extra one for you."

Reese peers into the tote bag, then holds it at her side, pleased. "It's confirmed," Reese says to Ames. "You have good taste in women."

Katrina leads them through the crowd. A brief thrill passes over Reese as she makes meaningful eye contact with a hot middle-aged butch in a white suit who looks like Robin Wright but is not Robin Wright, because this woman can lean against a wall more louchely than Robin Wright could ever dream of doing. But no, Reese! Do not be distracted! Reese breaks off eye contact regretfully and moves on, dutifully following Katrina and Ames who, Reese now notices, hold hands. Reese decides to postpone any feelings about this state of hand affairs for the moment. In the back of one of the conference rooms, beside a coffee bar, Katrina finds an empty couch. As the three settle in, Reese finds herself reluctant to be the first to talk.

"Do you want one of those fancy martinis?" Ames asks Reese, and Reese nods. Off to one side of the room stands a Ketel One bar, where bartenders fill glasses with premixed craft cocktails. Ames stands and lets go of Katrina's hand. "What about you? Can I get you something besides a martini?"

Indirect as it is, this is the first acknowledgment of Katrina's pregnancy, and Reese's attention narrows.

"Do you think they have any bitters?" Katrina asks in reply.

"I can see. I bet they have at least Angostura or Peychaud's."

"Some Angostura in sparkling water, can you ask for that?"

"Yes, I can do that."

It was as though they had decided to speak like the couple in that famous Hemingway story, both much too stoic to ever refer directly to anything but their drinks as their unborn child slowly sucks the air from a room.

But Reese is not a stoic and terse character in a Hemingway story. She is not one to say that hills look like white elephants when what she wants to ask, now that Ames has walked off and she has Katrina alone, is: *So! What the fuck are we doing here? How about this baby?*

Yet the baby isn't her subject to address. Not yet anyway. So instead, she compliments Katrina on her soft pink nails, and launches into a round of small talk. At some point, one of the nearby corporate men says the word "transgender." Then the other guy says the word "trans." It is impossible for Reese to tell exactly what they are talking about. But she has stopped talking midsentence to listen, and Katrina looks at her questioningly.

"Oh, sorry," Reese says, coming to. "I heard those guys say the word 'trans.' I'm, like, really curious about how trans stuff gets discussed by guys like that. They say trans like they are tasting the word for the first time, and that they are discovering that actually . . . you know what? It tastes okay!"

Katrina laughs and listens. When Ames returns with the drinks, Katrina and Reese are sitting silently, eavesdropping on the men in hopes of a trans reprise. At Ames's reappearance Reese sits up straight to receive her martini and napkin, and decides to launch in.

"So anyway, speaking of trans," Reese decides to say to Katrina.

"Does your work send you to lots of queer events like this, or is this your first time being out with one and a half trans women?"

Katrina frowns for a moment, looks around the room, as if trying to spot half a trans woman among the cocktail drinkers. Then a butterfly of laughter flutters out of her. "You mean Ames? Is he the half?"

"It's certainly not me," Reese says.

"Oh my god, Reese," Ames interjects from where he is perched on the couch's edge on the other side of Katrina.

"What?" Reese asks him. "Is it such an unreasonable question? It's what I always ask new people whenever we're about to engage in some intimate talk: like, 'Have you ever met a trans woman, or should we do the 101?' I like to establish a baseline. It's pretty much the only opening question I ever ask cis people, actually: 'What do you need to know to recognize my basic humanity?' "

Ames groans. "Reese, where is your chill?"

Katrina frowns and admits that no, she doesn't know very many trans women. The biggest impact a trans woman ever had in her life was a year or so ago, when a good friend's husband had an affair with a trans woman.

"One husband that you know of!" Reese says brightly. "I bet a lot more husbands that you don't know about have also."

Ames shakes his head. "Reese! Can you not?"

Katrina cuts him off, both hands steadying her drink. "No, wait, I like her approach to this conversation way better than yours!"

"Why? What was his approach?" Reese asks.

Katrina scrunches up her nose like a rabbit, then says, "I would describe it as getting me pregnant, then dumping a huge transsexual revelation on me with almost no time to process."

"Oh yeah," Reese says. "That's a classic. That's like the second most popular way to announce one's current, future, or past transsexuality."

Inwardly, Reese senses the moment coming under her reins. She doesn't want to do a whole getting-to-know-you thing. She wants to talk about the pregnancy. She wants to talk about why the three of them have seated themselves on a couch in the back of a Midtown hotel surrounded by bland carpeting and various attempts at gay branding.

Moreover, Reese knows how to team up with another woman to tease a man. Which is what she supposes Ames is to Katrina. Teasing men is very much in her wheelhouse. She finds the strategy to be an effective method to endear herself with other women, provided that she's careful not to outright flirt.

Ames does not defend himself. He shrugs and adjusts his jacket.

"Is it a classic?" Katrina glances briefly at Ames, but lets her doubtful expression come to rest on Reese. "Nothing about this has felt classic so far. I don't even know what to tell my friends. I haven't told them, actually. I don't know where to begin."

"What do you tell them instead?" Reese asks.

"What can I tell them? That I seduced my employee because he wore cowboy boots to work and looked good in a button-down?"

"I like her," Reese says to Ames.

"That's the second time you've said something like that," Katrina shoots back, before Ames can respond. "What did you expect of me?"

Yes, what did Reese expect? She supposed she expected a woman with whom she'd feel competitive, someone who might arouse Reese's own catty bitchery, who threatened Reese's supremacy in the areas in which Reese measured her own worth. That nameless amalgamation of characteristics that queers melded and tempered into a concept called "femme": creatures so territorial that they clipped their own acrylic claws with barely functional political movements like "femme solidarity" or "femme4femme" relationships so as not to rip each other to shreds. On one hand, Reese found the whole concept of the femme to be reductive and stupid and a little precious. On the other hand, Reese had no doubt that, inadequate as the femme rubric might be, she knew herself to be that thing that it sought to describe, and that thing was very real.

Reese was intimately acquainted with the moment of dismay that comes with first contact with another femme, the sudden contraction of space within a room, as if it could no longer hold both of them, a feeling that she'd seen best dramatized, dorkily enough, in the movie *Highlander.* Although to everybody else, those moments of introduction appeared as a passing and polite coolness, when emotionally it was as if Reese were compelled to shriek *There can only be one!,* unsheathe her blade, and charge screaming into a mystical combat that would end in the beheading of one femme or the other.

Amy had loved a femme for years. So Reese supposed that Ames would still love femmes. So, yes, Reese had expected Katrina would be a femme.

But that wasn't the person sitting with her on this couch. Not that Katrina wasn't feminine. But the woman who now sits across from Reese—wearing a simple red and black color-block dress with clean lines, and minimal makeup, the planes of her face interrupted only by a scatter diagram of freckles and bounded on three sides by shiny brown hair—triggers no sense of competition. In fact, as far as Reese can tell, the Venn diagram of Katrina's personhood overlapped with Reese's own at only a single point of contact: Ames. Which was hardly even a point of contact. Who was Ames? Reese loved Amy.

"Honestly," Reese answers, "I suppose that I expected a rival." It just slips out.

"I don't know whether to be flattered or disappointed," Katrina responds.

"Be flattered," Reese says. "I didn't mean to be insulting. I'm the worst. When I saw you holding hands with Ames, I had a moment. Normally a woman who casually claims my ex in front of me like that would find herself doused with holy water."

Reese smiles at her, hoping the inadvertent insult has passed. Katrina takes a sip of her bitter water and asks Reese mildly, "Are you friends with many women, Reese?" The question would have had more bite, maybe even bite that Reese deserved, but Katrina suddenly adds, "*cis* women, I mean." She says the word "cis" like she'd just learned it. Probably she had. Well, now they've both committed faux pas. So much the better.

At that moment, the crowd around them begins to buzz and move.

"Is the dinner starting?" Katrina asks.

A man passing by responds as he walks, "Sarah Jessica Parker just arrived. She's not going to the Met Gala this year, so she's going *big* with her fashion here."

"Thank you," says Ames to this unexpected docent, now hurrying away; then to Reese, "You two go gawk, I'll stay here and save our seats."

At the center of a scrum of people, Sarah Jessica Parker smiles tightly in a massive confection of silk. Two women beside Reese discuss whether it's the same gown they had seen in an Elie Saab show. Katrina looks bored and then suddenly Reese is very bored too. She remembers a certain definition of glamour: the happiness of being envied while not envying back your enviers. To her surprise, Reese has no envy to instantiate and fuel the glamour engine. She just sees a tired woman tolerating encasement in what appears to be a very expensive sissy dress.

Back at the couch, Ames asks how it was and Katrina replies, "Sarah Jessica Parker is all right, but I was hoping she'd arrive with her husband. I always had a thing for Ferris Bueller, but I didn't see him. Or are they divorced now?"

"God I hope so," Reese says.

"You hope they're divorced? Why?" Katrina asks.

"I love divorced cis women," Reese says. "Divorced cis women are my favorite people on earth. Have you ever been divorced?"

"You must know I have been," Katrina says.

"Yes, Ames told me. But I was trying not to sell him out for once."

Ames speaks up. "It's fine. I told Katrina all your secrets too."

Reese waves a dismissive hand. Her gel nails flash in the light. "As if you knew my secrets." Reese turns back to Katrina. "The only people who have anything worthwhile to say about gender are divorced cis women who have given up on heterosexuality but are still attracted to men."

Katrina leans in. "Really?" She's interested, Reese can tell. She's asked the question with a plain curiosity.

"Yes." Reese nods. "I mean, they go through everything I go through as a trans woman. Divorce is a transition story. Of course, not all divorced women go through it. I'm talking about the ones who felt their divorce as a fall, or as a total reframing of their lives. The ones who have seen how the narratives given to them since girlhood have failed them, and who know there is nothing to replace it all. But who still have to move forward without investing in new illusions or turning bitter—all with no plan to guide them. That's as close to a trans woman as you can get. Divorced women are the only people who know anything like what I know. And, since I don't really have trans elders, divorced women are the only ones I think have anything to teach me, or who I care to teach in return."

Speaking of divorced women, GLAAD chose Madonna to deliver a speech at the dinner, a very good talk in which she quoted James Baldwin, and then in the same breath, her own lyrics from a forthcoming album. That was how a true professional self-mythologized. Madonna's speech was followed by an auction, with a real auction barker. Men—only men—bid on items like a Delta flight with a sleeping cabin to an eco-lodge safari in Botswana, which went for somewhere in the neighborhood of twice Reese's annual earnings. Reese looked around the room for other trans women. She saw a cadre of them at a table nearby, actresses on a cable show, a couple of whom Reese knew glancingly, well enough to know that the year before, they were only surviving selling weed or turning the occasional trick. They were stone-faced throughout the auction. None of the money would go to trans people. GLAAD, like most of the big gay orgs, focused on messaging and lobbying; the money was not *for* trans people, it was to facilitate proper discussion *about* such topics as trans people.

Accordingly, the ceremony and speeches had been heavy with emphasis on how much everyone wants to see trans women allowed into public bathrooms. Reese couldn't give a fuck about public bathrooms. The Supreme Court had only made gay marriage lawful in the very recent past. These cis-gays buying themselves trips to Africa—their big victory had been domestic. They had rearranged possibilities for the American nuclear family and delivered unto themselves the gift of straight institutions: marriage, parenthood. Reese wanted the same for herself—no actually, she wanted *more*. *Who needs your public bathrooms? We're already in your bedrooms, fucking your husbands, and we'll use the master bath, thanks very much.*

As far as Reese was concerned, if you didn't want her in your bedroom, then maybe you ought to figure out how to get her a husband of her own, to be a mother in her own right. Otherwise, she'd do it her own way. Doing it her own way was, after all, why she was there.

After the dinner portion of the night, the crowd sifted back into the conference rooms, now darkened and lit with colored lights for the after-party—an adult version of the transformation a high school gym undergoes for prom. Reese suggested they take free drinks and find somewhere quiet in the giant lobby.

The lobby turns out to be prime real estate for people watching. Katrina, Reese, and Ames commandeer a bench with a strategic view of the comings and goings. A YouTube star with heavily contoured makeup throws a tantrum to the two pretty boys who make up his entourage. For some reason, former Republican-presidential-candidate John McCain's daughter has been invited and is now here, looking as straight as humanly possible while talking to some poor hotel employee. On the bright side, the hot butch in the white suit Reese noticed earlier orders a car, while a younger brunette, stupefied with pleasure at having been selected, hangs on her arm.

Beside Reese, Ames and Katrina gossip about the man and woman from their agency who had also attended the gala. Their talk turns to an incident that occurred last Monday at a company meeting, when Katrina's unit announced a new campaign for a dating site for wealthy men. One of the artists in the campaign had animated the announcement with two stick figures falling in love, but had put photos of Ames's and Katrina's heads on the stick figures. Ames is sure that this proves that everyone at the office is aware of their relationship. Katrina disagrees. That kind of teasing, she says, has always been part of the agency culture.

Although Ames and Katrina talk about their jobs as a matter of course, Katrina has not yet asked Reese what she does, a question for which Reese had prepared. She's annoyed that it has not come. Ames has accused Reese of class resentments before, but now Reese can't stop her defensiveness from welling up: She suspects that Ames has warned Katrina that Reese doesn't have a degree, that money has always been a struggle for her.

"Don't you want the people you work with to know about you two?" Reese asks. She's tired of dancing around the subject. "I mean, at some point with the baby . . ."

Ames grunts and Katrina shifts uncomfortably. Then Katrina takes a breath. "Yes. We may as well talk about it." Reese suddenly understands that Katrina means talk about it *now*, with her, not with the people at work. "I know Ames set this night up as just a get-to-know-each-other, but . . ."

"Right," agrees Reese. "Let's just talk about it. I don't know if this has to be awkward. I've been invited to be a third before, and for me, it always feels best when the agenda is up front."

"This isn't some one-night threesome, Reese," Katrina says.

"It's kind of insulting that you'd make that comparison, given that I'm the one who is supposed to share my pregnancy. That Ames has asked me to basically alter my life for you two."

Reese feels instant regret, the sense of already losing something that hadn't even been hers yet. Ames begins to apologize on Reese's behalf, but Reese speaks over him. "You're right. I'm sorry. It's a huge thing we're talking about. That's why I'm not handling well the anxiety of pretending this is just a casual night."

From where she sits, Reese sees Katrina at an angled profile. It's a strange angle to hold each other's gazes, but they do, and Katrina says simply, "I have reservations, Reese."

Reservations. Reese has been expecting it, but it still hits with an unexpected force. The prelude to a "no." The premature ending to what she'd begun to think could be real, despite all her intuitions. An ache opens up in her stomach. "I understand. It was a crazy idea," Reese says quickly. She needs to cut Katrina off. She can't bear to hear Katrina enumerate the reasons why Reese is unfit to be a mother, why not just this baby, but no baby would ever be hers. She was such an idiot. When would she fucking learn?

Katrina touches her leg then draws back. "Wait," she says softly, "hear me out." Now she rests a hand on Ames's knee to her other side. "Both of you."

"Okay," Ames says, though he has been silent for much of this exchange. For once Reese has a hard time reading his face, a face that has changed its shape, but whose expressions she usually reads instinctively.

"I'm the one who is pregnant," Katrina begins.

And again, the words hurt Reese; just listening is too much. She can't help herself. She blurts out, "Don't you think I would be if I could? Don't you think I wish my body could do that?"

Katrina's face doesn't harden. "I do get that, Reese. If I didn't understand that, do you think I'd have even considered meeting you? I mean, do you know how weird I felt when Ames just asked me to share my baby? Like I was some vessel for him to grow his ex-girlfriend's dreams inside?" She doesn't sound angry, but the words sting. "Do you realize how often I've been that? A vessel for someone else's dreams? Sure, just let the Asian lady carry our baby! You'll be like all the other nice white couples with your adopted Asian baby."

The accusation takes Reese's breath away. The unfairness of it. First of all, let's be honest: Katrina looks white. Second, are they playing Oppression Olympics? Ames begins to say it's not like that, but Katrina still has her hand on his knee and she takes it away roughly, a rebuke. "Let me finish," her voice remains soft. "I'm telling you how I felt. I'm telling you the things that your ideas made me feel. The angry ones and the less angry ones. But, I'm here. I called my mom, and I spent days thinking about it. I held on, even when I wanted to reject the whole suggestion. Because I tried to see things your way, Reese."

Reese blinks away the sting of precipitating tears.

"So try to see things my way in return," Katrina says. "Here is what I know. I know that I'm pregnant, and I know what being pregnant means for me. I'm excited. I told Ames this when I found out. I'm surprised to find I'm ready to take a chance on a family, with him, and I'm still ready. But we're all swept away in what that could mean in the future, and we haven't really thought what it means *right now*. I've been emotionally swept away too—How could I not be? For months I think I'm falling in love with this man, who is also my employee, and that alone is destabilizing. But then he responds to getting me pregnant by revealing he's a former transsexual? Of course I got knocked over."

"It feels weird discussing this in a lobby," Ames says, straightening and gesturing to a darkened hotel bar. "Can we, like, go in there to talk?"

Katrina doesn't move. "Why does it matter where we discuss this? If you can't bear to talk about it now, in a lobby, how are we going to live it together in the open for our whole lives?"

Ames looks at Reese for backup, but she just shrugs. She is impressed at Katrina's steeliness. Yes, she sees that this woman could easily be in charge when required, a boss. It makes Reese feel safer, that the onus to be honest for this strange meeting isn't all on her. In her head she reconsiders Katrina as a potential matriarch.

Ames sighs and slumps back down, waving his hand. "Go on, babe," he tells Katrina.

"Thank you. I've been pregnant before, and I still have no children. Nothing came of my earlier pregnancy. We're making the mistake I made with my ex-husband. He and I got emotionally attached to the idea of a baby. And now the three of us are making plans with the assumption that a body, my body, which has never produced a viable pregnancy, suddenly now will. There's no way any of us should count on it working out."

Reese begins to interrupt but catches herself.

Katrina sighs. "So, let me tell you, Reese, if you think I don't understand how it is to have a body that isn't a home to babies, I do."

Katrina sketches the details of her life during her previous pregnancy—in what Reese gathers is an attempt at clinical brevity and detachment—but Katrina cannot quite manage the distance required for detachment. Reese finds something deeply brave, nakedly vulnerable about saying these words in a Hilton lobby. Reese isn't sure that she could do it.

"When I miscarried," Katrina says quietly enough that both Ames and Reese lean in, "I, like . . . well, I pulled it out of the toilet."

"Oh my god." Ames can't help himself.

"I mean, I barely even know what I held, but even just touching something gave me a physical moment that made it real, to connect my emotions to," Katrina says. "Later on, when the guilt and grief hit, it helped me have closure or whatever. There was a while where I avoided supermarket checkout counters. All those tabloids with celebrities and their baby bumps on the covers."

"What did you do after you held it?" Reese asks.

"I flushed it," Katrina replies.

"Fuck," says Reese. She feels ashamed that this conversation has veered into territory too intimate for a first meeting, almost violating.

Katrina draws herself upright. "I was in the bathroom. I was shocked! There was a lot of blood and stuff. Then I cried."

Katrina puts her hand on her face, covering up some sudden emotion, then gathers herself when Ames squeezes her arm. Tourists pass by with luggage, loud and laughing. For an awful moment, Reese fears that Katrina might have taken that "fuck" as judgment. She can't think of what to say to make it right.

Ames must have felt the same, and in a reversion to the kind of awkwardness of which Amy was capable when Reese first met her, Ames asks, "I heard in Texas they passed a law that you have to give fetal remains a burial?" He pauses. "Or maybe it was just clinics? I can't remember."

"How is that helpful to tell me?" Katrina asks, pulling back from Ames, her voice going high. "I know that I failed the mother test. Everything about being a mother feels like a secret test, and I always come out unfit. What kind of burial do you suggest? Come on! They don't give you a guide for this shit! I can't imagine how bad it is when you have the actual baby to fuck up."

Reese again reddens with shame that Katrina has felt a need to justify anything, especially this thing that can never be Reese's own experience.

"I'm sorry," Ames says. "That was a thoughtless thing to blurt out. I was upset and not thinking."

"Well, it's upsetting!" Katrina says. "This is all upsetting! This woman I know described her miscarriage as a 'biological loneliness' and I admired her eloquence, but I also wondered if I was a remorseless psycho because I didn't feel the same biological loneliness—whatever that is."

"I'm sorry too." Reese leans forward. "I blurted out that question. But I feel the same. Like, if you feel unmotherly— I'm a tranny who just asked about flushing babies."

Katrina snorts. "That's what I mean! It's not about who you are! As far as I can tell, at least from the outside, motherhood is just some vague test designed to ensure that everyone feels inadequate."

"I mean, you are pregnant now, though. You're doing okay," Reese says.

"That's not motherhood."

"No, you're right. Further than I ever got, though."

None of them say anything. Reese knows motherhood insecurity well, although it's strange to hear a cis woman admit to suffering from it. A group of women from the gala swan by in mermaid gowns. "So here we are," Reese says finally. "Three failed mom-wannabes."

Katrina straightens, startled at the descriptor. "Can I ask you something directly, Reese?" Despite the claim to directness, Katrina focuses on her skirt, picking off a piece of lint. She doesn't want to look straight at Reese. "Why do you want to be a mom?"

Unbidden, the memory of the skating rink that Reese attended in her own childhood rises to the fore of Reese's thoughts. Although Reese told everyone in New York that she had grown up in Madison, Wisconsin, she had actually grown up in a little ranch house in Middleton. All the big Midwestern college towns seem to have one downscale twin, a suburb where the big-box stores, neon-and-concrete strip malls, and drive-thru chains can accumulate without threatening the Arcadian character of the college town itself. Like any good beta, Middleton took pains never to threaten her prettier, more famous sister—its city's motto was "The Good Neighbor City" and its chief attraction was the National Mustard Museum.

In the second grade, the family next door introduced Reese to figure skating. Some night, Reese doesn't remember why or how, she ended up in their neighbor Virginia's care while her own mother worked late at the Sub-Zero appliance factory offices. Virginia took Reese along with her daughter, Deb, to one of Deb's figure-skating lessons at the rink in Madison.

Reese was the only boy on the ice. She slipped around in her sweatpants and rented skates, arms flailing, a novel curiosity to the giggling girls in their sequined skating dresses. Her tiny heart fluctuated between elation, envy, and the thrill of losing herself in the same activity as all the other girls. On the car ride home, Virginia bought them Happy Meals—the boy Happy Meal that came with a He-Man cup for Reese, and Deb got the girl one, a pastel unicorn cup. Reese brainstormed all the ways she could ask her mother to go back to the skating rink, and in her young weary way, concluded that all of them would end with her mother's exasperated no.

That's not what happened. Over the next few weeks, her mother continued working late, sending her next door, and the lessons continued. For her birthday, Reese asked for a pair of skates, and got them. They were black, not white as they should have been, but her mother darkened when Reese pointed this out, so she hastened to correct herself: No, no, black is great, really, she loved black skates, she was just thinking about her new skating friends, the girls, and how they would want her to match them, that's all.

She skated for the next four years, largely chaperoned by Virginia. She was the only boy, looked after with a special kind of concern by the ice-skating version of soccer moms, who tended toward an entirely feminine, fussy sort of authority that Reese nestled into with satisfied sighs. The only moments of true pain came during the shows, when the skating rink raised money by having the kids put on a performance of *The Nutcracker* (at Christmas) or whatever Disney movie could be adapted (in the spring). Reese's costumes, sewn by the skating mothers, nearly matched those of the girls around her. It was only when she unfolded them that her heart sank: Where the leotard should have ended in a cute little frilled skirt, it instead transitioned awkwardly into a pair of black satin trousers.

After some time, Virginia learned to recognize these moments for Reese, and to help her steer clear of them. Reese remembered the ache of never wanting to get out of Virginia's car to go home, the joyful times when it was her turn to ride in the passenger seat as

Virginia shuttled her and a handful of other girls back and forth from local competitions. The way that Virginia included her with the other girls, complimented her on her grace, her form, the same as she did the others, so that eventually her daughter accepted Reese as one of them, and soon all of her friends did as well. The first time that Virginia just "forgot" and ordered five girl Happy Meals, instead of four girl Happy Meals and one boy Happy Meal.

Reese swivels on the bench to face both Ames and Katrina, nearly trembling, a runner taking her mark. "I can tell you exactly why I want to be a mom," Reese says. "So that when I have and love a child, no one ever asks me that question again."

"What question?" Katrina asks. "Why do you want to be a mom?"

"Yeah."

"How would being a mom make no one ask you that?"

"Because that's not the question that cis women have to answer. The moms I knew when I was little didn't have to prove that it was okay to want a child. Sure, a lot of women I know wonder if they *do* want a child, but not *why*. It's assumed why. The question cis women get asked is: Why *don't* you want kids? And then they have to justify that. If I had been born cis, I would never even have had to answer these questions. I wouldn't have had to prove that I deserve my models of womanhood. But I'm not cis. I'm trans. And so until the day that I am a mother, I'm constantly going to have to prove that I deserve to be one. That it's not unnatural or twisted that I want a child's love. Why do I want to be a mother? After all those beautiful women I grew up with, the ones who chaperoned my classes on field trips, or made me lunch when I was at their house, or sewed costumes for all the little girls that I ice skated with—and you too, Katrina, for that matter—have to explain their feelings about motherhood, then, I'll explain mine. And do you know what I'll say?"

"No, what?"

"Ditto."

Katrina listens, her face blank, braced as if facing into a wind. "I don't know, Reese. It doesn't sound like you're talking about all women, it just sounds like a certain kind of woman. Like, women now, here in this country—white women," she says when Reese finishes. "When my grandma arrived here from China, she wasn't encouraged to have kids. The opposite. She had to justify the basic desire to reproduce."

"Fine, cis white women," Reese concedes.

"But you say that like I'm being annoying," Katrina says, catching some aural cue from Reese. "I don't think I am. If you want to talk about this in terms of reproductive rights, it might be that you and I come from pretty different places. All my white girlfriends just automatically assume that reproductive rights are about the right to *not* have children, as if the right and naturalness of motherhood is presumptive. But for lots of other women in this country, the opposite is true. Think about black women, poor women, immigrant women. Think about forced sterilization, about the term 'welfare queens,' or 'anchor babies.' All of that happened to enforce the idea that not all motherhoods are legitimate. Or more to the point, take my own family: I'm *mixed*. My own mother was made to feel, by her own family and her husband's family and our neighbors in Vermont, that her mothering of me wasn't legitimate."

Reese had not expected to be questioned on her right to victimhood as a trans woman. Apparently, no one had informed Katrina that among queers, trans women were still a subaltern du jour. Perhaps Reese had grown accustomed to leaning on that a little too heavily.

"I'm not criticizing your feelings, Reese," Katrina says. "I'm telling you that I feel the same. Because everyone gets criticized about how they should or shouldn't be mothering. You don't have to tell me, because I already know about how women are made to feel that they don't deserve to be mothers—Chinese, trans, whoever. It's part of why this pregnancy matters to me. Why sharing a child, or giving up a child, isn't really so simple. So when I say I have reservations about this, it's not just logistics; my own identity is part of it, just like yours is for you. You think it's hard to be a mother because you're trans. I think it's hard to be a mother as the mixed descendant of Chinese and Jewish immigrants. We have difficulty with motherhood in common. But my question wasn't why this is hard. My question is: Tell me why you, specifically, you, Reese, want to have a baby. Ames has made a case to me. Now I'm asking you to make a case to me."

The challenge has singed Reese. There are so many reasons, but most of them are so simple, so embodied, that they feel inadequate to the question: She likes to hold children. To smell a baby's hair. To soothe a crying infant and feel his little frame let go of rigid fear to settle in her arms, the weight go slack and calm so that for a moment she both gives and receives a rare peace. To rock a baby and communicate with your body: *You're safe.* When she worked at the daycare she liked the thoughtless way a child would reach to take her hand. She liked watching kids puzzle out something new, their wonder, their awe and excitement, which was, when she let it be, contagious. She liked their sudden acts of altruism. She recalled this one kid at the daycare, maybe four years old, who built a tower out of blocks then tugged on her sleeve with the offer, "Do you want to kick it down?" He understood that the knockdown was the best part of building and he wanted to give it to her. Who else could give you something so pure but a child?

In the lobby, the group of trans women from the cable show whom Reese had noticed earlier swirl by in their gowns, and one of them gives Reese a nod. She might have stopped to chat, but something about Reese's face, or the intensity on the faces of these two people who sat with Reese stopped her.

Reese waits for her to pass, and when she responds to Katrina the words flow easily, borne by a current of anger, with none of her usual arch reticence. "I want to be a mom for the usual reasons. Most people have a hard time putting them into words. The kind of thing that people usually call a biological clock, which isn't a term that works for me, but still describes something I feel in my body. Yes, I agree with you. The women you're talking about, the marginalized women—they're told that they shouldn't *have* children, not that they shouldn't *want* children. The wanting of children seems to be an accepted universal fact for women everywhere. Not to play the trans exception card, but I'm sorry, it's not the same for transsexuals. It's not considered natural when I say that my biological clock is ticking, because I'm not granted a biological clock in the first place. I ache when I see other moms with kids. I'm so jealous. It's a jealousy of my body, like hunger. I want children near me. I want that same validation that other moms have. That feeling of womanhood placed in a family. That validation is fine for cis women, but it gets treated as perverted for me. Like, the only reason 'a man in a dress' would want to be near kids is not a good one. Let's come out and admit it: Everyone acts like moms are real women and real women become moms. Women who never have kids get treated like silly whores, obsessed with themselves, lacking some basic capacity to love."

Ames, silent until now, allowing the discussion to play out, interjects, "No one thinks that women without children are silly whores."

"What?" Reese is incredulous. "Have you ever seen any movie? Have you ever watched TV? Of course they do. But fine, I'll make that an *I* statement: I think that without a child, I'll forever be a silly whore. And I do have a capacity to love a child. And with no child to love, every day ends with a hunger unsated. Does that work better for you, Ames?"

"So much for queer liberation," Ames says, but he's bobbing his hands palms down in a gesture for her to calm down.

"Would it make you more comfortable if I said there's nothing wrong with being a silly little whore—it's just not for me anymore? Or can I answer her question now? Yes?"

He rolls his eyes. "Please continue, Reese."

"Thank you." She pointedly turns to speak to Katrina rather than Ames, and without quite intending, her body language attains a pose of near supplication, even as her tone stays hot. "I have a gift for mothering. All I do is mother people. I want to be a mom so bad that I make everyone my children. Other trans girls. Men too, actually. Sometimes when I think back on Amy—*Ames*—I think she fell in love with me because I mothered her as much as I dated her." Ames snorts, but Reese ignores it. "As a child, I needed so badly. When someone could meet that need, it was beautiful. It was the proper place for mothering. Now I need that proper place for myself. My sense of hope, my sense of a future, they are both reliant on having a child. I want to see what I cherish live on. Does that make it clear why I want to be a mom? Is that acceptable?"

Katrina pauses, then nods. It is a noncommittal nod, but a nod nonetheless.

Ames slumps back and lets out a long breath, audible even in the din of the lobby. "Credit to GLAAD," he says. "Tonight they have achieved their mission of facilitating yet another hard-hitting discussion on LGBTQ rights."

A short time later, Ames walks Reese to the corner. Reese has her jacket slung over her purse, but at the stoplight, she unfolds it and slips her arms into its sleeves. Katrina waits inside. "Maybe that didn't go super well," Reese says quietly. "Kind of stupid to think it would."

Ames shakes his head. "Might've gone better than you think." He reaches out and straightens the collar of Reese's jacket with absent familiarity. "I know Katrina pretty well. When she's disinterested or insulted, she avoids engaging. She'll never bother to challenge someone she doesn't care about. She's polite about it, but you can tell. That's not how she was tonight. She might not have said everything that you, or even I, wanted to hear, but she's seriously considering it. She must see something in you. She was really mad at me, but she didn't dismiss this idea."

"Yeah," Reese agrees. "Although, maybe you have a talent for getting women to give you second chances." The light changes and she slips past him, but he grabs her arm, and gives it a light squeeze to say goodbye. Across the street, it occurs to her that they did not kiss goodbye, not even a peck. This bothers her. She had years of habitual goodbye kisses with Amy. To leave without one makes her feel like she left something behind.

Coming up from the train in Greenpoint, she surfaces to a light mist and gets a text from her cowboy, who wants to come over. Normally, this would be an easy yes. But this time she hesitates, considers ignoring him, standing up for herself. She is proud that this defiance lasts until she is at her place, at which point her loneliness gets the better of her, and she recalls that no one has yet complimented her in her Marchesa dress.

Nonetheless, after her cowboy leaves, she finds that she does not resent him for leaving. Normally every one of his departures registers as a little failure on her part. But this time, as he shuts the door behind him, she experiences a moment of relief, luxuriating in the space to spread out in the cool of her own bed without his hot, hairy-legged, post-coitally-perspiring body beside hers. Most surprising of all, she discovers, as she drifts off to sleep, that her cowboy has faded from her mind almost entirely. Instead she is imagining life with Amy again. Weirder still, at the edge of the fantasy hovers Katrina.

CHAPTER SIX

Three years before conception

ONE OF REESE'S friends, a modestly successful designer, hooked her up with part-time work at a public relations firm that represented fashion brands. Reese quit the desultory waitressing to which she'd given the better part of a decade, though she kept a shift or two at the gym daycare, as it continued to put her in contact with kids and wealthy Manhattan mothers willing to pay outlandishly for a good babysitter. On Valentine's Day, for instance, Reese could ask as much from mothers desperate for romance as her friends who worked as escorts could request from their regulars.

Her new employment involved passing fashion samples to notable people in the hope that they would later be caught wearing the samples on their social media. Reese met the intended wearers only occasionally—usually, she'd just sit in the stockrooms of designers, waiting to pull product with a publicist, stylist, or entourage member.

Werner Herzog was the first famous person interested in the clothing she handed out who actually showed up in person. How he ended up on her agency's PR list remained a mystery; everyone's favorite Bavarian director is no one's favorite fashion icon. Herzog met Reese on the street outside the Bowery-based offices of the menswear brand Barking Irons. He wore an outfit of resolute anti-fashion: khakis, a shapeless button-up, and a navy blazer cut much too long—years out of style. He shook Reese's hand, a greeting that she disliked. An overly firm handshake could clock her, so she overcompensated with a floppy, limp wrist that undercut any semblance of authority. She felt much more at home with a kiss on the cheek. Nothing better for a Wisconsin girl than European manners. She wondered what he thought of trans women. Or any women for that matter. Were there women in his movies? She couldn't remember many. Perhaps some women died in a jungle over the course of one movie or another.

In the Barking Irons office, a loft space stylishly decorated in Gilded Age antiques, Herzog picked through t-shirts emblazoned with images of New York City lore, while the brand's founders, two local brothers, delivered a spiel on themselves and their branding, as they did whenever an actual celebrity bothered to show up.

Herzog nodded sagely. He told them that to succeed in anything, be it fashion or documentary film, one must scrap for everything—and that was why, despite his success, he made it a practice to accept free clothing. In the way that poor artists invited to upper-class salons a century ago were expected to be witty and entertaining, Herzog offered his benefactors at Barking Irons a truly Herzogian experience. In lieu of small talk, he announced that these new clothes were especially welcome as that very day he had experienced a horror: The hotel in which he preferred to stay while in New York City had been overrun by an infestation of bedbugs. He pronounced the word "infestation" with five syllables, overstressing the vowels in a manner that struck Reese as clearly habitual yet bordering on self-caricature. Werner Herzog played by Werner Herzog. With a demented urgency, he advised Reese and the two brothers that should they ever encounter such bloodthirsty vermin, they must immediately strip off their clothing, and place that clothing in a freezer turned down to "the temperature of zero for no less than two days, so that in the darkness and cold, all life will slowly drain from the parasites." Having thus paid for his shirts in trade, he gathered them in a paper bag, bid his dumbstruck audience thank you and goodbye, and descended in the elevator back out into the city street. For the first time in her life, Reese had a professional story that she couldn't wait to tell at parties.

Prior to this PR stint, Reese dreaded the moment at every social event—especially the ones with Amy's sensible and fully employed friends—when her turn came to say what she did for a living. *Waitress*, she'd say, and she'd watch the calculations whir behind the eyes of whomever she was speaking to, see them tally up a waitress's salary, what it cost to live in a two-bedroom by Prospect Park, and what Amy likely made; then, with the equation completed, they'd slot Reese into a position dependent on Amy's largesse. The girlfriend-mooch-child. Even if her interlocutor treated her politely afterward, engagingly even, Reese nonetheless begrudged the moment that pulled back the curtain to reveal her reliance on Amy.

With a job in PR, however, Reese began to anticipate the what-do-you-do interrogation with confidence—it didn't matter that she only worked part-time or that her role occupied a rung in the firm's hierarchy just above glorified intern or that she actually made less money than she had waitressing—proximity to fashion and the occasional celebrity anecdote put her on equal footing with Amy. Stories like Reese's were why people came to New York. Reese entertained the bizarre sense of having hoodwinked people into seeing her as a full-fledged adult, maybe even a successful one. It wasn't the same as seeing herself that way, but she enjoyed borrowing their eyes. After all, isn't that the Gatsby glory of the New York dream: telling the grandest story about yourself that you could hope to have others believe in the distant hope that you'll believe it yourself?

The idea of herself as an adult made other long-delayed considerations possible. She and Amy had been together nearly five years. Surely that counted as enough time for them to be a family now. The future beckoned. Or rather, maybe the future had arrived to the present.

In her twenties, she watched straight people progress in their careers or get married or discuss employer-matched 401(k)s. She had once confided to her fashion designer friend, a young gay man, of her sinking feeling that she had fallen behind. In response he bought her a book on the concept of queer temporality. The book was deadly boring.

In lieu of the book, Reese read as many blog posts as she could find on the subject. Her friend was right: The notion of queer temporality was comforting. Of course, she told herself, the flow of time and the epochs that add up to a queer life won't correspond to the timeline or even sequence of straight lives, so it is meaningless to compare her own queer lifeline to a heterosexual's lifeline as though they were horses on the same racetrack, released from the gates at the same moment. And that was just for your run-of-the-mill queer. Now imagine that you were trans! You would have to go through at least two puberties! By age thirty, the financial ads said, you should have saved two years' income for retirement. But at age thirty, the trans girls Reese knew held most of their investment portfolios in the form of old MAC lipstick shades they'd worn once; they spent workdays sending each other animated gifs and occasionally got trolled online by actual thirteen-year-olds.

Reese's own temporal anxiety congealed in the form of a dining room table. At one of her first jobs in New York, an attractive woman name Angela had taken an interest in Reese. Angela had been waitressing and bartending for most of her twenties, scraping by while trying to make it in photography. Reese liked Angela's photos: textured black-and-whites taken from jarring vantages. Over the course of the year that Reese worked with her, Angela began to date an upwardly mobile mechanical engineer named Chuck, who had cofounded a firm that secured a lucrative contract to weatherproof the city's new electronic parking meters, which through a previous design flaw, shorted out in the wet weather. By the end of the year Angela had moved into Chuck's brick townhouse in Jersey City. Soon after, she invited Reese to dinner.

Reese arrived to an upsettingly well-appointed interior. Greeting Angela in the living room—softly illuminated by recessed lights—she considered pretending that she hadn't actually brought wine, so as to avoid them seeing the twelve-dollar bodega brand. Immediately, Chuck apologized for the mess—of which Reese saw none but a box and some tools by a closed door. They had bought new faucets for the downstairs bathroom, Chuck said, and he had been overconfident that he could install them before Reese arrived.

"What happened to the old faucet?" Reese asked.

"It was hideous," Angela interjected.

Reese nodded stupidly. She guessed that Angela was her first-ever friend to replace a faucet that wasn't broken. "I'm sure the new ones are gorgeous."

Chuck sorted through the pile of tools, unsheathed a faucet from plastic wrap, and held it up for Reese to admire. It looked to Reese like any other faucet. Perhaps a bit more square.

"It's Italian," Chuck informed her.

"I can tell," Reese replied, unsure if she had spoken ironically or fawningly.

The impromptu tour continued. Angela showing off the house, the furniture, trailing her fingertips lovingly over the decor as she confessed excitedly to Reese the price of various odds and ends. At the dining room set, Angela announced, "This is my favorite. I always knew I wanted a table like this because my grandmother had one. I didn't see any in stores, so Chuck ordered this one custom as his own housewarming gift to me. We ordered it two months ago and it finally arrived." Her fingers stroked the wood tenderly and Reese followed suit. The wood had been sanded to a velvet touch, barely recognizable by feel as wood. "It's butcher block—it will last a century if we sand and oil it. You don't even want to know what it costs." The scrunchie in Angela's hair matched her napkin rings. Reese knew it was intentional without asking.

It was, indeed, a very beautiful and solid table. Reese's most valuable possession was her laptop. "When you are in your thirties," Angela told her, not unkindly, "you'll want one too. You'll want a table that will last your whole life." The table fixed itself with totemic power into Reese's brain. The butcher-block craftsmanship became for Reese an absurd-but-serious mental marker of a female bourgeois heterosexual temporality forever beyond her envious grasp: When a woman reaches a certain point in her thirties, she looks around and finds a good dining set with which to settle down.

One afternoon, after having lunch with Amy, Reese took the subway over to the Paul Smith store, where her boss had arranged for Mark-Paul Gosselaar to select knitwear samples. But Gosselaar was running late. She waited on a plastic chair toward the back of the store, surrounded by muted sweaters and the smell of new wool. She had her headphones on, so she didn't notice the man speaking to her until he loomed over her. Tall. A green field jacket. Floppy brown hair over a splash of grin. She emitted a little yip at the same time that her adrenal gland released.

Stanley.

He had lost weight, become lean. With his cheekbones showing beneath those pale eyes, his face had taken on a wolfish look. He ran his fingers down a sweater hanging near her face. She pulled off her headphones to hear him say "interesting spot for contemplation you've chosen."

"I'm working," she said quickly, getting her bearings.

"You work here now?"

"No, for a PR company that works with the store."

He widened his eyes. "Impressive."

She thought about deflecting the compliment, but no—let him think she was impressive.

"Is it in the fashion field?"

"Usually."

"Great! Help me pick out something here."

"I can't, I'm working! I'm waiting for Mark-Paul Gosselaar." She dropped the name intentionally, meaning it as a brag, but Stanley just asked who that was.

"Zack Morris! From *Saved by the Bell*!"

He laughed. "That's a deep cut."

"The expression 'deep cut' is a deep cut!"

"What?"

"The expression. It refers to vinyl records, you know. Not that I'm old enough to have ever owned one."

He didn't take the bait. "Whatever, you're the one telling me about vinyl."

Watching Stanley speak was like watching a movie she'd seen dozens of times—the familiarity of his expressions and gestures. She knew when Stanley would tilt his head, when he'd make that mock bashful expression and look sneakily to one side.

Just then, the store manager walked back with Mark-Paul Gosselaar in tow. Here was distant TV and the distant past come to life at the same moment. Reese stood suddenly. "Oh, Stanley, I have to work now."

But Stanley stuck out his hand to Gosselaar, who shook it, and asked Stanley, "You're Reese?"

Stanley pointed at Reese. "No, sorry, that's Reese. I'm just shopping."

Gosselaar took this in stride. He smiled, those good-natured nineties megawatts clouded only slightly by the beard and crow's feet that now surrounded them. Clearly the man had grown accustomed to strangers shaking his hand on little pretext.

"Nice seeing you," Reese said to Stanley, because the manager had pulled out a set of keys to brusquely unlock a door, and was by then holding it open for Gosselaar.

"Yeah," said Stanley.

But when Reese emerged from the storeroom twenty minutes later, she found Stanley still browsing sweaters. "I found the brevity of that encounter entirely unsatisfying," he said. "Now can you show me which sweaters Zack Morris took? I'm going to get those."

"I have to go."

He stood in her path. "Please?"

And this word, a simple "please," had occurred so infrequently in the vocabulary that he'd once used with her that she had to wonder whether he'd changed and how much. And this, in turn, made her curious, or at least curious enough to acquiesce.

.   .   .

That evening, Reese swept into Stanley's apartment, holding shopping bags of clothing, mostly his, but he'd bought some for her from
the various stores to which she'd taken him. He had sublet a loft in
Williamsburg, owned by a chef, who was spending three months
away on a culinary tour. That meant that Stanley was living among
the chef's tasteful belongings, making it difficult for Reese to suss
out clues as to the state of Stanley's life. A weathered wooden upright piano stood against a wall in the living room, and Reese
plinked a few keys. Along the other wall, shelves held glasses of all
shapes, and above that, a selection of liquor put the average craft
cocktail bar to shame. A collection of bottles of all colors, some
gleaming, others ancient-looking, and half of them with labels she
didn't recognize.

"Are you allowed to drink these?" she asked him.

"I'm allowed to do anything I want. I haven't yet, but I'll replace
the bottles of anything you use," Stanley replied. "Make me something. I haven't had a woman bring me a drink in a while."

An hour later, they were three drinks deep. She'd made a con-
coction of gin, Green Chartreuse, and some ancient floral liquor of
unknown provenance, along with a splash of orange juice from the
fridge. It wouldn't have been on a cocktail menu, but the fancy liquor made it drinkable.

She'd changed into a pair of tight, white high-waisted jeans that
he'd bought her that afternoon, and as she had when they lived together, she lay on the couch with her legs over his lap. He told her
about a trip he'd taken to Bolivia, where he drank ayahuasca, and
about visiting his vegan sister in Australia, where he'd adopted her
vegan diet for three months and lost a lot of weight. Then, sipping
his drink and gazing out the window at a view of the lit-up Williamsburg Bridge a few blocks beyond his balcony, he tentatively
began to speak with regret of the year of wreckage that followed
failure of his firm, his divorce, and of course, Reese's departure to
Amy.

After a long pause, she realized that he expected her to respond in kind. To confess her sins and ask for penance, to admit the errors that she had learned in his absence. Carefully she phrased a statement that she had just wanted to leave him alone, and that's why she hadn't checked in on him. He waved it away magnanimously.

"It's fine," he said. "I had a hard time after the divorce. Maybe I wasn't so kind to you either. Things are better now. This gig I'm starting with my friend's fund could last a year, and even if it doesn't pan out to a long-term thing, it'll still be lucrative."

The kind of money he hinted at was attractive to Reese. Yes, Amy did okay, but not in the realm of Stanley. With Stanley she'd have a dining set for every room.

He gave her a mischievous look and said, "Don't move, I want to do something." He stood up, his body looking taller than ever now that he'd grown lean. She obeyed, lying still on the couch, and he moved behind her, out of her line of sight. She heard the dry rustle of the big paper shopping bag that she'd left by the door. A moment later, he returned, and knelt at the couch beside her. She raised her head questioningly.

"I said don't move," he said.

"Sorry!"

"Keep your eyes on the ceiling."

Gently, he unbuttoned the top button of her new jeans. She wondered if she should stop him, whatever he was going to do.

"I still have a girlfriend," she said. "I'm in a *lesbian* relationship."

"I know." He didn't remove his hands as he spoke. "I looked at your Instagram a few months ago. You're prettier than her."

She ought not to have let a man compare her looks to her girlfriend's. Such an assessment devalued a lesbian relationship, demoted it to some kind of spectacle for his judgment. But also, no one thought she was prettier than Amy these days. Girls Reese grew up with used to call their sisters the smart one or the pretty one or the artistic one. Like a gawky little sister suddenly coming into puberty to hit a golden note, Amy had become the pretty one. Reese wanted to hold to herself for a moment or two the possibility of her own superior beauty.

The pressure of the tight fabric on her hips released with the slow descent of her fly. She found a spot on the ceiling, a faint crack in the paint, and remained still. A tickle shot up from her crotch. A half-nervous, half-aroused jolt that Stanley, more than almost anyone else she'd ever been with, managed to set off within her. His dry rough hands brushed below her navel as he slipped his fingers beneath the elastic top of her panties, and pulled them under her cock. She wasn't hard, the air was cool. For a moment, guilt tugged at her. But then, another, even worse, thought occurred to her. She couldn't remember the last time she had shaved. A mortification came over her, as strong as her guilt.

"Wait," she said. "Can we pause?"

He put his hand on her stomach reassuringly. "I'm not going to do anything that could be called sex," he said.

Of course this is sex. But she didn't say that. Instead she asked for a sip of her drink.

He reached behind him to the coffee table, and handed her the glass. "Just relax," he whispered. She propped herself up, took a sip, and glanced below. On her leg lay a satin ribbon that had tied shut a pajama set he'd bought that afternoon.

"All right," she said. She set her glass on the floor, wilted her shoulders, and let her eyes drift back upward.

"You know," he said, "I jerked off thinking about doing something like this to you a while back."

"I thought you said it wasn't sexual."

"I said it wasn't sex."

Satisfied that she would lie still, he took her in his hand, and slowly began to tie the ribbon around the base of her cock, wrapping it twice, then around her balls and shaft once each. She watched him, on the verge of telling him no. He had the fixated concentration of a surgeon. His eyebrows floated high on his furrowed brow, as if the actions made by his own hands had surprised him. Finally, he took the remaining two feet or so of ribbon, and laid it on her stomach, then pulled up her panties, and buttoned the waist of her jeans, with the zipper still down.

Carefully, he threaded the length of remaining ribbon through the open fly and held it. Then he stood up, looking down at her, at the ribbon hanging obscenely from the front of her jeans. He tugged on it lightly. "I wanted you on a leash like this," he said. He didn't move for a minute or two.

She stared up at him, defiant, turned on, the rest of her thoughts a white noise of guilt. When he moved to sit beside her on the couch, she spoke up. "I should probably go," Reese said. "I'll untie it my-self."

"I want you to wear it home. Wear it under the jeans I bought you."

"No, Stanley. We aren't playing these games again."

"But you want to. I can tell."

She shook her head.

His face went cold. "All right," he said. "I'm not stopping you from leaving." She forgot how he reacted to rejection. The unstated feminine injunction against leaving a man angry led her to reason that she could always untie it in the hallway or elevator.

"Actually," she offered as consolation, "it's kind of a turn on. I won't untie it yet. But I do have to go."

He softened but didn't speak. With the ribbon still dangling out of her fly, she gathered her jacket. At the door, she kissed him good-bye on the cheek. He nodded and said a stiff farewell, and shut the door after her. In the emergency stairwell, she untied the ribbon and put it in her purse, a Coach purse that, she realized, he had bought for her as well, back when they lived together. She'd used it for so long that the association with him had worn off.

She wondered whom she could tell about the incident. Not Amy or any of their couple friends. Only Iris. Iris was always telling sto-ries about her pseudo-johns. But Iris wouldn't keep the incident to herself either.

.   .   .

Amy went to bed early that night, while Reese stayed up watching
TV, her laptop propped up on her legs, idly browsing the Internet,
two screens going at once to drown out her thoughts. Her customary loop of social media and news often included a pit stop on hot
dad Instagram, or one of the trans porn stars she followed on Twitter. She was horny, she realized.

Quietly she padded to the bedroom and, from the doorway,
gazed down at Amy's face in the semi-dark. The light from the hallway fell across Amy's features, contrasting the planes of her cheeks
with the hollows of her jaw. A pang ran through Reese, half jealousy, half lust. Amy was just so fucking pretty.

In Amy's fourth year on hormones, a series of subtle changes
meshed in a way that they hadn't quite previously: The fat moved
up high on her cheeks, padding out her already delicate and sym-
metrical bone structure, the lingering muscles and sinew melted
and thinned, and her body took on a light, graceful affect. A blond
ponytail followed her around, worn high and hanging back respect-
fully, so as not to steal attention from her slimmed neck and collarbones. The plumpness of her lips was just unfair.

Pulling it all together: her nose job. She'd had it the year before.
When the swelling had finally gone down, the nose traced a straight
line down the center of her face. The line settled the planes of her
face elegantly—the keystone that locked the arch of her features
into place. Reese would never have said Amy's face lacked harmony
before. But after the nose job—Amy got so sheepishly gorgeous,
the beauty of someone who came to it late, hadn't internalized it,
and so carried herself a step behind her own elegance.

Health insurance had covered the nose job. Reese had talked
Amy into getting the surgery, even though Reese could have never
afforded any facial work for herself, and her own jealousy drove her
to curt imperatives on the subject. *You will get it. Stop delaying.*
Amy's dithering vigil in front of the mirror, accompanied with her
selection of celebrity nose photos (her favorite: Natalie Portman!

Such definition in those perfect nostrils!), fermented a nauseating envy in Reese's belly. But Reese continued to encourage Amy to go through with it on both principle and self-interest.

Amy's dysphoria centered on the ridge of her nose, which at certain pre-rhinoplasty angles, had given her a hawkish look. Reese didn't recognize the hawkishness as particularly masculine, but Amy could spend hours staring at pictures of herself, focusing on the supposed maleness of her nose while all of the other physical changes of transition melted away in its proximity. In fact, Amy's hatred of her nose was extreme enough to merit her the necessary letters from therapists to have it altered under the international standards for clinical gender dysphoria.

It was very Freudian, Reese thought, that this anxiety centered on the nose—the protuberant nose as phallus, the phallus as Amy's former self. But Reese didn't say this, because in truth, quirks of dysphoria did not follow a Freudian pattern—no, they sequenced themselves according to an alchemist's mixture of beauty standards, consumerism, and liberal doses of self-loathing. It took only a brief search of any transsexual forum to note, for instance, that a large percentage of trans women tend to focus dysphorically on the brow ridge, which thickens with exposure to testosterone during puberty and which avaricious facial feminization surgeons dubiously tout as an instant marker of a masculine face. More to the point, Reese maintained that foreheads drive trans women insane precisely because *there is a surgery to alter it.* The surgery created the dysphoria even as the dysphoria created a need for surgery. To know that surgery is out there, but that you can't yet have it, even as you stare in the mirror and want to die, means that the temptation of want will forever taunt you. Large hands, though? Yes, they suck, but short of lopping off your fingers, no surgeon has yet to devise a procedure to shrink them, so most of the women Reese knew just learned ways to minimize them and get over it, as Reese did herself. The instant that some surgeon invented a hand-shrinking procedure, though, Reese knew she would die rather than have that surgery denied to

her. Therefore, the fact that Amy's dysphoria had taken up resi-
dence in the nose, and that Amy *could* get a nose job paid for by her
agency's insurance, meant that in Reese's opinion, Amy *must* go
through with it, because otherwise, the nose would torment Amy
forever.

In addition to Reese's generalized one-size-fits-all-trans-women
opinions on plastic surgery, she had her own particular self-serving
reason to insist that Amy get a nose job. The day would come that
Reese could enroll on Amy's insurance. With a precedent set by
insurance already having covered one employee's gender-affirming
surgery, the path for a second widened. Reese would need it widened too, because she wanted more than just a nose job; she wanted
her long-awaited vagina and, yes, her brow reconstructed as well.
Just because she saw that the vagaries of capitalism, patriarchy, gender norms, or consumerism contributed to facial dysphoria didn't
mean she had developed immunity to them. In fact, a political consciousness honed on queer sensitivity simply made her feel guilty
about not having managed to change her deeply ingrained beauty
norms. Call her a fraud, a hypocrite, superficial, but politics and
practice parted paths at her *own* body. She would happily cheer on
any other woman who flaunted her orbital ridge in the name of challenging cis-normative beauty standards, but she would have the
first available misogynist dick of a surgeon burr her skull Barbie
smooth. As long as she tortured herself with a traitorously retro-
grade sense of what made a woman beautiful in her heart of hearts,
she would assuage herself with cis-possibility in her face of faces.

Reese sat down on the bed beside a sleeping Amy. She gazed at that
pretty face, with its lips parted slightly, innocent and unaggrieved.
The faint odor of lacquer that Amy seemed to emit, that Reese had
come to find comforting, clung to the sheets by her side. Amy
stirred. It had been a month since they had done anything but give
each other hand jobs. Reese leaned over to kiss Amy's cheek, while
slowly trailing a hand across Amy's hip. Amy opened her eyes.

"Hey," Reese said. "I can't sleep. I want some."

Amy gave a wan smile. "I'm sleepy, I don't think I have the energy. I can get you off, though."

Reese shook her head, and took back her hand.

"I'm sorry," Amy said, but she was already falling back asleep.

Reese wished Amy understood how the offer of an unreciprocated hand job made her feel like a creep, like she was some kind of pawing teenage boy. In the daylight hours, the thought of broaching the subject of their abortive sex caused tendrils of aphasia to constrict around her throat. *Remember Amy and Reese in their first weeks together? When Reese would come home late and Amy would slip down off the bed to crawl panting after her into the shower like some kind of kinky sleepwalker? Where did that go?* Reese wanted a dining set, but also maybe she wanted to have bruising sex all over that dining set.

Quietly Reese stood up and walked back into the living room. Her thoughts kept going back to Stanley as if toward a gyre. How stupid. He offered her nothing—he hadn't changed, his pull was the false newness of the familiar once again returned. Not only had Stanley possessed her before, but she'd had versions of Stanley in many other men. They could occupy her daydreams, at least for a week or two—keeping her anticipating moments of stimulation or excitement, instead of what was lacking in her life. A part of her knew those men were not love objects; they were just the vectors of least resistance into which a desire for the semblance—not to mention comforts—of womanhood sent her careening. Amy, on the other hand, was stability, was actual love. Unfortunately, Amy was sleepy, and had been both literally and figuratively every night for the past few months.

Back in the living room, Reese closed her laptop and switched off the TV, but couldn't quite find the energy to start the wind-down process for bed. Putting aside her anxieties for the night somehow required more work than just letting them spin on in their inertia.

Fuck it. She took her purse into the bathroom. She set it on the toilet to fish out her phone and Stanley's ribbon from where she had tucked it. Clumsily, she re-created the ties that she thought Stanley had done, snapped a picture, and sent it to him, with a message: *I wore the ribbon home, just like you told me to.*

In her office, Amy picked up her phone and typed in her passcode, pausing for a moment on the screen's wallpaper: a photo of Reese and her on the ferry to Fire Island from the year before. She scrolled to her favorites and called Reese. "Can you meet me for lunch? I need to tell you about something."

On the other end of the line, Amy heard Reese inhale sharply, then say cautiously, "What is it? Can't you tell me now?"

Reese's suspicion caught Amy off guard. "It's nothing bad, Reese, it's exciting news."

"Oh, can you tell me now?"

"Why can't you meet me for lunch?"

Reese didn't answer immediately. "I'm in Manhattan."

"For work?"

"Yeah."

"Okay, maybe we can just meet somewhere fast, like Union Square?"

Still Reese hesitated. Amy decided to drop it. By now, Amy told herself, she ought to know that when anxious, Reese wriggled evasively whenever Amy tried to pin her down. "All right, no lunch, but listen. Omar, from work, his sister works for an adoption agency that works with the foster system. They've always done LGBTQ stuff, but Omar said for the first time, a couple of trans guys adopted through them. Not a trans and a cis guy, *two trans guys.*" Amy emphasized the latter part meaningfully.

"But it's always easier for trans guys," Reese said.

Amy sighed Reese's name.

"I don't want to get my hopes up."

The screen saver on Amy's computer was of crystallizing fractals. When on the phone, she had developed the mindless habit of following the formations as they appeared, bouncing her eyes off the slight irregularities in the pattern. "Yeah, okay, I understand. But listen. There's an orientation tonight. Omar is going to tell his sister that we're coming. A new director at the agency has been pushing for trans and genderqueer foster homes, because so many of the kids in the system are queer. If we move soon, Omar's sister could introduce us."

"When's the orientation?"

"At seven at a Unitarian church. That's what I wanted to tell you. I'll take the rest of the day off. We can get ready for it together."

"I can't. I have work."

"What? Take off work! We've been talking about a chance like this for years!"

"My work is just as important as yours, Amy."

Amy sighed. She had accidentally poked right at that sore spot, hadn't she? "I never said it wasn't. I'm suggesting that I take off work too."

"Well, how about we meet at home at like four?"

What was going on? She had figured Reese would be rushing home already. Not this grudging response. Reese knew the situation as well as Amy did: Most of the private adoption agencies, the ones that procured babies from faraway countries, charged an adoption fee in excess of twenty thousand and up to forty thousand dollars. That was just the beginning of the costs. Amy calculated that if she and Reese went to the fanciest agencies and paid the fees, such a show of money might work like in expensive boutiques. As if their transness were merely an eccentric outcropping of a refined taste.

But Amy hadn't saved forty thousand dollars, and might not any time soon, especially not supporting Reese. She'd drain her bank account putting together half that, leaving nothing to raise the baby, much less the miscellaneous expenses and travel that two of her older coworkers had explained to her came with their own efforts to adopt.

This left adoption through the foster care system. And while foster care certainly allowed for LGBTQ parents by law, in practice, the heavy oversight and rights of the natal parents in the foster system meant that fewer queers than straights made it to the adoption phase. And until today, Amy had never heard of a double-trans couple getting anywhere at all.

But okay, whatever. Of course she could meet Reese at four.

At home, Amy had hoped to discuss their finances and time frame for a potential adoption, but instead, Reese arrived home in one of her wild, boisterous moods. Instead of preparing with a serious conversation, they ended up in the bedroom, raiding the closets to cosplay mom outfits for the orientation. Amy put on a jumpsuit and pulled her hair back into a ponytail. "Can I wear my black ankle boots? Or are the heels too much?" She turned her leg to better display the stacked heels to Reese. "Is that, like, not a wholesome mom look? Maybe I should wear sneakers? I want to be a MILF, but a subtle MILF, you know?"

Reese scrutinized the heels from where she sat on the bed. "Wear your white Nike sneakers and leave the ponytail," she told Amy. "Do, like, the sporty soccer mom."

"Yes. Soccer mom, good."

"I'm going to borrow your pearl studs, okay?" Reese asked, although she was already wearing them. Amy's own mother had given her the studs as a mixed gesture, after first years of deep resentment that followed Amy's coming out, during which she and Amy played a game of silent-treatment chicken. While the gift of the studs might have appeared to indicate that Amy's mother had swerved first, Amy interpreted in them a subtext: *If I must accept your womanhood, these are a strong suggestion of the kind of woman you should be.* Consequently, Amy joined her in silent-treatment armistice, but refused to ever wear the studs.

Reese hopped up from the bed and stood close to the mirror that hung on the closet door. "What are we going to tell them if they ask why we're there?"

Reese's nose nearly touched the nose of her reflection as she checked her brows, so Amy couldn't see her face.

"Why would they ask why we're there? It seems pretty self-explanatory."

"But if they press!"

"Reese, we are allowed to find out about adopting a baby. We can even name-drop Omar's sister."

Reese turned away from her reflection. "I know. But I feel naughty. Like we're passing ourselves off as just a normie lez couple. The deceptive transsexual, going like: One baby, please! Nothing to see here!"

"Like, what, they'll have the adoption version of trans panic?"

"Yes!"

"We are actual adults, Reese. We are not going to get in trouble. Now put your shoes on, sweetheart, so we won't be late."

But the same anxiety tugged at Amy. She had tried to picture to what kind of woman the voice at the adoption agency had belonged. She'd had an American accent, but Amy's mind's eye saw a disapproving and officious Englishwoman. *Enough with these transgender shenanigans! We've got real parents who need our time.*

On the way to the train, Reese kept laughing, giddy and nervous, her whole body coiled with impish energy, as if they were on their way to pull off a hilarious prank. Amy kept attempting to calm Reese down, but each attempt agitated Reese more. By the time they got to the Unitarian church, to the little room rented for the orientation, Amy couldn't explain Reese's comportment any other way: Reese was acting weird.

As she sat in the back, examining the other prospective adopters, Amy had to admit that she and Reese did not turn out to be very skilled at mom cosplay. No one but Reese wore heels or pearls.

Most of the couples occupying the rows of plastic folding chairs appeared to be straight couples. Back by the coffee machine, four men, who Amy read as two couples of bears, sat in a row, looking like the bench at a football game. Toward the side of the room a man with long thin hair and a Lemmy chop-stache sat, apparently, alone—a terrifying-looking prospective single father in Amy's opinion. One half of a dyke couple smiled at her and Reese, and Amy grinned back sheepishly. She thought she might start giggling, in a church laughter kind of way. Maybe Reese's nervousness was natural.

A young woman in a polo shirt began the presentation. Mostly it covered things that Amy had already learned researching the foster system online. Most of it she felt qualified to provide: She met the age and income requirements, and she'd even be able to provide a foster child a separate bedroom with a window—apparently a lot of kids shared rooms, and that caused problems. Amy hadn't before heard the figure that ninety-five percent of the babies in the foster system had been exposed to drugs. That seemed awfully high. But perhaps it was so. A man in a checked collared shirt raised his hand. "Do you have any data on the outcomes of the kids after they turn eighteen?"

The young woman giving the presentation, whose name was Consuela, grimaced perceptibly at the question, then recovered. "What kind of data or outcomes do you mean?"

"Like earning figures, college acceptance."

"You want to know how much money the kids grow up to earn?"

Amy inadvertently caught the eye of the man's wife. She gave a barely perceptible shrug: *He's like this.*

"I wouldn't put it like that," the man protested. "I just was wondering about the data."

"No," Consuela said. "We don't keep data on the kids after they turn eighteen." She hesitated. "But when thinking about kids who come from a background of neglect, separation, or even trauma, I would suggest that we engage with a more, um, robust, idea of what makes for success."

The presentation went on, but after that exchange, the enthusiasm in the room wilted. Everyone wanted a cute pristine baby, not some child with insurmountable baggage. Amy knew this to be true about herself, she wanted a kid who might somehow be mystically *hers*, who would imprint on her. It was selfish, she knew, but when is the impulse to create a little person in your image not selfish? Most of the people she knew with kids didn't conceive for the kid, they conceived for themselves, to accord with some notion of family, or purpose, or life stages that the child would bring them. Insert whatever worn-down cliché about life not having meaning until one becomes a parent. But whatever, she could get over that. No kid turns out as the parents had hoped. She sure hadn't.

Toward the end of the presentation slides, another woman entered and joined Consuela at the front of the room.

"I think that's Omar's sister," Amy whispered to Reese.

Reese appeared to ignore her.

When the presentation ended, Amy took Reese's hand. Her skin felt cold and clammy. "Should we go introduce ourselves?" she asked Reese gently.

Reese didn't respond, but her head drooped.

"Reese? Do you want to talk to her now?"

Tears welled in Reese's eyes. "I can't do this right now. You do it without me."

"I'm nervous already! I'm not going alone."

Reese dropped Amy's hand. She gathered up her jacket, draped it over her purse, then headed to the front of the room. Instead of stopping in the line to ask Consuela and Omar's sister a question, she sailed by, right out the door. Amy had to scramble to gather her own stuff, and only as Reese's heels clicked down the church hallway did she catch up. Reese was fully but silently crying.

"God, Reese! What is the matter?"

Reese waved a hand in front of her face. "Not here, okay? Not here, just take me outside."

But they didn't make it outside. Instead, Reese saw a dark little alcove furnished with a heavy bench, and darted into it. She mushed her jacket into her face. After a few minutes she dropped the jacket, and although her mascara had smudged and her eyes shone, the tears had ceased.

"It's intense," Amy said, flailing verbally at whatever had caused this outburst. "The idea of us being a family. Doing it like this. It's intense for me too. It's okay to have doubts."

Reese pulled her hair in front of her face and, as Amy had seen her do before in times of anxiety, began flicking the brushy tip against her lips. Reese inhaled the breath, and spoke on the exhale, her tone abruptly calm and flat. "I don't have doubts. I know what I want. I want to be a mother."

Amy put her hand on Reese's shoulder, but it felt lifeless, carved of wood. "Okay, I have doubts," Amy admitted. Reese stared straight ahead. Amy had the futile sense of trying to console a statue. Amy took back her hand. "You want to be a mother, Reese. Do you not want to be a mother with me?"

She could only see Reese's face in profile. Distantly, a man's whistling echoed down the tiled church corridor.

"I've been fucking Stanley this past week," Reese said.

Amy's thoughts wiped to blank. The total wash of denial. "I'm sorry?"

"All week," Reese repeated. "I've been fucking him."

Amy nodded. Then she stood up, slung her purse over her shoulder, and walked the length of the corridor, turned a corner, then encountered a pair of heavy, ornate doors on the right side of the hall. She pushed through them into the cool of a hushed and darkened sanctuary. There, she found a pew and sat quietly, her mind unquiet, her body in the kind of physical pain that only heartbreak can cause—pain that, like an acid trip, can only be truly apprehended while in the midst of experiencing it—as she waited for Reese to stop looking for her and leave.

CHAPTER SEVEN

Eight weeks after conception

I F YOU ARE a trans girl who knows many other trans girls, you go to church a lot, because church is where they hold the funerals. What no one wants to admit about funerals, because you're supposed to be crushed by the melancholy of being a trans girl among the prematurely dead trans girls, is that funerals for dead trans girls number among the notable social events of a season.

Who knows what people will say at a trans funeral? Will some queer make a political speech instead of a eulogy, so that for weeks afterward other queers will post outraged screeds about it on social media? How many times will a family member deadname or misgender the deceased from the pulpit, unabashed about it in his grief, peering out at this sea of weirdos who showed up unexpectedly to what he considered a family event? Did their son—er, daughter—really have all these friends? Which nice white cis person will remind the assembled mourners—a high percentage of whom are trans women themselves—that everyone must do more to save trans women of color, who are being murdered (*murdered!*), although this particular highly attended funeral is, of course, a suicide, because that's how the white girls die prematurely.

Afterward, the mourners will all file out and then break into little clusters, trading solemn hugs, some shoulders shaking, while others dart suddenly apart due to a just-glimpsed ex, so that the macro effect is like watching sperm wriggle under a microscope. Everyone will dress themselves in some shade of goth—in goth apparel you can look sad while also showing off fishnets and boobs. A few queer microcelebrities (as opposed to microcelebrities who are queer) will

grace the funeral; they will barely know the deceased, and to assuage a slight guilt over this, their names will be subsequently found
on the attendant GoFundMe campaigns and memorial funds.

Reese goes to the funerals. Pretty much every single one. She
attends for three reasons.

The first reason: not to miss out on the aforementioned social
importance of the gathering.

The second reason: Funerals remind Reese not to kill herself. Not
because she so badly wants to live, but because suicide as a trans girl
leads to a mortifying posthumous stripping of all that you cherished
by friends and strangers alike. If you are not there to stop them, the
loudest, brashest, and clumsiest of your semi-acquaintances will scoop
up all that was once you and simmer it down to a single mawkish
narrative, plucking out all that is inconveniently irreducible, and
inserting in its place all that is trite and politically serviceable. The
word "mortifying"—as in existentially embarrassing—has as its
root the Latin for "death," so if Reese seeks to avoid mortification,
she cannot kill herself: She simply must not die.

The third reason: Reese needs to know she is not a psychopath.
Because whenever she hears the news that another trans girl has
died, she is exasperated. *Oh goddammit, not again.* This reaction, of
course, causes her guilt. What's wrong with her? Everyone else
rends garments and keens. But look at Reese: There she is, at the
apartment where a cadre of the bereaved has gathered; she's brew-
ing coffee and refilling mugs, scrubbing dishes, setting out chips, so
that in her domestic utility no one will notice that she's a total psychopath unaffected by grief.

Attending the funeral is necessary for Reese to experience an
emotion beyond irritation at the dead girl. Funeral after funeral has
taught her to sit in the pews awaiting a moment of puncture: when
some tiny detail pierces the smooth carapace of her indifference.
Once, that detail was when the deceased-by-suicide's girlfriend
stood trembling in front of the crowd and finally conceded, "I am
humiliated that she is gone and left me here." Another time, it was a

song, high-pitched and echoing off the stone walls of the church.
Whatever that detail happens to be, when it finally penetrates Reese's
jaded and chitinous exoskeleton, for whole minutes at a time, the
rage, self-pity, and lacerating frustration toward the thwarted, vic-
timized nature of trans lives sears her directly, so that she twists and
wracks her body, her emotions pedaling like the legs of an upturned
beetle. To embrace that pain directly, to let the sorrow linger on her
vulnerable interior without caveats or irony or armor, offers a puri-
fication. In those moments, she knows that she is not a psychopath.
That she loved a friend who is gone.

When the moment comes to a close, when the funeral moves on,
she begins to armor anew, and by the time the queers have gathered
outside, she has repaired herself into a mildly irritated indifference
sufficient to exit and face them—outwardly cynical and, for once,
inwardly kindred.

Today's funeral is held for Tammi, who fatally wrecked her car.
That's the story that people have been kind to repeat. The phrase
"car accident" helpfully obscures the intentionality of the act. One
can believe that, yes, when you drive your car at ninety miles an
hour across a bridge, accidents do happen—had Tammi not spent
the previous Saturday making drunken hysterical calls in which she
slurred about no one loving her or caring when she's gone. Tammi,
whom many people loved, and after whom not a small number
lusted.

Reese first came across Tammi at Saint Vitus, a dank club that
primarily hosted music of the angry male variety. Every surface of
the interior was painted black and therein such ample moshing had
occurred over the years that the accumulated musk of sweaty post-
adolescent boys forever lingered in the circulation-free air. A
straight Tinder boy who was into noise had suggested meeting
Reese there one night, and she agreed, primarily because she'd
know immediately whether he was worth fucking or whether to flee
after a drink, and either way, her apartment was two blocks away.

Onstage, a cadre of boys hunched over keyboards. Among them, the only thing truly worth looking at in the whole club: a trans woman on guitar. Six foot three, tattoos jagged on lean porcelain arms, slashes of asymmetrical dark hair bisecting a face made up so expertly vampiric that had Elvira known about it, she'd have stopped by to learn something. The woman less played her instrument than throttled it every ten seconds or so, between which attacks she gazed with poised stillness at some unfixed point over the heads of the audience, listening to the reverberations of her own sudden violence, as a hiker who has shouted over an empty alpine lake holds quiet for the moments it takes his echo to return.

At least Tammi had been merciful in her method. No one had to find the body, save those qualified to do so: EMTs and firemen. Tammi's last grace was that flimsy veil of plausible deniability to deflect the charge of suicide just enough that her friends could tell themselves that perhaps, perhaps she had just been venting some frustration, and in the midst of that, lost control of the vehicle— that they had not failed her, that the epidemic of trans girl suicides had not taken another young lovely.

In the stone courtyard of the church, Thalia gives Reese a hug, then asks, "Want to hear a joke I thought up during the service?"

Reese does. The joke is this:

Q: What do you call a remake of a nineties romantic comedy where you cast trans women in all the roles?

A: Four Funerals and a Funeral.

Another girl, early in transition, wearing a black velvet dress, is standing near them. Reese recognizes her as one of those Twitter girls eager to offer theory-laden takes on gender. The girl has listened in on the joke and shakes her head—*insensitive!*—staring at them over her black-framed glasses with watery, wounded eyes.

Reese pulls rank. "Oh come on." She points to Thalia. "You know who gave Tammi her first shot? Thalia. Right in the butt. Who are you to say if she can make a joke or not?"

"Maybe just not where other mourners can hear it," the girl sniffs.

"Here's a better idea," Reese snaps. "Maybe don't stand around eavesdropping."

"Reese," says Thalia simply, "it's fine." Then to the girl: "Sorry."

The girl bobs a tight acknowledgment, then raises a brow at Reese, waiting for her apology as well. But Reese refuses. She is granite willing the girl to go away. Fuck that girl. Let her go to as many of these things as Reese has been to and see if she doesn't manage to develop a sense of humor. Eventually, the girl leaves, and almost immediately Reese regrets whatever enmity she made for herself in that unnecessary encounter. She's lost patience for the baby transes—never a good look on an older girl.

A little fountain burbles in the courtyard. It smells pleasantly of algae, and Reese moves closer, drawn by the cool of ionized air. Pennies flash in the pool at the base of the fountain, which seems blasphemous: wishing on coins in a church courtyard, when you could be inside praying for whatever it is that you want.

"I heard this thing"—Thalia holds the back of Reese's elbow, pulling Reese back to the present—"from Andy, who made arrangements with the funeral home. He went to those two older women who run that family funeral home in Bed-Stuy—those two nice black ladies who did Eve's funeral. After a few hours of setting things up, one of the two ladies asks him, 'I'm sorry, but was Tammi a transgender woman?' And Andy goes, 'Yeah,' and they, like, kind of exchange looks. One of them says they're going to change their plans and will be getting the body from the morgue within the next few hours to bring to their funeral home."

"Why? Why would it matter that she was trans?"

"The accident was out on Long Island, and I guess she got transferred to a morgue here. Apparently one where the morgue workers gawk at bodies of trans women—poke and laugh and shit."

This outrage, so fresh and yet unsurprising, punctures Reese anew. And yet, she can't quite enrage herself, because for once, other people beyond trans women—a pair of older black women who likely have concerns of their own—have cared enough to protect a dead queer trans girl's dignity.

"You could tell something was wrong with her a month or two ago," Thalia goes on, and Reese understands that she means Tammi. "When we went to wait at the Callen-Lorde purgatory together, she had completely stopped shaving. She wouldn't have been caught dead with a shadow like that a year ago—oh fuck, I'm sorry, very horrible expression for this moment. Thank Jesus Miss Twitter wasn't here for that too."

Reese's phone rings, and instinctively, she fumbles it in an attempt to silence the tones. A New York number. She gives Thalia another hug and finds an alcove down the block to call back the number because she's been fielding a lot of calls from vague acquaintances looking for logistics about the funeral.

A woman picks up. "Reese! Thank you for calling me back! Is there any chance you're free tonight?" A pause. "It's Katrina, by the way."

"Katrina!" The name, the pregnancy, her whole connection with Katrina, the yearning for a baby, seems like it should exist in a dimension that doesn't overlap with this funeral. Like running into one's teacher at the grocery store, it takes Reese a moment to close the dimensional gap and reorient herself. "I'm, uh, at a funeral right now."

"Oh, I'm so sorry. I'll call back."

"No, wait. What's happening?"

"Well, I was hoping I could talk to you. I might have . . . How do I say this? I might have betrayed Ames."

At this, the parabolic dish of Reese's focus swivels to aim squarely at Katrina. "Wow. That sounds very dramatic. Very romantic."

"No, not that kind of betrayal."

"That's a shame."

Katrina makes a noise of protest, then understands she's been teased and laughs graciously.

"Look," Reese says, "I'm actually really happy you called. The timing is a bit weird because of where I am. But we've got so much to talk about. I do want to get together." Reese holds her breath, waiting to see if she will get away with that "we," the "we" that couples use when they both own and take responsibility for a pregnancy. *We're having a baby,* say both men and women, often together, as if their roles were interchangeable and required equal commitment. Reese recognizes her own "we" is a little creepy, but fuck if it doesn't feel good to say.

"Oh, that is so nice to hear," Katrina says, sounding genuinely moved. "I can't interrupt a funeral, though."

But Reese has smelled something new and curious. Yes, she's supposed to take care of her friends tonight, but a betrayal of Ames? Katrina wanting to talk to her? Reese has had such opportunities seldom enough that when one comes, she knows to move. "Honestly, the girl was closer to my friends than me, so I'm mostly here for support." This is half-true.

"Who was she?"

"A trans girl from around."

"I'm sorry."

Reese *mmhmm*s in the mournful manner one properly receives a condolence, waits the necessary moment to avoid unseemliness, then asks, "So what's this betrayal all about?"

"Can we talk about it in person? I might have outed Ames to the whole company. I'm not sure of the etiquette for that. I'm happy to come to you to make things easier."

Reese moved into an apartment in Greenpoint with Iris a year and a half ago: a low-ceilinged ancient-brown-carpeted second-floor unit in a three-story building with asbestos siding that sits at the base of the Pulaski Bridge. The apartment had at some point in history been a one-bedroom, but by barely hewing to the New York real estate law that a room must have a window and a closet to qualify as a bedroom, a long-ago landlord had squeezed three bedrooms into the space by building a maze of walls. Each oddly shaped bedroom had exactly one window and a closet that protruded from the wall like a box.

Iris took the largest bedroom and in the smallest bedroom, she had placed a massage table and decorated the walls with tapestries and candles, turning it into a part-time erotic massage parlor. Iris had enrolled in massage classes the year before as she cleaned up and got sober. She had been working since then at a spa in Williamsburg. Iris divided up her male clients into two categories, daddies (positive!) and dickbags (negative!) and liked to detail at length their various behaviors for Reese after work. Occasionally, Iris offered good daddies who dropped the right hints the chance for sessions with happier endings at the apartment.

Reese lived in the medium-sized bedroom—what had once been a bathroom. Since the bathroom had a window, it had been made into a bedroom, and the living room closet made into the bathroom as building codes did not require bathrooms to have windows. Every night she rested her head on a pillow that lay in the space where the toilet had once been.

Reese and Thalia wait for Katrina in front of the McDonald's by the Greenpoint stop on the G train. Thalia came along without requiring an invite. Reese had earlier volunteered to keep her company that night, her motherly attempt to staunch both grief and Thalia's temptation to go out drinking with all the queers from out of town, both perennial ingredients in the recipes that Thalia fell back upon whenever she cooked up a truly messy evening. In return for allowing Reese to mother her so intrusively, Thalia felt entitled to the chance to witness and color-comment Reese's own messiness.

"So what's your plan here?" Thalia asks Reese, flicking through photos on her phone while they await Katrina. "You're just going to bring this nice pregnant lady back to Iris's amateur erotic massage parlor?"

"Amateurs, by definition, don't get paid," Reese counters. "I live in a *professional* erotic massage parlor, thank you very much. But I texted Iris to put away the massage table."

"And what did Iris say to that?"

"She hasn't responded." Reese retrieves her phone. "Oh wait, no. She texted. She says to fuck off, she's not hiding anything for Amy's baby mama."

Thalia laughed. "That sounds like Iris."

"Yeah," Reese sourly agrees. "It does."

"Why did she hate Amy again?"

"She didn't hate Amy. She just thought Amy was a snob. She was there the day when I met Amy." Amy and Iris's mutual distaste had begun the night that Amy launched into a tirade against the prevalence of Candy Darling–worship among trans girls. The rant revolved around Amy's oft-elaborated claim that trans girls never *do* anything. The best they ever hope for is for someone else to discover them, take an interest, and make them into a muse. But muses are passive. They have no agency and they reap no rewards—the rewards are reserved for those who use them for inspiration. Among the Factory girl trancestors, Holly Woodlawn and Jackie Curtis actually *did* things. Those two had a reputation for danger in their wit, vengeance, and unpredictability. They held Andy Warhol to account. But trans girls don't worship those two. Candy Darling? She was just some helpless languid blonde waiting around for a man to save her and make her famous. Iris, a languid blonde waiting for a man to save her and make her famous, had tolerated Amy's lecture in silence. When Amy finished, Iris coolly raised her skirt to reveal the photorealistic tattoo of Candy Darling's face that decorated her entire upper thigh.

"No," disagrees Thalia, "Iris definitely hated Amy. She told me."

"You two shouldn't be gossiping about me."

"We weren't gossiping about you, we were gossiping about Amy."

At that moment, Katrina ascends from the station and pops out her earbuds with a tug on their cord at the same time that she calls out a greeting to Reese. She's wearing yoga pants and an oversized duster sweater woven in a corporate approximation of a Native American pattern. To Reese's surprise, Katrina comes in for a hug. Katrina's shoulder blades slide delicately beneath her hands.

"I haven't been up to this neighborhood in so long! But *Girls* was filmed here, wasn't it?"

"Oh wow!" Thalia interjects. "Amazing you should mention that! Reese *loves* that show!"

Greenpoint's chance at being a cool area ended when Lena Dunham set the first season of *Girls* there, and it became associated with clueless white girls in both fact and popular conception. "It's the opposite of my favorite show," Reese corrects. "Meet Thalia. Thalia, Katrina—Katrina, Thalia." Thalia flashes Katrina one of her gorgeous smiles that knocks aside everything in its path.

Occasionally, Reese worries about the appearance of her living in Greenpoint—to live in Brooklyn and inhabit one of the few neighborhoods overwhelmingly inhabited by white people? It doesn't look good. Still, Reese likes Greenpoint precisely for its Polish people. Her apartment is located on the North End, along Newtown Creek, the Superfund site that separates Brooklyn from Queens, and the one part of Greenpoint that's largely retained its Polish residents. In South Greenpoint, on the border with Williamsburg, the Poles have sold their ramshackle buildings to developers and retired to Warsaw as millionaires. Her block hasn't yet succumbed. Living among the old Poles suits her. Elsewhere girls complained about aggression, catcalls, slurs, the constant fear of catching the attention of some man who realizes he's been attracted to a transsexual and has himself a good ol'-fashioned panic. But those old women pushing around their grocery dollies, the white-

whiskered men in faded windbreakers, they cannot trouble themselves to so much as glance at Reese. Any effort to get them to
consider such a thing as some American's gender presentation is
destined to break apart against the stony shores of a massive Slavic
indifference. The only women who approach her with anything resembling curiosity or friendliness are those who mistakenly greet
her in Polish; their faces slam shut when she responds in apologetic
English. Greenpoint is the only place she's ever lived where she feels
no injunction to put on makeup before a quick errand, because no
one deigns to take note of her one way or another.

"I hope you weren't waiting too long," says Katrina to the two
women. She doesn't expect a real response—lateness in the era of
smartphones having become a social rite for which one apologizes
without quite taking responsibility, as when you apologize for a
spell of bad weather to a friend visiting from out of town.

"No," says Reese, and she begins the walk north, toward her
apartment. Thalia politely steps a few feet ahead, allowing Katrina
and Reese to walk side by side—the sidewalk is too congested to
walk three abreast.

On the way, Katrina glances over Reese's shoulder at the Brooklyn Bazaar. "Do a lot of trans people live in this neighborhood?"

"What? Not at all. I've only seen a handful since I moved here,
and I don't know them."

The question amuses Thalia. She turns, taking a couple backward steps. "Reese and Iris are trying to escape the rest of us."

"Oh, okay." Katrina nods. "I asked because there's a sign that
says 'Tranny' right there."

Of literally all the things this cis lady might say in front of Thalia!

Reese flinches. Thalia's graceful body freezes rigor mortis–stiff
and she asks, "Did you say 'tranny'?"

Katrina points across the street. "Right there. Tranny."

Reese whirls. Pasted on the front wall of the Brooklyn Bazaar is
an amateurish black-and-white graffiti-style poster with a single
giant word: TRANNY.

Reese can't make sense of it. She and Thalia have come fresh
from a funeral. As she stands there gaping, anti-transgender bills
ferment in various state senates. Even the liberal media—*The New
York Times* and *The New Yorker* and *New York* magazine—have
taken to publishing anti-trans screeds penned by conservatives, the
editors disingenuously wringing their hands and pleading "balance" or "wait for the science." Radical feminists and Christian
fundamentalists have teamed up to insist that trans women are all
pedophiles, that such predators can't be trusted around children or
in women's spaces. Every year, the list of murdered trans women,
most of color, grows longer. Among those cases, the number of victims who were misgendered in their own obituaries is greater than
the number of victims whose murderer has been identified.

But all of that has been far away from Reese. She lives in Greenpoint specifically because it is all far away. That is news that lives on
the Internet. Not on her walk down the street. She spots another
similar poster: TRANNY. Only this one has an indistinct face and a
date. Suddenly, she realizes what the posters want to advertise: a
promotional tour by Laura Jane Grace, the transgender lead singer
of the punk band Against Me!, for the release of a memoir titled
with the same slur.

And suddenly Reese is furious. These rich trans bitches. These
fucking assholes who transition with hundreds of thousands or millions of dollars to protect them from ever hearing someone say
"tranny" to them on the street, so that one day, they can write *tranny*
on the streets themselves, and congratulate themselves on being so
punk. As if, in a climate of political dread, no one has ever written
jew, or *faggot*, or hung a noose, or painted a swastika where some
poor target tried to pass a small life.

Katrina looks back and forth, from Reese to Thalia, aware that a
minor drama largely illegible to her is being written.

"I guess it's the title of a memoir," Reese says, forcing herself to
shrug. "Laura Jane Grace," she adds to Thalia, who clearly can't yet
make sense of the poster.

"Oh, okay." The tension in Thalia's posture releases. "What an edgelord. Her and her transgender blues." Thalia spits the word "transgender" derisively, with a hard *g*.

"Who?" Katrina asks.

"A trans punk singer."

Katrina hesitates, then decides to address the moment. "I'm sorry I pointed it out. I didn't know it was a sore subject."

"It's okay," Reese says. "Thalia and I are both a bit raw today. Anyway, it's not *your* fault. Signs are meant to be read. So people should be thoughtful of what they put on them."

Katrina gives a slight nod, relieved that the tension has trailed away. "Speaking as someone in marketing, it's not what I'd have chosen. You have to imagine a high percentage of her audience is trans. Can you imagine a trans woman buying that book? I mean, what, is she going to read it on the subway? It'd be like holding up a label on herself. Or go into a bookstore and be like: 'Hi, I'm looking for *Tranny*.'"

This observation endears Katrina to Reese with unexpected force. That Katrina has imagined a trans woman buying the memoir and reading it, and how that might feel, required a descent into empathy three or four flights deeper than even Reese herself had taken.

In the apartment, Iris sits on a stool at the kitchen counter in panties and a tank top, sipping on white wine chilled with ice cubes. In a fig leaf of decency, she has at least tucked before Katrina's arrival. She's interrogating Thalia about the funeral, collecting information on who was there and what was said. She insouciantly dismisses those poor unfortunates on her years-long shit list with insults that make florid use of her abandoned English degree—insults being the only circumstance in which she puts it to use: *Those Truvada libertines! Ugh, I can't stand a hooker with a financial advisor! Listening to that dickbag's opinions is a form of self-harm! Her? She's like Starbucks— any idiot can enjoy her and, two hours later, forget he did.* Insults are

Iris's version of mourning. She and Thalia are putting on a show for Katrina's benefit, while pretending indifference to her presence. Where do they get the energy? At certain moments, when Thalia has wrested back the stage for one of her own monologues, Reese catches Iris regarding Katrina with undisguised curiosity.

Finally, Iris can no longer contain herself, and comments directly though obliquely to Katrina, "God, I wish I had subordinates to have affairs with me."

Katrina catches the inference and makes a face.

Iris says, "Oh please. I'm Reese's roommate and plus I have known Amy for as long as Reese has! Who else is she going to gossip with?"

Why, Reese asks herself, has she not taken any one of the thousands of opportunities presented to her to smother Iris in her sleep?

But Katrina collects herself almost immediately. It's impressive, actually. In the past Reese has brought over guests, perhaps those who have seen too much drag, who make the mistake of thinking that shade is an invitation to match Iris in her performance. Which is exactly the point at which Iris grows serious, while the interloper, still a step behind, bumbles alone through some embarrassing attempt at sassy.

"Did Reese tell you why I'm here?" Katrina asks.

"No . . ." Iris puts her fist under her chin in a pantomime of attentive listening. "But do tell."

"You don't have to tell her anything," Reese says to Katrina.

"How dare you," Iris says, but she doesn't break her pose.

"Oh my god, look at her," Thalia says of Iris. "It's like when a dog smells your food and freezes in a begging position."

"How dare you too," Iris repeats, still refusing any lapse in the discipline of her pose.

"I'm going to take her into my room away from your prying," Reese announces.

"Actually," Katrina says, "maybe a variety of opinions is the best. I mean, I came for trans etiquette advice, and here we are."

She makes a gesture around the kitchen. Iris sticks out her tongue at Reese in victory.

"And I never knew Amy at all," Katrina continues. "So I don't know anything about Amy when he was trans, or even before he was trans when he was Ames the first time—"

"James," says Iris.

"What?"

"Her name the first time was James. Then Amy. Now Ames. She didn't change back to her original name. Like, it's as though she couldn't fully bear to go back to being James after detransition, so she dropped the *J* and now she's Ames."

Katrina glances at Reese to see if this is indeed true, and Reese confirms it with a little nod.

"The way she picked her names is so psychologically indiscreet," Iris complains, emphasizing the word "indiscreet" to indicate the height of gauche. "She just parades all her issues naked in the front window."

"See, this is good stuff!" Katrina says. "This is the kind of info that I can't pull from Ames himself."

"Wait a minute"—Reese points a straw that Iris has left on the kitchen table at Katrina— "aren't you the one who's supposed to be giving us the lowdown on Ames tonight?"

At the weekly Monday all-staff meeting, the head of human resources, a young-for-the-position Southern woman named Carrie, announced that the agency's bathroom policy would be changing. Carrie came from the type of Southern culture where she pronounced the letter *H* in "white" and "wheel," ordered "mehr-leow" at wine bars, voted Democratic as much for obscure heritage reasons as politics, and at seventeen had the kind of debutante "coming out" that had nothing to do with the gay. "One final change this week," she intoned at the end of the company meeting. "About the law in my home state of North Carolina that prohibits transgendered persons from using the bathroom of their adopted sex. I happen to be personally very ashamed of my state for this"—she allowed a sorrowful pause for effect—"so I'm pleased to announce that the small bathroom across from the periwinkle conference room will now be designated gender-neutral." Carrie clapped for her own announcement and the meeting broke up. Ames had missed the meeting that day, and once back to work, Katrina forgot about the bathroom business.

But as Katrina gathered her things for lunch, Carrie knocked on Katrina's open office door, apologized for interrupting, and asked if they could chat for a minute. She was very delicate, so it took her a while to get around to the point, but she wanted to know if Katrina thought that one gender-neutral bathroom downstairs would be sufficient accommodation.

"I have no idea," Katrina told Carrie, baffled.

"Oh," said Carrie, "but you know, she works under you, so I thought maybe she might have communicated—"

"What?" Katrina cut her off.

"Ames, I mean. She reports to you."

"Ames is not a she."

"Oh, no, I know," Carrie rushed to say. "I'm sorry. You know, it's just that some other people have asked about it and, since it came out, people were talking about what our bathroom policy is."

"Carrie," Katrina said carefully, "you need to tell me exactly what you mean when you say 'came out.' What are people talking about?"

"Well," Carrie said, then smoothed out her skirt and dropped her conciliatory demeanor, "what I was told was that on your trip to Chicago, you told Dave Etteens and Ronald Snelling that Ames used to be a woman. Ames said as much to them too. Abby is the project manager assigned to Dave and well, he told her about it, and then it got around the rumor mill here. And I just want to handle this with dignity, for everyone's sake. The agency, but Ames too."

Katrina groaned and let her face drop into her hands.

Carrie ignored this rudeness and continued. "Anyway. I think it's good policy to have one gender-neutral restroom regardless. But since Ames is your direct report, please try to find out if we should designate one on this floor as well. I was thinking that the one by—"

"Carrie," Katrina cuts her off again. "Ames isn't a woman."

"No, I know," Carrie assures her. "I know. She is a man."

The way Carrie nodded, as if convincing herself, felt wrong to Katrina on an intuitive level. "Hold on, what are people saying exactly?"

Carrie grimaced a little. "That he used to be a woman, you know, that he is a transgendered man."

"Oh fuck." Katrina slumped back in her chair and stared at the drop-panel ceiling.

Carrie put her hand on Katrina's desk and leaned forward, concerned. "No! Katrina! He passes very well! It's not a problem for anyone here. I only want your help in creating a supportive environment. We don't have any policies yet for transgendered employees, so I think it's important to do this correctly now . . ."

Katrina's first urge was to call Ames. But the situation was humiliating for them both. Katrina couldn't face it on top of everything else. Instead, she thought to call Reese.

"Okay," cackles Iris, "so they think he was assigned female at birth? That he's female-to-male?"

"Yes," says Katrina with a sigh, "that's what I'm gathering."

Reese is enjoying this turn of events more than she should. "Can you blame them? That pretty boy. His beard hasn't recovered from laser, and oh my god, even after that pert little nose got broken, it must be easy for them to imagine him as a trans guy."

"Amy isn't that tall, right?" Thalia asks. "I've only seen pictures of her." Each of the women in that room has some favorite complaint about her body, through which she can't help but assess the bodies of other women. At six foot two, Thalia's was her height.

"Like five eight, maybe nine," says Iris.

"Perfect trans guy height."

"But you actually know trans men," Iris corrects Thalia.

Reese has to catch her laughter. This is really just so delicious. "Yeah, you know to clock a burly dude. Cis people are off looking for, like, Gwyneth Paltrow with a little mustache."

"In other words: They're looking for Amy." Iris's face looks as pleased as Reese feels.

Katrina's interest has snagged on a different detail. "Burly?"

"Oh yeah," say the other women in emphatic unison.

"If you want a manly man," Iris counsels her, "find yourself a trans man. They're the only ones you can be sure want to be that way, instead of compensating their way into it."

"Huh," says Katrina. The sails of Katrina's sexuality billow with new considerations.

"Thalia likes the FTM4MTF romance," Iris teases. "She's always got a boy panting after her. She's got a *dancer* right now."

"Really? Why didn't you tell me?" Reese's feelings get hurt when Thalia shares her love life with Iris but keeps it from her. "Lemme see a photo!"

"Tonight is not about me," Thalia snaps.

"Fine." Reese shifts focus back to Katrina to hide her miffed feelings. "So anyway, what advice do you want about this situation?"

"I don't know." Katrina pauses a moment to find the correct words. "I suppose I thought there were rules. I Googled what to do if you think that you have outed a trans person. I read a bunch of feminism blogs on it. There are strict rules. Apparently number one is don't out trans people in the first place."

"Yes," Iris says, "that is a good rule."

"Right, so I thought I'd come over and confess what I did, and you"—she indicates Reese with a little thrust of her chin—"would tell me what to do."

The word "confess" startles Reese. "I'm not a priest, Katrina! I'm not going to tell you to recite, like, ten Hail Transgender Marys and absolve your sins." This is what happens when the only trans voices out there are the loudest, shrillest trans girls constantly publishing dogmatic Trans 101 hot takes to rebuke the larger cis public. You get people thinking that in order to avoid offending trans people, you must locate and follow a secret guidebook filled with arcane rites, instead of just thinking about them decently, as you would anything else. You get one lady assembling an impromptu transgender focus group to assess how she should take the kind of basic responsibility that she clearly knows how to take in the non-trans-populated situations of her life, while another lady is going around gender-neutralizing bathrooms because she doesn't dare ask Ames what he prefers in a direct, respectful manner.

"Right, obviously not," Katrina says. "I was being a little facetious. So in all earnestness: Does detransition count the same as transition in terms of the respect it has to be given?"

This is a topic of fierce debate among the three trans women. Iris maintains a "yes, absolutely." Thalia agrees, but adds that everyone deludes themselves, including cis people, and the only way to force anyone to actively consider their gender is to equally disrespect all genders. In the abstract, Reese agrees on this principle of equality, but the fact is that Reese respects many genders, but doesn't respect Ames's current gender at all.

In her heart, she doesn't think Ames is a man. She just can't believe Amy's detransition is what it seems. How many times had she seen the way that Amy, even before detransition, used masculinity as a defensive cocoon? She'd learned to gauge it early in their relationship—Reese could tell how insecure Amy felt in any situation by how many traces of her days as a college bro she pulled to the surface. In those moments, the vitality of Amy's presence receded, and Reese knew that a certain level of numbing male armor had come over her.

Masculinity had always been what allowed Amy not to feel. Early on after transition, Amy had fled that numbness; she had been for a time, with Reese, gloriously there and present and fragile.

Amy had never shed her numbness completely, and later came to appreciate her own capacity for it as a useful tool. Iris, who excelled at sex work, talked about dissociation the same way: the superpower that let her succeed lucratively and heroically where the average mortal failed, succumbing to all the feels. Reese, however, didn't believe in that spin; she could never quite complete the dogmatically radical leap that would transform dissociation from coping mechanism to superpower.

In the back of Amy's closet—her literal closet, mind you, the one that they shared in their apartment—lurked a gorgeous men's Zegna suit, cut classically slim, in a deep black matte of fine carded wool. Amy had bought the suit her last year in college, from a resale shop where she pulled it off the rack, put it on, and with no tailoring necessary, discovered the Reservoir Dog in herself. In the post-transition culling of boy clothes, Amy had spared the suit, allowed it to survive, and granted it a clandestine life in the back reaches of the closet. Reese would have happily understood the suit as a sentimental keepsake, except for the fact that on rare occasions, she'd come home to find Amy actually *wearing* it, those malamute eyes a thousand yards away, slinking around like some kind of louche, androgynous James Bond.

Generally and specifically, Reese had no patience for this nostalgic boy dress-up. Reese, despite herself, succumbed to a grudging respect for Amy in Her Suit, if only for how completely shut off and thus invulnerable Amy became when wearing it. Though the next day, she made sure Amy felt sheepish and bashful, as you do to a hungover friend whose careless drunkenness the night before forced you into a state of resentful awe.

Detransition had been Amy's slow ossification across this unreachable distance. A place where Reese could no longer touch her to hurt her anew. *That is not gender,* Reese's guilt would argue, *that is pain.* All pain merits care, but not dogmatically egalitarian relativism.

·   ·   ·

Katrina and Reese sit cross-legged on a four-by-five-foot scrap of Astroturf laid over the black iron of the apartment's fire escape to make a combination balcony/front yard. Thalia talked Iris into giving her a massage, so it's just the two of them. Below, the rainfall from a brief thunderstorm earlier has collected into a sunken square of sidewalk concrete to create a perfectly quadrilateral puddle. A mother hurries along with a little daughter in tow, dragging her by the hand. At the puddle, the girl, with brown hair in a braid and a tiny pair of red galoshes on her feet, wriggles out of her mother's grasp and stamps the puddle, making a little splash. Her mother calls out her name: "Józefa, no, stop that, it is late." The girl ignores her mother, stamps again. Reese waits for the mother to get angry. But she doesn't. Instead, she pulls out her phone, kneels, and says, "Okay. We will film." The little girl jumps and splashes, and the reflections of streetlights shiver in the pooled water, while the mother films and says, "Okay, wait, one more, now jump, sweetheart, yes good, look at me!"

Reese and Katrina watch in silence from above. The moment elongates like pulled taffy. They are barely breathing, the two of them, their dark shapes two stories above, raptors transfixed by the scene. The mother, still kneeling, shows her daughter the video, the light of the phone illuminating the girl's pleased face as she watches her recently past self giggling in the tinny audio. When the two walk away, they seem lighter. The mother no longer pulls at her daughter. A truck coming down the Pulaski Bridge engine-brakes with a loud fart, they turn the corner, and Reese exhales.

"Ooof," Reese says.

"Yeah."

"That hurt me to watch."

"It hurt me to watch you watch."

"Thanks, I think."

Katrina snuffles, pulls her shawl around her. "So now what?"

Reese's machinations fire up, but just as quickly sputter out. Her head tilts back against the shingles of the building, and a wave of resignation comes over her. She has nothing left to think about Ames, no more advice to give. "I don't know, Katrina. I'd just tell Ames you outed him before someone at work does. He's not new to gender hijinks."

"I mean about the baby. That could be us."

Reese wants to say the right thing, but has no idea what that could be, so waits, hoping Katrina will go on.

"Your friends, Iris and Thalia, you know, when you were in your room changing, they jumped all over me. Told me what a great mother you would be."

"Oh, so that's it. They acted so weird when I came back out."

"It's just a question if you can find a place for yourself in this."

"Yeah," said Reese. "I want it. But I'm afraid I'll resent my place."

"It doesn't mean you won't be a mom too."

Reese nods. She can't bear to meet Katrina's eyes when she speaks. "There are moms and then there are moms. I know another trans woman. She had two little girls before she transitioned. They're four and six now. Do you know what those girls call their mothers?" The question is obviously rhetorical.

Reese goes on. "Mommy and Mommy Lucy. The trans woman, she is Mommy Lucy, the mommy who needs a qualifier. Not Mommy. When there is a woman who carried the baby biologically, and a sort-of dad, and his transsexual ex-girlfriend, which of us do you think will be the mommy with no need of a qualifier?"

"So it's all or nothing, then?"

"I'm not in a position to be setting terms. You are."

Katrina reaches out and grabs Reese by the wrist, not at all gently. She pulls Reese's hand, and fumbling, holds it in both of hers, against her chest. It's a gesture of such intimacy, but when Katrina speaks, her tone is hurt and angry. "You think you're the only one who thinks this is unfair? You think I'm not being treated unfairly? The only one whose expectations have been disappointed? When I found out I was pregnant, I thought I had what you wanted:

a baby with a reliable man. But that's not what I turned out to have, and I'm getting over it."

Katrina's chest is hot through her shirt against Reese's hand. Reese speaks, "Whatever you are, I'm lower."

"Tell me something. Do you resent me for being pregnant?"

"Yes."

She drops Reese's hand.

"I thought so."

"I'm jealous. God, I'm so jealous. And resentful too."

"I want to figure out how to be something to you, Reese, or with you." For a moment, Katrina appears ready to mount a second, more impassioned argument, but instead, in a deflated voice, she says, "Well, I don't know how to do that if you're just going to be resentful and jealous. Being pregnant isn't as magical as you think."

Reese rolls her eyes. Cis women are always complaining about the burden of their reproductive ability, while secretly cherishing it. Hysterectomies are widely available, but even women who don't want children aren't exactly lining up to get them.

Wind stirs the water in the puddle beneath them. When Reese speaks, she doesn't respond directly. "There's that Reagan-era saying that weed is a gateway to hard drugs like heroin. I feel that way about a vagina. It's a gateway drug. I used to want surgery; but I'm pretty sure that would just have been the gateway to wanting a uterus. And if I had a uterus, that would be the gateway to wanting a baby in it. I hear how that sounds. You add it all together and it sounds like my deepest desire is to go shopping for some other woman's organs. I don't lie to myself about my situation. If I want a baby, I have to take one from some other woman. Can you imagine how that feels for me? I gave everything for my womanhood and here I'm talking about taking things from women. I'm bitter bitter bitter about being in that place."

Katrina pauses, then asks, "Why do you have to use these words? 'Take'? 'Give'? This isn't a zero-sum game. I'm not even offering to *give* you anything. I'm inviting you to join me, to put in commitment and work. I don't think of a child as something given back and forth, and I actually think you wouldn't either. That's not how families work." Katrina gestured to where the mom and girl had been on the sidewalk. "You think that scene doesn't make me ache? That's a scene that you build, not a scene you take from someone else. That's what I want to build with other people. With children and mothers."

Reese pursed her lips, as if Katrina had invoked something sour. "Do you remember that I just went to a funeral? I've been doing this for the better half of my life. I know how things turn out when it comes to trans girls. Believe me, there can only be one mommy. You'll see. It'll be the one with the right body for it."

Katrina opens her mouth. Abruptly she laughs. "I can't believe that I'm more willing than you to think openly. Maybe the way you're seeing things isn't working. You're so sure how things are, how to do things. But the way you do things ends in funerals. Maybe instead of saying what the inevitable outcome is, just make a fucking leap. Because maybe I'm ready to. Maybe try recognizing the chances you have, recognize this chance with me, and be a mom if you want to. In a few weeks, my doctor is supposed to call and initiate care. I'll get an ultrasound to hear the heartbeat. Why don't you come along?"

CHAPTER EIGHT

Three years before conception

AMY SPENT A week tortured by her iPhone's location-sharing service. She and Reese had turned it on one day in order to find each other in a park, then forgotten about it and left it activated. Amy rediscovered Reese's shared location after Reese's confession about Stanley. That discovery twinned with a second: When Reese claimed to go to work in Manhattan, the little white circle with an R at the center that represented Reese on Apple Maps instead traveled to Williamsburg, an area Reese usually made noises about avoiding. The first time Amy spotted the R in the Williamsburg area of the map, she figured that Reese had gone errant on a shopping mission, but the following day, the little R returned to that same location. The third day, Reese went about her normal business, her R visiting locations that Amy could identify as retail brands with a client relationship to Reese's firm—but the fourth day, a Friday, the R again returned to Williamsburg. When Amy came home that night, she feigned casualness to ask whether Reese had been to Brooklyn that day.

"No," Reese replied. She stood at the kitchen counter intent on peeling a mango. Reese had discerning tastes when it came to mangoes—according to Reese, units of disappointment should be measured in the difference between a good mango and a bad mango. A friend forgetting to call you on your birthday? Four mango units.

"Oh. Ingrid told me that she thought she saw you on the train," lied Amy.

"No," said Reese, dangerously licking mango juice off the blade of a chef's knife. "I was down on the Lower East Side all day."

Amy nodded and discreetly looked at her phone. There was Reese's *R:* safely tucked into their apartment.

Jealousy is like a hangover: When you are in the midst of it you want to die, you are poisoned, useless. Nothing stretches before you but an expanse of ashes and regret; yet despite the intensity of your suffering, no one feels sorry for you, no one cosigns your fury. No sympathy for you! Look how wantonly you indulged! Of course it hurts, but your suffering is nothing unique, everyone has suffered like that, so get ahold of yourself, show some backbone and discretion, for god's sake. Don't go making any major decisions. Jealousy and hangovers, as common wisdom goes, are temporary.

But torture is temporary too, and torture nonetheless breaks its victims. The poor guys on the lowered end of a CIA waterboard wouldn't confess if it were possible to tell themselves that, actually, this drowning is merely temporary.

All weekend, Amy stayed transfixed by the *R*. She would look at Reese, then check the *R*, a compulsive instinct to confirm that the *R* and Reese were inextricably linked, that she really had seen the *R* travel to Williamsburg multiple times over the preceding days. Despite a desperate urge to shout accusations, to indulge in her trembling emotions, Amy redoubled her stoicism, and rebuffed her mind's calls to go on the attack. She would not be one of those jealous lovers, interrogating her beloved. She refused. For both their dignities.

On Monday, when Amy went to work, the *R* hung around the apartment until around noon, when it crept northward, to Williamsburg, where Amy had concluded that Stanley must reside.

One million mango units.

In Amy's cubicle, the air seemed to have lost all pressure so that she breathed in a vacuum. Despite how her phone hurt her, Amy couldn't find the will to stop looking at it. Her bargaining went unheeded by her fingers: *Put the phone away, Amy, don't look at it.*

Okay, well at least turn off location-sharing permissions with Reese, so
you stop flaying yourself. No? Well, maybe at least just, like, look at
Instagram? It was like giving "sit" and "stay" commands to a cat.
Her fingers stirred themselves only to tap the glass when the screen
saver darkened the LCD. After some period, they languidly moved
on their own. Amy watched them call up the Uber, watched them
punch in the cross streets where Reese's *R* lingered.

A young guy showed up outside the office in a maroon BMW.
Uber had kindly upgraded the transportation for Amy's disgraceful
jealousy reconnaissance mission. A truly impressive car in which to
behave sordidly.

In her senior year of high school, Amy had a crush on the captain
of the girls' field hockey team, a little pixie girl, who wore her hair
in a slick ponytail and moved like a dancer across the grass, thread-
ing among larger opponents with her pleated skirt whirling so that
the white shorty spandex she wore beneath flashed sexily. They were
basically a combination of cheerleader and schoolgirl fantasy outfits,
those field hockey uniforms. Her secret-fetishist-cross-dresser heart
skipped in time to those spandex panty flashes. Finally, just before
summer vacation, Amy made out with the field hockey captain at a
party.

The next day, the captain invited Amy to a café in a little strip of
town that the popular girls had deemed the hangout spot that year.
Amy had shown up, thrilled. But the captain had not come alone. A
small cadre of girls had assembled themselves at a sidewalk table
leaving open a single chair for Amy, as though conducting a job
interview—the captain flanked by her lieutenants. A brief preamble
of greetings occurred, in which it became clear that Amy's affec-
tionate giddiness and hopefulness about the previous night's make-
out would not be reciprocated. With an expression of polite sadness,
the captain informed Amy that she didn't want a boyfriend, she
wanted a summer of fun; and she got the sense that Amy liked her
better than she liked Amy, so she wanted to be up front. Her lieutenants nodded in accordance. Amy tried not to blush and feel stu-

pid. She couldn't manage to make eye contact, and nodded while she looked at the streetlights, which were of an antiquated ornate design.

At some point, Amy saw that the girls expected her to verbally agree, to pledge that yes, a romantic relationship would not be forthcoming, and any future make-outs could only occur organically and drunkenly, if at all. Amy opened her mouth to say what was expected, but just then a guy who went to a different school, but with whom Amy had played guitar a couple times, drove by in a red BMW convertible. He drove with the top down, his popped collar looking like the preppy handsome villain in a John Hughes movie, complete with two summery babes, one on the passenger side, one in the back seat. Ska-era Sublime pumped from the stereo.

"Ben!" shouted Amy. "Hey, Ben!"

Ben braked into a roll, and without thinking about it, Amy propelled herself up and away from the humiliating breakup interview, sprinted across a lane of traffic, assessed in a split second that the car was a two-door coupe, but that nothing, not even a lack of doors must interrupt the boldness of this moment. Amy took a leap, vaulting the side of the car, clearing the door with ease, and came to rest with a rangy athletic grace beside the back-seat blonde, who smiled ingratiatingly at this unexpected excitement bestowed from above.

"All right, all right," said Ben, like a baby Matthew McConaughey, and stepped on the gas, so that the Beamer peeled out, streamers of blonde trailing. It was, in high school boy terms, a really cool moment. Even the captain's lieutenants betrayed her. They gossiped that when she had tried to break up with James, he didn't even give a fuck. He just hopped into a convertible car without saying a word, without even opening a door. The whole thing was yet another little deus ex machina that turned Amy's anguished dissociated yearning into the act of an aloof coolness, cementing Amy's reputation as a broody James Dean to be reckoned with, but furthering her from any possibility of anyone she knew ever seeing past that.

Years later, the deus ex machina had returned, another slick reddish BMW to chariot her through a crucial moment of humiliation.

"All right," said the Uber driver when she slid in, assessing her curled hair and the way her work skirt had snagged and ridden nearly up to her ass. He punched the gas and they were off.

"I need you to drive fast," Amy told the driver, a young guy who had a Dominican flag hanging from the mirror and reggaeton playing softly, a compromise with the tastes of Manhattanite Uber customers ordering a luxury car. "Can you do that?"

He grinned. "Oh, hell yes."

As the RPMs revved, the stereo automatically adjusted the music volume higher to compensate, giving the man a beat to which to drive. Still, flying cinematically across lower Manhattan cannot actually occur without the necessary movie permits and advance planning to facilitate it, so they less shot through lower Manhattan than crept their way through it, with her driver honking and gesticulating heroically.

"Why the rush, though?" he asked at a stoplight.

"My partner is cheating on me," Amy said, divulging to him the purpose of a mission she hadn't at that point even permitted herself to acknowledge.

"Oh, you have a boyfriend?" The tone made his disappointment clear.

"Sort of," said Amy. She had stopped declaring herself a lesbian to strange men a long time ago.

"Sort of?" Then he answered his own query. "Yeah, I guess you won't have one after you catch him, huh?" At this conclusion he redoubled his efforts.

On the Williamsburg Bridge he finally had the room to show off his car's acceleration, and so he did, hitting seventy miles an hour before braking hard and wrenching the wheel to the left at the backup at the entrance to the Brooklyn-Queens Expressway, slurring his car across a lane, cutting off a Maytag appliance truck and barreling out the exit chute onto Broadway.

Amy checked her phone. Reese's *R* was moving. It was heading northward.

"Oh shit," she cried. "They're on the move!"

"Are they running? Did they get a tip-off that you're coming?"

For a moment, Amy almost forgot to be miserable. A tip-off? What did this guy think this was? But then it occurred to Amy that if she could see Reese's *R*, maybe Reese could see her *A*. Maybe Reese had been tracking Amy's movement for months! Maybe that's why she felt safe to cheat whenever she wanted! Amy had tagged herself like some sort of research dolphin! No. C'mon. That's paranoid. Right? Totally paranoid. But . . .

The *R* was moving too fast for Reese to be on foot. Was she on a bus? No! She was in his car!

"They're gonna get away!" she cried. "We have to follow them."

"Okay," said her driver. "But you have to update your destination in 'location' in the Uber app. I can't just drive where you say."

"What?"

"I won't get paid except for the destination in the phone. Create a second destination."

"But I don't know their destination!"

Her driver shrugged. "I can't go except for where you put in."

This was bullshit! In the movies, you get in a taxicab and shout "Follow that car!" Uber ruined everything.

"I'll give you cash for the extra."

He shook his head sadly. "That's not the way Uber works. I could get in trouble."

She didn't know what to say. They'd had a rapport! Okay, no, she hadn't really flirted with him when he gave her the chance, but . . .

"Fine, how do I change destinations?"

"Well, actually what would be best would be to add a second destination, since we are basically almost at yours."

"I don't know how to do that!" Amy wailed.

"I'll show you," he said, and pulled over.

"No! Don't pull over, they'll get away!"

"It's faster than telling you!" he cried back.

She shoved her phone to him, and absurdly, he began to explain, step by step how to add a second destination to the Uber route.

Goddammit! she wanted to scream. *My heart is breaking and there is no pathos in this world!* Instead, as he went through the steps she said, "Okay, yes, thank you. Yes, I understand now. Yep. They were on the corner of Bedford and Metropolitan when I last looked. Let's put that in as the second destination. Yes. That's great. Perfect."

Of course, by the time he handed the phone back to her, and turned his attention back to the wheel, the *R* had crept farther north. The green flag waved and a race commenced: Amy's smartphone typing skills as she updated the location on the fly against Reese's indeterminate travel.

"I think they're going to the park," Reese cried.

"Which park!?" The driver had returned to her team, ready to fly ahead.

"McCarren."

"I'll take Franklin north!" he shouted. "It's faster, I promise!"

Yes, he's right! Amy and her driver traveled north on the map, her trajectory parallel with Reese's *R*. Soon enough they would pull even, and then it was just a matter of cutting over and heading them off. Amy's pulse raced. Love is a battlefield, but also a car chase.

Earlier that month, Amy had come home from the adoption orientation to an empty apartment. She wandered from the foyer to the dining room to the kitchen, shell-shocked, not understanding. In her mind, Amy expected Reese to be waiting at home—sorrowful, repentant. Or even angry. But an empty apartment? It had not occurred to her, and the cold fear that she had gone to Stanley's pierced her.

She opened Reese's closet: The clothes were still there. In the front closet, Amy pulled out the suitcases. Did Reese have a bugout bag? That just didn't seem like Reese. Reese was not a prepper type. Even if prepping was just to run, after admitting to cheating. She unzipped both suitcases they owned, to check if cash or toothbrushes, or whatever, had been stashed in one. But no, the suitcases were empty.

She was kneeling on the floor, zipping back up a blue suitcase, when the front door opened.

Reese saw Amy on the floor with a suitcase. Her eyes widened, then she screamed, "No!" and came down upon Amy, tore the suitcase from her and sent it tumbling across the wood floor. "No, no, no." Reese clutched at Amy, pulled her closer. "Don't go, don't, please."

"What? I'm not going. You were the one who wasn't here!"

"I went back to wait by the train stop for you! For hours!"

"I took a car."

Reese's eyes showed red and raw. "You had a suitcase out." She had a hurt, little-girl tone.

"I was seeing if you were going to leave."

Reese shook her head, and her nose flared, a sign that she was holding back tears.

Look how sad Reese was at the thought of losing Amy! Relief radiated out through Amy's limbs, bright and hopeful. So intense that it almost compensated for the anguish of her whole night thus far. When Reese asked if she wanted to process, to talk, Amy—now confident—shook her head and said they should sleep, and talk in the morning. She couldn't bear the thought of losing this relief raft. She grasped at it, and even managed a wan smile when turning back the covers and getting in tentatively beside Reese. Amy settled in with maximum care and tenderness, as though getting into bed beside someone who'd just had surgery and needed comfort but couldn't be jostled.

Amy expected that Reese would understand that since she was the one who had wronged Amy, she had the responsibility to initiate the emotional processing. The next morning, however, Reese showed no inclination to process. It seemed unfair to Amy that she would have to do the work of bringing it up, of showing herself as hurt and in need of explanations and comfort. Reese ought to have been the one to debase herself by having too many feelings. That was the least she owed to Amy. Reese ought to have been eager to give it to her, unsparingly and unstintingly. Instead, Reese took a glassy approach, a brittle pretending that everything was already as before.

They ate breakfast at the little wicker-and-glass table in the nook beside the kitchen; over toast, Reese talked about a cat she had seen the previous day, hiding and meowing under a car. The topic struck Amy as so inane and avoidant that she got up and began scrubbing dishes so that Reese couldn't see her face. And on it continued like that all weekend, until Monday, when Amy first discovered the *R*, which gave her a concrete symbol to fixate on.

Well, we shall sure as fuck emotionally process now, Amy thought when the BMW turned right, down Twelfth Street. Amy's projected trajectory and that of the *R* would collide at the Bedford corner of McCarren Park.

In the winter of the last year of her relationship with Reese, Amy began to call dominatrices for phone sex. This was a stupid habit, not for its expense, but because she expended the majority of her emotional reserves holding back an urge to inform these dommes that she was actually a very beautiful and desired transsexual, not just your average submissive phone-sex sissy. Of course, that was exactly the kind of fantasy in which submissive phone-sex sissies liked to indulge.

After she had been at it a month—claiming that she couldn't sleep, quietly slipping out of bed, wrapping herself in a nightgown, and sitting on the floor of the kitchen to dial—she ended up talking with a dominatrix from Detroit, who was clearly a man in India using a bad voice modulator over VoIP to slide his tone up about 80Hz. The encounter was so steeped in gig-era, digital-age poi-

gnancy that Amy stayed on the line for a whole half hour—
indulging her own fantasy of domination at $2.99 per minute,
indulging this Indian man in the fantasy that he was a dominatrix.
The next morning, however, she felt even more stupid than usual.

Reese would have been delighted with this story—but Reese
was the exact person Amy was afraid to tell. Had she not lost, sometime in the last year, the ability to tell Reese exactly what she wanted
in bed, she wouldn't have had to tell the dommes. Early in the relationship, she and Reese had been switchy and kinkier. She'd bought
Reese a black latex dress, and Amy could practically orgasm just
rubbing the silicone polish on Reese's curves, never mind when
Reese put Amy over her knee for a spanking. That early dynamic fit
Amy well: Reese topped in the kinky things that Amy liked, and
Amy, who had almost no genital dysphoria, was happy to put Reese
on her knees or fuck Reese in the mornings—the kind of vanilla
affirmations that Reese needed. But slowly the kink stopped, and
Amy, wheedling for more, ramped up her soft boyfriend act, putting in more work to affirm Reese's gender, while getting less of
what she needed. She didn't just want Reese, she wanted to blush
before Reese. But she couldn't say this to Reese. The words locked
themselves in and refused her attempts at eviction.

And so the dommes. After the Indian guy, and a tally of her
month's phone sex expenditures, Amy decided it'd just be cheaper
to see a domme in person; and for once, she wouldn't have to convince that domme, sans evidence, that she was more than your average sissy, that the domme was herself lucky to be seeing Amy.
Unfortunately, because the trans community and the queer dommes
who would have been perfect for Amy overlapped, Amy couldn't
actually hire any of the women that she'd lusted after at parties.
Instead, Amy went on Eros. Her first time, she hired a domme who
combined mindfulness meditation, acupressure, and BDSM. The
woman tied up Amy quite creatively, including braiding a rope
through her hair, then pressed on sensitive points on Amy's body
until she cried, stopping if Amy couldn't maintain the correct

breathing patterns and postures through the pain. The experience, while intense, remained clinical, the approach a little too therapeutic. Mindfulness Domme did acknowledge that most of her clients were not, in fact, beautiful transsexuals, but Amy's beauty didn't appear to move her one way or another. Some clients were tall, some short, some hairy, some young, and yes, some beautiful. A professional and standardized application of pain made most of them cry the same way.

A month later, Amy had reevaluated. She felt only a little guilt about wanting to see dommes, because she believed that if she could simply achieve the needed release, she could return to Reese a whole girlfriend. Mindfulness Domme did not give Amy the needed release, because Amy's issues, Amy decided, were mommy issues.

With a conscious self-irony, Amy had read a Freudian self-help book for women. While reading she grew increasingly earnest, and found herself persuaded by an explanation for her sexuality that appealed to her: She'd never had a girlhood, and so never had the proper bonding and separation *as a woman* from female authority—i.e., her mother. Following this view, Amy was constantly looking for female authorities who would possess her in order to heal a maternal lack from her childhood.

In a Freudian thrall, Amy again went on Eros, this time to hire a maternal domme, to spank her and then cuddle her. And this was how Amy found herself in the elevator, heading up to the twentieth. floor of a building on the Upper West Side, with a plump olive-skinned woman in her forties, who wore a lacy camisole under a blazer and introduced herself by resignedly sighing, "I guess I'm calling myself Kaya these days." She avoided eye contact with Amy, even as she led Amy into her own apartment, so that Amy thought that perhaps Kaya found it distasteful to have a female client, or perhaps a trans woman.

In a low-ceilinged foyer decorated with mirrors and fabric flowers, Kaya disappeared into the kitchen, returned with a bottle of water, and tentatively pointed the cap toward a bedroom. "You're so pretty, I feel like one of my friends is playing a trick on me," Kaya admitted shyly, gratifying Amy, and relieving her of her doubts. "I don't do this work very often and they still don't approve. But if you're for real, take off your clothes and leave the money under the Kama Sutra book on the nightstand."

This was everything that Amy had hoped for. Someone to actually cherish her, to admire her, from a position of feigned authority. Amy slid off her dress, slinky, and bent over her purse, which rested on a chair, as obscenely as possible to extract the four bills.

"You want mommy to show you what happens when her little darling is a bad girl? That's what you wrote in your email," Kaya said from the doorway.

"Yes." Amy breathed. She tucked the money under the Kama Sutra.

"I hope you don't have anywhere to be," Kaya said. "I'm not a clock-watcher."

For much longer than the agreed-upon hour, Kaya rubbed Amy and cooed over her, and spanked her and scolded her. Demanding to know who had given Amy permission to shave herself, and then bending Amy over her lap to finger her. Amy sighed, felt entitled to let go, to give in to Kaya's touches. At one point, facedown in Kaya's lap, Amy could smell Kaya's wetness. Kaya shifted and apologized. "I'm sorry. I'm really into this," Kaya said. "I wanted to do this to my ex-husband. He lives in Florida, down with my two sons."

The admission was so intimate, so unprofessional, so inappropriate, that Amy almost came, but abruptly Kaya held Amy to her large soft breasts, called her baby girl, told her that mommy was going to take care of her.

Afterward, as Amy gathered her things and discreetly placed a tip on a pillow, Kaya told Amy to come back next week. "We can work out a deal, maybe not even money. I just like this."

They saw each other twice more, but to her surprise, Amy enjoyed herself more when she paid. She had never before felt so entitled to the sex she wanted, and the entitlement came as a revelation.

Most of her life, she had expressed her desires only with the maximum exertion of will and fortitude, straining to keep playing whatever creep show was happening in her head to keep herself turned
on, while putting on an external veneer of interest in her partner.
Only with Reese had the two ever merged, but still, she rarely managed to talk dirty with any kind of abandon, terrified at what might
tumble out of her mouth if she opened the sluice gates more than a
crack. At four hundred dollars an hour, however, the compunction
to hold back crumbled, and so there Amy was, sucking on Kaya's
tits, calling her mommy, while Kaya wiggled a finger in her and
asked if she was old enough to be such a dirty slut. But at the price
Kaya asked for the second and third time—a hundred dollars and
some takeout Thai—Amy once again found herself shy. A hundred
dollars and some Thai food didn't offer enough value for Amy to
feel entitled to her own desires. Instead, Amy found herself needing
to be reassured that Kaya would say what Kaya wanted, if Kaya
didn't really find Amy kind of burdensome, if Amy didn't ask for
too much emotional labor? Then alone, packed into commuters on
the train, returning home from Kaya's place, came the sadness:
Why couldn't Amy just ask the women in her life for what she
needed? Why did she need to pay to feel like she deserved what she
liked? Even Kaya just wanted to give it away to her! What kind of
fucked-up trans-misogyny or late-capitalist angst or trauma had
colonized her? She had never been able to ask her mom for validation as a girl, had never been able to ask her girlfriends for the pleasure she needed when she was a boy, and even now, with a girlfriend
who obviously needed sex with her, it was easier to just jerk off to
the thought of Kaya, to knowingly leave Reese lonely, than for
Amy to make herself vulnerable to Reese. No wonder Reese went
back to Stanley.

Tiny raindrops pricked the windshield of the BMW as it pulled up
to McCarren Park. Even after nearly a decade in New York, Amy
had still not bothered to learn how to decipher eastern weather. In

the Midwest, Amy read the weather instinctively. She could smell
the wind and know whether it had come in West from the plains, or
bore the bite of Northern ice. She could spot iron banks of thunder-
heads in the distance and know exactly how long she had before
they arrived. She could watch the vividness increase in the hue of a
flower to sense a tornado brooding. The clouds and sky yielded
their information to her willingly.

In New York, however, nature offered her senses only an exhausted soup. She assumed that natives read the weather off the
Hudson as easily as she could read the Great Lakes. But she couldn't
stir herself to care about New York. She lived there because it was a
place to live, a place that offered the opportunities and resources of
a metropole, not because it awoke her soul. Rhapsodizing over New
York was for overly romantic foreigners. Your Irish novelists. Your
French theorists. Your Chilean poets. What was there to say about
New York that anyone from the Midwest in possession of a television hadn't heard or seen thousands of times before? The cultural
shadow of New York stretched its cloak beyond the Mississippi. The
Midtown skyscraper occupied a place in her psychic heritage beside
the strip mall. In high school, she heard about the gold-lamé-clad
hipsters flocking to a Bulgarian bar before she heard about the club
that attempted to copy that fad, which opened two miles from her
house. New Yorkers were only unique in one regard: their audacity
to recognize their own provincialism, yet still persist in foisting it
upon the rest of the nation. She had been intimate with New York
and gotten over New York long before she arrived there.

Reese's *R* and Amy's location practically overlapped on her
phone's map. "Here, I need to get out here," Amy blurted to her
driver, though she spotted no one who looked like Reese. In the
park, a group of softball players had halted play and conferred, their
hesitant heads tilting back to guess whether the sky meant to rain in
earnest.

Her driver pointed to a fire hydrant's no-parking zone. "I'll drop
you there."

But when he braked to a brief stop behind a black Explorer, Amy popped open the door.

"Careful!" he shouted, but she was already out. The sound of what he said next got cut off by the door closing with a luxuriant *thunk*. He would understand. Sensitive missions require evasive maneuvers.

In work pumps with two-inch heels, Amy skipped between two parked cars, onto the sidewalk, scanning the black spike-topped bars of the wrought-iron fence that surrounded the park for an entrance gap. In a half run, half prance to accommodate her heels, she set off along the perimeter and ducked into the park, fifty yards south. Casting her gaze about, she saw no sign of Reese. Two teenage girls, both in white tank tops, met her searching eyes. The larger girl, her hair in a braid, held a joint and openly gave it a puff, defiantly—as if Amy would care. They were dykes, Amy registered, but they hadn't registered her as a queer. Just some lady in business clothes. The thought flitted away largely unexamined, unusual for Amy, because she often fixated on how she read to other queers in public. For a moment, she tried to see herself with a semblance of humor or distance, this woman in a hurried semi-dash from a BMW. The humor didn't stick. She hurt too much, the emotions clung too close for that kind of breathing room.

On her phone, the *R* logo had moved slightly to the south. The raindrops fattened. Scattered groups of people began to stand, to collect their belongings. Amy set off south, hunting the *R* by way of her phone.

By the southern edge of the park, a wind shear swept across the grass. A woman was getting out of a silver Audi SUV when the gust took her by surprise—she wore a full-skirted gingham dress, and shifted her purse to hold down the fabric of her skirt, which flapped upward. Amy owned a dress like that. Actually, Amy owned that exact dress. That was Reese. Reese was wearing her dress.

A wet dream of a housewife dress, with a structured nipped-in waist and the discrete petticoat that gave it the curves of an inverted goblet. It was the kind of dress in which men picture Betty Draper, waiting docile at home with a drink and a blow job at the ready. And that was how Amy saw it too—her own jerk-off fantasy bent back and draped over her own body. Except that the very male gaze of that vision had always poisoned the dress for her: No matter how many people told her she looked great in it, somewhere deep down her very joy in it made her feel like a man. Reese, however: Full, soft Reese, appeared to wear it psychically unencumbered, as though she not only could thoughtlessly kneel at the door to deliver an ice-clinking drink and a BJ, but had plans to.

Now, finally! Something to be angry about! Reese's cheating obviously caused Amy the most terrible anguish, the reasons for Reese's cheating implicated Amy; they threatened the stability of Amy's whole life. You don't go charging at a beast that dangerous. You circle it softly, you eye it cautiously, looking for weakness. But a dress taken without permission? That was a rabbit. You just march over and break its neck.

Reese opened the back door of the SUV and rummaged around, and during that time, Amy exited the iron-barred enclosure of the park and closed the distance between the two of them. Reese stood back up holding a folding red umbrella, and futzed with it. A tall man rolled out of the driver's side, and said something to Reese— still fumbling with the umbrella—then rolled his eyes, took the umbrella from her, opened it, and handed it back to her. To Amy, the man was a study in neutrals. Nothing on his body popped with any kind of color—his hair and skin ran the gamut all the way from birch to pine. Amy examined his big oafish handsomeness. This was the kind of man Reese had professed to find very desirable, which Amy couldn't quite believe, because the concept of attraction and such a man remained unacquainted with each other in Amy's version of the universe.

Neither Reese nor he noticed Amy, who had stopped on the edge of the sidewalk, along the fence.

"You stole my dress for a date with him?" Amy said quietly.

The man—Stanley, Amy knew—heard her, but Reese had turned toward the McCarren Hotel.

He whirled, spotted Amy, and narrowed his eyes. "What?"

"I'm not talking to you," Amy said. "I'm talking to her."

Now Reese turned. Dawning was slow to arrive. She appeared to require a moment to process Amy in the defamiliarized context. For Reese, to have a lover of years, her close domestic companion, appear on the street where you do not expect her—a lover whose face is twisted in anger, her body shaking, her shoulders pulled in tight, clutching her purse as though someone meant to take it from her, her hair bedraggled by the damp—no, maybe Reese could truly not place her.

This momentary pause infuriated Amy. In that second of hesitation, Amy decided that her own lover had been so taken by this sourdough lout that she had forgotten about Amy. "I want my dress back," Amy said, without bothering with how unreasonable she sounded. Without observing at all how that bizarre demand lost her the moral advantages of the moment.

Reese blinked. "What? Now?"

"Yes. Give it to me," Amy insisted.

Stanley laughed. "What?" he said again.

"Amy," Reese said. "Don't."

"Don't do what? Cheat on you with a man? It can't be that. That appears to be totally cool to do."

Stanley bobbed his head in a slow nod. "Oh. I get it. That's who you are."

"Yeah, *Stanley*, that's who I am," Amy shot back.

"Listen," Stanley said, and indicated the McCarren Hotel, "we were going to go for a swim at the pool here. How about you come too?"

"How about you shut the fuck up and let me and my girlfriend talk?"

He widened his eyes as if slapped, and might have responded, but Reese stepped in front of him, a slight movement that cut him off. "How did you follow me, Amy? How did you know where I was?"

Ugh, that was so Reese: She got caught cheating, and she acted like she was the victim. "If you don't want to be followed," Amy replied, "then you shouldn't steal my things." She heard how petulant she sounded—how weak and beside the point.

Reese turned to Stanley. "Stay here. Please. Stay here."

He shrugged. Reese came close to Amy, not quite close enough that they both stood under the umbrella—Amy remained in the rain. "Let's not pretend this is about the dress. You followed me and caught me with Stanley. Now what do you want to do about it?"

"What do I want?" Amy repeated, incredulous. "Since when is it up to me?"

"Since you're here. Since you came here and forced things."

"I want you to feel bad about what you're doing to me!"

"I do, Amy. I really do." Reese's face, however, remained placid. The tolerant expression of an adult refusing to give in to a tantrum. A look that infuriated Amy.

"You don't look it! You don't look upset at all."

"What do you expect, Amy? We're standing on the street. I don't want a scene. So let me ask again. What do you want to do now?"

Yes, what did Amy want? She wanted an apology. She wanted Reese to take her home. For Reese to hold her and tell her that she had made a mistake. That she needed Amy. Needed Amy's forgiveness. But those wants were eons away from this moment. They were not what you asked of this woman staring at Amy with a stony face. This woman who had no remorse. More than anything Amy wanted to shock Reese out of her superior calm. "Right now?" Amy asked, meeting Reese's hard glare. "I want to punch him in the face."

The declaration had the intended effect. Reese's eyes widened, and she darted a quick panicked look toward Stanley.

"What's that?" Stanley asked. "You want to punch me in the

face?" The words rolled around his mouth like a lozenge and he grinned, a strange eager grimace.

"Just stay the fuck out of it, dude," Amy snapped. Her voice came out from somewhere in her chest, low and angry. She sounded like a man. She heard it immediately, with a stab of shame. Something clicked across Stanley's eyes, so that he saw the scene before him with a new clarity, as occurs at the optometrist during an eye exam: *Look at the top line. Do you see him now, Stanley? Do you see the man challenging you?*

"No, *dude*." Stanley leered, loosely pulling his frame to full height. "I don't think I will. I don't like little faggots threatening me."

Faggot? For a moment, the misgendering threw Amy off. Was he calling Amy a man or not? If Amy was a faggot, didn't that make Reese a faggot, which would make him a faggot? But she had no time to ponder inconsistencies. A change had come over Reese. She looked genuinely frightened, and began pushing Amy away from Stanley, whispering, "No, no, no." Was Reese afraid that Amy would hurt Stanley? No, of course not. Quite obviously, Reese was afraid of Stanley. Around the perimeter of Amy's consciousness flickered an awareness that there were people out there much crueler, with minds much touchier, more defensive and fragile, who kept themselves more ready and prepared for violence than Amy herself could ever tolerate. One did not escalate with people such as that. Reese still held the umbrella as she pushed Amy away and the rod pressed against Amy's face, painfully. Amy took a step to the side, so that Reese clumsily fell forward past her.

Stanley had closed the distance in one or two long steps. "I know all about you," Stanley said, flicking his hand toward Reese. "She told me all about her little bitch girlfriend, when she came to get dicked down how she needed."

Was that true? Had Reese complained about Amy to him?

Reese had hold of Amy's arm now, was tugging her away. Amy

wrested herself from Reese's grip, and balled her fists. She had a sense that she would look stupid trying to fight in a tight skirt and heels. She could barely get her legs more than a foot apart. As Amy tensed her arms—the gestural prologue to a shouted *Come at me, bro!*—an expression of naked scorn came over Reese's face. In some future moment, Amy would find the shame of this moment intolerable, the image of herself reflected in Reese's scorn—scorn for the posturing vestigial instinct of a once-male, indignant with the rage of insulted masculinity, dressed ridiculously in the outfit of a demure woman. But in the present Amy didn't have the time nor inclination to gather up the implications of Reese's expression. Amy's anger had a blinkered momentum unto itself. She could as much parse the meaning of Reese's scorn from inside her rage-fugue as count the passing floors while falling from a skyscraper. Meanwhile, Stanley had stepped closer. He really was very big. "Yeah, I know all about you. You were the one who moved her out of my apartment. You came into my apartment and took what was mine. You violated my space and stole from me. I have a lot I owe you." He seemed to be talking almost to himself now. Working himself up.

"Stanley!" Reese shrieked. She pushed past Amy's shoulder to throw herself between them. Casually, Stanley grabbed her as she came and flung her into a heap on the grass behind him. Reese was larger than Amy, and he tossed her without strain. Fury roared over the chorus that pleaded for caution at the edge of Amy's mind. Amy hit Stanley then, striking with a guttural bellow as Stanley turned back away from Reese. Closed fist, solidly on his jaw, near his ear. Stanley staggered, taking a step backward. Reese screamed, and Amy looked away from Stanley, over at her. Then Amy saw white, like when she was a kid, lying on her back in gym class, staring up at those big aluminum-caged halide lights that left trails across her vision, even with her eyes closed. The concrete of the sidewalk cracked against the side of her face, and a thump to her midsection stole all breath from her. She gasped but her lungs would not fill. Short breaths in the fading halide light.

She cracked her eyelids, and saw Stanley opening the door to his SUV. "Reese, get in the car," he commanded. But Reese, still on the ground, ignored him, and half pulling herself up, moved toward Amy.

"Faggots," Stanley spat. Amy heard the jingle of his keys, the slam of a car door, and the ignition. She opened her mouth to pull in more air. And when she exhaled, it was a loud deep sob. The shock of what had just happened, how quickly, pressed away all will. Her white blouse was turning transparent in the rain. Her skirt had ripped, and her legs and panties were showing. Her tuck had come partially undone—balls out the side of her panties, hanging dainty and vulnerable over the damp concrete. She pressed her legs together in shame. People in the park had stood up to peer and drivers had stopped, trying to make sense of the scene through the streaks of their windshield wipers.

Stanley leaned on the horn, shockingly loud and still close. A Camry accelerated jerkily out of his way, and he pulled out. Humiliation poured all over Amy, and she sobbed again, feeling the glare of the gawkers. She pushed herself up with one arm, knees bent, pressed together and off to one side so that her weight shifted onto her hip; a ridiculous pinup pose, but one that kept her legs tightly together. She sobbed a great loud honker from deep in her diaphragm that she heard further reveal her as a man. None of the gawkers made a move to help. The two dyke teens had scrambled up at the early shouts of the scuffle. Now watching the scene from between the bars of the fence, they traded looks of baffled disdain, far from the faces of allies, and nothing even resembling kinship. Some transvestite or whatever had picked a fight and made a spectacle. So weird. "Go ahead and stare!" Amy squawked, her voice thick and phlegmy. She made eye contact with a mother, who had a young son by the hand, and had paused as they fled the intensifying drizzle. Let's feed the nostalgia of these fucks. McCarren Park like it was two decades ago, with some real edge again. Transsexuals getting called faggots and stomped.

"Amy, stop. Shhh, stop." Reese's hand was on her forehead, her face over Amy's. "You're bleeding."

"Go away!" Amy cried. There was blood and snot in her mouth. Reese tried to tug Amy's skirt down, a futile attempt at modesty, but Amy pushed her hand away.

Reese's nostrils widened. "Amy, you're hurt."

"Go away!" Amy shouted again, heavy and wet.

Reese ignored her, pulling Amy's hair away from her face, so Amy grabbed her hand. "This is your fault."

Reese rocked back on her heels, looked around at the people staring. "Fine, Amy, fine." Then she stood, and stiffly began to walk away. Amy hadn't quite believed that Reese would walk away. Yet there was the back of her, stiffly moving away in Amy's dress, the red umbrella blooming above her head with a grotesque festivity.

Amy curled forward and moaned. Her fingers went to her face and came away sticky with blood. She sobbed again. Then felt around her face. Came across the sting of split skin over her brow, then her fingers moved on. They touched her nose and she half felt, half heard the dried-wood creak of cartilage shifting and a sensation like rubbing a hair between her forefinger and thumb. Then eye-watering pain radiated outward from her face and she yelped involuntarily. Her nose was broken. The nose for which she had fought so hard, for which Reese had fought so hard to get covered by insurance. Ruined. She was ruined.

A man got out of his car and approached her, but she screamed again, a deep tear of a scream, that stopped him mid-step. He called out to her instead. "Should I call the police?"

Oh god no, not the police. The question sobered her. "No." she shook her head and pleaded, "No police." Her voice came out heavy and thick.

"Are you sure? What do you need?" He hesitated between two cars.

"Hospital." She grunted and pushed herself up, feeling around for her missing heel with her right hand, the other hand over her nose.

Tentatively, the man approached her again. He wore a windbreaker; he was older, silver hair and iron-gray mustache. "There's an urgent care round the corner. Can I walk you there?" A slight accent.

"Yes," Amy managed to say.

The man knelt and gently took her heels from her. "Let me carry these, you just lean on me. Can you walk? I'll walk you there." He held out an arm for her to pull on.

When she stood, the driver of another car honked at his empty car, which blocked the road. He glanced back and told her to hold on, that he had some tissues in his car. She waited—holding the rip in her skirt closed with one hand, and covering her bloody face with the other, less for the bleeding and more so that she couldn't see the gawkers staring at her—while he pulled his car to the end of the block, turned on the flashers, and returned with some Kleenex.

She balled up a handful and dabbed her eye. It came away red. Her nose ached now, and it too bled, but she didn't want to touch it directly or dab at it. The man peered at her brow. "It's actually not that bad. Head wounds bleed a lot once they get going, so it seems worse than it is."

"Thank you," she said for the first time, grateful to him that what he said might be true. "Thank you."

This time when Amy came home to her apartment, she opened the door to Reese popping up from the couch. A stream of tenderness engulfed her, Reese burbling, apologizing, weeping, promising to change, even at one point sliding down to her knees while hugging Amy, so that Amy had to disentangle her from around her legs—everything Amy could have ever hoped for that first morning. Yet even as Amy listened with something like gladness, and although the drama seemed to occur just beyond the bandage that covered her nose, she watched it all from across some new distance. "It's okay, we'll be all right," Amy kept hearing herself say. And it wasn't that she didn't believe it—in fact, the way she said it sounded very believable—it was that she and the person making these assurances didn't quite seem to be one and the same.

On the first day that Amy had to go back to work, the thought of putting on one of her cute little work outfits struck her as completely intolerable. How could she believe in the demure little office worker she had been playing? Some other character had revealed itself, an angry man who postures and shouts, "Bring it, bro," a possessive brute who would look asinine and ridiculous in heels and a blouse. She selected a pair of beat-up jeans and a hoodie—with a broken nose front and center, no one at work would question her outfits. Over the next few days, many of the feminine grooming habits she enjoyed revealed themselves as silly. Why bother with makeup when your nose lists to the left? She felt much more comfortable dressing in a loose androgynous manner, all boots and dark neutrals, letting the nose look tough on her behalf, so that no one asked any questions, so that no opinions ventured into her vicinity.

She had, of course, long come to understand that masculinity dulled her, that it dissociated her from herself. But honestly, that's all she wanted at that point. A pocket of space to separate herself from the bright emotions of shame and fear, a veil between herself and the curious eyes on the subway and at work, a sheath over the sharp edge of furious betrayal that lacerated her whenever she met Reese's gaze; and likewise, a sheath over that awful longing for Reese as she had so innocently seen her before Stanley. A week before Reese's birthday, Amy stopped taking her anti-androgens. She and Reese took their last shot together on the night of Reese's birthday, before they went out for sushi, and that brief return to the vividness of estrogenated emotions so scalded that the next week, Amy faked taking her shot. She never took one again.

Two months later, she got a new job at an advertising agency, and confessed to Reese that she'd actually applied under a male name. When they fought about it, she shouted, in that same deep bellow that had emerged in front of Stanley, "Didn't you want a man? Isn't that what you're into? That's what I remember!" Only this time, she didn't feel ridiculous. She felt righteous in her anger, replenished and intoxicated by it. She punched a cabinet, and it yielded to her fist, the wood veneer door caving in with a satisfying, terrifying splinter.

Reese left her shortly after.

CHAPTER NINE

Ten weeks after conception

REESE HAS ALREADY been to Katrina's apartment three times. She even slept over one night, in the second bedroom—the baby's future room. She awoke in the morning to poached eggs with Katrina, in a borrowed silk robe, while trying her best to ignore the confusing intimacy of a half sleepover/half post-unconsummated-hookup vibe. Yet despite having now spent hours in the apartment, only tonight does Reese finally place the sense of déjà vu that comes over her when she looks through the bank of windowpanes that make up one wall of the living room. They overlook a narrow brick balcony, which is itself hung in a deadened air shaft.

"*Friends,*" Reese says aloud, suddenly placing the déjà vu. She walks over to examine the banks of glass panes, then whirls to let Katrina in on her discovery. "These windows—they look like windows on the set of Rachel and Monica's apartment on *Friends.*"

"I know," replies Katrina. She pops open the plastic container holding the delivery sushi—fish for Reese, vegetarian rolls for Katrina in her pregnancy—from the place down the block. "I'm sure it's on purpose. They added them when they remodeled this whole building. I think they saw a perfect way to tap into the nostalgia of Gen Xers. Give them the New York experience they saw as teenagers on TV."

"Who wants to live in *Friends?* That show is a Disneyland of New York."

Katrina pours the soy sauce packets into little ramekins. "You don't have to spend much time in marketing to understand that even though New Yorkers are snobs about it"—she smiles apologetically at having to implicitly include Reese among her misinformed fellow snobs—"they secretly like the television fantasy version of the city. Who wouldn't like to live in a huge loft on a waitress's salary?"

"Okay, I see the appeal," Reese concedes.

"If you put a couple *Friends* replica apartments in a remodeled building in Fort Greene and have it overlooking the airshaft, then, when sad ladies are in the middle of a divorce and need a comforting place, they subconsciously can rent a spot in *Friends*—a show that comforted them as a child."

Reese doesn't mull Katrina's point too deeply, instead she thinks about the words "sad ladies": how when Katrina seems like she's bullshitting through some borderline show-offy intellectual riff, her thoughts often curve back around in a scorpion's tail to reveal an emotional barb. When, Reese wonders, did Katrina learn to dress up her feelings like that? Was it a defense or a skill, or maybe both?

Reese presses her fingers against the cold panes of glass to peer down over the balcony into the concrete bottom of the gloomy air shaft. Beside Reese, the plants Katrina has hung to catch the daylight that penetrates the air shaft at certain hours give off a lush, living scent. The air in the apartment is thick and dark, but soothing, as on a forest floor.

"You're a sad divorced lady susceptible to nineties *Friends* nostalgia? But I thought you left him?" Reese asks.

"I did. But that doesn't mean I didn't suffer over it and want comfort and familiarity. Every time he told me I was making a mistake, I believed him—I just believed it was a mistake I had to make."

Reese understands exactly. She tells Katrina, "You should paint the walls purple. Weren't the walls in Monica and Rachel's place some awful nineties color scheme? Purple and green or something?"

Katrina makes a face. "Gross! I would never!"

Katrina's kitchen and living area are one big room with high ceilings, just as in the *Friends* apartment set, only the room is smaller, and Katrina's kitchen has a counter dividing it from the living space.

With a little click, Katrina ignites the flame of a stick lighter and touches it to the wicks of a clutch of candles in jars hunched together on the counter. Satisfied with the lighting effect, she picks up the plate on which she has arranged the sushi and carries it into the living area. On the plush cream rug beside the coffee table, she kneels, places the plate on the floor, then quickly grabs it again, and pops back up, turns, and puts it on the little table in the eating area beside the kitchen.

Reese watches this maneuver bemused. "What was that cute detour on the way to the table?"

Katrina reddens a little. "I like to eat on the floor when I'm by myself. I call it an indoor picnic."

"That's adorable. We can have an indoor picnic if you like that."

Katrina shakes her head. "No, I'm silly."

Reese leans over the counter and grabs the ramekins, places them on the rug, and settles in beside them. "I'm going to have an indoor picnic," she announces, looking over to Katrina at the table. "I know you want to join me."

Katrina gives a shy but pleased smile. The backs of her knees push away her chair as she rises. She carefully picks the sushi plate back up, then bends and sets it in front of Reese before lowering herself onto the rug, so that her bare feet, toes polished dark red, are tucked sideways behind her butt, and her body weight rests on a hip. "When I first moved in here," Katrina explains, "my ex kept most of the furniture. We bought it all to fit our old place. I was the one who was leaving, and I didn't feel entitled to take what seemed to belong to that other space—or if I had, it would have felt mean-spirited. So I didn't have anything and ate sitting on the floor the first weeks I was here. The first night, I remembered that once when I was a little girl, we had to leave our house because it needed some structural repairs. My parents rented a place in Burlington, which was supposed to be furnished but wasn't. It was too expensive to get furniture just for two months' rental. But instead of showing me her worry, my mom told me that on very special occasions, a family could have indoor picnics. She put the food on a tray and spread a blanket over the bare linoleum, and made like it was just as fun as eating in a park. When Dad came home a week or two later with a table he'd scrounged somewhere, I was disappointed. When that memory came back to me I cried, maybe 'cause of the divorce, maybe just because of nostalgia. Now, when I'm alone, I prefer to eat on the floor and think of my mom."

This is the moment when Reese names the sudden softness and need that she has been developing for Katrina a "mom-crush."

Is there such a thing as a mom-crush? Certainly there is a friend-crush, and of course, a typical crush-crush, but Reese would call what she feels for Katrina a mom-crush. Every morning for more than a week now, she has woken up thinking about being a co-mom with Katrina, picturing her future self five years hence, in hopeful domestic scenes. For instance, this very day, on the way to Katrina's, she imagined Katrina and herself in the grocery store, deciding whether or not it is okay to make Kraft mac and cheese for their child. Her own mother often made Kraft mac and cheese, tossing in a half stick of butter and pouring in whole milk, so that the barely curled macaroni noodles shone creamy in their fluorescent-orange glow. Once, her mom made real baked mac and cheese, with white cheddar and breadcrumbs on top. Reese turned her nose up at it, spooked by the pale color of the cheese. Five years from now, Reese imagines, Katrina will argue for making real mac and cheese for their child, and Reese will have to explain that no, Kraft mac and cheese is the pinnacle of food science, and one does not forsake the pinnacle of food science merely because it is unnatural.

The imagined scene animates Reese, and helps shush the whispers of a new fear: that Katrina, in her own subtle late-thirties flailing, harbored fantasies that queerness would save her. That in the whirlwind of divorce, pregnancy, and unexpected transsexualism, Katrina had become unmoored, and, drifting and fumbling in the darkened water of a fallen heterosexuality, had brushed against an opportunity for queer parenting and held fast to it. There was a utopic aspect to the way that Katrina talked about co-parenting, the way that recently out queers proclaimed their romantic loves and predilections with the most fervor, still innocent of the thorns inherent to queer life. In her more paranoid, cruel moments, Reese braced herself for Katrina's coming abandonment, the way that a queer girl tries to moderate her desire for the heterosexual college girl who has been excitedly returning her kisses in the wake of an asshole boyfriend leaving her.

But after that adorable little indoor picnic thing? The image of a future together that it conjured? Fine, Reese gives herself permission to stop resisting. She's never had a mom-crush before! Yes, all her past crushes turned sour and curdled into resentment or addictive limerence, but they weren't mom-crushes, were they? Maybe a mom-crush was all she ever needed, and if not, who cared that maybe she was lying to herself? Let that hunger—for a family, for a child, for others to make a place in their lives for her—quiet itself a spell in anticipation of a coming satiation. Sometimes the wonder over the object of a crush is indistinguishable from the simple relief that you are still able to leap into one at all.

A week later the two women walk into Buy Buy Baby, a two-story chain store that sells motherhood as a lifestyle. As the automatic doors shush closed behind them, Katrina slings her jacket over her purse, and then, to Reese's surprise, takes Reese's hand in her own, and intertwines their fingers. It creates, to Reese, a confusingly dyke-coded moment: two women walking into a Chelsea store to create a baby registry.

The suggestion that their new partnership, that of raising a child, could bleed into romance has haunted the past few weeks. Katrina

and Reese had even begun to joke together about the necessity of
Ames to the project—that perhaps he had already made his big
"contribution," and they could take it from here.

This hand-holding, however, is the first time that Katrina has
initiated any kind of intimate touch. Reese isn't sure how she feels
about it. Maybe Katrina herself needs the emotional support physically, and Reese wonders whether, in proper lesbian fashion, they
really ought to stop and process this moment.

But Katrina isn't stopping: She keeps a firm grip on Reese's hand
and leads her past a fleet of strollers, where a few of the particularly
sporty models stand spotlit on pedestals, the way a dealer's prize
Corvette lords it over the anonymous sedans at the Chevy show-
room. Past the strollers, following a fence that encloses what seems
to be an acre of baby clothing, stands a lounge adorned with a large
REGISTRY sign. There, a young woman in a flowered blouse sits
behind a large desk. The woman doesn't yet look old enough to be
a mother herself, which Reese finds comforting—perhaps without
personal mothering experience, this woman will not detect Reese's
motherly lack. Katrina, still holding Reese's hand, announces their
intention to create a baby registry with the tone a groom uses to
claim that he and his betrothed shall be wed on the morrow. The
woman behind the desk surveys the apparent couple standing before her with a practiced nonchalance, offers them water, and leads
Katrina and Reese to a low couch in a little lounge area beside her
desk. There, she hands them a tote bag of brochures, free samples of
baby goods, and a large bar-code scanner. Katrina eyes the scanner
doubtfully, and the woman explains that any item in the store that
they scan will be immediately added to their baby registry.

The vibe of the little in-store lounge reminds Reese of her visits
to a medical spa for Botox or laser. There lingers the faint suggestion that this is a place where other women understand what you as
a woman might need and will be prepared to provide it to you—but
with the good taste and discretion never to ask directly what might
bother you about your body.

"I just have to put down some information," the woman says. "Starting with your due date?" Reese realizes that the woman is speaking to her. That between Katrina's business attire and Reese's loose dress, these two lesbians have a quasi butch-femme thing going, and the femme is the one assumed to be with child.

Katrina also realizes this, but rather than correct the woman, she gives Reese's hand a squeeze and says, "When did the doctor say?" This is a little gift from Katrina, a tiny way of sharing the pregnancy. The only problem is that Reese doesn't remember Katrina's exact due date. "Ummm," says Reese, stretching it out, waiting for something to come to her, or something else to happen.

"Was it the fifth? December fifth?" Katrina interjects, the threat of a smirk hovering at the edges of her face.

"Yes," Reese says after a moment of hesitation, "that was it, December fifth."

"Great, December fifth," says the woman. She approves. That gives them plenty of time to fill their registry.

The idea to create a baby registry came from Maya. The week before, Katrina had a Skype call with her mother scheduled for a time when Reese happened to be over at her apartment. In a seemingly spur-of-the-moment tone, Katrina asked to introduce the two of them.

Reese's first instinct was to decline. Unfortunately, there was no graceful way to say no. Especially since Katrina attributed her mother's new West Coast chill as instrumental in recognizing how raising a child with Reese and Ames might actually be a situation Katrina had been looking for all along, but been blinded to by her heteronormativity. That was the word Katrina had started to use— "heteronormativity"—which Reese figured must be a new arrival to Katrina's everyday vocabulary. Katrina had learned the word, but not yet the queer cynicism that made such words impossible to say aloud without first dunking them in a bath of irony. But whatever! If heteronormativity was what allowed Reese and Maya to enthusiastically endorse transsexual co-parenting, then let's all get tickets to heteronormativity!

"Of course, I'll meet her," Reese said, pushing down her reluctance. "I'd love to! She'll be our child's grandmother. Just let me maybe touch up some makeup beforehand?"

Katrina shook her head, excited. "You look great! Anyway, she doesn't care about that."

"No, but I care," Reese insisted. "Please. It'll give me better confidence."

On Katrina's laptop, Reese saw an attractive and plump woman, wearing black-framed glasses and a wrap blouse in white. Reese couldn't track much physical resemblance between Katrina and Maya, but after a few minutes, shared gestures and expressions began to pop up. Maya had been holding her phone in her hand to talk initially, but eventually set it down wide-screen on a coffee table, propped up on something, creating a tableau. Maya sat back on a plush white sofa with her legs and bare feet curled beneath her. Light streamed in through a window offscreen, illuminating her face and hair from one side; behind her was a bright open kitchen, with what appeared to be pots hanging from an indoor trellis. The scene was very California chic, which, since Maya was an interior decorator, must of course have been intentional. As she talked, Maya ran her fingers through her thick hair, and flipped it from side to side, which increased the sense of her luxuriating in her surroundings.

She kept the conversation to a get-to-know-you talk, and then recounted for her daughter a new installment in an ongoing saga with a difficult client up in Mendocino who wanted to turn one of the crumbling old wind pumps on his property into a meditation room. Reese felt a little jet of jealousy fire up at the way these two women chatted: their easy familiarity, barely sketched allusions to past events. Reese had never had a breezy conversation with her mother, much less talked frequently enough that either could just drop in on events of each other's lives. She wondered if this was what her relationship with Maya would be like? She could barely imagine a relationship at all. She'd never had a mother-in-law. She'd never even met any of her boyfriends' parents. Amy had kept Reese away from her own mother, ostensibly for Reese's protection. At some point in one of her stories, Maya cut herself off, "Oh, I finished that book you sent me! Last night. Reese, did you read it?"

"Which book?" Reese asked. She had only been half paying attention.

"Confessions of the Other Mother," Maya replied.

"My copy is on the shelf by the kitchen," Katrina added helpfully and pointed. "It's essays by non-biological lesbian moms. They write about how the second mom gets treated. I know you worry about that, so I wanted to be sensitive to that. The book was good, so I ordered Mom a copy too." Katrina had a way of making her voice soft when she was feeling her own compassion.

In the kitchen, Reese's knees popped as she crouched by the shelf to locate the book: a pastel-yellow cover and an illustration of a bullet bra and a pacifier. She flipped it over and read the blurb. *These tales examine what it means to be mom and not-mom at the same time . . . the feelings of envy and loss of would-be but infertile mothers learning to accept their easily pregnant partners.*

Maya had read this? Katrina had read this?

Reese felt seen, even exposed.

Still, despite her mom-crush, the label of Lesbian Mom struck Reese as off-key. She couldn't quite fake politeness through her vague dismay at yet another suggestion that her own journey into queer parenting must begin with advice from the cis lesbians who disdained her motherhood. Why, whenever she proclaimed her desire for motherhood, did people point her to a political movement that had banked thirty years making it clear that it didn't want her around? Also, more obviously and perhaps pertinently, she had never slept with Katrina and had no plans or desire for that. They were not a lesbian couple. They were a mom-couple, with mom-crushes. Very different. It was important that Maya understand that.

"Actually," Katrina said from the couch with her virtual mom, "Ames picked that one out."

Ames has, of late, been brainstorming prodigiously about the logistics of their triad. He has taken to saying that every generation must reinvent parenting, and he, Reese, and Katrina, will be part of their own generational reinvention. As part of his brainstorming, he told Katrina about a friend of his and Reese's in Chicago, a successful doctor named Quentin. Quentin was a trans guy with a long-term cis boyfriend. After Quentin got a plush job at the downtown campus of Northwestern Memorial Hospital, he bought a gorgeously crumbling Victorian in Rogers Park—the nondescript northernmost neighborhood along the lakeshore of Chicago. The house had its own little compound, with a small yard surrounded by a rotting fence through which neighborhood kids would slip to pass down a path that ran alongside the adjoining building and allowed them to trespass onto one of the few private beaches in the whole city. After he bought the house, Quentin had the interior remodeled into two living spaces, one upstairs and one downstairs, each with its own living room, kitchen, and master bed and bath, just as anyone would do in order to divide a house into a duplex. But instead of adding any doors between the two units, they were openly joined by a grand wooden stairway that traversed the two open shared living areas, both with fireplaces and exposed beams. When the remodel was done, Quentin and his boyfriend moved in downstairs, and a lesbian couple—Irene and Heidi—settled in upstairs. The cis boyfriend donated sperm to each of the two women, and they simultaneously each carried a child—a boy, Ambrose, and a girl, Justine—born a few weeks apart. The foursome raised the two kids together, the dads downstairs and the moms upstairs, with the two children having the run of the place, moving freely up and down the stairs between dads and moms, always with a grown-up around to pay them attention or answer a question or look at a drawing or whatever. Quentin and the other adults all took the last name they gave the children, so any of them could show up at any official proceeding, and the name alone would confer parenthood.

Most intriguingly, the parents never told Ambrose and Justine that this kind of family unit wasn't how most or even *any other* families had arranged themselves. So until the siblings went to school, they understood their family as the norm and, by that point, had so incorporated the idea of four parents into their concept of family that they seemed to feel an assured smugness at their abundance of parents compared with their schoolmates' paltry one or two.

Quentin, however, kept the setup quiet—a queer familiar version of stealth. He was an unassuming patriarch, content to revel in what he had made for himself, tacitly rejecting any calls to explain himself—other families were not required to explain their existences, and so neither would he. What Reese and Amy gleaned was primarily through observation—what they saw over the course of a few evenings early on in their dating life, when they visited with a friend of Amy's who had grown close to Quentin.

"It's just that, sometimes if you can imagine the concrete logistics of a situation," Ames said to Katrina when Reese was over with the two of them. "You can then begin to envision yourself in it."

"But what exactly are the logistics to envision, Ames?" Katrina asked. "That's where I get hung up. Are you suggesting we remodel a house? That our situation needs an architectural solution?"

"Well, that's why I mention Quentin—" Ames began, but without even planning to, Reese cuts in.

"No."

"No, what?"

"I'm not doing that. Even if you magically had a mansion to divide into two, I'm not living in the basement, or whatever, while you and Katrina cohabit above me. That is humiliating."

"Look! Forget the house! I'm not talking about a house. I'm saying if we want to break an old pattern, we need to envision a new pattern in its place. If we want to break the pattern of typical two-parent, even queer two-parent nuclear families, we have to think through the logistics of the replacement. I'm not one of those people who thinks all problems get solved by some human-centered design. We're proposing a family, not a tech start-up . . . but it's also true that part of being queer can be a design problem. I mean, Jesus, just look at our sex toys."

He had lots of ideas, many abstract thoughts about parenting, and hypothetical solutions to their dilemma. For instance, he suggested that Reese put her name on the baby's birth certificate, along with Katrina's, so that Reese would be a legal parent, and he would be a parent by blood, each of them establishing kinship in one way or another. He had so many schemes! Enough that Reese began to suspect that his logistics had become a way for him to avoid emotional realities: an eagerness to fix problems rather than feel them. Here's the name of a family lawyer who specializes in queer families. Here's the hormone regimen required in order to induce lactation in trans women. Here's the prescription necessary from Callen-Lorde: Double the estrogen and progesterone doses to mimic the levels of pregnancy. Here's an order of domperidone from an online Canadian pharmacy to increase prolactin levels.

Katrina would run Ames's ideas by her mother, which at first alarmed Reese, then slowly she began to feel good about it. This is how families work! This is what she was always missing! A mother to oversee her mothering. Yes, of course! How lucky to have Maya.

Which was why, in their initial conversation, when Maya told them to stop listening to Ames, Reese laughed and agreed.

"He has too many ideas!" Maya said. "It's all so abstract! Even this book! So abstract! When it's three in the morning and the baby is crying or sick, and you are bone-tired, who cares what your family structure looks like? All three of you are going to be too tired to care whose name says what on what legal piece of paper."

"I'm already getting too tired to care," interjected Katrina with her hand on her stomach. For once rather than jealousy, Reese felt compassion. She'd seen Katrina in the mornings now, fatigued by that first trimester.

"You know what you two should do?" Maya advised. "Go make a baby registry. When you're in the store together, looking at cribs and clothes, you'll get a much clearer idea of each other's mothering styles. You'll see where you're compatible and where you're going to fight. Because you will certainly fight. I promise. Stop philosophizing about the meaning of family. Get a jump-start on the real work of making one."

"That's a good idea," Katrina said, and Reese nodded.

"Yes, I know it's a good idea! You should listen to your mother more! Maybe if you put something appealing on the registry, I'll even approve of it, and generously get it for you." She winked, and Reese, in that moment, wanted to be her daughter.

So now here are Katrina and Reese, scanning bar codes on swaddlers and wearable blankets. Even perusing the socks area had brought them close to choice overload. Who knew infants needed so many styles? Especially since it seemed that a baby would outgrow each sock size in a matter of months. In front of a stand of socks for nine-month-olds, Reese experiences a wave of sentimentality for the impossibly tiny infant socks. *Where does the time go; the days when her baby's feet could be measured by her thumb were so few, so precious,* she imagines she will one day lament.

"Oh my god," Reese tells Katrina. "I'm, like, missing the days when our baby was just an infant, and she's not even born yet."

Reese and Katrina tend to use "she" pronouns for the baby, even though they had yet to find out the sex. Katrina has a pretty solid grasp on the difference between sex and gender and Reese isn't one to think that sex doesn't matter. Even if her kid turns out to be trans, it's helpful to know in which direction that trans will travel.

"Premature nostalgia is better than what I'm feeling."

"What are you feeling?"

"Consumer fatigue. I knew this shit was going to be expensive, but oh my god, looking at this crap, it's overwhelming. UGG makes fucking baby shoes! Fifty-five dollars!"

"For Sale: Baby UGGs, never worn."

"We are living the saddest short story ever told," Katrina snorts, then points to the swaddlers. "Can we just dress her in those wearable blankets for the first year? It's not like she's going to care if she isn't in designer clothes, and it'll cost a fortune to have to buy all this every three months. Let's just put her in blankets, they'll last longer."

Reese shrugs. Now that she has seen that Coach makes little baby shoes, her inner brand whore is crying out to scan them onto the registry. But, really, it would just be in terrible taste to let her first mothering disagreement with Katrina be over whether or not to dress their kid in designer brands. They'd have all of the teenage years for that shit.

Downstairs, a glass case displays the breast pumps: sleek electronic affairs that look as though they've been designed by Steve Jobs–era Apple. Smooth, white curves, with a minimum of buttons.

"Fancy! They even have an app! Can we share one?" Katrina asks. "Or do we each need our own?"

"We should each have one," Reese says. "For two reasons. One, you have cooties. And two, we don't know what the living situation is going to be, and neither of us wants to take the G train to pump every night."

Katrina had been surprised when she learned that trans women could make milk. Reese had grown uncharacteristically shy when Katrina asked questions, and it was Ames who ended up explaining the hormone regimen that made it happen. The reason why Reese knew how to produce lactation in trans women was too confusing in the context of actual breastfeeding. The majority of discussions about Reese's own capacity to lactate had all been with men. Men who were all fascinated by it—probably because it meant somewhere, deep down, they understood that their bodies too had that potential. In fact, in a drawer somewhere, Reese already had a breast pump, a gift from the cowboy who wanted to include it in their mommy-pregnancy role-play. But that pump was manual.

Together, Reese and Katrina decide on identical baby-blue Spectra automatic breast pumps, the kind with a rechargeable battery. And this choice, made with their bodies pressed close and faces near to each other in order to read the informational placard, contemplating the future care of their breasts, forms one of the most unexpectedly intimate moments of Reese's life.

Sometimes, Reese wants to talk with Katrina about the eroticism of motherhood. Even this store. Look at it! A sanctum of femaleness, of private domestic acts. Maternity clothes to cover a changing body. Photos and products designed to encourage touch, nurturing, care. Everything packaged in the same soft, pale pastel colors women choose for lingerie when the male gaze is subtracted from the equation. The ghost scent of baby powder dusting the space. Queers—hell, even straight people—had all begun to call each other "daddy" in bed, but for Reese, there had never been a word more taboo, more soft, more intimate than "mommy." If masculine displays of overt horniness have always been more celebrated than their feminine counterparts, the mommy vs. daddy dirty-talk dichotomy only heightens that disparity.

Katrina must have been thinking something parallel. Something about protective female allegiances, the pleasure of cultivating shared nurturing devotion. "This is nice," Katrina tells Reese. "Being here, doing this with you. I would run screaming from this store if I had to do this on my own. My friends who have babies complain to me about it being lonely. Their bodies are like these miracles—they are amazed with themselves, anxious and excited. And their husbands don't get it. My friend Beth, her husband drinks a lot, and once she asked him to lay off of it while she was pregnant, and he got furious. He was like, 'What does you being pregnant have to do with me drinking? Why should I have to stay in?' He thought it was *unfair*."

"I have the opposite problem," Reese says. "I'd be happy if you shared even more than you do. I want to know everything about your pregnancy, because then it feels like mine too, but asking makes me feel weird and like I'm prying about your body."

"That's perfect because I'm probably just going to keep complaining more and more. Starting a couple weeks ago, brushing my teeth has made me feel like I'm going to puke, and I've been suffering through that in silence because it feels too banal to bitch about."

"Girl, bitch away."

"I won't take you for granted. I promise. It's so good to be here with you. My friend Diana has been having IVF treatments and she's so worried and also so alone. They managed to get three embryos fertilized, and she's already emotionally attached to them. This is their second round of IVF. The first time, when one of the embryos got damaged in the freezing process—she called me crying, sobbing like she'd lost a child. It was really pretty heartbreaking and her husband acted like she was being crazy and irrational. The day they transferred an embryo she had to tell him not to be an emotional moron, because he had made plans to go indoor rock climbing that night. She was like, 'You are staying in with me and your maybe-unborn-child tonight' and he was like, 'But, babe, your procedure is in the morning, and my plans aren't until five.'"

Reese snorted at the idiocy of men. Ames, at least, had spent enough time as a woman not to totally revert to complete emotional tone deafness. In fact, she supposed that's why he hadn't come today, why he had been giving Katrina and Reese their space. Had he been there, Reese might have slipped into the role of resentful third wheel. No, in fact, his stereotypical male absence was probably an act of astute emotional perspicacity on the order of Amy's. Maybe, gender aside, he'll be a good dad.

·   ·   ·

"What do you think of this crib?" Katrina asks. They have wandered into the furniture area. She runs her hand along the rail of a stark white crib that comes paired with a matching changing table. The crib is designed by a Danish company. Scandinavians seem to have cornered a disproportionate slice of the high-end baby product market.

"Oh, I didn't think we'd use a crib," Reese says offhandedly. "I never had one."

"Of course we need a crib. Where will she sleep otherwise?"

"In bed. Babies are happier in bed with their parents."

"What? No way. That's how babies get crushed. You roll over on them in your sleep."

Reese feels a flash of irritation. This is something Reese knows about. For all her mother's absences, her carelessness about the task of child-rearing, Reese's mother had insisted on the danger of cribs. It was the one thing her mom was very proud of—she had Reese in bed with her all through Reese's infancy. It was an eighties parenting thing. Babies shouldn't be alone at night. Later on, certain science confirmed it: Babies in cribs in the other room had elevated cortisol levels, and some childcare experts theorized that infants exposed to stress hormones nightly at such a formative age could end up locking in baseline stress levels for a lifetime.

"When I worked childcare, I talked about this with mothers," Reese says. "It stresses babies out to be separated at night. You give them separation anxiety. There were studies, even. It's also way better for the mom. When you have to nurse, you just sleepily hold the baby, and then fall back asleep. Getting up, putting something on, sitting up, that makes you wake up completely. It fucks up your sleep rhythms. Besides, the only times people roll over on babies is when they are drunk or high."

Katrina makes a face. "What do you mean when you worked in childcare? I thought you worked at a gym daycare."

"I did! That's childcare."

"It's not exactly the same as a degree in child psychology."

That was mean. No, she doesn't have a degree. Obviously Reese knows her own credentials. Reese chews her lower lip. She wants to say something cutting, but the hurt has come out of nowhere. Instead she looks away, staring hard at a rocking chair. The intimacy of the store dissipates, leaving in its place a cold, stupid, and banal consumer trap.

"I'm sorry," Katrina says. "I'm grumpy."

Reese nods, but still refuses eye contact.

"It's just that we have to do things the same way," Katrina says by way of apology. "We can't have a crib at my place, and she sleeps in your bed with you. We need consistency."

And this is Reese's whole complaint. That in the end, when it comes to final say in how the baby will be raised, Katrina, the natal mom, will have that last word. Second-place mom, Reese, would be allowed suggestions only.

Reese responds as she so often does when she finds herself in a position of strategic weakness: with a combination of passive aggression and grudging submission. She raises the bar-code scanner and pulls the trigger. It emits a little beep as a complicated network meshes to send the important data through space and time: Enter one Danish crib to a particular registry.

"Thank you," says Katrina.

That night, Reese sits at the little glass laptop desk in her bedroom, logs in to buybuybaby.com, and sees that Katrina has removed the crib from their registry.

CHAPTER TEN

Eleven weeks after conception

A SLEEK WOMAN OPENS the door of the apartment. She wears ripped jeans and a loose tank top, woven of some mutant technical performance cotton. Her hair is up in a clip, and perched on a delicate nose are a pair of swoopy black-framed glasses that angle along the same steep slope of her cheekbones. The combination of hair and glasses together gives the impression of a costume chosen for an extremely sexy woman to wear in order to indicate that, no, it's not what you think, dear viewer: This woman is smart! As is always intended with that disguise, Reese couldn't help notice that this woman is, in fact, very sexy.

"Come in, you two!" cries Sexy-Smart, and she welcomes Reese with a hug that, in its unexpected affection, Reese would put somewhere between suddenly discovered long-lost relative and cult leader thanking you for your impending sacrifice. The woman introduces herself as the host of the party.

"I love your place," Reese says generically, without even yet having fully stepped inside, simply noting how from the door, in the evening angle of the light, the windows made long boxes of illuminated gold that draped diagonally over invitingly feminine living room furniture. Sexy-Smart looks confused.

"This is Kathy's place," she corrects Reese. "I'm Kathy's yoga instructor, but she lets me use her apartment for my dōTERRA parties." She doesn't give her own name.

"Kathy is such a good real estate agent," Katrina says helpfully. "So of course she has a cute place."

That afternoon, when Katrina called Reese to invite her to a dōTERRA party thrown by her real estate agent, who was also one of Katrina's good friends, Reese agreed to attend without totally understanding the situation.

What Reese did understand was that Katrina was extending an invitation for Reese to meet her friends, a variety of invite that almost never came from any of Reese's usual cis crushes. She never met their families or their friends. Never traveled for holidays. The last two Christmases, she did the same thing: bought a tiny pine tree, set it on her dresser, and decorated it with a string of lights from her local dollar store. Then she spent Christmas Eve alone, thinking about her erstwhile lovers while taking selfies reading beside the tree, as evidence for the trial in which her counsel would plead that no, Reese was not sad, she didn't care about being alone, like that famous t-shirt said, she was SINGLE AND LOVING IT.

Therefore, although Reese played it cool, the lifting of the quarantine between Reese and the rest of Katrina's friends carried momentous and solemn import.

It was only on the way to the party that it occurred to Reese that she had no idea what a dōTERRA party was. "What's a dōTERRA?" Reese asked.

"It's an essential oil company," Katrina said. "We'll have to sit through a presentation, but at the end, I think we make face scrubs."

This information did not illuminate the situation for Reese. Making face scrubs with a real estate agent? Is this cis culture? What's next week? Nail art with your financial planner?

"I have to admit," Reese now confesses to Sexy-Smart Yoga Instructor, "I don't know dōTERRA."

Sexy-Smart beams at Reese; she has that habit of charmingly touching the person whom she addresses on the arm. "Oh! A virgin. Don't worry, I'll take care of you." She winks. You really must be sexy to successfully land such a nakedly mercantile wink on a target like Reese. But this woman lands it, and Reese, despite all her cynicism and familiarity with informal sex work, can't help but experience a moment of involuntary relief and gratitude that she will be losing her dōTERRA virginity to such an amazing woman.

By the time that Reese has munched on some appetizers and had a glass of chardonnay, she's gathered that dōTERRA is another entry in the ranks of companies reliant on a model of party-plan direct sales—it's like Cutco knives, Mary Kay, or Tupperware— only it targets, with its upscale essential oils, the anxiety of those wellness-obsessed women who are just a little too beholden to middle-class propriety to permit themselves to take up crystals and anti-vaxxing screeds. So Reese will be sold essential oils this evening. She doesn't even mind. She's just happy to meet Katrina's friends, discussing either kitchen remodels, recalcitrant husbands, or recalcitrant children. As they mill about, they do not have the air of tremendously moneyed people, but Reese detects that alien assurance of educated folks who have always had jobs, or at least a clear path to earning. A temporality that said yes, another paycheck will arrive somewhere soon on your way to the next life event.

Ensconced in a nook by the window, snacking off a plate of crudités, Katrina confides to Reese that she and some of the others are trying to be supportive of Kathy, who has been getting into some weird intersection of capitalism and witchy shit, post-breakup with her long-term boyfriend. "We did a sound bath last month," Katrina whispers confidentially. "Fifty bucks each. At this ridiculous, opulent penthouse in Tribeca. We all lay on blankets for ninety minutes, while these people that Kathy met at Burning Man came and played steel drums arrhythmically and held tuning forks above our heads. They said the vibrations would clear our auras."

"Did it work?" Reese asks.

"At one point the Irish lady with dreads playing a steel drum, the one leading the ceremony, instructed us that we should 'follow the psychic dolphins through the crystalline waters of our minds.'" Katrina repeats this phrase in a surprisingly good Irish accent. "This older woman next to me snorted derisively, which broke the spell.

She was like, 'Really? Mind dolphins?' and I started giggling and couldn't stop, for like a half hour. I don't know when the last time that happened to me was, but that much giggling was totally purifying. I left with a very purified aura."

"It's nice that you support her," Reese says.

"Kathy is a sweetheart." Katrina shrugs. "She was my friend before she was my real estate agent. We've known each other for a long time. Some of her family is still in Taiwan, and when I went on a business trip there two years ago, she even came along and they showed us around."

"So everyone is just doing this for Kathy?" Reese asks, waving a hand at the scene around her.

"Just the women I know. I think the others want essential oils. They really do smell nice."

A few moments later, Reese finds herself included in a conversation with Kathy herself, who does not look witchy at all; she looks like a real estate agent—which of course she is—the kind of blandly pretty face that belongs in a headshot beneath a photo of your suburban house. Another youngish woman, who speaks in a husky, honeyed voice—though Reese can't tell whether from chardonnay or habit—is recounting with excitement that her husband will be away at a bachelor party that weekend. The party is somewhere upstate, and the woman works herself up describing her husband in flannel, drinking whiskey, and tacitly, of the anticipation of his returning home, smelling of woodsmoke and replenished masculinity, to ravish her. The woman wears an immaculate cream skirt, so crisp it looks freshly starched, even though she claims to have come directly from work. There is an audacity in wearing a cream skirt so crisp: Cream is even less forgiving than white; a single stain on cream and the whole skirt looks vaguely dirty, whereas a single stain on white just looks like a single stain. Reese once read in a fashion magazine that, at the turn of the century, the leisure class wore immaculate whites to show that they did no work, the same-classed fashion that gave the feminine gender heels, corsets, and long nails. Thus, Reese has to surmise that this cream-skirted woman has not actually married a ranch hand, so most likely, her husband is another NYC white-collar worker.

How is it, Reese wonders, that a bunch of New York men wearing flannel and slamming whiskey in a cabin is seen as a sorely needed release of their barely tamed and authentic manliness, but when she, a trans, delights in dolling up, she's trying too hard? It's not that Reese thinks her desire to dress up reflects some authentic self. It's just that, unlike bros, she's willing to call dress-up time what it is. Meanwhile, this starched woman has practically soaked her panties over the homoerotic escapades of her man upstate. Can you imagine if Reese confided in these women, with the same apparent horniness, about her Truvada birth control regimen? Social disaster! She decides for the ten thousandth time that heterosexual cis people, while willfully ignoring it, have staked their whole sexuality on a bet that each other's genders are real. If only cis heterosexuals would realize that, like trans women, the activity in which they are indulging is a big self-pleasuring lie that has little to do with their actual personhood, they'd be free to indulge in a whole new flexible suite of hot ways to lie to each other.

Sexy-Smart clinks on a wineglass with a spoon to ask for everyone's attention, which mercifully averts Reese's building desire to tender her opinions on gender to someone. "And now, the moment we've been waiting for," Sexy-Smart says seductively, although, from the way that the women seem content to stay in the kitchen eating snacks, there is no way that anyone has been waiting for this moment. "We can move to the living room for the dōTERRA essential oils demonstration!"

Shuffling with the herd into the sunset-drenched living room, Reese and Katrina take a comfortable love seat, and the other women settle in on the couch, chairs, and plush rug, in the way Reese remembered from middle school sleepovers, everyone finding a spot to watch the TV. Only instead of a TV there's Sexy-Smart handing out brochures, and instead of blankets or pillows, each woman sets beside her a designer leather tote handbag in differing brands but the same essential boxy style, the sort that gets sold at Nordstrom to women who aspire to vacation in the Hamptons. Reese feels entitled to be judgy about boxy tote handbags, because she herself carries at that moment her own boxy Coach tote and her secret self aspires to aspire to vacation in the Hamptons.

Sexy-Smart opens a copy of the brochure she has passed out, indicates a blank box, and tells the assembled women to write all of their ailments—both physical and mental—within that square.

Nice try, Yoga Lady with the perfect body! No way is Reese going to tell these cis women the stuff that troubles her—lack of womb, desperately sad need for sex with fuckboy men, a sourceless despair that arrives punctually at five o'clock every evening, a weird spot on her inner thigh. Instead she writes *lack of energy*, a compromise in between that she hoped would make her appear flawed and relatable enough to ingratiate herself with Katrina's friends, while revealing a genuine vulnerability. She peeks down at the woman sitting cross-legged on the rug at her feet. The woman has written *binge eating, no sex drive*. The frank confession shocks Reese. A flash of shame for how judgmental she'd been toward these women.

When the other women read their ailments out loud, many of them also share problems that are nakedly vulnerable: depression, back pain, postpartum depression, insatiable appetite, mood swings and irritability, insomnia. Who were these women, who trusted that there wouldn't be some silently judgmental bitch among the others? And what did it mean that Reese was that judgmental bitch? Only Katrina appears to noticeably hedge her vulnerability—*stress at work, hormonal*—and Reese wonders if it was her own caginess that led Katrina to withhold vulnerability in her presence. Reese hasn't been in such a ritualized gathering of straight cis women in a long time. Since when did they have the self-assuredness to trust each other?

Reese listens, trying to understand what is happening. Ultimately she decides that they don't seem to be sharing their problems out of an excess of self-confidence or trust. Mostly they sound weary, near resigned, fanning just an ember of genuine openness to the hope that an essential oil could solve their issues. Which is to Reese, the most incredible aspect of all. How bad must things be to place faith in highly scented snake oil? Reese would expect a similarly motley list of misery in a room full of trans women, but at least trans women—with all the necessary contact to medicalized bullshit that transition entails—would be cagey about sharing their ailments, whether to a doctor of Western medicine or to a huckster of essential oils, no matter how fit either looked in her ripped jeans and tank top. Due to their apparently cushy, enviable, and alien lives, these women haven't developed a morbid and highly skeptical subculture to temper their credulity. She would like to introduce some doubtful lesbians into the next essential oil spiel.

About halfway through Sexy-Smart's sales pitch, a generically handsome and tanned man arrives—the kind of white guy who might have a bit role as a doctor in some television drama.

"As a yoga instructor, I'm not really versed in the medical chemistry of essential oils," the yoga instructor explains to the room with an expression that conveys genuine regret for the inadequacy of her career choice. "So I brought my boyfriend to tell you how essential oils really do work. He is a celebrity acupuncturist and uses dōTERRA essential oils with his patients."

Prior to that moment, Reese had not realized that the adjective "celebrity" applied to acupuncturists.

The yoga instructor steps to stage left of the living room, allowing her boyfriend center stage, in front of the flat-screen TV. "Hi, ladies, my name is Steve. And it's true: I'm an acupuncturist. I practice traditional Chinese medicine." He looks at Kathy as he says this, then smiles. "But some people just call me the most satisfying prick in town."

Reese gapes. Just like that, all of his handsomeness has vanished. Reese waits for one of the other women to tell him off. Do you know what would happen if a man walked into a room of queer women

and declared his prick satisfying? The prospect was hideous to contemplate. Death by outrage. But instead of sentencing him to die by
lethal callout, the assembled women laugh politely. Even Katrina.

Steve winds up into his dōTERRA sales pitch, a narrative about
how his girlfriend, the gorgeous yoga instructor, had been such a
bitch before she started using essential oils. But after she made oils
a daily habit, she chilled out and he liked her much better. Reese
glances around the room—surely now, the women will rise up! The
revolution is now!

The revolution is not now. The women listen, or even nod politely, draped docilely around and below him. Steve stands too close
to one of the women sitting on the rug, in Reese's estimation of
proper personal space. His crotch—the most satisfying prick in
town—bobs at her eye level. He waves his hands as he speaks, and
a few times it seems as though he might pat her on the head. The
woman at Reese's feet, she of the eating disorder and low sex drive,
takes out a pad of paper and makes notes as Steve speaks; very sin-
cere notes, Reese observes, on which oils, in particular, had made
his yoga instructor girlfriend less of a bitch.

At the end of his speech, Steve offers to prescribe the proper essential oil for each of the women's ailments. But with Steve in the
room, the women list different problems than those they'd shared
earlier. When it's Katrina's turn, she smiles, pauses dramatically,
then looks around the room at her friends, making eye contact, then
asks, "What's good for pregnancy?"

A moment of gasps follows, and Steve responds by pointing at
his girlfriend and saying, "Don't give her any ideas." Sexy-Smart
hides a wince.

But then Kathy is half singing, half wailing "Oh my god!" and
getting up and embracing Katrina. Then so is the woman in the
cream skirt, and others that Reese hasn't yet been introduced to.
Even Sexy-Smart, despite her interrupted sales pitch, is cooing and
vying for a hug.

"But who's the father?" Kathy asks, when the cooing dies down.

Katrina points at Reese. A room full of confused faces turns to Reese. Kathy tilts her head, as though trying to look under Reese, for whatever father Reese might be sitting on and hiding.

There is a second in which Reese instinctively fears that she's been outed and says suddenly, "We're co-mothers." Then she says, "But I'm not the actual father." Then, aware of how odd that sounds, she concedes another piece of information: "But I am trans."

If an oracle had foretold that Reese would voluntarily come out at a dōTERRA Essential Oils direct-sales party, she would have understood it figuratively, a puzzle like the one the witches gave to fool Macbeth—because the literal possibility of a forest traveling up a hill existed beyond the realms of even outlandish farce. A dōTERRA-party-coming-out is Reese's Birnam Wood.

Yet now, it has happened. She has come out at a dōTERRA party, although she's not sure what she has come out as, or how much more coming out she still has to go.

There is a moment's silence to take this in. But Kathy, being the hostess, knows exactly what social grace the situation requires and she executes it properly. Which is to say she coos loudly and happily and swoops in at Reese for the congratulatory embrace.

The woman in the immaculate cream skirt (whose name Reese has forgotten and can't bear to ask again, and so she has named her the Empress of Dry Cleaning), Kathy, Katrina, Reese, and two other women have left Kathy's apartment for a café specializing in Italian desserts. It is an impromptu celebration for Katrina's pregnancy announcement. They all smell like essential oils.

Reese has a healthy droplet of peppermint under her nose that Steve wiped there with his bare finger, and which he said would open up her sinuses. Everything smells like freezing candy canes, but since her sinuses weren't stuffy to begin with, she can't opine as to the efficacy of his celebrity medical technique.

The Empress of Dry Cleaning knows the proprietor of the dessert place, a darkly handsome man in his midlife. Fireworks of smile lines burst across his face at every small pleasantry uttered by the Empress. Reese sees the effect the Empress has on the poor man, and really, who can blame him? She must be in her thirties, but it is not just her clothes that are perfectly pressed: Everything about her is apple crisp and seems newly made. Her skin, Reese imagines, must smell like dryer sheets.

He has put the women at a big table by the kitchen, and has been bringing out all sorts of delicate Italian desserts special for them, all of which taste to Reese like York Peppermint Patties dressed up in pretension, although the other less aggressively anointed women note for each other many other complex flavors, none of which are peppermint.

Finally, the Empress of Dry Cleaning announces, "Okay, I can't wait any longer. I have to know everything." She is trying to be excited and bubbly, socially proper for some kind of impromptu baby shower, but the phrasing suggests a note of concern. Katrina explains with much less of a sales pitch than Reese was expecting. It's not exactly like Reese wants Katrina to lie to her friends, but she doesn't even try to soft-pedal it. Reese's sense of her own gender does not allow her to make sports analogies, but like, Katrina is doing the thing where the guy who throws the ball does so with no spin whatsoever. What is Katrina doing? She has to know this is a weird thing to tell her friends. That she had an affair with her employee, who turned out to be hiding that he was a former transsexual woman, which is why he mistakenly thought he was sterile, and now Katrina is going to raise the baby with him and his ex-girlfriend, another transsexual.

Katrina's friends' smiles have dimmed, and the creases of worry between their eyes have deepened.

"It's not as weird as it sounds," Reese says, trying to make her voice bright.

"Yes, it is," Katrina says, "but that's okay; that's what I want to express. That, yes, it's like, not how most people get pregnant, or how most people raise a family. But we've thought it through. It's exciting. I'm excited not to do the heteronormative thing."

And suddenly Reese gets what is happening. That word "heteronormative" reveals the game to her. She thought that she was the one coming out. But no, Katrina is coming out as queer to her friends. That's why she's being so aggressive about it. This is the path of the baby queers. The borderline confrontational assertion: *This is what I am, got a problem with it?* It is delivered with all the zealotry of the recent convert, who has yet to be bludgeoned into weariness and compromise for her ways, who believes that the new religion holds the answers lacking in her old one. Even more revelatory to Reese: Katrina is defiantly *excited*! She thinks this queerness makes her *interesting*!

Katrina's friends trade discreet but doubtful expressions. They are still a few steps behind. "So the man"—Kathy tries—"the father, I mean, he is a man?"

"What?" Katrina says.

"She means is he coming or going?" clarifies the Empress of Dry Cleaning, then adds for Reese's benefit, "No offense."

"It's fine," Reese says. Though she doesn't like it and so says, "He was coming then he was going, but then he came back again. Pretty clear, right?" She smiles sweetly.

Before the Empress can say no, Katrina jumps back in. "He was born a man, and transitioned, then transitioned back."

"So he was cheating on you, Reese, with you, Katrina?" Kathy asks.

"No," says Reese. "We broke up years ago. We dated as women."

"Ah," says Kathy, clearly not getting it. "So how did you, Reese, get back into the picture?"

Before Reese can say anything, Katrina tries again to explain: How she doesn't want to be a single mother. How Ames had suggested a queer family. How actually, queer families have all these opportunities that she didn't realize she was missing back when she was married, and that she sensed were missing in her marriage with Danny. That she always had an affinity for queerness, although because it wasn't cut-and-dry gayness, she had never known what to call it.

Oh, is that how it happened? thought Reese. *Now she's spinning it.* But even more than spinning it, Katrina seemed to believe it. She'd re-narrativized her divorce. Those amorphous diffusely unhappy reasons she needed to divorce Danny? Now it was that she had recognized, but been unable to name, a need for the possibilities of queer relationships.

One of the other women, a cute plump girl, whose dōTERRA confession had been irritation and low moods, broke in. "I feel like I get that. Like, you realize when you get married how much the institution changes things. I remember that in the first few months I was married, how often, if I was out by myself, people would be like, 'Where's Max?' and I would want to be like, 'Max and I have a marriage where we don't have to account for each other.' And maybe I even said that a few times, but eventually, it was just easier to be like, 'He knows I'm out.' Everyone says that you can make marriage what you want, but sometimes the institution of marriage really wins out. It'd be freeing to just make up your own rules."

This, to Reese, was the straightest, most married thing anyone had ever said.

But Katrina says, "Exactly!"

The other women are coming around. Reese sees suddenly why Katrina might be so good at her job. In the span of time it takes to consume a few dessert items, Katrina had begun to convince these women of the soundness of child-rearing with transsexuals.

The Empress of Dry Cleaning is the one holdout. As everyone else offers their tentative endorsements, she frowns as if the thought pains her, and says, "I just don't know. I think everyone wants something queer now. It's like a fad. And a lot of us end up getting hurt."

Kathy pats her hand with sympathy and says cryptically, "That wasn't your fault, you know, but the difference is that Katrina has a choice." At this, at the hint of old gossip, of some past brush with queerness, Reese perks up and looks at the Empress of Dry Cleaning with new interest. She tries to imagine what kind of queerness the Empress could have gotten into. Look at her, she's so fresh and pert—there is no stink of deviance to her at all. Maybe she's the kind to go for some butch player and get her heart broken.

Katrina leans forward toward the Empress. "I know, I know, I was a little worried how you'd take it, but like, this is different, everyone knows what's happening."

"I'm sorry," the Empress says. "I'm trying to be open-minded. Maybe I'm, like, triggered, or something." She gives a wan smile. "Oh god, I'm making this about me. No, that's not okay."

The Empress remains the only woman present with whom Reese has not managed to establish rapport, the only one who looks at her with suspicion. And everyone else regards the Empress with some expression of concern or sympathy. Reese can't quite figure out a way to ask what happened, and so makes a mental note to ask Katrina about the Empress's history with queerness when the two of them are alone.

A half hour or so later, Reese tries to make a show of paying the check, but to her relief, the women deny her this gallantry—each tossing a shiny credit card onto the check. "No," says Kathy, with the social grace that Reese is growing to appreciate from her. "It sounds like you're going to be a mother too, so we ought to be celebrating you as well. No way you're going to pay." Reese is grateful for this too; there has been little talk thus far of Reese's own impending motherhood. As expected, her motherhood is already an afterthought to Katrina's—though she tries to accept that these are Katrina's friends, and so naturally, they would pay attention to Katrina.

As the women rise from the table, Reese glances at the door. She stifles a gasp and reaches out to hold Katrina by the arm. "Wait," she whispers, turning her body so only Katrina can hear. "Wait with me a second."

Katrina frowns. "Are you okay?'

Reese jabs her chin toward the door in a rough gesture. "That's him," Reese says. "That's my cowboy— No! Don't look. Help me decide what to do. Should I say hi? I haven't ever run into him in public before. What is proper affair protocol?"

But Katrina looks at the handful of people lingering over where the cakes shine beneath the glass counter. "Who?"

"The tall guy in the brown jacket. The handsome one with the stubble."

Katrina swallows. "Not the guy, like, between the glass dessert counter and the door?"

"Yeah, that guy. Oh shit, what should I do? Do you think he's here for me?"

Reese has been holding Katrina's arm lightly, and now Katrina steps back suddenly. She regards Reese with a strange, alarmed expression, peering hard, as though at some object disobeying the laws of reality, flickering in and out of this dimension.

Then Katrina turns to the cowboy. He meets her gaze, nods, and smiles amiably. A moment later his eyes flick over to Reese, and his face goes hard. Alarm, then fury, trembles in the briefest of moments through the tiny muscles of his face, before the Empress lays her hand on his arm and leans in for a peck on the cheek, at which he composes himself.

"No, he's not here for you. That's Diana's husband," Katrina says quietly.

Diana, right, that's her name. I guess she has a cowboy after all, Reese thinks inanely. Then the window in which inanity remains a possibility shuts closed—a surge of adrenaline hits, carrying with it a squall of panic. Reese tenses her body, in full fight-or-flight mode—the faces around her blend, break into shapes, and dial back into ultra-sharpened focus. Her evolutionary response has not evolved to meet the moment. Eons of lizard-brain instinct tell her to flee wildly—the exact wrong thing to do. She requires grace or poise or wit. Instead, her body pours on the sweat, her heart rate ascends into the triple digits. In slow time, the cowboy forces his face into a smile for his wife and pushes open the door for her. He turns and catches Reese with a hard questioning look. Then Kathy is behind him, offering up pleasantries, which he gathers himself to return—and then three women in workout gear walk in, blocking Reese's view, and her cowboy is gone.

"He cheated on Diana with a trans woman a year or two ago," Katrina says quietly, from beside Reese. "Was it you?"

"No! No, that wasn't me," Reese says, trying for insistence, but the panic makes her voice waver, as though she isn't sure. She tries to remember if she knew which girl it was. As though if she could name the girl to blame it on, she'd be absolved.

"Diana went to college with me," Katrina says, fidgeting with her purse. "She was my roommate's younger sister. I've known her for a long time. I know most of her family. When he was diagnosed after that affair, it threw everything into turmoil. I thought things were okay now."

"That wasn't me," Reese repeats.

Katrina continues to hold Reese with that strange look. "Maybe it's not your fault. Maybe you couldn't have known. What did he tell you about his wife?"

Reese exhales to calm herself, consciously, she forces her shoulders to release down. "I don't know. He told me some. You know how men are."

"I don't know." Katrina shakes her head. "I don't know if I understand either of you, why you'd do that." The way her wonder shades those words sounds to Reese like doubt, almost a whispered insult.

"Don't tell Diana," Reese says, trying not to plead. "It doesn't have to be a big deal. I can never see him again. It's a dumb affair. People have them."

"I don't know," Katrina says, then repeats, "I don't know. I'm going to call a car. Do you think you could give me some space for a few minutes?"

Reese nods. Outside, she walks past the cowboy and his wife, willing herself to stare at the ground, afraid that recognition might show on her face. Diana, blinding in her gorgeous skirt, calls out a bright goodbye. Reese waves without looking, pointing vaguely. "My car is waiting down the block," she protests lamely, then redoubles her rush away. Around the corner, she ducks into a bodega, breathes deeply by the Doritos. The clerk asks if she's okay, so she nods decisively and grabs two bottles of Corona, in case she needs to get buzzed in the very near future. After buying them, she fumbles them in her purse, and the clerk makes a sour face. Only in leaving does she realize that this makes her look desperate, that it calls attention to her in a way she normally makes a habit to avoid. She still isn't processing information well.

She considers going back to find Katrina, but instead calls her own car. Whenever she tried to mend feelings in the wreckage of a panic, she made things worse. It hurt, the fear, but if she could make it through, experience told her that this could be okay. This is just how things go. It can be salvaged. Nothing has yet happened. She and her lover just locked eyes across a restaurant. No one said anything. It wasn't Katrina's business. Don't panic, don't rush to fix everything. Everyone just use a little goddamn discretion and things will be fine.

What Reese didn't understand but began to grasp as the cramped shared ride disgorged her at her apartment, was that things had already fallen apart. The lack of drama in the moment had suckered her into underestimation. Years of queer meltdowns had convinced her, wrongly, of the unmistakable current of action that accompa-

nies a true meltdown. Like, when Amy punched Stanley. That was
the kind of meltdown Reese had come to expect. Not a series of
glares and a car home alone. No polite manners and certainly not
well-adjusted adult emotional regulation of rage.

The cowboy calls as she cuts a lime for her beer, but she can't
bear facing him right then and lets the call go to voicemail. Then he
texts: *WHAT THE FUCK WERE YOU DOING WITH MY
WIFE*. A follow-up: *Are you a fucking psycho?* Yes, this is more in
line with the drama she expected. The voicemail contains a lot of
shouting about Reese being jealous and trying to ruin his life with
her *Fatal Attraction* bullshit. Reese has never seen *Fatal Attraction*,
so she doesn't totally get the reference, other than to gather it's
clearly another way to call her a psycho. She admires that about her
cowboy: He's something of a cinephile. His message ends with a
warning to stay away from him, and most of all, to stay the fuck
away from his wife. She watches a trailer for *Fatal Attraction* on her
phone, which makes the insult sharper, but also, she can't help but
notice that Glenn Close, the Reese analogue of the movie's affair, is
clearly hotter and more magnetic than whichever actress plays the
threatened wife.

She imagines that her cowboy must be stalking the streets somewhere, shouting in a park. No way could he yell like that in his own
place, with his wife around. She takes her second beer to the window and gazes past her own reflection onto the parked cars. A small
man walks a small terrier of some sort, but otherwise, the sidewalks
are empty. In a moment of fantasy, Reese tries to calculate whether
the cowboy might show up at her place, might try something to hurt
her. But no, that isn't his way. He will simply withdraw himself from
her, withhold himself, perhaps indefinitely. That has always been
the best way to hurt Reese anyhow.

Iris answers the door and glares at Ames from under her rumpled
hair, a silk robe wrapped haphazardly about her. "What the fuck,
Amy, it's one in the morning."

Before Ames can answer, Iris gestures him in.

"Do you think you can wake her? I don't want her to wake up to a man in her bedroom."

Iris rolls her eyes and jerks her thumb. "Up the stairs, Freddy Krueger."

Ames follows Iris down a linoleum corridor and up a flight of stairs, into a cozy space with geometric rugs. "Hold on," Iris instructs, and then goes into a room dimly illuminated with some sort of colored LED lighting, from which Ames hears the murmur of a distinctly male voice, then Iris reemerges and goes into another door. A moment later, Reese comes out, blearily staring at Ames. "What the fuck? It's one A.M."

"Thank you!" Iris says. Then she glances in her room. "Maybe we can both put on some music so we don't hear each other?"

Reese waves her hand. "Yeah, girl, get back to it."

Iris glares once more at Ames then shuts her door behind her.

Reese asks if Ames wants some water. She's wearing a camisole and a pair of cotton sleep shorts. Without waiting for a response she walks past him, trailing a hand on his lightly, then pulls two glasses from a shabby doorless cabinet and fills them in the sink. "You're in trouble with Ir-is," she sing-whispers, drawing out Iris's name.

"Same as always."

"I think you interrupted her mid-fuck." Some sort of slow, bass-heavy darkwave cranks up from behind Iris's door, sex music for goths.

"Well, next time answer your phone. Katrina's flipping out. I wanted to hear from you what's really going on."

Reese hands him a glass of water. "I didn't answer my phone because I finally fell asleep."

Reese takes him back into her tiny room, where there isn't any place for Ames to sit except on the bed beside her. He notes the floral bedspread. It's very girly, and it depresses him. This little room, the hopeful nod to girlishness from a woman he's known for so long.

On a makeup table, he sees the same jewelry chest in the shape of a book, the same chest that she had when they shared an apartment, and the little makeup mirror from Costco. He'd had an identical mirror—they had bought them together.

Reese hands him a pillow, puffs one up for herself and puts it against the wall to lean on. The pillow has little centipede footprints of mascara from her eyelashes. Like always.

"So?" Reese says.

"She's really upset. Can you at least tell me your side of the story?"

"Are you upset too?"

"Yeah. I stormed out, I was furious. With both of you." But he doesn't feel furious. He feels nauseated, needy. He wants to put his face in Reese's lap. For a woman to run her fingers through his hair and say that he has tried so, so hard, that she sees how hard he's tried.

Ames can't find a place to set down the water she gave him, so he drinks it all, then leans over and puts the glass on the floor. Just then, from through the wall, comes a series of cracks, and then the burst of Iris's laughter.

"Oh wow," Ames says. "Is she being flogged?"

Reese shrugs. "I can't see Iris bothering to buy a flogger when guys have perfectly serviceable hands to wear out first."

"Can we take a walk or something?" Ames asks. "This is the exact wrong soundtrack"

"Where to?" Reese answers her own question, "But oh, we could go down to the river? There was a work-stoppage order where they're building the skyscraper, and they have been leaving the fence around it wide open. You can wander right up to the water to get a view of the Midtown skyline."

The tower's skeleton rises huge above the water, dark against an indigo sky. In each of the empty rooms hanging in the air, a light-bulb burns bare, warding off squatters and thrill seekers. From the ground, the visual effect of all those hundreds of suspended bulbs makes it seem as though a firework has been fixed mid-explosion against the night sky.

Reese has thrown on a pair of fleece UGG knockoffs over a pair of pajama pants, and has a lightweight trench coat draped about her shoulders. A breeze abrades the black water's surface, and tiny waves lap against the rocky revetment where Newtown Creek flows into the East River. Reese leads Ames through the construction debris to sit in the lee of the wind behind the sleeping body of a bulldozer. She pulls her knees to her chest, and wraps her long coat around them, making herself into a gray boulder in the dark shadow of the machine. Ames can't help but fastidiously touch the treads of the bulldozer, testing how dirty he'd get leaning against them. With a shrug, he sits beside Reese. "So," he says, "who is this guy?"

Reese peers off over the river toward Manhattan. "He's my boyfriend."

"The way Stanley was your boyfriend?" As Ames says it, an old resentment wells up. A fear that has been with him, and that he's been trying to ignore. He's afraid of Reese's men. The way she finds them, and what she wants from them. The things they can give that she never wanted from him. After Stanley had broken Amy's nose, Reese had apologized, she'd begged, she'd displayed her guilt. But she'd never given Amy what she really needed: the security that it would never happen again. Amy had never trusted that another Stanley wasn't on the way, invited in by the woman who supposedly loved Amy, a man ready to call her a faggot and break her face. And she was right to be afraid because here he was again, breaking things in new and unexpected ways.

"Is this about Stanley?" Reese says slowly. "Because if it is, then you've already decided what's going on and it's useless for me to explain."

"I can't help feeling that your men, somehow, they always manage to hurt me."

"You can blame me for cheating on you with Stanley, but nothing that came after was inevitable. You detransitioned because of you. Not because of my men. I won't take the blame for that."

"Maybe you made me compete with them."

She peers at him in the dark, then laughs, unhappily. "Is that what this is about? This whole thing? Give me a baby, because none of my men can?"

Ames rubs at the light stubble at the side of his chin, trying not to take the bait. "Will you at least tell me about this guy? So I don't only hear it from Katrina?"

Reese pauses a moment, then accedes. She'll tell him the truth. Why not? So here it is sketched as quickly as she can: her cowboy, what she knows about his wife, how he's the same as all the other guys, hiding her away in hole-in-the-wall restaurants, walking a few feet in front of her in public unless she protests, at which point he protests—unconvincingly—that he is ashamed of the affair, not that she is trans. All the shit that Ames already knew because Ames had lived it, both vicariously and on his own.

"What about the HIV?" Ames asks.

"What?" The question takes Reese aback. "What about it, who cares? I'm on PrEP and he's undetectable."

"Katrina is freaking out about it. She's close with Diana. Apparently she feels like she was the one who picked up the pieces when this guy—what's his name, Garrett or something?—seroconverted. She spent a lot of time up in Diana's relationship. Katrina was going through her divorce, and Diana went back and forth with her a lot about leaving her own husband. He seroconverted with a trans girl, you know."

"Yeah, I know. Again, so what?" Reese feels a surprising pang at the news that Diana considered a divorce. Then she reminds herself that, even if divorced, her cowboy would never have gotten over himself to be out with a trans woman.

"So what," Ames says, "is that Katrina has spent a lot of time hearing about that couple's anguish from Diana's point of view. About some trans girl who ruined her friend's life. And then when they decided to have a baby, Katrina learned about what it means to wash sperm. About IVF treatments. And then, here's you, a trans girl he's cheating with again. Katrina is not taking it well."

"Is she having an AIDS panic or something?"

Ames pauses. "Yeah. She wouldn't call it that. But that's what it is."

Reese snorts. "How retro."

"That's what I told her. She was so starry-eyed these past few weeks. This whole idea that what she'd needed her whole life was queerness. And now she's having the most basic freak-out. Talking how you put yourself and her and the baby at risk."

"At risk of what?"

"HIV I guess?"

"Can you talk her down?"

"I tried. She told me to leave."

Reese closes her eyes and leans back, exhausted. With her eyes still closed, she raises her hand and rubs her eyebrows, unwrinkling a knot of stress. Into her silence, Ames picks up a stone and tosses it toward the river. It falls short. He's angry but doesn't want to show it, especially since he's still all jumbled up over who he's most angry with. "Still, I just can't believe it's happening all over again. Three years ago, you said you wanted to raise a family with me, and I felt like we were going to do that, and then you threw it away with a shitty man. And now, once again, we're on the brink of a family, and you throw it away by cheating with some shitty man. How many times are we going to do this? When are you going to change?"

Two men on dirt bikes drive by the construction site, the flatu-lent engines loud in the night breeze, and Reese lets them pass be-fore she speaks. "I'll change when it's worth it to me to change. The actual question is whether this thing with Katrina is real enough for either of us to bother to change. For you to change too, for you to get back in touch with yourself. For Katrina to change too, because apparently she needs to."

Ames exhales. His shoulder blades hurt where they press against the treads of the bulldozer. "I haven't even told you everything. Katrina asked me to leave because I yelled at her." He picks at some mud on his shoe, collecting himself.

"And why did you yell?" she asks, awaiting the blow.

"Because she was crying and talking about ending the pregnancy."

After Ames walks her home, Reese lays in bed, slowly growing more and more outraged. AIDS panic? Has Katrina been listening to eighties-era Jerry Falwell sermons? It's bad enough that Katrina somehow has entitled herself to feelings about Reese's sex life, to judgments over Reese having slept with some other bitch's husband—but AIDS panic? In a situation in which only one person has HIV and it's undetectable? What the actual fuck?

Her landlord hasn't yet turned off the heat for the season. The pillow in Reese's bed sticks to her face, the sheets cling hotly. She flings off the bedding, opens her one window, turns on a little fan, and flops back facedown, with her arms at her side, beached-seal style. There is no chance that she will be able to sleep. She opens her laptop. She herself has never gone to therapy, but many of her friends have, and they enjoy repeating to whoever will listen the things their therapists say about them. By osmosis, Reese feels that she too has gone to therapy of sorts, and picked up ways to deal with anger and upset. One of her strategies is to write the bad feelings in a letter addressed to the object or source of those bad feelings. The point of the letter is not ever to send it, but to examine those bad feelings.

So Reese drafts an email to Ames and Katrina.

Reese has lived in a queer zeitgeist for so long that those years have honed instincts beyond her conscious control. Just as her fingers know how to apply eyeliner through muscle memory, her queer experience has instilled an instinct toward political righteousness as the surest way to win an argument, even between two individuals. Your roommate wants you to do the dishes? Okay, but doesn't your roommate understand that your mom once worked as a domestic maid (for three months while on a break from college), and, actually, this demand to do dishes is a traumatic attack on your class status and upward generational mobility?

Reese is a veteran of the horrific social gore that results when individuals fight personal battles with unnecessarily political weaponry on a queer battlefield mined with hypersensitive explosives. As a veteran, she usually steers clear of such tactics, an adherent of the Geneva Conventions. Unless of course, in a moment of hurt or outrage or vengeance, her bloodlust gets the best of her and she goes looking for maximum gore. In those cases, she might draft a letter like the one she now writes. A letter that hews to the deadly formula taught to her by her own rare defeats in verbal battle, those rare painful instances when she couldn't help but imbibe her foe's delicious ratio of seventy percent irresistible truth telling to thirty percent emotional poison.

This whole sharing-a-baby enterprise is nothing but an elaborate exercise in the gentrification of queerness. Your whole queer kinship spiel, Ames, is nothing more than an overpriced and underspiced fusion restaurant with Edison bulbs and brightly colored graphic design to allay gentrifiers' fears of foreigners while congratulating them on their culinary adventurousness. Neither of you can handle spice. You can tell, because Katrina is throwing a fit over HIV and infidelity, both of which are delicious for anyone who has a taste for authentic non-gentrified trans flavors.

In fact, HIV is one of the original trans flavors! Check your recipe books. Back in the eighties the big institutions looking at AIDS noticed a population with wildly high rates of infection—a population that wasn't captured in the usual categories of "gay" or "Men Who Have Sex with Men." A certain kind of people slipped through the gaps, people who went by all sorts of names: transvestites, drag queens, sissies, cross-dressers, transgendered, transsexuals, fairies, and on and on. But institutions require categorical names in order to function—the guys at the CDC can't be writing a new grant or reworking studies every time a nancy starts calling herself a nelly. So they assigned a name to this population: the umbrella term "transgender"—and since transgender women wanted access to resources, that's what we ended up calling ourselves. But make no mistake, HIV and the invention of transgender women are inextricable. Transgender is the name selected to recognize a vector of disease.

But maybe it couldn't have been any other way? Don't HIV and gentrification always go together? How else do you forget a plague? Isn't HIV exactly the symbol of an indigestible queerness that even the most assimilated queers haven't figured out how to break down? No, those wounds have never healed, they have only been built over and moved past—only been gentrified. No wonder Katrina choked when she caught even a whiff of HIV flavor.

At this point in her rant, Reese's fury begins to sputter. The more she thinks about it, the more she loses her grip on righteousness, and the more the hurt of betrayal licks at her. Maybe motherhood with Katrina would never have worked in the first place. If Katrina would give up over this, maybe it was inevitable that she would give up at some point anyway—she was just waiting for the spell to break. And Reese doesn't want a fight. She wants Katrina to understand that Reese hasn't done anything wrong—or okay, nothing that is really any of Katrina's business, certainly nothing on the level of ending life plans. They have a child together! Sort of! How could Katrina put their baby at risk? Reese sets her laptop to the side of her in bed, her email still open, half-written. Isn't this what this exercise was for anyway? To burn out her anger before she does something stupid? To show her what really matters? A despondence indistinguishable from sleep overcomes her.

Five hours later, she wakes to the repeated bamboo-clack alerts of her phone as a series of texts from Ames roll in. Clearly he's awoken to his own sense of righteousness, ordering her to fix what she's done, that she needs to apologize if she wants to appease Katrina and remain a potential mother in this situation. His righteousness refuels hers. A strange instinct, one she hasn't before experienced in such a sustained tone, growls low in her chest, an instinct that other women might call the mama bear instinct, but that is too new for her to have named—a vague deep sense that Ames *is threatening her baby.*

Shifting over in the sheets, her shoulder presses against the laptop. She flops over, opens it up to her half-finished letter, and without even bothering to end unfinished sentences or sign it, she hits Send.

She's still lying in bed when her phone announces another text from Ames.

You are such a hypocrite.

Katrina never responds at all.

CHAPTER ELEVEN

Twelve weeks after conception

J ON AND AMES see each other roughly twice a year, whenever something goes wrong in one of their lives. They had been on the baseball team together in college and shared a dorm room their senior year. When they lived together, Jon disliked discussing his emotions with anyone able to cross-check those feelings against the events in his life. Instead, when his emotions got to be too much, he called up another boy who went to school thirty minutes away and they would meet at a café to pour out their hearts to each other over breakfast. After college, Jon moved to New Jersey, where he worked for a family-run architecture firm, at which point Ames became a person who lived at an ideal distance from Jon's daily life to discuss the matter of emotions.

These biannual bilateral feelings summits have been a tradition for nearly fifteen years now—with the exception of a strained period of time during Amy's early transition. Their relationship as buddies could not withstand the threat of heterosexuality. In deference to Amy's professed womanhood, Jon opened doors for her, kissed her cheek in greeting, and complimented her appearance, which, while tremendously sweet, upset them both, and caused them to miss their previous ease and freedom. Theirs had been a masculine bond. Neither responsible for the other. Ames had imagined that were they ever to have been caught in a crisis—say a flash flood—each would swim manfully on his own without even a glance back, secure in the other's competence.

In Amy's transition, this confidence in the other faded. Jon began to wait in a gentlemanly fashion with her outside of restaurants to make sure she got safely into her cab, telling her to text when she got home. On one hand, Amy appreciated that Jon understood that the world is cruel to transsexuals in a manner that it is not with men, but on the other, Amy wished that Jon still regarded her as a co-equal who required no protection.

A year into Amy's transition, Jon got married. His wife, Greta, attempted to make Amy into her friend. She invited Amy to parties in New Jersey and Amy would drink white wine in the kitchen with Greta and the other wives, conflicted: grateful to be included on the correct side of the gender-segregated socializing, while acutely aware that her actual friend was on the other side of the kitchen wall, oblivious to her plight. Eventually, Amy began sitting in the living room with Jon, rather than in the kitchen with Greta, and so Greta stopped inviting her to the parties.

In detransition, their meetings returned to the earlier pattern. Jon accepted Ames as a man once more as readily as he had accepted Amy as a woman. The switch caused Jon so little pause that for their first few reunions together as two men, Ames suspected that Jon had doubted Amy's womanhood all along. But after a short time, it became apparent that those doubts were misplaced. Jon was simply a creature of absolutes. Which is why, this time, it is Ames who has called for a summit of feelings sharing. Ames's desires and wants have been lost to him in a fog of indecision. Perhaps Jon's absolutist perspective might hold an answer.

After Katrina got Reese's letter, Katrina offered Ames an absolutist choice of her own. Ames arrived at her apartment that night to find her sitting in front of a cutting board, on which she had crumbled a block of Gouda cheese into bits. He sat down across from her and she launched her thoughts: It seemed obvious to her now that their plan to raise a child with Reese was misguided. She, Katrina, had been swept up in the excitement of a baby, of the newness of being queer, and even if Reese was right—and probably she had been: Katrina was willing to acknowledge that she had overreacted to the HIV news, maybe even for homophobic reasons—that did not change the clear fact that Reese was not a person to be relied on, that Reese's affair with her friend's husband, and Reese's subsequent cruel letter ruled out her participation in their family.

Ames noted the way Katrina said "their family." How she presented it as a fait accompli, a thing that existed already, for the purposes of her argument.

Reese had not sent a thoughtful letter, Katrina went on, and this comparing of Katrina to a gentrifier who couldn't handle spice? Which of them had grown up eating her mother's Chinese food and which had grown up eating fried bread in Wisconsin? Please! Reese was not the only one who knew how to weaponize identity!

Katrina glanced down at her cheese as she made this argument, as if her assertion might be undercut by its presence.

Anyway, Katrina concluded, if Reese had disqualified herself, and she had, Ames now faced a decision. After the divorce, after Ames's coming out, Katrina has come to the conclusion that she needs stability in her life. Especially if she is to have a baby dependent on her. She cannot bear another jolt to her idea of herself, or her plans for how to live. Therefore, she planned to schedule an abortion in the coming week. Ames must decide what he wants. He could either commit to be a parent and raise a child with Katrina or she will plan to end the pregnancy. She will not uproot herself even one more time. Moreover, she said calmly, if she had an abortion, she didn't see how their relationship together could continue.

Jon and Ames meet at a café on the Lower East Side. As always, Jon has driven his SUV in from Jersey and arrives twenty-five minutes late because he circled around looking for parking before giving up and paying at a garage.

Jon goes first. He wants to quit his job, but he has a six-year-old son, and Greta has gone back to graduate school for an MBA. They will have only one income for the next couple of years. "Greta takes for granted that I'll be at the firm forever, so that she can go to school, for what, the third time now?" Ames has learned to be tactful when Jon complains about Greta, because Jon turns touchy and protective of his wife if Ames ever agrees with him. When it is Ames's turn, Jon listens. Jon has recently shaved his head, and its bareness reveals an expressive topography of furrows as he frowns.

When Ames is finally done, Jon says, "Okay, I can't say I get this whole thing emotionally. I'm trying to follow you at least intellectually. I think you kind of just need to be honest with the women in your life about what you want. But that's what I don't understand either: Do you want a kid or not? Alexander is about to turn seven. And at some point, I have to realize that my kid is his own person; he doesn't make me who I am. That's trite, but if I get my sense of self through Alexander, I'm going to end up being one of those dads who ends up in a brawl with the referee and a bunch of other dads at his Little League hockey games. It kind of sounds to me like you're doing the gay version of that."

"I'm not even at the stage of getting my sense of self through my kid's accomplishments," Ames corrects him. "I'm at the stage where my sense of self would be changed by the very existence of a child."

Jon grazes a hand over his head. "Okay. Putting the women aside, do you want to raise a kid or not?"

"I don't know. That's the problem. I just feel blank. I have for a while."

Jon shrugs at Ames. "Have you ever tried to make somatic decisions?"

Ames laughs, which Jon takes for incomprehension. "It's this thing that Greta does," Jon explains, "where you take two options, and you say them aloud and you see how each feels in your body. Sometimes your body knows what your mind doesn't."

"Yeah, I know what somatic exercises are," Ames says. "I just didn't expect you to know."

"Why not?" Jon asks, affronted. "I'm very sensitive." Then he suggests that as a somatic exercise, they drive to the batting cages and work out some aggression, like they did in college. Maybe that will shake something loose in Ames.

· · ·

Jon refuses to pay the outrageous prices for parking at the batting cages at Chelsea Piers, so he finds, on his phone, a warehouse with batting cages way out in Queens. Aging major league paraphernalia hangs beside local Little League team flyers all over the walls of the entranceway. Inside, old-school pitching machines shoot out balls with a satisfying *chunck*. The building's interior is separated into lanes by heavy cargo nets and the lanes are occupied either by guys in their twenties who have the look of ex-athletes and smack consistent line drives at the pitching machine, or dads coaching their sons.

While Jon pays, Ames grabs a bat, shares a terse nod with the old-timer behind the counter, then Velcros closed a batting glove tight to his left hand and takes a few practice swings. The old ritual comes to him without thought. Ames's shoulders hum with loose energy as the bat goes round and he waits for a cage to open. He finds a perverse comfort in the way his body reacts, a bodily experience below thought. Maybe Jon really does know something of somatic therapy, in his own way.

Back when Amy and Reese lived together, on certain spring and summer evenings, Amy would walk down to the Parade Ground at Prospect Park, where the high school boys, mostly Dominicans, played baseball. She came for the *thwack* that occurred when a ball thrown hard and straight struck the leather pocket of a glove. She longed for that sound. She longed for her own high school past that snapped forward out of time's stream at the necromantic power of baseball's *thwack*s and *plonk*s. She'd sit on a bench, far enough away that the boys—or their dads—wouldn't make eyes at her, and she'd listen as the sounds of the game raised the ghosts of muscle memory. She could feel the batter's step forward, readying the pendulum of body weight to swing to the timing of the pitcher's windup. At every heard *thwack* the muscles in her arm came alive, remembering how her glove jerked back at the impact, how they sprang to snap a throw from third to first. All that smooth power her body had once had, ready to obey her every thought. She had missed it. She missed how obviously impressive it had been. The way women noted that impressiveness with their eyes and other boys chose her as their friend. The ease with which it all had been given to her.

Back before all this gender shit, her body was like a good dog. Maybe it wasn't fully her, but her dog did everything she wanted: she moved so fast, pulled himself up trees, sprinted through forests and across fields, giddy and waggy. She was lucky to have gotten a dog like that. She didn't deserve such a good dog. She'd thought she'd have that dog forever—when they were both old, he would lay at her feet like a canvas duffel, loyal and obliging and charming to the last.

Now, as Jon sends the ball into the chute, Ames's bat flashes round, and after a few minutes, it is indistinguishable from practice at college: the two of them silent, the *chunck* as Jon feeds the ball into the machine, the *tsing* as it hits the aluminum bat, so that their conversation becomes a wordless call-and-response—*chunck-tsing, chunck-tsing, chunck-tsing,* and on and on—until Jon breaks the meditation with a "my turn."

Jon selects a thirty-five-inch bat, gigantic by the standards of today's major-league players, who finesse their bat speeds and swing paths with smaller, lighter bats. But Jon bats as he always has, in the way of the old players, using his heavy frame to club the ball whenever it gets near him.

When Amy transitioned, she lost her dog. There was just her. She and her body were one and the same. Every sensation simply belonged to her, unmediated. It was supposed to be good. Sometimes it was. She didn't have to guess what was going on from her dog's behavior. But without a dog to hurt for her, on her behalf, her life as a woman arrived with pain; pain that had to be endured, withstood, pain that was the same as being alive, and so was without end.

As Jon bats, Ames tries to listen to his body. He has not thought about his dog in a long time. Does he still have a dog? In his detransition, he supposed he'd get his dog back, but he didn't. He has simply lost the vibrancy of both pain and pleasure. The world has receded to a tolerable distance, the colors unsaturated, while the dog stayed dead. In a certain cowardly way, he supposes that he has avoided thinking about it, hoping that this is enough. But of course, he has lived the last three years of his life in a way that requires so little of him—an office job of moderate ambition; a relationship that, as much as he really believes he loves Katrina, came to him without quite searching for it; friends who know him well, but not too well. Only now, with this baby, this work of his traitorous, animal body, does he need an inclination of his truest feelings. When Jon wears himself out, Ames takes a second turn. The bat goes round and round, and each time it is a prayer, beseeching the dead to speak.

When he goes over to Katrina's that evening, he throws himself to his knees and presses himself against her, kissing her belly, her inner thighs, cultivating his want, sussing out his edges, feeling for a way to let it speak to him, even as his hands are all over her, and he's murmuring over and over how much he wants her, how hungry he is for her. It has been in moments of desire with her that he's felt the most vibrant these past years, sweet moments when the distance between his body and his self narrows. At first she protests, but then he feels her body release, give in to him, and she laughs softly. "Easy, easy, all right. I've missed seeing this in you."

The sex comes easily, his body doing what he asks of it, and she sits on top of him, while his hands hold the parts of her waist that get so plump and soft and inviting when she's sitting like that. But even with Katrina, his mind doesn't connect, not fully. Not in the heavy saturated way of his years as a woman, and he can't help but think, doubtfully, if he's lying to Katrina. Maybe she deserves something better. More than just a proficient facsimile of a man in tune with himself, but the truth of it: a man who wants her with a body in synchrony with his mind. Even if he accepted her offer to raise a child with her, perhaps the child deserved better too. A parent whose presence was unquestionable, because it was true. Perhaps

Katrina may or may not figure it out, but a child certainly would. Children make studies of their parents, decipher them, propose theories about their behavior, turn them this way and that, examining every flaw, and continue to do so long after the parents themselves are gone. In stories, at the therapist's office, at holidays—the study of the parent never ends. Ames's child will know him. It is inevitable. And finally, there, an answer: He does not want his child to know him as he is.

After sex, he tells Katrina that he has an answer. That he has made a decision, but in turn, she must make a decision about him. He will raise a child with her. They can be parents together—but he cannot promise that he won't someday decide to live again as a woman. He cannot promise her that kind of stability. He cannot promise that he is sure of who he is, and so he cannot promise that Katrina or their baby will have an unchanging constant as either a partner or a father. And while he wants to promise consistency in his ability to be a provider and lover, he knows from experience that he can't promise that either. It's not up to him. As he changes, so too do the opportunities offered by the world around him ebb and flow. Katrina sits up in bed. Her skin is still faintly dewy, as it gets after sex. She breathes in and says finally, "I can't say I'm surprised."

He shifts, reaches out to her, but she says, "Give me a second," and turns her face away from him. Then, with her hand over her face, she gets up, naked, walks into the bathroom, and closes the door.

Ames's phone rings, a number he doesn't recognize. He silences it, but whoever it is calls back. Then again, and this time he answers.

When Katrina exits the bathroom, she has a robe wrapped around herself, but he is putting on his clothes. She widens her eyes; she cannot believe what she is seeing. Is he really getting dressed to leave?

"That was Reese's friend Thalia," Ames says. "She told me that Reese is in the hospital. A suicide attempt."

Have you ever heard of Wim Hof? He's this weird-ass Dutchman, known as the Iceman, who developed a method to withstand extreme pain. Among other superhuman feats, he climbed Mount Everest in just a pair of shorts, submerged himself in a block of ice for two hours without his core body temperature dropping, and ran a marathon across a desert without drinking water. He's in his late fifties and looks like an ancient Northern European hermit or an extra from *Game of Thrones*. He's usually filmed shirtless in frozen landscapes, icicles entangled in his beard, exhorting listeners in his staccato Dutch accent: "The cold trains your power. Your mind must deal with the elements. You must be healthy electromagnetically." His followers, as near as Reese can tell, are bros without girlfriends who read Kerouac between MMA workouts and don't own sheets.

Reese discovered Wim Hof a couple of years back, through a Grindr hookup. She went to a guy's apartment and he seemed normal enough—he worked at Saks and answered the door in a button-down with French cuffs. He offered Reese vodka, and they commenced to make out. After about ten minutes of dry-humping on the couch, they moved to the bedroom, where he stripped Reese to her bra and panties. Then, abruptly, he walked into the bathroom, took a five-minute icy cold shower, and after toweling off only cursorily, got into bed with her. His skin was so cold that she felt as though she were embracing a corpse. But the guy fucked like a god.

Afterward, he admitted that he'd always had trouble maintaining erections. So he started doing this thing called the Wim Hof method—a combination of breathing exercises and cold endurance trials, beginning with cold showers and moving to immersion in frozen lakes—intended to help adherents withstand pain and even control autonomic bodily systems, like blood flow or adrenaline. After a few months on the Wim Hof training regimen, her Grindr date claimed to have taken control of his erections again. The price was simply to freeze himself beyond performance anxiety before any intimacy. As Reese lay under the covers beside his finally warmed-up body, he pulled out a laptop in order to show her a half-hour Vice documentary on Wim Hof. It was a typical Vice piece: a credulous white guy doing things that he ought not to, filmed in a neutered gonzo style. But Wim Hof intrigued Reese—not for his physical feats of endurance, but for his apparent grief.

In 1995, he said, his beloved wife had committed suicide. She had jumped out of an eighth-story window. Beyond that, Wim Hof offered very little about his wife. To fill in details, the documentarians had Hof's adult son share that his mother had been a clinical psychotic with eleven different personalities. Wim, however, disclosed nothing negative about his spouse, other than the fact that the pain of grief had almost ended him. In his mourning, the widowed father of four began jumping into frozen ponds—holding himself underwater until the diamond-sharp needles of cold began to dull, until the pain of loss began to freeze as well, until his body succumbed to a lower state of consciousness, a place of purity numb to memory and thought. Wim Hof began to crave this cold place, began to love the cold, this place beside pain but not in pain, a place that pulled him "back into his inner nature, the way it was meant to be."

The duration of his forays beneath the ice and grief began to increase. If he went into the ice frequently enough and stayed down long enough, his pain never quite fully thawed. Scientists who have studied Hof have observed in him an uncommon amount of heat-producing brown fat, and have noted the similarities between his regimen of cold endurance and the Tummo form of Tibetan meditation, despite Hof never having studied Eastern religion.

Reese let herself become captivated by this Wim Hof character, even as she found him ridiculous. She enjoyed his take on stoic masculinity—the tragic man who loves a woman enough that the loss of her makes submersion in a frozen pond appealing by comparison. Would that all difficult women be loved so deeply.

When Reese got home from her Grindr date that night, she entered her shower stall, pulled shut the curtain, and turned on the cold water. Horrible! Good Christ. Never do that. That kind of bullshit, Reese decided, is for repressed men who otherwise have no outlet for emotions like grief. Women need not bother themselves.

Except that years hence, at Riis Park Beach in May, when the water along the Rockaways is still so cold that to let waves break against your ankles numbs your toes into strangers to each other, the ocean will call to Reese.

In the warmer months, weekends at Riis Beach become a queer ubiquity. Reese, however, has always preferred the luxury and romance of empty beaches, which one can find without much trouble by going to Long Island on weekdays. She acquiesces to attend Riis out of social necessity rather than true excitement. The queer beach, in Reese's estimation, combines the worst parts of a high school lunchroom with the worst parts of a nightclub—only everyone is also nearly naked.

For trans women: To tuck or not to tuck, that is the question. Reese never tucks. Her math is solid, tight as a geometric proof: to go untucked, to bare her little dickprint for all to see, is brazen enough that she can otherwise wear a tight one-piece without seeming too prudish.

Thalia, beside Reese, wears only a pair of boy shorts—but tucked—and is sunning her perfect little boobs golden. Thalia has always had, in Reese's estimation, the best collarbones in Brooklyn; she recently gave up eating any animal products, and between her new diet and the sun, they've taken on the soft gloss of burnished teak.

Reese showed up at Thalia's house the night before, trying to hold it together, to maintain the righteousness of the letter she had

emailed to Ames and Katrina, but she fell apart after only ten minutes, sobbing about the cowboy, and AIDS panics, and how she'll
never get another chance to be a mother.

Despite her amazing collarbones, Thalia's shoulders are not the
most comfortable upon which to cry. Because Thalia grew up with
a self-described histrionic Greek stereotype for a mother, whenever
Reese got histrionic, Thalia turned edgy and furtive, insecure about
the adequacy of her own emotions in response.

But for once, Thalia's reassurances did not falter. "Babe," she
told Reese, "just sleep over, okay?" And she led Reese to her bed,
fed her an Ambien, and tucked her in to sleep. Reese woke in the
morning to instant coffee steaming beside the bed and Thalia already dressed.

As Reese sipped, Thalia announced that she had spent the night
thinking about Reese's problem, and that it was not in fact a problem, but a solution. Ames and Katrina had indeed been the issue all
along. Reese was a queer, if she was going to do a queer family
model, she ought to do it with *real* queers. "Ames brainwashed
you," Thalia insisted. "He made you think this is your only chance
to have a child. But why should that be? Queers have kids all the
time."

"Not trans women."

Thalia listed off five trans women who had children, but Reese
protested that they had all had children *before* they transitioned.
They had been *fathers*.

"What about Babs?" Thalia countered. Babs was a trans woman
who had married a trans guy and the two of them moved to south-
west Florida, where the trans guy got pregnant. "You could pull a
Babs!" Thalia suggested brightly.

Reese shook her head unhappily. Everyone knew that rules
didn't apply to Babs. Babs was like if the Most Interesting Man in
the World from the Dos Equis beer commercials were actually a
trans femme. One of those nonbinary beauties whose impossible-
to-properly-gender gorgeousness was so discomfiting that, faced

with her, people took an involuntary and alarmed step backward, as if they had just opened the door to their house and glimpsed inside to see all their belongings ablaze. One could not include Babs in any kind of meaningful comparison. Babs and her daughter were probably riding around the mangrove forests on a pair of manatees or something, even as Reese and Thalia discussed them.

"Look," Thalia finally said, after Reese had refused any hope that a Babs comparison might offer, and so forced Thalia to move on to a more aggressive line of argument, "I can't make you stop feeling sorry for yourself." She raised her voice to cut any attempt for Reese to disagree. "But," Thalia continued, "I can drag you to Riis with me. It's supposed to be the first warm day of the year, so everyone is going, and maybe there you will remember you have friends who aren't detransitioners and yuppies."

Thalia is right. They arrive at a beach clear of both Ames the Detransitioner and Katrina the Yuppie. But Reese cannot twist this lack into a benefit. Something has curdled in her overnight. Ricky, the trans boy with the motorcycle whom Reese had once dated many years back, sits beside Reese on her towel and recounts his spring, mentioning a series of protests he helped to organize in response to bathroom bills and the banning of trans children in schools and sports. Reese has not attended any protests. Ricky's monologue, though seemingly about his own exploits, is a manner of gentle prodding that he has mastered the last few years, as he'd entered his thirties and made the move from party boy to trans activist. Reese reads his meaning plainly: What has happened to you, Reese? Why don't we see you anymore? Aren't you one of us? In fact, don't you have a responsibility to us? She is unable to respond clearly to this subtext, and dissembles, unwilling to talk to him about anything so square as the child or family that preoccupy her, then lapses into silence.

He waits a few moments, then makes an excuse, and goes off to talk to a group of guys admiring each other's swim shorts beside a boom box thumping Latin trap. Reese watches him go. She wishes she had said to him: *I am angry. I don't care about your protests. They are not enough.* Then she feels ashamed of herself. Why does she deserve to be so angry? What has she truly lost? Quietly, to herself, she answers her own question: *I have lost a child.*

The statement jolts her. She hears in her own voice a latch sliding into place. She says it again, phrased slightly differently, *I have lost my child.* Is it grief she feels? Is grief even a feeling to which she is entitled? Reese stands up suddenly. Thalia ignores her. She is engrossed in conversation about bathtubs with a topless and tattooed redhead. Both of them love bathtubs, but neither of them has one; they are cursed with shower stalls.

Reese walks up the slope of the beach, away from the water, toward the remains of a concrete jetty. The queer section of the beach occupies one of fourteen bays that make up Jacob Riis Park, and it is, to Reese, the most squalid and forlorn section of them. Decades before, this ugly, unwanted, out-of-the-way stretch must have been the only place queers could bathe with each other unmolested. But as queerness has grown cool, the last bay has become the most packed and popular of the beach, with straights setting up camp alongside the queers, unwilling to miss out on whatever makes this stretch of sand so apparently desirable, even if they remain uncertain as to what that thing is.

Overlooking the queer beach the moldering sea-bleached concrete of what was once Neponsit Beach Hospital decomposes, a former tuberculosis sanatorium now chain link—closed from the public. From the jetty, Reese walks west along the fence, grasping on to it occasionally to steady herself in her flip-flops while she moves along the edge of its concrete bar as she would traverse a balance beam.

The fence around the abandoned hospital strikes Reese as unnecessary. Not a windowpane remains unbroken in the facade, already so vandalized and graffitied that to deface it further would only waste effort, the delinquent equivalent of pissing in the ocean. Toward the end of the fence, Reese grips the chain-link with her fingers and peers in. "I lost my baby," she tells the building. It feels crazy to say aloud, but still, she has the sense that the building hears her. How many people suffered in that building? A century's worth of sanatorium patients and then, after it became a municipal nursing home, the elderly. It must be full of ghosts. "I had a miscarriage," she tells the ghosts.

Is this a lie? Can she lie to ghosts? Won't they know the truth? Anyway, is it really a lie? She had planned for a baby, and now she had lost a baby, before it was even born. What else is that but a miscarriage? Perhaps it was a trans version of a miscarriage, but she doubted that ghosts required gender to be explained to them. They had moved beyond all that. "Miscarriage," she says again.

Katrina had had a miscarriage. And with this thought, Reese feels another stab of something like grief. At what point, she wonders, does a mother go from wanting *a* child to wanting *this* child, *her* child? When does that transformation occur? Reese remembers that Katrina had felt relief at her miscarriage. Perhaps that first time, Katrina had miscarried *a* child, not *her* child. How else would she be willing to do it again? Reese herself had always wanted to be *a* mother to *a* child, and yet, it is only now that she realizes that, without quite noticing, she wanted to be *this* mother, to *that* child. Attachments had formed that had almost nothing to do with identity. Perhaps, even, the important thing was *that* child. It was, perhaps, too late for Reese to be *this* mother, but Katrina could still have *that* child. Somehow this was the worst thought of all. If she really wanted to be a good mother, she had to admit she had been wrong. The child was everything. Reese would disappear. Ames and Katrina could have her baby if that's what it took. She experienced a moment of Solomonic self-satisfaction. Not that she knew her Bible all that well, but wasn't the true mother she who would rather give up her baby than allow it to be sawed in half? The wind blew sand through the empty hospital and Reese turned to gaze at the ocean, freezing beyond the frolicking queers, and she recalled suddenly the Wim Hof method.

. . .

Among the queers of Brooklyn, it will become a generally agreed-upon story that the first truly beautiful beach day of the season was ruined when a certain pale, aging, once-popular, still-haughty trans woman traumatized an entire community by throwing herself into the freezing waters of the Atlantic Ocean to drown a la Virginia Woolf in full sight of everyone who had just come for a good time.

At first, she is the only one in the water past her ankles. Then she wades in to her waist. By the time the water hits her navel, a few onlookers on the shore have noticed the woman in the red bathing suit walking slowly into the sea. They watch her with consternation. She goes alone, with none of the excitement or shrieking that ought to accompany a polar plunge. By the time she is up to her neck, she has caught the attention of a few small crowds. Two hundred feet out, she rises slightly, on a sandbar. Small waves break over her arms. Then she steps off the far side of the sandbar, and goes under.

Four men make the rescue attempt. Three turn back before the sandbar. In the water, in the cold, their bodies won't respond. Up and down their legs, nerves go incommunicado and muscles turn to lead. The sandy bottom can be seen, but cannot be felt. Only Fredrick, a rent-boy muscle queen in a neon-blue speedo who has been drinking Nutcrackers the color of antifreeze for the past hour, presses on. Between his mass and a blood alcohol level that would keep plumbing running in the dead of winter, he splashes forth to Reese. At the sandbar, his broad back rises from the water and he scans for the woman. She is floating on her back, hair fanned out, lips blue, inhaling and exhaling hard.

He dives, comes up, plants his feet, grips her arm, and hefts her, fireman-style, to his shoulders. She opens her eyes, startled.

"Hey!" She pushes against him.

"I have you!" he bellows.

"No, no," she wheezes out. She is so cold, it is hard to get her lungs to push out enough air to speak. "Wim Hof method."

"Huh?" he shouts, churning with her toward land. On the beach, people cheer. What a rescue.

"Wim Hof method! I'm fine. Wim Hof method."

They rise at the sandbar, and he sets her on her feet. The heat of the sun is only a distant memory. The air too has turned arctic. "Can you walk?" he asks dubiously.

"Yes, yes," she says. Her ears ache from the cold, a terrible pain like from eating ice cream too fast, but encircling her whole skull. She hears people shouting, and suddenly is aware of how many people are watching. She can't believe it. She was only in the water, like, what, five minutes? But she can't focus on that now. Instinct has reasserted itself and she needs to get warm. Nothing else matters. Wim Hof was right. He discovered, in our backyard ponds and on banal coasts, the lair of a terrible god, a place beyond self-pity, beyond grief.

Reese is on the shore, wrapped in a towel, fending off Thalia's worry, which has turned to rage. Reese's skin is blue and her teeth clack. She has only a few moments to try to explain herself, uselessly, in between Thalia's imprecations, before the paramedics arrive. The lifeguards haven't yet come out for the season, but someone who witnessed Reese's submersion has called an ambulance and reported an incident of self-harm. What is happening? the newly arrived beachgoers ask each other, as the ambulance lights flash at the end of the boardwalk. The rumor goes around: Another trans woman has tried to commit suicide. They nod sadly, knowingly: Isn't this kind of performance just what trans women do? Throw themselves in front of trains from crowded platforms? Film themselves downing fistfuls of pills on Facebook Live? Broadcast and perform their pain no matter whom it triggers? Don't even trans women expect this from each other?

The paramedics—two young guys, one white, one black, equally fit—have Reese wrapped in one of those shiny Mylar reflective blankets, and have pulled the ambulance out to a patch of asphalt near the road, away from the beach. Reese has denied her swim was a suicide attempt. But she has regained her wits enough to know better than to shout "Wim Hof Method!" at paramedics responding to a supposed mental health crisis. It was a polar bear swim, she tells them. One of the guys interviews Thalia, then comes back.

"She says you've lost a baby," he informs Reese, "that you've been upset about it. Does that have anything to do with what just happened?"

How dense are these guys? Why would they remind a grieving mother of her lost child? Besides, her clothes are still down at the beach; she's sitting there untucked in a one-piece. "I'm trans, duh," she snaps. "I can't have a baby."

The men exchange glances, and Reese understands she has miscalculated. Transness is not the most direct route to non-suicidal credibility. The guy who interviewed Thalia has also asked some other people what happened, and everyone has described the same scene: a woman walking soberly and purposefully into a sea of lethal cold, refusing to turn back no matter what they shouted. Reese lets out a little derisive laugh. Who did they think she was to wear a bathing suit for that? Did they think she had no sense of theater or gravitas? Can you imagine Virginia Woolf being so undignified as to put on a bathing costume to walk her intolerable despair into the river? If she wants to be taken seriously when she walks tragically into the sea, she needs a big skirt weighed down with stones, not a polyester one-piece.

The paramedics tell her that they want to take her to the hospital, and she refuses. She's got the worst insurance that's still legal; she can't pay for an ambulance trip. Nonetheless, they say, she should go to the hospital. They can't make her go, they admit, but in a mental health crisis in which a suicide attempt has been reported, she must speak with proper authorities. She has the option of doing an evaluation at the hospital or waiting here for those authorities to arrive.

"Like what other authorities? The police?"

The white guy shrugs as if to say, *this choice is your doing.*

She imagines speaking to police on the side of the road while a sizable portion of Brooklyn's queer population files past on the way home from the beach.

She waves her hand angrily. "Hospital," she commands.

Reese enters the waiting room with a drawn, tight expression. She wears the cover-up and flip-flops that she had worn to the beach, an off-kilter outfit that seems a cruel joke to Ames. One that confirms the suspicions that one might have of anyone emerging from the psychiatric ward.

Thalia stands, rushes over to Reese, and hugs her. Ames hangs back with Katrina, waiting for Reese to notice them. He's apprehensive, and Katrina, beside him, gives Ames's hand a nervous squeeze.

When Reese catches sight of the two of them, she pulls away from Thalia, her face darkening. A slight sunburn reddens her face and her skin stretches tight over her cheekbones. Her eyes move wildly from Ames to Katrina, then back to Thalia.

"I called them," Thalia says simply. "I didn't know if you could pay or what you might need."

Ames knows Reese well enough to know that she is wavering between anger and gratitude, that she hates being seen in such a compromised position, but that anyone who comes down to a hospital in Midwood must, somewhere inside of them, care about her. Perhaps if it had just been Ames, she might have let herself go to anger, but with Katrina there, Reese's teeth flash as she gives Katrina a nervous smile.

"I didn't do it," she says, and Ames realizes that she is talking to Katrina. "I wasn't trying to kill myself."

"Okay," says Katrina simply. "Thalia said that. But she also said you've been upset. Anyway, you don't have to explain anything. I drove here. I can give you a ride."

"Thank you," Reese says. "I want to explain. This is humiliating, but I'm glad to see you."

There are papers for Reese to sign, insurance information for her to verify before she's discharged. Ames asks if she needs help, or money, but she shakes her head. He stands beside her at the reception counter anyhow. When she's done, he asks if she will please give him a hug. He intends the request as a gift—to spare her having to ask for one herself—and because, honestly, he needs one too.

Katrina drops off Thalia first. Thalia gives Reese a kiss goodbye on the cheek as she gets out of the car, and thanks Katrina for the ride. Then, to Reese's surprise, Thalia turns to Ames. "Take care of her," she instructs him, and before Ames can respond, she turns and strides her long strides away from the car.

"She's a good friend," Katrina says, pulling out. Reese sits in back, and Katrina has to duck forward to see Reese's face in the rearview mirror. Reese nods without responding.

"Do you want some food?" Ames asks. "Or just to go home?"

"I want to go home," Reese says. But then, a minute later, as Katrina turns the wheel and pulls into the traffic on Bedford, Reese says, "But I have to explain myself. I will never sleep if I don't. And I never expected to have you two here, to have this chance."

"Please," Ames says. He is glad she's spoken. His curiosity had grown to the point of morbidity, but he was afraid of Reese's temper, and was being careful to remain solicitous of Katrina, who'd surprised him, after Thalia called, by telling him that she would drive him to the hospital.

"I'm sorry about the letter," Reese says, more to Katrina than Ames. "I was really angry. And I'm sorry that Garrett is your friend's husband. I should have put it together sooner."

"You were partly right," Katrina says. "I wanted the good parts of queerness without the hard parts. At the first hard part, I had a panic. It was homophobic. I'm embarrassed." She leaves the rest of the letter unaddressed. Then, after a long period of silence, Katrina adds, "I didn't tell Diana."

Reese nods. Then after another stretch of time without speaking, she adds, "I won't see him again. You don't have to worry. The messages he left me are not the kind of thing you say if you ever expect to see someone again. He's scared of me now that I know his friends and could ruin his marriage, and that's not sexy for him. He can't treat me however he wants anymore."

"She'll probably leave him eventually," Katrina says. "This is the season for it. For a while everyone was getting married. Then everyone was having children. Now it's divorces. Diana always likes to do what's in vogue in the moment."

Reese laughs, but without force. She asks Ames to turn up the heat in the car. In her beachwear she's grown chilly. But not in a meaningful Wim Hof sort of way. Ames obliges, and directs a stream of air to the back seat.

At the next stoplight, Reese says, "I didn't go into the water for attention."

"I never thought that," Ames assures her.

"Yeah, but that's what the doctor at the hospital clearly thought. He didn't say it right out, but I could tell from his questions. Like, 'how cold was the water really?' And when I guessed the temperature was in the low fifties, he said that that water was never cold enough to kill me, only give me hypothermia. Instead, he suggested that I was making a scene in front of people at the beach for attention. Not even a cry for help. Just a cry for attention. It is literally the most ungenerous, most embarrassing conclusion that he could have come to. It makes me guilty that you came, because now it seems like I did it for attention, to get you here. And because I'm glad you came, it must really seem like that was my plan all along."

"So why did you go into the water?" Ames asks, trying to pitch his voice softly to make the question more tender than its blunt construction.

Reese sighs and gazes at the street passing by. Shadows cast by telephone poles and streetlights swing over her face as the car moves. "I was really sad. It was this exercise for numbing grief that I heard about. A real exercise. A method by this guy Wim Hof. Don't ask me to explain him. I already had to explain him to the doctor."

"Grief?" Ames asks.

"Yes, grief. The loss of a baby." Up front, Katrina glances briefly at Ames, a moment of sadness, or alarm, but Reese doesn't seem to notice. Katrina just grips the wheel as Reese keeps talking. "I haven't memorized the stages of grief but isn't acceptance one of them? I'm trying to accept that I won't be a mother to this baby I've grown attached to. That I won't be part of your family. But I am trying to see good things. It was nice seeing you two holding hands in the waiting room. That baby is going to have really caring parents, the kind that show up. And I'm trying to accept that's good enough. Even for me."

Ames knows how much Reese is giving up to speak like this. But still, Katrina doesn't say anything, and Ames hesitates, torn. He wants to console Reese—but the decision as to their future parenthood belongs to Katrina. He owes it to her to let Katrina speak as she wants or not at all. When Katrina does finally speak, it is only to ask whether the best way to Reese's at this time of night is via the Brooklyn-Queens Expressway.

After work on Monday, Katrina and Ames walk to the subway arm in arm, linked at the elbow with their hands in their jacket pockets. Heavy clouds have begun to blow over Brooklyn and above them, building tops move in and out of the peachy sunlight. At street level, dusk has come to stay.

"Just after lunch I got a phone call," Katrina says. "It was a nurse-midwife from my doctor's office. She said that by now they had expected me to call and initiate care. Like to direct them about what kind of experience I wanted for my pregnancy."

Ames doesn't understand the question that well. "Did she say what your options are?"

"Like, do I plan to have a doula? A nurse-midwife? Do I have a hospital in mind or am I going to give birth at home? They don't really initiate care too early in the pregnancy, she said, unless a woman is having a hard first trimester, but I'm approaching the second trimester, I'm older, and at risk; and they hadn't heard from me, so she followed up."

"What did you say?"

"Well, she was very chipper. It was sort of like she was welcoming me to the official part of my pregnancy. She suggested that I still needed to schedule a Doppler to hear the baby's heartbeat."

He stops on the sidewalk. She stops with him, but doesn't turn. She is holding herself very erect. "Katrina," he asks, "are you okay?"

"I couldn't bear it," she said. "The thought of hearing a heartbeat. The woman, she heard it in my voice, and, like, her entire demeanor changed. She clicked out of this whole happy welcome thing into, like, professional mode. Like counselor mode."

"Yeah," says Ames. He's heard a recording of a baby's heartbeat before. The rabbit-fast whooshing of a tiny creature. Such a sound is happening right now, he realizes, inside Katrina—they just lack the ability to detect it. They are still linked at the elbow, and he feels too close to her, physically. But he makes himself hold on to her, and then after a moment, he wants to be closer again, so he takes his hand out of his jacket and puts it in her pocket, beside her hand.

"I've been so afraid to call," Katrina says. "Every day I tell myself to call my doctor, to ask about what's happening inside my body. I can barely bring myself to search online for information. How late is too late, what an abortion entails. When I have to decide what. I've been paralyzed about it. And then, this woman called me. It was just because that's her job and probably a calendar told her to, but it felt like it was meant to happen. She walked me through what happens in an abortion, told me that the sooner I did it, the easier it would be. She helped me schedule it, so all I had to do was call a number to confirm."

They are standing on the sidewalk facing each other, and other pedestrians are breaking around them, like water around a snag in a river. Ames puts his hand on her arm and they step under the awning of a Cajun restaurant. "Did you call that number?"

"I can't do this, Ames," she says. "I need the stability of a partner who can promise that he's more or less going to be the same person. I need the stability of someone who can help provide for a child. I want to know what my future will look like. I want to be able to do that for my family too. And you told me you can't do that. So what choice do I really have?"

Ames braces as the future crumbles before him, their own private earthquake. "You have no choice," he sighs. "And yet, the choice is yours. My choices are the same way."

Katrina scheduled her procedure for four in the afternoon. It is now eleven A.M. and Reese, Katrina, and Ames sit in the living room of Katrina's apartment.

Yesterday, Ames begged Katrina to let him accompany her, and finally she acquiesced. To his surprise, Katrina responded that, if Reese wanted, Reese could come too.

"That's generous of you," Ames had said carefully. "Are you sure?"

"No," Katrina corrected him. "It is the opposite of generous. Misery loves company. I don't want to be alone in losing a baby today."

"Are you being ironic?"

Irritation flashed on her face when she responded. "Do you think I have the energy for irony, Ames? Just invite her. She can come if she wants, and not if she doesn't."

Reese declined the invitation at first. In her mind, she had given the baby up to Katrina, and now, it was with dismay—perhaps even horror—that she had to acquiesce that the baby's mother had the

right to abort. That another woman could end the existence of a
baby that she had come to imagine, softly, tentatively, at the center
of her future life. She had found her emotions and, in the two days
since Ames told her about the abortion, had veered in the direction
of pro-life politics. Never before had she found her thoughts trend-
ing to the personhood of an unborn child.

And thus, she declined the invitation. Out of confusion, and a
distrust of herself and the self-service of her own motivations. And
above all out of grief.

But after thinking about the invite for a few hours Reese called
Ames again. "Why would she invite me?" she wondered aloud to
him. "Is it possible she wants us to talk her out of it? I tried to imagine myself as her, and that was the only motivation I could imagine.
Maybe she invited me because some part of her wants to change her
mind, but feels either too proud or too scared, and can't admit it to
herself. So she has invited someone who will do it for her." Even as
she spoke, Reese could again hear the twisted conservatism of her
position. She'd told other women to fuck off with their opinions
about her body, her hormones. They meant almost nothing to her,
her readiness as thoughtless as slapping away a mosquito. But what
if it was never about politics? Maybe she just always wanted what
she wanted: hormones then and a baby now. A nimble mind can
always uncover the politics to justify its own selfishness.

"I don't know," Ames said. "But Katrina is not you. I do best
with her when I believe she means what she says. But you always do
whatever you want. Even Katrina must realize that by now. You'll
say what you want to her, regardless of what I think, and some part
of her must have known that when she invited you."

Katrina has turned off the heat for the season, but the weather is
cold and drab, so the air in the apartment carries a damp chill.
Kindly, she offers Reese a blanket, and wraps one around herself.
Reese accepts and covers her bare shoulders with the scratchy wool.

"Please, Katrina," Reese says, at length, and somewhat without segue from the small talk they had been making. "Please can't you wait?"

Katrina shakes her head. "I already missed my chance to do it with the pill. Now they have to use a vacuum and if I wait more, dilation. The longer I wait—" She pauses and pulls the blanket over her face, so Reese thinks she might be crying, but a moment later, she pulls it back down, eyes still dry, and her face expressionless. "I just can't take the risk. I just can't handle the uncertainty, I just can't."

Reese refuses to let herself respond. She does not trust herself to speak on the subject of risk. Which of them has it in them to risk and which doesn't. To her surprise, Ames, who is sitting beside Katrina, holding her hand, speaks up.

"Do you remember, Reese," he asks, "what you used to call the *Sex and the City* Problem?"

"Yes, of course. I remember my own bullshit, thank you very much."

Katrina, thankfully, smiled at this.

Ames turns to her. "Do you, Katrina, remember how much you liked that reference when I told you about it? I pretended that I had come up with it myself, but actually I stole that from Reese."

"Yes, I remember." Katrina nods. "Although now it makes way more sense, because I kept asking you about different episodes of *Sex and the City*, and you could never remember them. I was like, 'How does someone come up with a life philosophy about a show he doesn't seem to have watched?' It makes sense that you got it from Reese. It's obviously her style."

"Yes," Reese agrees sadly. "I am much more culturally relevant and funny."

Ames accepts this in the way he's always accepted being teased, although this teasing has the somberness of a joke cracked at a wake. "Okay, let me ask again: Reese, do you remember how the whole idea of the *Sex and the City* Problem for you is that no generation of trans women has solved the *Sex and the City* Problem, and that every generation of cis women has to reinvent it?"

"Yes."

"Well, what if this is our solution? Maybe this is so awkward and hard and without obvious precedent because we're trying to imagine our own solution, to reinvent something for ourselves, whatever kind of"—he pauses, and looks down at his own feet, the boots and jeans he wears—"whatever kind of women we are."

"Maybe," Katrina says.

Reese hears this, an indefinite to Katrina's tone, and she raises her head, eyes shining in the dark circles. "Yeah," Reese agrees, "maybe."

Katrina gets up to make some tea. The kettle boils, and she pours out three cups and returns with them. The three of them sip in silence as the clock ticks. They are together, and miles from each other, their thoughts turning to themselves, then turning to the baby, each in her own way contemplating how her tenuous rendition of womanhood has become dependent upon the existence of this little person, who is not yet, and yet may not be.

ACKNOWLEDGMENTS

THIS BOOK IS a story of trans feminine culture in the new millennium. As a result, I am indebted to the trans women everywhere who have changed their whole lives to create our cultures. I want to thank every trans girl I have met in the years that I wrote this book, but especially those who lived in New York, Seattle, the Bay Area, rural Tennessee, and Chicago.

Thank you to the specific trans people who made this book possible: Theda Hammel, Harron Walker, January Hunt, T. Clutch Fleischmann, Cecilia Gentili (in a book about trans moms, she is trans mom to so many girls in NYC), Morgan M. Page, A.J. Lewis, Sophie Searcy, Crissy Bell (to whom goes credit for the "four funerals and a funeral" joke), Casey Plett, Sybil Lamb, Davey Davis, Aubrey Schuster, Jordy Rosenberg, Cyd Nova, Ambrose Stacey-Fleischmann, Ceyenne Doroshow, Gaines Blasdel, Dean Spade, Calvin, Hilt, Beau, Lex, and Sophie. May Emma, Bryn, and the other trans women lost during the writing of this book rest in power.

There have been so many other women (especially moms!) who have taught me so much. Pike Long, Charlie Starr, Rebecca Novack, Julia Reagan, Florence Menard, Julia Moses, Courtney Lyons, Rachel Lewallen, Siobahn Flood, Allie Grump, Alice Eisenberg, Kendra Grant, Elan, Yvonne Woon, Sarah Schulman, and Katie Liederman all made a difference in the shape of this book. Thinking about the relationship of sex to sex work was also a part of my writing, and to that end, I want to thank the sex workers and sex work activists in NYC in general, but specifically Chloe Mercury, The Villainelle, and Mistress Blunt.

I suppose the boys can get some love too: Dan Pacheco, Mike Casarella, Akiva Friedlin, Jon Philipsborn, and Jacob Brown.

In a book about transness and pregnancy, what are the odds to have gotten a trans editor in Victory Matsui, and a pregnant editor in Caitlin McKenna, both of whom happen to be brilliant? My editors truly made this a better book. And then I was lucky enough to have Emma Caruso come in at the last moment and put the finishing touches on their work. My agent, Kent Wolf, has the best hair in publishing, which I think must be how he has been so successful in advocating for me—well, great hair and that he is kind, smart, and quietly badass. Thank you to Chris Jackson and the One World team for taking a chance on my writing. Jackson Howard, thank you for seeing something in my writing and kicking off this process.

Believe it or not, I have an actual mother to thank: Suzanne Torrey, thank you for a lifetime of wisdom. Thank you as well to my father, Scott Peters. David N., this book wouldn't exist without you. I am grateful to Olive Melissa Minor for joyously spending the first half of her life with me, for both our marriage and our divorce, and the lessons of each reflected in this book. Lastly, to Chrystin Ondersma, my future, whose thoughts, words, and love cannot be separated from the text.